Pride Publishing books by K. Evan Coles and Brigham Vaughn

Single Books
Wake
Calm

The Speakeasy
With a Twist
Extra Dirty
Behind the Stick

By Brigham Vaughn

Anthologies
Right Here, Right Now: The Soldier Next Door

By K. Evan Coles

Boston Seasons
Third Time's the Charm

The Speakeasy

WITH A TWIST

K. EVAN COLES &
BRIGHAM VAUGHN

With a Twist
ISBN # 978-1-913186-08-1
©Copyright K. Evan Coles and Brigham Vaughn 2018
Cover Art by Cherith Vaughan ©Copyright September 2018
Interior text design by Claire Siemaszkiewicz
Pride Publishing

Published in 2019 by Pride Publishing, United Kingdom.

Pride Publishing is an imprint of Totally Entwined Group Limited.

WITH A TWIST

Dedication

With a Twist and the *Speakeasy* books came upon us out of the blue as we wrote the second book in the *Tidal* series. It wouldn't have been possible without the incredibly supportive people in our lives and some scene-stealing secondary characters.

For my husband, who is patient (usually) and encouraging (always) of my endless scribbling.
For my son, who makes me laugh every single day.
For the people in and around my life who inspire me, let me be weird and make me feel brave.
And for Brigham Vaughn, who puts up with my thousands of questions, listens to my rants, indulges my kooky humor and is always ready to put pen to paper when our stars align.
— K. Evan Coles

This book is for my friends who were patient when I was too busy writing or editing to spend time with them. For the people who cheered me on and had faith in my writing long before I did. For my parents who are the best patrons of the arts a writer could ask for.

And, mostly, for K. Evan Coles, who got me into reading and writing gay romance in the first place. I wouldn't be here without you! It's been a wonderful—and occasionally frustrating—journey. There's no one I would rather have done it with.
— Brigham Vaughn

K. and Brigham would also like to thank:

Their patient beta readers Shell Taylor, Jayme Yesenofski, Rebecca Spence, Kade Boehme, Allison Hickman, and Sally Hopkinson. You helped us mold the story you see before you today. We could not have done it without you.

And the Speakeasy Crew who just won't stop talking: Will, Jesse, Kyle, Carter, and Riley. Those boys have got a whole lot more company these days.

Chapter One

June 2014

Will Martin set down his empty mug and flipped to the next page of the *New York Times*. A familiar profile caught his attention and, despite his better judgment, he read the caption below the photo of two smiling and laughing men in tuxedos.

The year's hottest gay couple cut a fine figure at the Met premiere last night. Riley Porter-Wright and Carter Hamilton are still going strong. The couple appeared oblivious to those around them as they talked during intermission. They were joined by the former Mrs. Hamilton, who seems to have forgiven Mr. Porter-Wright for stepping into her place. Also there was her new paramour, Robert... The ex-Mrs. Porter-Wright was nowhere to be seen. The couple have been spotted at —

Annoyed, Will threw the newspaper on the coffee table. Everywhere he turned there were reminders of his ex-boyfriend Riley's happiness with his new love. Well, long-time love, really. Will had competed with Riley's best friend, Carter, the entire time they'd been together.

But how could Will have competed with a man Riley had loved since college? Riley had left his wife to explore his bisexuality and Carter had ultimately done the same. Will had been foolish for thinking he could offer Riley more than a man who had known him for a decade and a half could.

Will scrubbed a hand through his hair and stood. *I need a change of scenery right now*, he thought and glanced around the living room of his stylish Manhattan condo.

His laptop screen glowed at him from his desk by the windows. He'd planned to take the morning off and enjoy the gorgeous early June weather, but with edits looming over him and reminders of Riley lurking around the edges of his consciousness, relaxation seemed out of the question.

"Fine, fine," Will muttered under his breath. "Work it is."

He filled his cup with coffee, doctored it with cream and sugar and took a seat at his desk. He pulled up his manuscript and scrolled to the place he'd left off — Bernard Schwartz's appointment as Chief Counsel of the House Legislative Oversight Subcommittee.

Half an hour later, Will's phone trilled on the desk and he blinked to clear the haze from his brain. *Riley* flashed across the screen. *Speak of the devil*, he thought, then immediately chastised himself. Riley wasn't the problem. Riley loving Carter instead of Will wasn't even the major issue. Will's habit of falling for emotionally unavailable men then struggling to get over them was something he desperately needed to change.

Not wanting his ex to sense the turmoil in his head, Will made sure to keep his tone pleasant. "Hey, Riley."

"Hey, Will. How have you been?"

"Good. Making solid progress on my book." Will sat back in his chair.

"Oh, that's right, you're not teaching during the summer semester, are you?"

"No, I decided to focus on my writing. I'm in the midst of edits, so I'll be spending the summer cursing at a computer screen while I try not to tear my hair out."

"What a rewarding career," Riley said teasingly.

Will chuckled and relaxed a little. He'd always enjoyed Riley's sense of humor. "I must be a masochist for voluntarily subjecting myself to college students *and* editors." Will taught legal history at New York University and had published a handful of well-regarded books on the topic. He suspected Riley hadn't called to ask about his writing, however. "How's work? Is your father still pretending you don't exist at the office?"

"I think he's hoping I'll leave Porter-Wright Publishing, to be honest. He and Geneva were polite when Carter and I took the kids to the company picnic but I'm sure it's only because they were afraid of looking bad."

"Appearances above all else," Will muttered. He and Riley had always had that in common. Although at least Will spoke to his mother occasionally and kept in contact with his sister, Olivia. Riley's relationship with his parents was far worse. "How are things with you and Carter? And the little Hamiltons?"

"Really good." Will could hear the smile in Riley's voice. "We all spent last weekend in Southampton at the beach house."

Riley sounded so happy every time they talked about Carter and his kids. Will's heart ached, knowing he could never have made Riley that happy, but on the whole he was glad Riley had found the contentment he'd searched for.

"Anyway," Riley interrupted his thoughts, "I called for a reason. You know Jesse Murtagh and Kyle McKee, right?"

"Vaguely. I met them at Carter's birthday and Jesse again at your holiday party last winter."

"Right. Well, they're opening a speakeasy in a week or so."

Will laughed. "A speakeasy? That's intriguing."

"It's basically ready to go, and they've been inviting friends in to see it and try the cocktails. I called to see if you would like to meet me there tonight. I thought we could grab some drinks and catch up."

"Just you?"

Riley hesitated. "No. Carter will be there with Jesse and Kyle. Along with six or eight of our friends."

Will stifled a sigh. "Riley..."

"Hey, I know it's going to be awkward. But it's been six months. You and I are doing pretty well with our friendship. So, stop being a fucker and come."

Will couldn't prevent the laugh that escaped him. "Well, when you word it that way, how can I possibly resist?"

"No, I don't mean to be glib. I know this isn't easy for you, but I don't want to lose you as a friend." Riley sounded earnest. "I'm asking a lot, but I'd like for you to be able to hang out with all of us. And hey, maybe you'll meet the perfect guy there."

Will snorted. "I'm definitely not looking for the last part, but sure, I'll come. What time and where am I meeting you?"

* * * *

Later that evening, Will glanced around Lock & Key, a pub on the edge of the upper West Side in Morningside Heights, where Riley had arranged for them to meet. The floors were scuffed and slightly gritty under his feet and the tables and chairs had seen better days. The pub was entirely ordinary and not at all what Will had expected.

"Have dive bars become your thing?" he asked, mystified.

Riley laughed and clapped him on the shoulder. "This is not our destination for the night. Someone Kyle used to work with owns Lock & Key. The speakeasy is underneath."

Will raised an eyebrow. "*Under Lock & Key*? Clever."

"What can I say, my friends are punny." Riley grinned. "Come on, follow me." He strode to the end of the bar and opened an unmarked door. Will followed more slowly. At the end of a hallway was an old-fashioned phone mounted on the wall.

Riley picked it up and spoke. "Let me in, you fucker." He fell silent for a moment then tipped his head back and laughed. "That *is* the passphrase, you jackass!"

Riley hung up the handset and turned to Will, merriment clearly written across his face. "Jesse," he said, as if that was explanation enough.

In truth, it probably was. Jesse Murtagh was one of a kind. Part of a powerful media family in Manhattan, he was also pansexual and the biggest flirt Will had ever encountered. Not to mention charming and incredibly handsome—no wonder Carter had been attracted to him. Like Will, Jesse had been left in Riley and Carter's wake once they'd decided to get together, but Will suspected Jesse had been far less affected.

"Are you coming down or what?" A door opened at the end of the hall and Jesse appeared, a smile lighting his face and making his bright blue eyes twinkle. He glanced over at Will and gave him an appreciative grin.

"Glad you could join us tonight, Will. You're looking good."

Will chuckled and stepped forward to offer Jesse his hand. "It's good to see you too." Irrepressible flirt notwithstanding, Jesse had a compelling presence. Broad shoulders capped off a tall, lean body and the closely-cropped beard he sported framed full lips. Not Will's type, but easy on the eyes.

"Think you can manage to not storm off this time?" Jesse asked, raking a hand through his dark-blond hair.

Riley groaned. "Jes…"

Will smiled, despite his stab of discomfort at the reminder of the dramatic ending to his and Riley's relationship six months prior at a Christmas party. Will had finally realized the futility of his feelings for Riley that night and caused a scene in front of a small group of their combined friends, including Jesse and Carter. *Ugh.* It hadn't been one of his finer moments.

"I think I can behave tonight," he said aloud. "So, a speakeasy, huh? What made you decide to open that?"

Jesse held open the door and allowed Riley and Will to precede him down another long, narrow hallway.

"Why not? Kyle wanted to open a bar. We looked at a ton of locations and were bored by all of them, but when our friend Matt mentioned the space under Lock & Key, it all fell into place. Who doesn't want to own an underground, secret bar?"

"I can't say it's ever crossed my mind," Will admitted. They reached the end of the hall and Riley pushed open another unmarked door to reveal a stairwell. Although well-lit, the walls were painted black and totally bare.

"This is the problem with you, Will," Jesse said. "You're so buttoned up. You need to live a little."

"Well I'm spending the evening at a speakeasy with you," Will said as he followed Riley down the stairs. "Will that do for now?"

Jesse laughed. "Touché."

Riley pushed open a door at the bottom of the steps and the sight of the bar rendered Will mute.

In sharp contrast to the run-down bar above, the speakeasy was stylish and welcoming. Open shelves on the walls were filled with bottles of liquor. Inlaid floors were topped with sleek leather and metal furniture, and candles in votives glowed on the tables. The mellow music and subdued lighting lent the space an atmosphere of sophisticated relaxation.

Astonished, Will glanced over at Jesse. "This is incredible. I'm impressed."

"You have good taste, I'll give you that." Jesse grasped his shoulder and squeezed. "C'mon, let me get you a drink."

As Will crossed the room to the bar, Riley slipped into a spot beside Carter on the leather sofa. Will tried to hide a wince as Carter reached for Riley's knee and squeezed it without pausing in conversation.

"Wistful or vaguely nauseated?" Jesse asked as he took a seat on one of the bar stools.

Will glanced at him. "Excuse me?"

"Was the look because you wish you had that with Riley or because you're grossed out by two people being disgustingly in love?"

"A little of both, I suppose." Will had nothing against relationships, but they were starting to seem like a pipe dream for him.

A man appeared behind the bar and Will easily recognized him as Carter's friend, Kyle.

"Will, right?" he said, holding out a hand. "Kyle McKee."

"Yeah, hi. We met at Carter's birthday dinner."

Kyle smiled. "It's nice to see you again."

They shook and Will gave Kyle a once-over. Kyle was easily six feet tall, with broad shoulders, thick dark hair trimmed short on the sides, and heavy but well-groomed brows over dark eyes. Unlike Jesse, Kyle was very much Will's type. Except for the suspenders he wore over his crisp gray shirt and his rolled-up sleeves. Kyle pulled them off better than most, but the look screamed hipster too much for Will's tastes.

"Great place you have here." Will glanced around. "I like it."

"Thanks." Kyle's eyes crinkled at the corners when he smiled. "I'm pleased to hear it. A speakeasy wasn't quite what I had in mind when I told Jesse I wanted to open a bar, but I'm glad I decided to go for it."

Jesse grinned. "When will all of you learn my ideas are always brilliant?"

"Probably never." Kyle turned back to Will. "So, what can I get you? We have a wide selection of beer, wine and cocktails." He slid a leather-bound book in Will's direction.

Will perused it for a moment before he closed the cover. "You know what? Surprise me. Make me a cocktail."

"Hmm. I can do that. Anything you particularly dislike?"

"Anything too sweet. And Amaretto."

Kyle scrutinized Will for a moment before his eyes gleamed. "Got it."

Will watched with interest as Kyle pulled a glass out of the freezer and mixed together cognac, Cointreau and lemon juice in a shaker with ice. A few moments later, Kyle poured it into a glass, topped it with a twist of lemon and slid the drink across the bar to him. "Sidecar. Tell me what you think."

Will raised the glass to his lips and took a sip. He found the drink refreshingly cold and a perfect blend of sour and sweet with a fresh citrusy taste balanced nicely by the cognac. "That's delicious."

Kyle grinned. "Excellent."

"C'mon." Jesse picked up a tumbler filled with amber-colored liquid and a large spherical ice cube. It clinked pleasantly as he moved. "Let's go hang out with the guys."

The majority of the patrons were part of Riley and Carter's group, spread out across two leather sofas and a handful of chairs that made a square seating area around a finely crafted wood coffee table. Riley leaned forward and set his martini glass down. Will placed his own drink on a table and pulled up a chair.

"Everyone, this is Will Martin. Some of you met him at Carter's birthday and a few of you met him over the holidays. I'll introduce everyone, though."

Will gave him a brief smile. "Thanks."

"You know Carter, obviously." Carter nodded in greeting and Will returned it. "Next to Carter is his sister, Audrey." A tan blonde woman gave him a smile over a martini glass filled with something frothy and yellow. "And Audrey's husband, Max." An attractive, bearded man with brown hair and light brown eyes raised a pilsner glass in greeting.

Riley continued around the circle. "Gale, Jarrod, Henry and Miles are friends of Carter's." The men waved and murmured their hellos.

"You seem outnumbered here, Audrey," Will said.

She grinned at him. "I'm not complaining. My brother has some very good-looking friends."

Her husband elbowed her. "What am I? Chopped liver?"

"Never, darling. But I see you every day."

Kyle seated himself at an empty chair across the group. "You're a law professor, right, Will?"

Will nodded and took a sip of his drink. "Yes, at NYU. I'm spending the summer working on my latest book."

"What do you write?" Max asked. "I'd love to hear about it."

Will chuckled. "You may regret you asked, but I'm currently writing about the Chief Counsel of the House Legislative Oversight Subcommittee."

"So, political law then?"

"I couldn't totally avoid the family business," Will said dryly.

Audrey frowned. "You have a family member who's a politician?"

"My father." Will made a face. "And a Republican at that."

"How does that work at family dinners?" Audrey asked. "I thought my parents and Carter were bad, but at least they're not pushing discriminatory legislation."

"I haven't spoken to him since college, to be honest." Will took a fortifying sip of his sidecar. "I see my mother and sister on occasion, but never when he's around."

Riley shot him a sympathetic smile.

"Sorry to pry," Audrey said with an apologetic glance. "I've been battling my parents about them shutting Carter out and that's difficult enough."

"Ancient history." Will waved off her apology. "What do you do, Audrey?"

"I chair several philanthropic organizations. And I recently got involved with PFLAG." She exchanged a look with her brother.

Jesse leaned forward. "Beautiful *and* socially aware? Be still, my beating heart. If Max hadn't met you first..." Jesse took a sip of his drink. "That goes both ways, Max."

Max chuckled and Carter rolled his eyes. "We've had this discussion before, Jesse. No hitting on my sister *or* my brother-in-law, please. And definitely not both at once."

A chorus of laughter rose. Riley chimed in with a humorous comment as Will relaxed back in his chair and sipped his drink, enjoying the banter flying around the room. He'd been far too antisocial since the breakup and he was glad he'd taken Riley up on his invitation.

* * * *

A few hours later, Will reluctantly excused himself. He'd had a wonderful time and had enjoyed the witty conversation. It had left him feeling lighter and more relaxed than he had in a while. "I'm going to head home. I have an early game of racquetball planned with Charles tomorrow. I had a great night," Will said. "Thanks for inviting me, Riley. Carter."

"I'm glad you came," Carter said with a nod. He offered Will a sincere smile that crinkled the corners of his hazel eyes and Will grudgingly admitted he could see Carter's appeal. His jealousy had blinded him too much to appreciate Carter's broad-shouldered, long-legged build and handsome face before.

Will said goodnight to everyone and Jesse stood to shake his hand. "Please come back any time. I'll add your name to the list, so even if Kyle and I aren't here, you'll be let in. We do have a seat limit of forty and try to keep private events on the smaller side, but feel free to bring a friend or two. Especially if they're hot and single." He winked. "And maybe save that for when I'm here."

"Jesse!" Carter sounded exasperated and Will couldn't hide his smile.

"I'll keep that in mind," he said.

"We're trying to turn this into a regular thing," Kyle said. "Riley and I had the idea of meeting here the third Thursday of every month. Nothing formal, and if you can't make it, no problem, but it would be great if you could join us."

"I'll try to make it," Will said. "And thanks for a great evening. You make a mean sidecar."

"Any time," Kyle responded.

Will turned to leave. "I'll walk you up," Riley said. He fell into step behind Will.

"Tell Charles I said hi," Riley said as they walked up the stairs.

"I will."

"How are he and Gabe doing?"

"Good. They're both pretty busy right now. Charles is teaching classes this summer and Gabe is looking into opening another restaurant." Charles was an ex of Will's, and one of his closest friends and a colleague at NYU. Charles had married Gabe the summer before, and Gabe owned a high-end Vietnamese restaurant in Tribeca, not far from Will's home.

"You're welcome to bring them to Under anytime," Riley said. "If you think they'd be okay with that."

Will pushed open the door leading into Lock & Key. "I'm sure Gabe will be. Charles is still holding a bit of a grudge," he said. Will and Riley's breakup had rocked Riley's friendship with Gabe and Charles.

Riley sighed. "I deserve it."

"No, I should talk to him. You and I have mended some fences. There's no reason he needs to continue to shut you out." Will walked through the exit of the bar and turned to Riley when they stepped onto the sidewalk out front. "Thanks for inviting me tonight."

"I'm glad you came. I know it was asking a lot but—"

Will cut off Riley's statement. "I meant it when I said I wanted us to be friends. You're happy with Carter and *I'm* happy for you. Honestly, it's been great hanging out with you guys and your friends."

"I'm relieved to hear it," Riley said with a smile. He leaned in, then hesitated and Will closed the distance to hug him.

"Have a good night, Riley."

"Night, Will."

Riley disappeared back through the door of Lock & Key and Will sighed. Hugging Riley left him with a bittersweet feeling, but he was glad he'd come to check out the speakeasy. And he'd meant it when he said he'd try to come back on Thursday evenings in the future. He'd needed some time to lick his wounds and recover, but his self-imposed isolation only made his loneliness worse.

He glanced up and down the street. There wasn't a cab in sight so he pulled out his phone and brought up the Lyft app. He leaned against the wall of the brick building while he waited and a few minutes later a car slid to a stop in front of him.

Will made small-talk with the driver as the car traveled from Morningside Heights back to Tribeca. When they got caught in a traffic snarl near Central Park West because of a protest, Will took out his phone to kill the time. He was scrolling through articles on a news app when his phone vibrated in his hand.

Mom flashed across the screen and he hesitated before he accepted the call.

"Hey, Mom," he answered.

"Will." Agnes Martin's voice sounded strained, with none of the usual groomed sophistication it typically held.

He straightened. "Is something wrong?"

"Will, your father…" Her breath hitched. "I have some news. Your father has been ill lately."

Serves the old bastard right, Will thought grimly. "Ill?" he said aloud.

"Tired, losing weight, stomach pain. At first, we blamed his stress. He's been working so hard lately—"

Yeah, probably passing more anti-LGBT legislation, Will thought.

"But when we noticed some yellowing of his eyes, we got concerned. We were hopeful it was a gallbladder issue, but after some testing, we were referred to an oncologist."

His breath caught. *Oncologist? Shit.* "He has cancer?"

"Yes. He has something called a — a non-functioning neuroendocrine tumor. Pancreatic cancer. It's quite large and the doctors are concerned it's spread to some nearby lymph nodes. It's stage III and the — the prognosis isn't good."

Will took a moment to let the words sink in, but didn't feel much of anything about the news. A wave of guilt washed over him. "I'm sorry, Mom," he said gently. She loved his father and while Will had many, many issues with William Martin Sr. as a father and an elected official, he had always treated Will's mother well. There had never been a hint of infidelity and after Agnes had suffered a serious car accident years ago, Bill hadn't left her side until she'd recovered. "I know how hard this must be for you."

His mother sniffled. "I can't lose him. I know you and your father have your…differences but — "

"We don't have *differences*," he retorted. Any goodwill he'd felt dissipated. "He detests me. He thinks I am less deserving of the same basic human rights he affords everyone else. That's more than an ideological difference, Mom, that's a complete lack of respect for me as a human being."

"Come to Garden City," she blurted out and the words rang in his ear for several seconds before he could process them.

"What? You must be *kidding*," he said. "You can't think I'd come to Long Island to sit by his deathbed and hold his hand." He winced. His cruel words served only to remind Agnes her husband was probably dying. "I'm sorry, Mom, but I can't do it. I can't pretend like everything is fine between us. We haven't spoken in over ten years and it's not only because *I'm* pissed at him. He's the one who cut me out of his life, remember?"

"He wants you here," she said softly. Agnes had used the same tone during Will's years growing when she tried to get him to do something he didn't want to do.

Will sat back in his seat. "Really?"

"I asked him if you could come home and he said yes."

Well, that was more plausible than Will's father specifically asking for him to come home. He sighed. "I-I don't know. I suppose I could come for a long weekend or something. School's out and I could work on my edits while I'm there."

Agnes went silent for a moment. "I hoped you'd stay longer. Your father is undergoing surgery next week, but it'll be exhausting for all of us. If the surgery doesn't work, we may only have a few months left with him." Her voice broke.

"You want me to spend the entire summer in Long Island?" he asked, incredulous.

"Please, Will. If you won't come for your father, come home for Olivia and me. Your sister and I need you. We can't do this alone."

Will glanced out of the window, surprised the bright lights of the city were blurred by tears. He wasn't sure who they were for.

"I'll think about it, Mom."

Chapter Two

Despite having lived in Freeport, New York, for three years, Senator David Mori was still acclimating to his new home village. His twin sister, Isabel, didn't seem very sympathetic about his observation.

"You decided to move here," she said. Amusement danced in her green eyes. "No one forced you to up and leave the city."

Despite David's request that his sister not make a big deal about their birthday, Isabel insisted on making steak-frites for dinner and his favorite dessert, vanilla Bundt cake. She'd come over earlier that afternoon with three big bags full of groceries and homemade biscuits for his dog, Mabel. The Husky-Inu mix was currently snoozing on the deck, her belly full of Isabel's creations.

He looked up from a bowl of strawberries he'd been hulling. "Thank you for your wisdom, Captain Obvious. I remember the trek out here with the moving van perfectly well."

"God, me too." Isabel screwed up her pretty face in a grimace as she stirred a bowl of frosting. "I had no idea your comic book collection had grown so large! I think I pulled every muscle in my body hauling boxes that weekend."

David's heart squeezed, but he couldn't hold back a smile. "Sorry. If it makes you feel any better, we moved Dad's collection out here, too. I think more of the boxes were his stuff than mine."

Isabel smiled too and flicked her ponytail over her shoulder. "Well. That's to be expected. Dad had a head start on his collection."

David glimpsed a familiar flash of pain on Isabel's face. It had been years since they'd lost their parents, but the ache was still fresh.

"So, what's not to like about this little town?" Isabel asked. She set the frosting aside and he admired the pretty picture she made in her simple black sundress. "It's lovely, and everyone I've spoken to seems perfectly nice. Did someone make a crack about your Asian-ness?"

David's race sometimes garnered attention from the District Eight voters of Long Island, but he was hardly the only Japanese-American in the county. People were seldom overtly rude. "Not to my face, no. I don't dislike anything about Freeport, which is a village, incidentally."

"But the city boy in you isn't at home here?"

"More like the city boy in me is still getting used to everything being very quiet and clean with nothing out of place."

Isabel rolled her eyes. "I can't believe you're complaining about this."

"I'm not!" David laughed. "It's just different. Back in my old neighborhood, I used to go down the street to the market every morning for coffee and a newspaper.

Here, my newspaper is delivered, bright and early, before I've even *had* coffee. Today, I stepped outside to go for a run and it was so close to the door I stepped on it, turned my ankle and fell right on my ass." He sniffed when Isabel burst out laughing.

"Poor baby. Is your butt bruised?"

"Not as much as my pride."

"Did any of your neighbors see?"

David made a face. "Oh, God, I hope not. I'll bet Mrs. Cohen did—I'm not sure she sleeps." Mrs. Cohen, a lovely middle-aged lady who lived two doors down, doted on both David and his dog.

Isabel clucked at him. "Don't worry. Things always roll off your hard candy shell. Besides, it's good to show the mortals around you're one of them."

David frowned. "Oh, come on. They know I'm a regular guy underneath the business suits."

"Now you come on." Isabel eyed her brother. "I know you're a nerdy boy from Glendale, but that's because I grew up with you. People who didn't…" She stepped forward and brought a hand up to smooth David's dark hair back from his forehead. "Davey, you're like an anime super-hero to them. With your degrees and giant brain, not to mention this face—"

"You're one to talk." David took Isabel's hand in his. "You have at least twice as many degrees and I *know* you're more beautiful."

"I'll give you the first," Isabel countered, "but I'd also lay odds most of the planet would vote you as the prettiest Mori, babe."

"Hey, don't sell yourself short."

"I'm not! I value my accomplishments as much as I do yours. But you can't deny you're bigger than life. You're six-foot-two, ripped, and we both know there's a reason three different modeling scouts tried to recruit you when we were in college."

David groaned in exasperation, but Isabel shushed him. "That said, you light up a room when you walk in. Right or wrong, charisma is one of the main reasons people listen to you and vote for you, and think you're on the right track to do something worthwhile."

"That doesn't change the fact I'm a man, Is. Just like them." He waved toward the kitchen windows. "I didn't get into politics to stroke my ego—I got in because I want to make a difference."

"I believe you can, and so do your voters." Isabel squeezed his fingers. "Those people out there admire you already. Let them get to know you—the real you who sometimes trips over the newspaper and falls on his ass. They'll come to love you like I do and Mom and Dad did."

David's throat tightened and he nodded. He leaned in so Isabel could press a kiss to his cheek, and breathed a sigh of relief when she turned her attention back to the cake and icing on the counter.

"Okay, let's dress this bad boy up so we can eat it."

"Allen's coming, right?" David checked the clock on the wall and frowned at the time.

"He said he'd be here by seven," Isabel replied. "He had a web-conference with a client in Scotland this afternoon and wanted to get some paperwork done before he drove out." She flashed David a smile. "You know how he is about cake—he'll be on time."

He turned back to the bowl of fruit. "Well I'm saying it now, then—if he isn't, I'm eating his share of everything."

Isabel's husband showed up thirty minutes later with two bottles of very good Syrah. Allen immediately jumped into helping with the dinner preparations while they talked about David's recent voting record. Generally, David tried to avoid discussing political policy with his family. His conservative views had often been in opposition to his parents' liberalism and were a one-eighty-degree turn from Allen's progressive leanings. Allen was unabashedly curious about David's work, however, and an incurable gossip when it came to his senate colleagues.

"How's your mentor treating you, by the way?" Allen asked. "And tell me again how that works between you two, anyway, because I've always assumed Martin is vehemently anti-gay rights. Does it even come up?"

"LGBTQ issues definitely come up when we're working—there's no way around them in this day and age," David replied. "Bill's mentioned my status as a gay man on occasion, but more like he's trying to figure things out than anything else." He smiled when Isabel snorted a laugh into her wine glass.

"Poor bastard got the short end of the stick, huh? Bad enough he has to mentor the gay boy, you had to be *hāfu*, too."

Allen scowled. "Is, stop."

Isabel scowled right back. "What for? David and I are mixed race, honey, it's not like we don't know it. In the States we're too Asian and in Japan we're too white."

"I know *hāfu* means 'half' but it's weird to throw it out there like that," Allen persisted.

"Don't sweat it, man." David took pity on his brother-in-law, who never knew how to react when he and Isabel spoke frankly about their mixed ethnicity. "Is and I have known we were different pretty much since we could talk. Kids asked us all the time why our dad was 'a Chinaman' even though our mom was white.

My race hasn't come up with Bill," he added, with a glance at his sister. "I mean, he knows my background, but I don't get a feeling he gives a damn."

"Well, that's promising in a weird sort of way," Isabel replied. She shrugged when Allen appeared bewildered. "It's bad enough Senator Martin is a homophobe, Allen — at least he's not an obvious racial bigot, too."

"Jesus. I don't know how you do it, David." Allen reached for the open bottle of wine and refilled his own glass. "I'd bust a blood vessel on my first day."

Isabel gave her husband an indulgent smile. "That's why you're a transportation engineer, honey — because autonomous cars are cool as fuck."

David and Allen burst out laughing. "I'm not sure Senator Martin is a homophobe, by the way," David said when he'd finally caught his breath again.

"Do you *have* to call him by his title?" Isabel asked with a grimace. "I mean, it's so formal. Does he call you Senator Mori?"

"Sure, when we're in the middle of business on the floor or working a crowd. It's who we are, Is — Senators William Martin Sr. and David Mori. Off the floor, we're just Bill and David."

Isabel swirled the wine in her glass. "That's a relief. I get you respect him because he's got decades of experience, but he's your peer, not your boss. It's weird enough you followed him out here to freaking Long Island, for God's sake."

"I didn't follow him — I had to move out of Queens to run for the seat."

"Yeah, yeah, and you moved to Stepford," Isabel teased. "What makes you say Bill Martin's not a homophobe? He and the rest of the jackasses you work with are still stalled on GENDA even though the New York Assembly's passed it six years in a row."

"That's about to be seven years," David corrected. "It'll probably pass the Assembly again next week."

"So, what's the problem?" Allen wanted to know. "Gender Expression Non-Discrimination Act extends human rights protections to transgender people who, hello, are also voters. Don't Martin and the rest of you care?"

David frowned. "Of course I care. People shouldn't fear losing their job or home because of their gender identity, whether they're registered voters or not. I talked to Bill about it last week, when we knew the vote would be coming up. He assured me he'd be ready when the time came and he's surprisingly neutral about the whole topic."

"Maybe he doesn't feel strongly about transgender people," Isabel suggested.

"That's kind of my point. How can a homophobe not care about a population of people who are controversial even within the LGBTQ community? Some of my most liberal-minded friends are completely weirded out by even the idea of sex-reassignment."

"That is interesting," Isabel said. "I'd definitely assume he'd be more outspoken about it, even with you."

"But you like Martin?" Allen asked.

"I respect him, yes, and like him. Despite our differing views on some social issues, he's had an admirable career and I've learned a lot from him."

"He really doesn't give you shit about being gay?" Allen's expression turned dubious even as David shook his head.

"I don't think he especially *likes* that I'm a gay man, but he seems to understand it's what I am." He brought a hand up to rub his nose. "I will say on the few occasions we've talked about my sexuality, it feels a little like he's doing research."

Isabel scrunched up her nose. "Creepy."

"It's complicated," David allowed. "And gotten even more so the longer I've known him. I get the feeling something's going on with Bill, especially recently."

"Like what?"

"Well, he's been out sick quite a bit the last couple of weeks and working from home. Sure, people get sick, but he almost never misses a day, unless it's for travel. And tomorrow, he's invited me to his family's home for a 'working brunch'," David said, making quotes in the air with his fingers. "Not that I mind, but if I'm going to see the man Monday morning anyway, what's so important it can't wait?"

"Well, at least you'll be fed," Allen put in. "Hopefully you get something tasty like eggs Benedict instead of organic muesli and almond milk."

"I ate muesli and almond milk for breakfast this morning, you bozo." David tossed the crispy end of a French fry at Allen, who somehow managed to catch it in his mouth. Isabel nearly fell out of her chair laughing, and it took a minute before any of them could formulate anything near real words.

"You're such a dick," David told his brother-in-law, who fist-pumped like a boy.

Isabel smiled and pushed back her chair. "Why don't you boys clear the table, while I get some coffee started? Then we can see about demolishing that cake."

* * * *

David pulled into Senator Martin's driveway the next morning at five minutes to eleven. He powered down the engine of his Tesla S60 and sat for a moment, his gaze fixed on the elegant white Colonial house before him. His habitual need to be early usually served him well, but today he wasn't so sure.

He hadn't lied to Isabel and Allen the night before when they'd asked how he got on with Bill Martin. Bill acted the part of mentor to David with understated skill, and they worked well together, even when they disagreed on policy. David hesitated to call Bill his friend, however, and he wasn't at all sure showing up on the dot for brunch would ingratiate him to his hosts.

"Too late to do anything about it now that you're sitting in the man's drive," he murmured to himself. He reached for the small bag on the seat beside him and climbed out of the car, feeling suddenly younger as he approached the door and rang the bell, like a gangly teenager in his navy-checked shirt and light blue khakis, rather than the self-assured man of thirty-four his sister had described the day before.

That awkwardness faded as the door opened and David came face-to-face with Agnes Martin, who gave him a welcoming smile.

"Good morning, Mrs. Martin."

"Good morning, David, and please, call me Agnes." Agnes' brown eyes were lively as she waved him into the house. "Bill made some cold-brewed coffee last night and just poured out some glasses, so your timing is impeccable."

David waited until the door had closed behind him to present her with the little bag. "I recently discovered a fudge shop near my place and brought some to share."

Agnes' eyes grew round as she peeked into the bag. "Oh, how thoughtful of you."

"There's penuche and chocolate, and I can attest to both being some of the nicest fudge I've ever had."

"Well I adore both, and so does Bill, though he's not supposed to have too many sweets right now." Agnes gave David a conspiratorial grin. "I'll have to keep these in a hiding place so he doesn't clean me out!"

She led him through the house and kept up the cheerful chatter. The home's interior was elegant, and there were homey touches scattered about in the form of family photographs and fresh wildflower arrangements.

They found Bill in the kitchen, standing at a large island with several tall glasses filled with ice and a carafe of coffee. Bill glanced up, his gaze steely but his smile sincere.

"Hello, David."

"Hello, Bill."

"Care for a coffee?"

"Yes, thanks."

Bill filled one of the glasses and held it out to David, then gestured at the coffee service on the island. "I hope you brought your appetite," he said as David picked up a small pitcher of cream. "Agnes has made enough food to feed half a dozen people."

Agnes rolled her eyes but smiled. "It's funny, but I didn't hear you complaining while I did the actual cooking."

"That because I'm not an idiot," Bill said with a short laugh. "You made at least three of my favorite breakfast foods, so I'd be out of my mind to complain."

"Is there anything I can help you with?" David asked. He smiled when Agnes waved him off.

"Oh, no dear, I wouldn't hear of it, and we're nearly finished here anyway. Bill, would you hand me the spoon by your left hand? The one I've got here isn't big enough."

Agnes and Bill Martin were a study in contrasts both physically and temperamentally. Where Agnes was warm and vivacious, Bill was formidable and composed.

Agnes was a fine-boned beauty, and the light caught the silver strands threaded throughout her golden-brown hair. While petite, she had a regal bearing that gave her the illusion of being taller than her actual height, particularly next to Bill's six feet, four inches. Bill cut an imposing figure, due in part to his broad-shouldered physique, but also to his craggy good looks and piercing blue eyes. David had never known Bill to raise his voice above speaking volume, even when visibly angered. Instead, he focused his attention on whomever he addressed with laser-like precision, using his gaze and quietly powerful tone to convey his displeasure.

David sipped his coffee and chatted with his hosts. He spent only a little time with Bill outside of typical work settings, and even on those occasions — like parades and fundraisers — they still played their parts as political creatures. Today was a rare opportunity to spend time with his mentor outside of their jobs and, as he watched Bill and Agnes together, his earlier bout of nerves disappeared completely.

When Agnes was satisfied with the preparations, their housekeeper appeared to help bring the platters of food outside to the patio. Greta, a cheerful, middle-aged woman with dark-blonde hair and smiling eyes, shooed Bill and David out first.

"Safety first, sir," she added with a grin that could easily have been taken for a smirk.

"Of course." Bill led David out to the patio. "I dropped a platter of bacon *once* in the twenty-five years Greta has worked here," he muttered, "and she refuses to let me forget it."

David admired the large pool and surrounding rock gardens while Agnes and Greta filled the patio table with food, and was pleasantly surprised when Bill asked about his home.

"It's a lot bigger than I need right now with only my dog and me, but I won't complain," David said. "Plus, there's a sundeck off the back of the house facing out onto the canal and that makes for some beautiful sunsets."

Bill chuckled. "I'd imagine so. It's a pity you don't have a family to enjoy it with." His expression turned calculating and slightly hard. "Though I suppose that's no longer outside the realm of possibility for the people of your community."

David nodded. He'd heard a lot worse before and Bill wasn't wrong. "True. Family options have become more varied in recent years."

Both men paused and glanced Agnes' way when she cleared her throat.

"We're ready," she said and while David hadn't thought much about eating, his stomach rumbled as he got an eyeful at the food.

"David, Bill tells me you're not vegetarian, but if you'd like something lighter on breakfast meats, the whole-wheat pancakes are very good, if I do say so myself." Agnes smiled as Bill pushed her chair in. "There's also a ham and spinach strata and pastrami hash with potato, along with the usual pork products Bill simply has to have."

Bill plucked a piece of bacon from one of the platters before seating himself. "She says all this like she doesn't eat them herself."

"Everything looks fantastic," David assured Agnes, and he nearly laughed when she nudged the platter of pancakes toward him. "I had a protein bar on my way out of the house earlier this morning and didn't even recognize how hungry I am."

Agnes frowned. "That's no good, David. I understand you're a single man, but there's no good reason you can't learn a few tricks in the kitchen to make your own life easier."

"Oh, I'm handy enough around the kitchen," he assured her. "I had my family over yesterday and put off running some errands until this morning."

Agnes raised her brows. "Your family is in town?"

"My sister and her husband," David said. "We had dinner and they stayed the night instead of driving back to the city. They're going to do some exploring on the beach today before going home."

"Oh, I'm glad they're close by. Do you see them often?"

"My sister and I try to have dinner together at least once a month." David laid down his fork and used his napkin to wipe his mouth and considered how to continue. Talking around the topic of his parents only made things more awkward for everyone.

"It's just Isabel and me now," he said and gave Agnes a small smile. "My parents—"

"Bill told me of your loss," she cut in gently. "I'm so very sorry, dear."

David glanced at Bill and found his expression unreadable before he looked back to Agnes. "Thank you, I appreciate that."

"I'm glad you and your sister have each other," she added, her expression so knowing his heart ached. "Are the two of you especially close?"

"Yes," David said with a grin. "But we're fraternal twins, so we've never been anything but really, *really* close."

"Oh, my goodness, I can't even imagine having twins. I have no idea how people do it."

Bill huffed out a laugh. "Agnes, we have two children."

"Yes, but they were spaced nearly three years apart, dear," Agnes replied. "We didn't have two infants, two toddlers or two potty trainings happening at the same time."

"We had two teenagers at the same time," Bill returned. David wanted to laugh at his long-suffering expression. He knew of the adult Martin children from Bill's bio, but not much beyond their names and professions.

"At least only one of them proved truly difficult at the time." Bill sighed. "Christ, I thought for a while Olivia would end up in juvenile detention."

"Don't be so dramatic," Agnes scolded and turned to David. "While it's true Olivia was the more high-spirited of our children —"

"She shaved her head, Agnes."

" — our son, Will, got into trouble when the mood struck him, too."

David grinned and cut into his pancakes. "Did he also shave his head?"

Agnes laughed. "No, no—he was far too fond of his hair to actually get rid of it, but he did dye it some fantastic colors when he entered his teens. I've been talking to Will about visiting us soon so perhaps you'll get to meet him yourself."

They passed a pleasant hour dining and talking, though David noticed Bill didn't eat very much. By the time Greta returned to help Agnes clear the table, David had made up his mind to suggest returning the brunch favor by hosting one of his own.

"Let me help you clean up," he offered and began to stand, only for Bill to shake his head. David realized why when Greta turned her bright grin on them.

"We've got it covered sir," Greta said. David bit back a smile at the almost forced cheeriness in her voice.

"I told you," Bill murmured. "She won't allow me near the plates unless I'm in a seated position. Best thing is to let her take charge and stay out of her way."

"I'll remember that," David said. "Thanks for an enjoyable afternoon, Bill. This is very different from how we normally spend time together."

Bill nodded. "You're welcome. I've meant to talk with you about something for a while now, but my schedule shifted. Now I find myself hurrying to complete things before—well. I just find myself hurrying."

David furrowed his brow. Those few words were enough to set off a prickle of concern. "Forgive me if I'm overstepping, but is everything all right?"

Bill shook his head. "No. Everything's not 'all right'. Agnes and I are driving to Philadelphia tomorrow." His eyes flashed with emotion despite his low, steady voice. "I'm having surgery on my pancreas this Tuesday, and I'm not sure I'll survive it."

Chapter Three

Will's head pounded as he turned the Zipcar rental into the driveway of the stately home he'd grown up in. He parked in front of the detached garage and turned off the engine. He'd agreed to come and get the house ready for his father's return. A medical supply company would be arriving this afternoon to set up a hospital bed and he had a few telephone calls to make to coordinate with the in-home nursing service.

Since his mother's call, he'd received a flurry of texts from his sister, laying out what needed to be done. Olivia and his mother actually *did* need help. Will couldn't leave them in the lurch. But he still had to force himself to open the door and retrieve his laptop and suitcase from the trunk.

On leaden feet, he followed the curved brick path leading to the front door. The lawn was neatly trimmed and flowers bloomed in the beds surrounding the house. An American flag fluttered in the light breeze. A black iron railing topped the portico at the foyer, though no door led out to the small balcony. Will had spent a good portion of his childhood clambering out of the window to read there anyway.

He ignored the trembling in his fingers and fitted the spare key in the lock to open the door. He'd had to dig the key out of the back of a desk drawer where it had languished for years, dragged from apartment to apartment until he'd finally settled into the condo in Tribeca.

The front door opened into a roomy foyer decorated with heavy antique wood furniture and Persian rugs. To the left was a large formal living room. To the right, a stuffy dining room. Little had changed in the past ten years, beyond fresh paint and a few new decorative accents.

The seven-bedroom house was far too large for his parents alone—it had been too much even when Will and Olivia had lived there—but his great-grandparents had it built in the nineteen-thirties and he couldn't picture his parents ever selling it.

The house was exactly as he remembered—large, traditional and the last place he wanted to be.

A familiar middle-aged woman appeared in the hall, wiping her hands on a towel as she peered at him. "William?" Her face lit up. "Your mother said you were coming!"

Greta had worked as the family's housekeeper since Will's childhood, but unlike his troubled relationships with his mother and sister, he'd never had an ambivalent relationship with Greta. Will smiled. "It's nice to see you, Greta. How have you been?"

"Very well, thank you." She beamed at him. "Your mother keeps me updated on you. Are you still teaching at NYU?"

"I am. I'm very happy there."

"I'm so pleased to hear it. Oh, before I forget, your room upstairs is ready. There are fresh sheets on the bed and towels in the bath. Let me know if there's anything else you need."

"I will. Thanks, Greta."

After Greta excused herself and disappeared down the hall, Will sighed. He hefted his suitcase and walked up the familiar set of stairs. They were ones he'd raced up and down as a kid and played on until Greta had gently scolded him to find somewhere else to stage mock battles.

Although the downstairs had become a semi-public space with his father's staff members and the occasional colleague coming in and out, the upstairs was reserved for family. The hallways were lined with framed portraits of the Martin family throughout the years. He passed one and winced at his buck-toothed smile from before he'd had braces.

Will's bedroom was situated at the back of the house over the addition. He'd moved out everything personal years before and found it decorated in neutral colors now. The sitting area still housed a desk beneath the window, however. At least he'd have a pleasant place to get work done.

After he unpacked, he returned to the first floor, laptop in tow, debating where to set up. Will eventually settled on a small table in the sunroom with a view of the backyard and sparkling blue pool. Something brushed against his ankle and he looked down to see a small black cat winding around his feet.

"Hey there, kitty," he said, reaching down to pet it. He didn't recognize the cat, but Agnes was a long-time animal lover and harbored a soft spot for cats. She was on the board of every animal welfare organization in the area and donated to an equal number of shelters.

She'd always had several house cats and at least one or two strays who were too wild to sleep anywhere but the garage. Even the strays were taken to the vet for testing, shots and neutering.

The black cat found a sunny spot near Will's feet and a few moments later a contented purr filled the room. Will considered himself more of a dog person, but as he worked he had to admit the cat made for pleasant company and took the edge off his anxiety about being there.

He'd gotten midway through compiling a to-do list when Greta reappeared. "I'll be heading out shortly, William. Is there anything I can get you before I go? Lunch? Something to drink?"

He turned and smiled at her. "I appreciate it, but I'm all set. You could call me Will, though, you know?" he teased.

She smiled back but shook her head. "You've been William Junior as long as I've known you."

"I suppose William is better than being called Junior," he pointed out.

She clasped her hands together and pressed them to her chest. "Oh, it's so good to have you here."

He had no idea how to respond so he cleared his throat instead. "Thank you. Why don't you head home? I have everything under control here."

"Oh, that reminds me," she said. "Senator Martin's office has been cleaned — top to bottom — and my nephews came to rearrange the furniture. There's plenty of room for the hospital bed." A shadow flickered across her face. "I hope he'll be able to move back upstairs soon."

Will swallowed. He'd done some online research and, coupled with what his mother had said, it didn't sound promising. Survival rates for pancreatic cancer were incredibly low. "Olivia said the surgery went well and they'll be home tomorrow."

"God willing," Greta said. She shook herself and smiled at him. "Now, you have a good afternoon."

"You too, Greta," he said absently. He'd fallen deep in thought by the time she left the house a short while later.

Will spent the remainder of the day converting his father's office into a sickroom. Will's grandfather had built the large addition on the back of the house and originally intended it as a den, but Senator Martin had made it his office for years. It had a separate entrance off the backyard and allowed him to meet with staff members without having them constantly traipse through the rest of the house.

Although Will disliked his father's politics, he couldn't deny Bill was a hardworking public servant. He'd always treated his position as a sacred duty to his constituents rather than a means to power or wealth. Will couldn't fault him for that. He'd never felt the same burning desire to be a part of it, however. That had been the first of Senator Martin's disappointments in Will.

After checking off the last item on his to-do list, Will slumped on the sofa in the living room and contemplated what to do with himself for the rest of the evening. The house seemed large and echo-y with no one else there.

His father had gone under the knife six days ago. Olivia's latest update had sounded promising and surprisingly upbeat. Their father should be able to leave the hospital as soon as the doctor released him the following morning, and they would drive home from Philadelphia. With the home medical care squared away, Will had little to do until they arrived.

He decided to take a shower before heading out into Garden City to find someplace to eat. He wasn't looking forward to dining alone, but he'd lost track of the people he'd grown up with on Long Island and was cut off from his life in Manhattan. He felt out of place, like a stranger in his hometown.

Once showered and dressed, Will hopped into the Zipcar and headed into the village, hoping his favorite Italian place from his youth was still open.

* * * *

The following day, Will was hard at work on his edits when he heard the front door open. "Will?" a familiar voice called out.

"In here, Olivia," Will replied and stood to greet his sister.

She peered at him from the foyer. "Can you come out? We need your help getting Dad inside."

Olivia was tastefully dressed and made up, but Will could see she looked weary as they crossed the room toward each other. There wasn't a strand of her sleek chestnut hair out of place but there were shadows under her brown eyes and a strained tightness around her mouth. She appeared older than her thirty-six years.

"Sure," he agreed, although he felt nowhere near as confident as he sounded. He followed Olivia out to the garage and a gleaming black Town Car.

William Martin Senior — better known as Bill to friends and family — sat in the back. His skin was sallow and his face haggard. Will froze at the sight of his father. For the first time, he looked old.

"There you are," his mother said. She looked tense and tired too, but her hug was warm as Will embraced her.

"Will." His father's tone indicated his surprise. Guilt flared briefly in Will as he realized his father had doubted he'd come.

"I told you he'd be here, Bill," his mother said. "He came yesterday to get everything ready."

Bill nodded tightly. "That was good of you."

Will couldn't remember the last time he'd heard his father praise him and he had to swallow before he could speak. "What can I do now?"

"I'm fine, but your mother is insisting I get some help walking to the house," he said tersely. Will could imagine how difficult his father found admitting he needed help of any sort. "Come here, George," he said gruffly.

Will glanced over at the driver who hurried to the open door. It hurt to watch his father struggle out of the car with the young man's help, and a pained expression crossed Bill's face when he stood.

"Will, get his other arm," Agnes directed and Will took the spot at his father's side.

Bill stooped and his flesh seemed to hang off his bones, as if he'd shrunk inside his formerly powerful frame. For the first time, Will stood taller and straighter than his father, but Bill's grip on his forearm was like iron.

Will and George maneuvered Bill out of the garage and onto the sidewalk, but when Will turned to head toward the front of the house, his father balked.

"Around the back," he snapped. "Less chance of someone seeing. I don't want this in the papers."

Will quelled a biting comment and turned toward the rear of the house.

In the bright summer sunlight, his father's steely hair looked thin and his skin even more sallow. His once-arresting features seemed softer than the last time Will had seen a picture of him, and for the first time his wrinkles made him look aged, rather than distinguished. His blue eyes were still piercing as he glanced over at Will.

Will managed a small smile of encouragement and something he couldn't identify flickered in his father's gaze.

By the time they crossed the patio and into the new sickroom, Bill looked exhausted and he sank heavily onto the hospital bed set up at one end of the room.

"Did you have to get a bed with rails?" he groused. "I'm not going to fall out like a child!"

Agnes raised her hand and smoothed it over William's hair. The tenderness of the gesture made Will look away. "If the nurse says you can keep them down, that's fine," Agnes said. "But the hospital bed will be easiest on you for your recovery for a little while. You'll sleep more comfortably."

"Why don't you lie down for a while, Daddy?" Olivia said. "I am sure the nurse will be here soon, but you can rest until then."

Will cleared his throat. "I confirmed with the agency and someone should be here within the hour."

"Thank you." His mother flashed him a tired smile before she turned back to her husband. "Bill, won't you relax for a bit at least? You don't have to sleep but you should be lying down."

Bill muttered under his breath, but he sounded alarmingly weak and Will saw him waver. Bill swung his legs up onto the bed with a pained grunt, clutching his side. "God damn it."

Agnes removed his shoes and covered him with a light blanket while Olivia fluffed the pillows behind his head, then handed him the bed controls.

Once settled, Bill waved them off. "If you want me to rest, don't hover around. I'll call if I need you."

Will followed his mother and sister out of the room, then went to close the French doors to the room. "It was good of you to come, Will," Bill said gruffly to his retreating back and Will turned back to his father. Unsure of what to say, he nodded and a moment later, Bill closed his eyes.

When Will joined his mother and sister in the hallway, Olivia burst into tears. Agnes held a hand out to her, but Olivia shook her mother off and walked quickly away.

Will looked helplessly at his mother. She offered him a wan smile and squeezed his upper arm. "It's been a rough week. Go after your sister. I'm going to make some tea."

After poking his head through several doorways, he found his sister in the sunroom, her hand pressed to her mouth to stifle a sob. Will wrapped his arms around her and pulled her close. He rested his chin on the top of her head as she cried against his chest. After a few minutes, she stepped back, wiping at her eyes.

"Liv..." he said helplessly. "I wish I knew what to do."

"I'm glad you came. I couldn't do this alone." She pulled a tissue from the pocket of her trousers and dabbed at her eyes.

"I know. That's why I came — for you and Mom."

"Don't you feel anything for Dad?"

"Very few things that are positive." Will swallowed. The interaction he'd had with his father had shaken him. He didn't know what to make of the frail older man who seemed relieved to see him. It didn't fit the image in his head of the angry, scathing father who'd told him he was no longer welcome to come home.

"He's not a monster, Will!" Olivia snapped.

"I don't want to have this argument right now," he said sharply, then softened his tone. "Look, Liv, I'll stay for a week. I'll help you and Mom get him situated, then head back to Manhattan. I'll try to come by every couple of weeks if you want me, but I can't promise anything beyond that."

She frowned, her lips thinning with displeasure. "You're very selfish."

He opened his mouth to reply but stopped. Will was tired of feeding the cycle of arguments about his relationship with their father. He forced himself to take a deep breath and respond with something more productive. "Tell me what I can do to help right now."

"I don't suppose you've learned to cook recently?" He shook his head. "Fine, then will you go to the grocery store and pick up some things for the next few days? Mom didn't want Greta hovering so she gave her the day off. Dad's on a very restrictive diet and we made a list at the hospital of what he'll need."

"Of course." Will would agree to anything that got him out of the house.

"I'll email it. When you get back, I'll make dinner, then head home, unless Mom and Dad need something else."

"You're leaving me here alone?" Will's tone was incredulous.

Olivia rolled her eyes and he suddenly remembered teenaged Livvie—the reigning queen of eye rolling. "You'll survive. I have children, remember? I've been gone for a week, already. I'd like to see my family."

"How are Adam and Jocelyn?"

"They're doing well. Jocelyn has started horseback riding lessons."

"They teach six-year-olds how to ride horses?"

"Yes, but she's nine, so that's a moot point."

He winced. "Sorry. That means Adam's...eleven?"

"Yes. He'll be twelve in August." Olivia gave him a stern look, and the resemblance to their mother was spooky. "This would be a good opportunity for you to get to know your niece and nephew better, you know. I don't know if Dad will be up to having them visit, but maybe you can come over for dinner some night."

Will nodded. Over the years, he and his sister had met occasionally in Manhattan. He'd assuaged his guilt over not being involved in their lives more by sending gifts and the occasional card. But gifts were no substitute for actually being there on a regular basis. "I'd like that."

Olivia's expression softened and she stretched to kiss his cheek. "Okay, I'll send you the grocery list in a moment. When do you think you'll leave?"

He glanced at his wristwatch. "I can head out now."

"Thanks. Sorry I snapped at you earlier. I hope you know we're all grateful you're here."

* * * *

Will and his mother ate a quiet dinner together while Bill slept. Neither of them spoke much and Will could see the strain on his mother's face as she pushed the roasted chicken and salad around on her plate. She ate very little of it. She took him up on his offer to wash the dishes and disappeared into his father's room with a quiet "Good night."

After finishing the dishes, Will collected his laptop from the sunroom and thought about how to spend his evening. He was in no mood to check out the nightlife in Garden City — such as it was — and he didn't want to leave his mom home alone with his sick father. He could read, he supposed, although at the moment it didn't hold much appeal.

A bookshelf with brown leather-wrapped photo albums caught his eye. *What about a trip down Memory Lane?* he wondered. The urge surprised him, but it had been an odd day all around. He picked a couple of albums, unplugged his laptop and carried them all up the stairs to his bedroom.

After setting the laptop on the desk, he sprawled on the bed with the albums in front of him. Apprehension crackled through him as he flipped the cover of the earlier one open. *Is it a good idea to dredge up the past?* he asked himself, half-tempted to close the damn thing and forget about it.

He paused when a picture of Olivia with pigtails and a wide, gap-toothed grin caught his eye. Her goofy expression made him smile. Next to it was a picture of the two of them on a park bench eating ice cream. And another with their mother at the beach. Will couldn't remember that specific trip and he wondered if his father had taken the photo. More likely, his Aunt Cora had, or his mom's best friend, Elizabeth. Senator Martin's schedule had been busy and hadn't allowed him to be a hands-on parent.

And yet, the next few photos belied that fact. In one, Bill helped a seven-year-old Will build a soap box derby car. Will remembered his father's obsessive focus on building the perfect car, but also the way he'd helped Will steady the tools. The photos showed some of those moments, father and son laughing together.

Will continued flipping and spotted more photos with the senator than without. Maybe his memory wasn't entirely reliable.

He chuckled when he got to a photo of him and his sister dressed up for Halloween. He'd dressed as a Supreme Court Justice — *God, what a nerd,* he thought — and Olivia as a gender-bending Jack Skellington from *The Nightmare Before Christmas.* Much to his parents' chagrin. They'd tried to steer Olivia into something they considered 'more appropriate' but she'd stood firm. Although she was only three years older than Will, he'd looked up to his sister.

Funny that, as adults, the rebellious one in the family had fallen into step with them and Will — the more easygoing kid until his teens — had become the black sheep.

He flipped through page after page of both albums, the images from family vacations, holidays, school events all creating a vivid slideshow of his life growing up. He paused when he got to one photo. Shortly before it had been taken, Will had realized he felt attracted to one of his friends in his Boy Scout troop.

The happy, smiling, laughing Will in earlier images now looked uncomfortable in his own skin. He stood apart from everyone else in the troop. Will flipped to the next page and noticed the pattern continued. Olivia — despite her rebellious façade — seemed happy and content. Will looked sullen and apart from his sister and parents.

Will covered his mouth with his hand and stared at the array of photos showing his gradual distancing from his family. He'd had no idea his growing certainty about his sexuality and worries about their reaction had caused him to behave so differently.

How much of the estrangement was due to his own fears and stubbornness?

* * * *

The following afternoon, Will wandered downstairs to fix himself a sandwich for lunch and came face-to-face with Greta, who stood on a small step stool, dusting the light fixture over the granite island.

"Can I get you something, William?" she asked.

"I'm just going to fix myself a quick lunch, Greta."

"Are you sure you wouldn't like me to prepare it?"

"I'm sure. It'll only take me a few moments. Thank you."

He'd finished piling roast beef and horseradish Cheddar on bread and was debating between an apple and potato chips for a side when the doorbell chimed musically.

With his mother upstairs and Greta on the stool, Will wiped his fingers on a dishtowel. "I'll get the door, Greta," he said before she could step down.

Will made a beeline for the door and pulled it open. He froze when his gaze met that of a gorgeous man roughly Will's age. He had thick, glossy dark hair and slightly hooded eyes more black than brown. He had a strong chin and jaw, chiseled cheekbones and warm golden skin.

He stood almost eye-to-eye with Will and had broad shoulders. His tailored sage-green checked shirt showed off his lean torso and his khaki trousers hugged narrow hips and long legs. He was, quite frankly, one of the most gorgeous men Will had ever seen.

He was maybe Asian and *definitely* hot.

Will wet his lips and the stranger smirked a little. He looked Will up and down and held out his hand.

"David Mori. I'm here to drop some paperwork off to Senator Martin. You must be William Jr."

"Will," he managed faintly. He shook David's hand, his skin buzzing from the warm contact. "It's — call me Will."

Chapter Four

David did his best not to stare at William Jr. as they shook hands, but he nearly flinched away from the odd tingling sensation he felt where their skins met.

He'd seen photos of William Jr. — no, *Will* — around the Martins' home, but they depicted a sweet-faced boy growing from toddlerhood into his late teens. Fully adult Will was, as David's sister would say, stupidly attractive. He'd inherited both parents' good looks, including Bill's athletic physique and Agnes' regal bone structure.

Tall and rangy, Will appeared lean beneath his gray Henley and dark jeans. He had a square jaw and the artfully styled brown hair his mother had spoken of so fondly. His large blue-gray eyes were almost dazed. He was checking David out — ogling him, really — and to say this surprised David was an almost comic understatement.

Where the hell is this coming from?

Bill and Agnes had talked at length about their children during his last visit, detailing educations and careers, and expressing affection for Olivia's children and pride in Will's accomplishments. They hadn't mentioned their son being gay or bi, though, nor had anyone in Bill's social circles.

David dropped Will's hand. "All right if I come in?" He gestured at the briefcase slung over his shoulder and tried another smile. "I need to unpack the docs and organize them a bit—shouldn't take me more than a minute," he added, keeping his tone even in the face of Will's wide-eyed stare. "I have a card from the senator's staff and a few others signed by his colleagues, too."

The tips of Will's ears turned pink and he immediately backed away from the door, gesturing for David to follow. "Of course, yes, come in. I expected a delivery man or one of the neighbors and not...well, not someone like you."

David quirked a brow and stepped into the foyer. "Someone like me?"

"Someone from my father's office." Will shrugged and shut the door. His features were pinched when he turned back to David. "I suppose it's too much to expect him to wait a few days after major surgery before he starts back at it again, but how can he when you people enable him?"

Well, shit. David wanted to escort himself right back out of the door. Of course, Bill's family would be feeling protective of him right now—he was fortunate to be alive. In the meantime, his son had definitely regained his composure and decided to focus his irritation on David.

"He's barely been home twenty-four hours—how did you even know he'd come home?"

David didn't bother correcting Will's mistaking him for a member of Bill's staff. "Agnes messaged me yesterday evening," he replied gently and licked his lips at the surprise streaking across Will's face. "I asked her to keep me updated on your father's surgery, and we've been swapping messages since your parents drove to Philly."

"You text message with my mother?"

"Just about Bill," David assured. "Your parents have no idea I planned to come by today. Bill didn't ask for these files. I used them and the cards as an excuse to stop by to see how he's doing in person." He watched the tension in Will's face ease. "So, how is he? Doing, I mean."

"He's fine."

"I'm glad to hear it. Agnes seemed stressed out in her messages and I didn't know what to think." Sympathy panged through David as Will crossed his arms and sighed.

"Okay, no, he's not fine — he's miserable. The surgery was successful in the sense that everything happened as expected. My father's now missing parts of some internal organs, and he's weak and in a lot of pain and snapping at everyone. Generally, he's making life difficult for my mother and sister and anyone else who stumbles into his path. Not that his behavior is necessarily out of character," Will grumbled.

David raised his brows. *What is this guy's problem?*

"I'm sorry to hear that," he replied carefully. "I imagine this has been difficult for you all. Bill expressed a lot of concern for you the last time we spoke." He paused when Will's face twisted, his bitterness almost palpable.

"I doubt that. My guess is he's more concerned about his reputation than any of us. You know he made us take him in through the back door? So no one would see him in such a weakened condition." Will shook his head. "Bill's career is the great love of his life, and he's trying like hell to make sure his own health doesn't keep him out of the office."

David didn't bother to hide his scorn. Will might be hurting, but he had no idea when it came to the things Bill and David had discussed at brunch over a week ago. Frankly, David suspected he knew Bill better than his own son.

"You're wrong. Bill worried about Agnes and your sister and her kids. He worried about you, Will, and how you and Olivia would manage to care for your mother if his surgery didn't go well."

Will scanned him up and down again, this time with derision, and David pulled himself up straighter. "Who *are* you, anyway? Besides a glorified gopher?"

David drew in a deep, calming breath, and forced himself to count down from five in his head. He willed his anger away and studied the storm of emotions in Will's eyes.

"Someone who knows Bill well enough to excuse his son for reacting out of fear," David said, his voice low. "Regardless of what you think, your father is genuinely concerned for his family's well-being."

"Did he tell you the thing no one in the family talks about? That his son is gay?" Will mashed his lips into a thin line when David shook his head.

"It didn't come up, no." David's stomach fell at the raw pain in Will's face. "There are limits to how personal I'll go when discussing my life with colleagues, but Bill and I rarely discuss my being gay either, other than when it's pertinent to work we're doing."

Will's jaw dropped slightly as the words registered, and his expression hardened. "You—how the hell can you work for him?" he breathed. "The way he votes and the way he treats people like us—"

"Senator Mori!"

Shock replaced the anger in Will's face. David cut his eyes toward Greta, who was bustling toward them.

"Hello, Greta."

Greta's brown eyes were suspiciously bright as she came forward to clasp David's outstretched hand, but her smile remained steady. "Goodness, I had no idea you were at the door, sir—William, you should have called me," she chided gently, and David nearly groaned as Will's cheeks flushed red.

"It's all right, Greta," he soothed. "I stopped by to leave some things for Bill and ask how he's doing. I'll be out of your hair in a minute, I promise."

"Nonsense." Greta reached for David's briefcase. "Give me your things and I'll let Mrs. Martin know you're here."

"I'd rather you didn't, ma'am, if that's all right." He smiled. "This is a time for the family to rest and recuperate and I don't want to intrude."

"David? David, how lovely of you to stop by."

David turned to meet Agnes Martin's gaze, and wanted to clench his fists at the mixture of sadness and relief he saw in her expression. Agnes seemed to have aged ten years in the last week and a half, but she stood straight and strong and gave him a smile that nearly broke his heart. Immediately, he crossed the foyer to take hold of the hand she extended toward him.

"Hello, Agnes. Your son was telling me about Bill's recovery."

Agnes looked past David then to Will, who moved to stand by his mother's side.

"Yes. By the Grace of God, Bill's getting stronger every day." She turned back to David and squeezed his hand. "I'm so glad you and Will had a chance to meet. He's doubtless downplayed his role in all of this, but he's been a tremendous help. I would never have managed without him and Olivia."

Will's face had paled when David glanced at him, but his voice was steady as he spoke to his mother.

"Mom, I'm glad I could help. You know that."

Agnes regarded her son with obvious pride. "Well, your father will never say it, but he's grateful to you and your sister. We both are."

She looked back to David and brought her free hand up to rest on his arm. "Come. I'll bring you back to see him."

"Well, hang on now." He held his ground as Agnes tried to move him, even after she cocked a brow in his direction. "I stopped by to check in, but I had no expectation of seeing Bill today. I imagine he's fatigued and I don't want to add to that. Are you sure it's a good idea for me to go in?"

Agnes patted his arm and gave him a disarming smile. "Of course I'm sure. Bill's bored with seeing only family every day — he'll welcome the chance to talk about something other than his health."

She caught Greta's eye. "Would you bring some tomato juice for Bill and iced tea for David and me when you have a moment, please? I'm afraid I can't offer you more than that," she said as Greta headed off. "Bill's diet is severely restricted and I feel terrible eating things in front of him he can't have."

As Agnes led him out of the foyer, he glanced back at Will. He stood alone where they'd left him, head bowed, hands on his hips, and his mouth downturned.

David regretted having to cut their conversation-slash-argument short, but shelved those thoughts upon entering Bill's temporary bedroom. Bill had lost a significant amount of weight since the surgery and he appeared frail in the steel and plastic hospital bed. His complexion was slightly sallow against his dark blue tracksuit, but David glimpsed anger in his mentor's fierce gaze. In that moment, the resemblance between Bill and his son was unmistakable and unsettling.

"Hello, sir." David stopped a respectful distance from the bed and braced himself. He couldn't help smiling when Bill's expression abruptly shifted and became wry.

"Aren't we past all the politeness and PC garbage?" Bill chided, his voice quiet. "You ate a half-pound of bacon the last time you were in this house, David, and one of Agnes' cats peed on your shoe — I think you can dispense with the honorifics."

David moved to one of the chairs by Bill's bed with a chuckle. "All right then. I've brought you some paperwork and Get Well cards from your colleagues and staff."

Bill let out a rumble. "Reports of my death have been grossly exaggerated."

"Oh, dear," Agnes clucked. She took the window seat on the opposite side of the bed and gave David a wink. "It's never a good sign when Bill quotes Mark Twain — please do your best to distract him."

David set about following Agnes' directive and talked quietly about work. He stuck mostly to light topics and office gossip, but they discussed policy too, despite David's discomfort at playing the enabler Will had accused him of being.

Agnes stayed close, working on an embroidery project while Bill nursed the glass of tomato juice. She always had a quick reply when Bill turned to her for a reaction, and she seemed content.

"I should go," David said after about an hour, when Bill's energy flagged and he turned snappish. David pulled his briefcase into his lap. "You need to rest and I'm sure Agnes would like some time to herself, too." He paused when Bill held up a hand.

"Did you meet my son?"

"I did, actually." David laid his case flat on his lap. "Will let me into the house and we introduced ourselves." *After a fashion*, he added silently.

"I see. So he's aware of your political affiliation?"

"Not officially. But he knows I'm your colleague and I'm sure he inferred my party."

"I imagine that went well. How rude was Will when he identified you as a member of the GOP?" Bill smiled wryly when David hesitated. "Very rude, then. He inherited his mother's quick temperament, I'm afraid, but his...*gift* with words is all me. Much as he hates to admit it."

David furrowed his brow. Bill certainly had his son's behavior pegged. "We only spoke for a few moments. There wasn't time to finish the conversation we'd started."

"Hmm. That means my son regards you as an enemy operative." Bill grunted, then seemed to lose his energy all at once. His lids went to half-mast and he sank farther into his pillows. "He'll assume you're bound and determined to vote against your own people's best interests unless you correct him."

"I always have the best interests of all my constituents in mind," David replied slowly. "I may not agree with everything the voters want, but I got into politics to make people's lives better, not the other way around."

"Yes, well that's where you and I differ," Bill said. "I'd be lying if I said I always acted in people's best interests, because it's just not damned true. Sometimes, I acted in my interests and not theirs. Especially when I didn't agree with the way people led their lives."

David said nothing as Bill closed his eyes. "I have a habit of putting my own ambitions before people's happiness," Bill said. "See that you do better than I did while you have this job. Put people first and yourself second, even when it hurts to do it."

"Yes, sir," David murmured. He waited a moment, but Bill's breath slowed and evened out, so David caught Agnes' eye.

"Let's let him sleep," she suggested, then stood and gestured toward the door.

He stayed quiet until they were safely in the hall. "I'm sorry," he said. "I should have waited until next week to visit."

"Don't be ridiculous." Agnes shook her head. "Talking shop with you is no doubt the thing Bill's enjoyed most since his surgery. He'll be annoyed when he wakes up and finds you gone, of course. Of all the issues involved in his recovery, it's the fatigue he hates most."

"Really?" David couldn't help asking. "He's bothered more by that than the diet?"

Agnes covered a laugh with one hand. "That shows how young you are, dear. Of course, you'd miss eating well." She sighed and tucked her hand into the elbow he offered as they walked toward the foyer.

"You must come back later in the week for dinner. Bill is gaining strength every day, and I'm sure Greta and I can arrange a meal both of you will enjoy."

David agreed to come back, and Agnes promised she'd keep him up to date on Bill's progress. He kept an eye out for Will as they neared the front door, hoping with equal parts dread and anticipation they'd bump into each other again before he left.

A dark kind of fatigue settled over David as he drove his car out of Garden City. He'd spent less than two hours with the Martins and it wasn't even five in the evening, but he needed time to recharge.

He'd read up on Bill's procedure, and understood how much the surgery took out of its patients when they were lucky enough to survive. He'd expected Bill to be less than healthy, but it pained David to see him so diminished and weak. Add to that Agnes, who'd appeared to be bearing the weight of the world on her shoulders, and Will, who'd stared at David with such outrage...

"Jesus, what a clusterfuck," David muttered. He slowed to a stop at an intersection when the traffic signal turned, and quickly took steps to pull himself out of the dumps.

He tapped a key on the steering wheel to activate the voice commands and connect the car to his cell phone. "Call *Tony Cuban*," he told the car, and restrained himself from speeding the rest of the way back to Freeport and one of his favorite restaurants.

He made a stop for a six-pack of ale, then collected his order — Coconut Striped Bass with beans and rice and a Ropa Vieja sandwich. He breathed a sigh of relief and headed home to walk his dog.

"I may have to call in late tomorrow," he said to Mabel once they'd sat down together on the sundeck after a long ramble around the nearby park. "I know it's in your nature to disapprove of human laziness, so I brought you steak. I'll even eat the sweet potato fries if you don't want them."

Mabel made a low, huffing noise David knew all too well. He took a long pull of his beer and gently scrubbed her thick black scruff with the fingers of his free hand. "Yeah, yeah, I get it — put up or shut up."

He stared out over the water, breathing in the salty air but not seeing the low-hanging sun. He still couldn't wrap his head around his unfortunate meeting with Will Martin. David couldn't remember any time a conversation with someone he barely knew had gone so wrong. Worse still, he'd probably meet Will again, and how the fuck would he handle that?

However, he should *want* to run into Will again, if only to clarify his own politics as a moderate Republican and an out gay man. The idea of having to watch Will's handsome face twist with distaste, though... David felt a little sick and a whole lot bummed out even thinking about it.

As she often did, Mabel seemed to sense his mood. She rested her muzzle against David's thigh and let loose a rumbling growl.

"Next time, I'm bringing you to the Martins' as my date," he said. "I solemnly swear not to use you as a canine shield *if* you keep the cats from peeing on my shoes, okay?"

Mabel yawned then and thumped the deck beneath them with her tail. David laughed at her antics and let go of the tightness he'd carried in his chest since meeting Will.

Chapter Five

"Senator Mori, please, come in."

Greta sounded very pleased as she welcomed David into the house. Will stifled a sigh and set his tablet on the side table in the sunroom. The man was handsome, but, with the exception of LGBTQ issues, he frequently voted like a typical moderate Republican robot. Will hadn't worked out exactly how he'd been roped into having dinner with his father's colleague, but, unfortunately, he couldn't back out now.

Actually, Will mused, *I know exactly how I was roped into this.* Agnes Martin had said they were having a small dinner and insinuated it would be rude of him not to join them. By the time Will realized his mother had invited David, he couldn't refuse. Even if Will had had been able to, he owed David an apology. He had been rude to David the first time they'd met.

Will had also googled him and been relieved to learn David wasn't ultra-conservative but he still couldn't wrap his head around a gay man aligning himself with a political party actively trying to damage their community. If Will was being honest, David's relationship with Will's father bothered him more. He was envious and resentful of the closeness they had. And hurt. Why did his father appear so much more accepting of David's sexuality than Will's? The rejection stung bitterly and made Will want to lash out and make David feel as terrible as he did.

But no matter how he felt, it didn't excuse his behavior. He stood and headed for the foyer.

Will caught a glimpse of David, who stood talking with Greta. If only the man weren't so infuriatingly good-looking. Will couldn't think of the last time he'd found a man so attractive, even Riley.

To Will's surprise, David wasn't alone. A medium-sized black and white dog with fawn-colored stripes on its legs and a tail that curled up onto its back stood by David's side. He held the leash loosely in one hand.

"Hello, David." Will stuck out a hand for him to shake. David's expression was friendly and his hands were large and strong around Will's long, narrow fingers.

"Nice to see you, Will."

"You as well." Ignoring how good David's skin felt against his, Will dropped his hand.

Greta patted his arm. "I'm going to go help your mother get food on the table."

"Thanks, Greta. I'll walk David back to the patio in a moment." After Greta disappeared down the hallway, Will turned his attention to the animal sitting calmly at David's feet.

"I see you brought a date," Will said with a small smile. He was such a sucker for dogs. Not to mention hot men with dogs. He crouched and held out a hand. "Hello there, gorgeous."

"Her name's Mabel."

She sniffed him delicately before pushing her snout into his hand in greeting. He laughed and looked up at David as he scratched Mabel behind the ears. David stared down at them with an expression both perplexed and amused.

"She's beautiful," Will murmured. "Husky mix?"

David nodded. "Husky and Shiba-Inu mix. Or so said the guy I got her from. She's mixed like me."

Will blinked at him and David laughed softly. "Sorry. I'm Japanese on my father's side, and a whole range of European countries on my mom's. My brother-in-law is always on me about the jokes my sister and I make about being mixed race. The jokes make him uncomfortable."

"Your candor took me by surprise." Will cleared his throat. "How old is Mabel?"

"Two—no, two and a half. I've had her since she was a pup."

Mabel let out a whine and licked Will's forearm as if pointing out he'd stopped petting her. Will chuckled and resumed.

"Do you have any pets, Will?"

He shook his head and gave Mabel a final pat before he stood. "I live in Manhattan and my building doesn't allow it."

David nodded. "I think she's enjoying the move from Queens to Long Island. She seems to like the beaches and canals quite a bit."

"When did you move from Queens?"

"A few years ago. On your father's recommendation, actually."

"Hmm." Will made a noncommittal noise. He wasn't sure what to make of the relationship his father and

David had. David's race wasn't an issue. Neither of his parents had ever shown themselves to be racially intolerant, although Will had a vivid memory from high school of arguing with his parents about why using the term 'Oriental' was really, *really* inappropriate. At worst, they were occasionally clueless, but even then, they'd listened to his argument and made an effort to change.

Sexuality was a different story, however. How could Bill be vehemently against his own son's sexual orientation but have no problem working side-by-side with a gay man? And inviting him to his house for meals? Will bristled, but he forced himself to tamp down the irritation. That reminded him, he still needed to apologize to David.

Will cleared his throat. "Uh, before we head back to the patio, I wanted to say I'm sorry about the way I behaved when you were here earlier this week. My temper got the better of me, and I hope you can forgive me."

"Of course. No hard feelings." David gave him a warm, open smile.

"Thank you."

Will's mother appeared before he could say anything else. "What on earth are you two still doing in the foyer? Let David in, Will."

"I was getting to know his dog, Mabel," Will said, feeling slightly abashed. Apparently, all of his manners *did* go out of the window when he encountered David.

Agnes regarded the dog with a soft sound of delight. "Oh, she *is* lovely. Even prettier than the pictures you sent me. I am so glad you asked to bring her. You probably felt like you needed a guard dog to fend off the cats. I am so embarrassed Fluffers used your shoe as a litter box."

A laugh escaped Will before he could stop it. "That old thing is still alive? I haven't seen him around outside and I assumed he'd died."

Agnes frowned at him. "Fluffers is very much alive. Just getting a bit senile these days. Thankfully, David was very gracious about it."

David chuckled. "One should always expect the unexpected when it comes to pets and kids."

"You are correct." Agnes smiled at him. "Now, I want both of you to come back to the patio. Appetizers are on the table."

* * * *

Greta cleared away the appetizers and served Caprese salads. She had worked overtime to help Agnes figure out meals compatible with Bill's new diet. No longer able to handle large meals or high fat, sugar and fiber, he needed to eat five to six smaller meals throughout the day. His father had taken to the restrictions well, but Will had caught him looking longingly at the wine. His doctors had recommended he avoid any alcohol except a very small sip on a special occasion. It had to grate on Bill, who had always enjoyed wine and, in fact, had a rather extensive wine cellar in the basement.

"You're an author, Will?" David asked.

"I am. I teach law history at NYU and write. I'm working on a book about Bernard Schwartz."

"The CEO of Loral Space & Communications? He played a part in some big campaign donation and China missile technology scandals, right?"

Will shook his head. "No. The legal scholar and historian. He was before my time, but he served on the law faculty at NYU and is a legend there."

"I'm afraid I'm not terribly familiar with his life. What made you interested in writing about him?"

Bill spoke before Will could formulate a thought. "Schwartz was extremely prolific with his writing. He did a great deal to help lawyers like myself understand the inner workings of the Supreme Court. I look forward to reading Will's take on his life. His previous books were excellent."

Will set down his fork. "You've read my work?"

Bill scoffed. "Of course I have. If you had taken a look on the bookshelf in my office, you'd see all of your books there."

Will swallowed hard, surprised by how much that meant to him. "As my father explained, Bernard Schwartz's life is incredibly interesting. In the late 1950s, he served as Chief Counsel to a special House Legislative Oversight Subcommittee looking for misconduct in federal regulatory agencies. His zeal for investigation got him dismissed from the subcommittee."

"Fascinating," David said. "When will the book be out? Are you finished with it?"

"I'm in the midst of edits right now," Will said. "I have a release date scheduled for November."

Greta cleared the salad plates and brought out broiled chicken with a light herb sauce.

"David, where are you living on Long Island?" Will asked.

"I bought a place in Freeport, right on a canal. It's a beautiful area and Mabel seems happy. She likes harassing the shorebirds."

Will chuckled and glanced under the table at the dog, who lay sprawled with her head on David's shoe, lazily wagging her tail. Because of the fenced yard, David had let her off her leash. He'd obviously done a great job training her, too, as she hadn't once begged for food.

"I need to check out more of the local attractions," David said. "Do you have any suggestions?"

"There's Sagamore — Theodore Roosevelt's home," Agnes said. "Old Westbury Gardens and the Long Island Aquarium. Block Island is actually part of Rhode Island, but it's very close and extremely nice. Oh, and Duck Walk Vineyards offers lovely guided tours."

"Walt Whitman's birthplace is on Long Island," Will said. "He's an important local resident of the LGBTQ community."

"His homosexuality has never been proven," Bill said.

"Really?" Will glanced over at David before turning back to his father. "'A tenor large and fresh as the creation fills me, The orbic flex of his mouth is pouring and filling me full' doesn't sound homoerotic to you?"

"While I'm impressed by your memorization of poetry, Will, I am not sure it's the best dinnertime conversation," Agnes chided before her tone turned cheerful. "David, there's the Nassau County Museum of Art and the Vanderbilt Museum and Planetarium. You might like those."

Will gritted his teeth. It took every ounce of his determination to leave the topic alone. His gaze met David's across the table and saw a flicker of something in his expression. Compassion maybe.

Guilt swept through Will. How awkward for David to be stuck in the middle of Will's terrible relationship with his parents. Bill was David's mentor and David seemed to have a good relationship with Agnes, too. Will's distaste for the man's politics wasn't a license for Will to take his frustrations out on him.

Will cleared his throat. "It's usually quite crowded, but Jones Beach State Park is nice. You may have to check and see if they allow dogs during the summer season, though. Some beaches here have restrictions."

"Oh, yes, I'm aware." David shot him a grateful look. "I'll have to check that out, thanks."

They had finished their entrée when Bill pushed back from the table. "I'm afraid I'm going to have to excuse myself."

Agnes leaned forward. "Are you ill?"

He gave her the ghost of a smile. "I have pancreatic cancer, my dear, I could hardly be called *well*. But I'm fine, just tired. I hope you'll forgive me, David."

"Of course." David half-stood. "Can I assist you?"

Bill shook his head. "Will can walk with me."

He worded the request more like an order, but Will stood without hesitation. His father's exhausted expression quelled any urge to argue. Will helped his father to his feet and did his best to support him without making it obvious.

Once perched on the edge of the hospital bed, Bill blew out a breath. "I'm afraid I overestimated my energy today."

"Is there anything I can get you?" Will asked. "Water? Pain medication?"

Bill shook his head. "The medication schedule is iron-clad. I have a goddamn pharmacy to swallow every day, but it all has to happen at specific times."

"I'm glad you have Mom to keep you in line."

Bill managed a small smile. "I'm glad you're here to help her. She appreciates it, you know."

Will nodded. "Well, uh, I guess I'll head back out if you don't need anything." He turned to go but his father stopped him.

"There is one thing you can do for me."

"What's that?"

"I suspect you and David got into it the other day. He's a good man, Will. Don't take your dislike of me out on him."

"I'm not—" Will swallowed his own words. Was that what he'd done? He changed tack. "I'm trying. I apologized to him when he got here. And I'll do my best. I can see he's someone you and Mom care about. I simply disagree with his politics."

"You always were a passionate, stubborn one. From the moment you were born." Bill's smile turned almost wistful before he cleared his throat. "I have some bottles of wine in the cellar that will be wasted otherwise. Why don't you and David split one and see if you can come to some agreement? You're welcome to any of the bottles down there. Lord knows I won't be drinking them anymore."

Will nodded. "Thank you."

Bill yawned. "Leave me be now. I need my rest."

Will left without another word, trying to digest his father's words. On his way out of the room, he caught a glimpse of a handful of familiar spines on the heavy wooden shelf. His books. Odd, he'd been in and out of the room dozens of times in the past week and hadn't noticed them. Maybe his resentment of his father had blinded him.

David and Agnes were quietly talking when Will stepped through the French doors onto the patio. His mother turned a worried look on him. "Should I check on him?"

Will shook his head and took a seat. "He's resting. He seems fine, other than being tired."

"I worry about him."

Will reached for his mother's hand over the table and squeezed it. "I know, Mom."

They were all relatively quiet as they finished the meal with a scoop of berry sorbet.

Agnes stood with a smile and excused herself. "I'm going to go check on Bill. I'm sorry to cut the evening short, David. We'll have you back again when Bill is feeling stronger."

David stood. "If there's anything I can do…"

She smiled and clasped his hand. "I appreciate that. You're a good friend to both Bill and me."

Agnes walked to Will and he leaned down when she moved to press a kiss to his cheek. "Do be nice," she said quietly.

With Agnes gone, he and David were left alone, except for Mabel snoozing on the warm patio.

David cleared his throat. "I should head out."

"Actually, would you like to have a glass of wine with me?" Will offered. David raised an eyebrow at him. "My father offered his wine cellar as a way for us to make peace."

David grinned. "Sounds like Bill. It's not a bad suggestion."

Will couldn't stop himself from smiling back. "I'm willing to give it a shot."

David glanced at the napping dog. "Do you think I should leave her there?"

"She seems content and the yard is secure. Unless you think she'll dig up my mother's peonies, I don't see why not."

"She doesn't show much interest in digging. Lead the way to the wine cellar I've heard so much about."

His smile sent a wave of heat through Will. His voice came out rougher than intended. "Follow me."

The wine cellar was located in the finished basement and encased in glass. The temperature and humidity controlled environment held hundreds of bottles of wine. If Will could give his father credit for one thing, it was his knowledge of wine that he'd passed on to Will.

Will held the door open for David and their shoulders brushed as they stood side by side, staring at the racks of bottles. The space suddenly seemed small, eaten up by David's large, handsome presence. Will's breath sounded unbearably loud in the quiet room and he cleared his throat. "What kind of wine do you like?"

"Hmm, reds mostly. Bolder, spicier ones like Syrah or Malbec." He brushed his fingertips across the bottles. Will could smell the clean, crisp scent of David's cologne.

Will perused the selection in front of him for a while, taking down a bottle and reading the label before returning it to the rack. Distracted as he was by David's presence, the words seemed to swim in front of his eyes. He spotted a familiar logo and reached for it gratefully.

"How about this?" he finally asked and handed the bottle to David. "It's a red blend from the local vineyard we were talking about earlier."

"Fruity, with some spicy nutmeg and clove notes," David read off the label, then gave him a slow smile. "Sounds great."

A fully equipped bar stretched across one side of the finished basement. Will located a wine key and attacked the bottle's cork while David retrieved stemware from the hanging rack above the bar area. Will wiggled the cork loose and poured the deep garnet-red wine into the large Cabernet glasses. "This probably should be decanted and allowed to breathe for a while," he said apologetically.

David shrugged. "I think I can live a little dangerously."

Will raised his glass and held it out to David. "Here's to living dangerously then." David clicked their drinks together and his bright smile was like a punch to the gut. Will took a sip of the wine to cover his reaction. As promised, it was rich and fruity with a spicy finish. Will preferred whites, but he found this vintage pleasant and was glad David seemed to enjoy it.

Will took a seat on one of the comfortable leather bar stools and looked at David. "I know I already apologized once, but I feel badly about my behavior the other day and at dinner tonight. I know I've been a moody bastard. It's hard when I see how well you two get along. He rejected me and embraced you and I haven't dealt with it well. But I don't mean to put you in the middle of the relationship I have with my parents. Being home is bringing out the worst in me, I'm afraid."

"Why do you do it?" David said. "Antagonize your father like that?"

Will's laugh was a touch bitter. "Me antagonize *him*? Oh, I don't know, maybe because he's ashamed of having a gay son? Because when he walked in on me and my boyfriend, he flipped out and told me he never wanted to see my face again? He disowned me, David."

"I'm sorry. I can't imagine how difficult that was for you," David said. "Do you think it's possible your father has changed some?" he added, his tone gentle. He laid a hand on Will's forearm and his warm touch stirred something in Will. But his words made Will draw back. He moved to pick up his glass, and forced David to remove his hand.

"I think that man will go to his grave the same stubborn asshole he's always been," Will muttered before he took a healthy sip of wine.

David observed him for a moment, his brows drawn together in a faint frown. "Do you know what your father said to me the other day when we were talking?"

"I can only imagine." Will's tone was dry. He took another sip of his wine. On top of the light dinner and wine during the meal, it warmed his stomach and he welcomed the mellow glow.

"He said something to the effect that you had identified me as an enemy operative."

Will huffed quietly, amused by his father's choice of words, half-offended by the unflattering picture it painted of him.

"He also said you'd inherited your mother's quick temper and his gift for words."

"That's probably accurate," Will grudgingly acknowledged. His mother *did* have a quick temper and the senator was formidably eloquent. "But it doesn't change anything."

"I'm not saying it does." David captured his hand, and Will felt compelled to meet his gaze. This time he didn't pull away. "I'm saying...hell, I don't know what I'm saying. Maybe just that it's been a long time since you and your father last spoke. Ten years, give or take, right?"

Will nodded.

"Maybe he's changed. He may not be thrilled to work beside a gay man, but he's been unfailingly decent to me since we met. I'm not saying you have to agree with your father's politics, but maybe try to let go of the idea you have about who he was then. Take the time to learn who he is *now*. You may not have much time left."

Will stood, agitated. "Why is everyone acting like my father's death will change *anything* between us?"

Something raw flared in David's dark eyes. "Because it *does*—death changes everything. People in your life who you count on, who you take for granted will be around forever, are gone. You can't share news with them, or cry on their shoulder, or argue over who stole the last donut, or share a good bottle of wine. All those moments are lost and you can never get them back."

Startled, Will stared at David, who dropped his gaze to the glass in his hand.

"I lost my parents a few years ago in a car wreck. One day they were fine and the next…" He shook his head, his jaw tight. "Anyway, we got along pretty well, my parents and my sister and me. They were supportive of us, even when they didn't always understand our choices or decisions. Despite what you'd expect from the parents of a young woman living in New York, they always seemed to worry about *me* more. Who can blame them, I guess—I'm a gay politician who votes purple in a blue state."

David huffed out a laugh, but his expression was earnest when he looked up again. "I'd like to think they'd be proud of the man I'm trying to be. But I can't ask them and I miss talking to them more than I ever imagined. You can still talk to your father, Will, and maybe learn some things about him that surprise you."

"I see your point," Will said softly. "And you have my sympathies about losing your parents. But my relationship with my father is complicated and I can't forgive and forget the things he said to me."

David grimaced. "I'm sorry."

"I can't ignore the fact my father voted *against* marriage equality in New York a few years ago."

"I know how hurtful that must be."

"Do you?" Will swallowed another mouthful of wine.

"Well, the marriage equality bill was before my time, but yes, I do."

Will scoffed. "You're a Republican too."

"Whoa, don't paint us all with the same brush. I'm nothing like the Tea Partiers. Hell, your father is more conservative than I am, but he's nothing like the ultra-conservatives out there right now, either."

"Look, I'm not saying you're all the same, but I can't wrap my brain around conservative gay people. Or conservative minorities. It's shooting yourself in the foot," Will argued. The wine made his tongue loose and while he hated to admit it, excitement flickered through him. He was actually enjoying the argument with David.

"I respectfully disagree. I can support more socially liberal causes while remaining fiscally conservative. I believe *that's* in my best interest."

Will raised an eyebrow. "So you're essentially a Libertarian?"

David shook his head. "There *are* some similarities, but no. I'm not a fan of the flat tax model or unfettered capitalism. Nor am I anti-gun control. The last thing I want is guns in the hands of people who can't be trusted with them. But I don't think banning them wholesale is the answer either. Like with most issues, I think it's a matter of finding the right balance."

Will's heart sped up and he swallowed hard. A man passionately arguing a well-thought-out position had always turned him on.

"The Republican party has made a drastic shift to the right but that doesn't mean it has to stay that way. There *were* actually moderate Republicans until Barry Goldwater."

"You're the last of a dying breed. There is no turning back from the direction we're heading in. The Republican party is imploding and I don't see any way back from the brink," Will countered. The air around them practically crackled with the tension and he felt flushed and aroused by the argument.

David pushed aside his wine glass and leaned in. "Don't be such a fatalist. I'm certainly not the only moderate Republican in the New York Senate."

Will made a disparaging sound. "Too bad none of you have the balls to stand up to the ultra-conservatives. They've hijacked your party and are about to send it off a cliff!"

"That's a gross generalization! Just last week we—"

Will grabbed David and pressed their lips together. David went still against him and for a moment Will thought he'd made a huge mistake, but then David groaned against his mouth and grabbed the back of Will's head. They kissed hard and messily for a few moments, both of them attempting to control the kiss. They slid from the stools to stand and Will gripped David's hip, pulling their bodies closer together.

David shifted, pressing Will against the bar. He deepened the kiss, delving into Will's mouth with a skilled exploration that made Will's head swim. Will reciprocated, squeezing and kneading David's firm, muscular ass. David's cock hardened against his own arousal.

Need flashed through him. It had been so long since touching someone had felt like this. The few lackluster encounters he'd had since Riley had left him unsatisfied. He wasn't even sure he even liked David, but Will's skin was on fire and all he could think about was getting closer to him.

David pulled away, kissing along Will's jaw. Will moaned and slid his hands up David's back, pressing their bodies even closer together. David worked his way lower, kissing and nipping at Will's neck. He allowed his head to fall back to give David better access. David brushed the collar of his shirt aside and bit the juncture between his neck and shoulder.

Will shuddered and goosebumps rose along his skin. He turned their bodies to pin David to the bar, then reached between them. He slid his hands across David's torso, exploring the hard body under the soft fabric. Will could feel the ridges of his abdominal muscles.

"Oh God, we shouldn't be doing this." David groaned against Will's throat.

"I know," Will admitted.

David kissed his mouth again, hard. "Your father…"

"I don't want to hear you talk about my father while you're kissing me," Will said, shutting David up with his mouth. He devoured David, enjoying the spicy taste of wine on his tongue and the heat of his mouth. He needed more.

He slid a hand lower, rubbing at the hard length trapped beneath David's trousers. David made a pained sound and kissed him harder. "Oh God, Will…"

Will dropped to his knees and reached for his belt buckle, but David stilled his hands. "I can't." David looked down at him with a pained expression. "Not here. Not in your father's house."

Will stood with a scowl, aroused and frustrated all at once. The irritations from dinner returned, boiling to the surface. Without even trying, his father was interfering. He'd had fun debating and flirting with David, but this was an abrupt reminder nothing in Will's life was in his control anymore. Couldn't he even get off without feeling as though he was completely under his father's thumb? In this house, he couldn't be himself, even for a moment.

"It would be fucking nice if I could actually live my life without my sex life being dictated by my father's presence," he hissed. Will recognized his overreaction but couldn't stop the vitriol falling from his lips. Was it too much to ask he get ten minutes of relief from his father controlling every move in his life? Ten minutes to break the creeping tension that had threatened to strangle him since he arrived? "Clearly I made a mistake. I'm sure you can find your way out."

He turned on his heel and strode toward the stairs, straightening his rumpled clothing as.

"Will…" David called after him, but he kept walking. Will knew he was being a jackass, but he was afraid to open his mouth again and make a bad situation worse. He'd calm down, then apologize for acting like a jerk.

Fuck! So much for finding some common ground with David.

Chapter Six

David eased his car into the driveway of the Freeport house and blew out a breath. He was relieved to be back after almost a week in Albany and suspected his dog shared the feeling. The State Legislature had been in session four days, which meant he'd split his time between his office in the capitol building and the Senate chamber while Mabel had stayed cooped up in David's one-bedroom rental. The apartment building employed a very competent dog walker who paid daily visits to the pets in residence, made sure they were exercised and supplied them with fresh water and food, but none of that alleviated David's guilt at leaving Mabel in a less than familiar space.

"You feel guilty because you are a sucker," he muttered to himself, then switched off the car's ignition. "Mabel doesn't give a damn where she naps as long as it's warm and dry and there's a bowl of kibble within easy reach."

As always, the k-word worked its special brand of magic on Mabel. She poked her head up from the backseat and as David turned to look at her over his shoulder, she leaned in to bathe his face with her tongue. He laughed.

"Yeah, I'm glad to be back, too." He put a hand back to scritch between her ears. "What do you say we get out of the car, huh?" David made his eyes wide when Mabel jerked backward and away from him. "Huh, Mabel? Should we put the bags inside and go for a walk?"

Mabel braced her legs on the backseat, her dark eyes shining. She let out a trio of sharp little barks that told him how much she liked his idea.

"Okay, okay," he crooned, then grabbed his duffel from its place on the passenger seat.

They'd left Albany after three p.m., and driven through heavy traffic along the Taconic State Parkway. Now, as David hustled Mabel and their bags into the house, seven p.m. approached, and he wanted nothing more than to finish Mabel's walk, then fix a quick snack and enjoy a glass of good wine.

David wrinkled his nose. Maybe wine wasn't such a good idea, as it reminded him of the awkward-turned-disastrous dinner he'd suffered through with Will Martin and his family.

Fuck, what a mess.

Quickly, he clipped Mabel's lead to her collar and walked her toward the back of the house, determined to shake off his melancholy. Exiting the house through the sun deck door, he guided Mabel along their street and waved at Mrs. Cohen when he saw her in the window. They turned onto Main St. and walked another block to the entrance of Cow Meadow Park, and David shifted his brain into auto-pilot.

He stared out at the canal and the purpling sky as he and Mabel made their way to the now empty fishing pier. Despite the warm summer night, his mood had soured. He hadn't gotten Will out of his head, though he'd certainly tried, and worse, he didn't know if he was angry at Will or simply pitied him.

Will had seemed...lost during the dinner at Agnes and Bill's house. His apology had sounded sincere and he'd been genuinely taken with Mabel, but the moment Will got near his parents, every ounce of charm drained right out of him. He vacillated between hot and cold during the meal, and while Agnes maintained a fragile kind of civility among the men at her table, the family's old resentments roiled just below the surface.

David had made up his mind to leave after Bill and Agnes retired, but then Will had offered him a glass of wine and those damned expressive eyes of his had taken David off guard.

Heat born from both desire and chagrin blazed across David's face. He'd been drawn to Will from their first meeting, but had misjudged the depth of their chemistry. The longer they'd talked, the more he'd wanted to hear. He wanted to understand the pain and anger Will still felt after years of estrangement from his parents. To know this troubled, infuriating man better, despite the fact that Will seemed determined to dislike him. Their attempt at making peace over wine had failed, and before David knew it, they'd been in each other's faces, voices ringing loudly against the wine cellar's walls.

Then Will had kissed him and Christ Almighty, David's skin had practically caught fire. He hadn't been intimate with another man for a while — the demands of his career and the scrutiny that came with it made him careful when it came to dating. And it had been far, *far* too long since he'd known the level of desire he experienced while practically manhandling Will. David had nearly hauled him up onto the tabletop after Will grabbed his ass.

David shivered now and pictured Will on his knees, reaching for David's belt, his face flushed and mouth kiss-swollen. Too bad David had had no idea how to keep his mouth shut to prevent the night from going straight to hell.

David frowned and turned toward home. "C'mon, girl," he murmured, tugging gently on Mabel's leash to signal it was time to go.

Helplessly, he played the scene over in his head, recalling the disgust in Will's face before he'd stormed off. David had stared after him in disbelief, certain he wouldn't leave David there, breathless and hard and fucking *humiliated* in his mentor's house. Will had done exactly that, though.

A chill had fallen over David as he'd placed an order for a Lyft back to Freeport, like he'd been doused with cold water. He felt...reduced, somehow, and small. Like he had no business showing his face in the Martins' grand old Colonial house. Quickly, he'd straightened his clothes and snuck back upstairs to retrieve Mabel from the backyard, then led her out through a gate on the side of the house without a word to anyone.

Mabel whined, signaling she'd sensed David's wordless distress. His heart was racing, and he held Mabel's lead so tightly his fingers tingled. Immediately, he stopped walking and squatted down beside Mabel. For a long time, he simply petted her, taking and giving comfort by running his fingers through her thick fur.

He waited for his heartbeat to even out before he leaned in to press a kiss to the top of Mabel's head, and smiled when she got to her feet.

"Let's go home, pretty lady—we need some food."

* * * *

Despite sleeping poorly, David went to his office near Freeport's center early the next day and brought a box of muffins and a tray of coffee to share with his staff. He needed to be in Albany again on Monday and had a ton of work to catch up on, so he shoved aside his fatigue and focused his energy on doing his job. At two p.m., his assistant stuck her head in his door.

"Hey, boss, you want something from the deli next door?"

David glanced up from a legal brief and gave Kerri an indulgent smile. Like many of his small staff, she was actually a few years younger than David, but insisted on mother-henning him at every turn. "No, thanks— I'm not all that hungry."

Kerri pursed her lips, seeming to think for a moment as she closed the distance between the door and the desk. "How about an avocado smoothie from the juice place down the street?"

Before he could demur again, David's stomach rumbled loudly enough for Kerri to hear and she flashed him a big smile.

He laughed. "You did that on purpose."

"I might have, yeah." Kerri shrugged, clearly unashamed at the manipulation. "But you're the one who's fasting."

"I had a muffin and coffee when I got here," David protested even as she waved him off.

"I'm headed in that direction, so I'll grab a smoothie for you. I sent a metric ton of phone messages through to your tablet," she added, nodding at the iPad by his elbow. "I don't think there's anything too pressing, but I did want to let you know Senator Martin called. He'll be in Albany on Tuesday and Wednesday and wants to talk some things through with you."

David drew his brows together. "Are you sure that's what he said?"

"He was very emphatic." Kerri's expression sobered. "I knew you'd be interested in his plans seeing as you've kept up with him and Mrs. Martin during his recovery."

"Thanks, Kerri. I appreciate that."

David rubbed his forehead with one hand while Kerri gathered up the correspondence he'd worked on. He flipped through the messages on the iPad until he found Bill's, then sat staring at the words.

Following last week's dinner, he'd made a conscious effort to back off slightly with Bill and Agnes. He answered their texts and email promptly, but had turned down a second invitation to Sunday dinner to avoid running into Will again. David didn't feel up to pretending nothing had happened between them and he certainly wasn't spoiling for another argument, but he felt like a shit for ghosting.

Screw your ego, and Will's too. You're better than this, David thought. He sat straighter in his chair and picked up the receiver on his desk phone.

David left the office after five p.m., finally feeling the effects of his sleepless night. Later, he'd blame the sleep deprivation for walking right past Will, who stood on the sidewalk in full view of the building's front door.

"David!"

For a moment, he considered ignoring the familiar voice, then forced himself to stop. He turned to face the one person he'd tried to push out of his thoughts for the past five days and damned if Will didn't look delicious. He was like a preppy nightmare in his white Oxford shirt, army-green trousers and a pair of white Converse. David quelled an urge to kick himself.

"What are you doing here?" he asked.

"Well, that's not very welcoming. Don't I even warrant a hello?" Will flashed a crooked grin that David would have found charming a week ago. Now, it made his stomach twist.

"Hello." He clasped his briefcase with both hands, holding it in front of him like a shield. "You didn't answer my question."

Something in David's demeanor seemed to penetrate Will's blithe manner and he abruptly sobered. "I checked you out on the New York Senate website and found your office address. I'm...heading back to the city tomorrow and I wanted to talk before I go."

"Why?"

Will drew in a deep breath. "I wanted to apologize — yes, again — for the way I behaved the other night. I overreacted about a lot of things, and I know that. But don't let my poor behavior impact your relationship with my parents. My mother said you turned down her invitation for Sunday, and I hate to think you'd skip it rather than deal with me. I'll be gone by then, anyway."

A chill passed over David. "I didn't turn down the invite because of you, Will," he lied. Slowly, he eyed Will up and down, then turned to leave. "Have a safe trip back to the city." He'd already started moving when a touch brushed his wrist.

"Wait!" Will's cheeks were pink when he turned back, and for all his perfect styling, his expression was unhappy. "Okay, I know we keep getting off on the wrong foot—"

A soft, mean-spirited laugh bubbled up in David's chest. "That's a hell of an understatement."

"Believe it or not, I don't mean for it to happen." Will licked his lips. "My parents keep telling me you're a great guy, but I'm starting to think you and I are literally like oil and water and don't have a fucking clue how to mix."

"Who says we have to?" David shrugged at Will's aggrieved expression. "We have no obligation to get along, so what does it matter if we don't?"

Will ran a hand over his hair. "You know how sick my father is. He's a tough old fucker, but the odds are stacked against him. And as much as I hate being in that house, I need to be available when my mom or Olivia need me, which, I've gathered, is quite a lot. So, I'll be back."

Will dropped his hand and stepped closer. "I'm not sure why my father has bonded with you, but the fact remains he has. You're important to him and my mom, David, and you're right here on Long Island with them. You and I are going to have to spend time around each other and I don't want to make your life difficult purely by virtue of being in the same room."

"So, when you said you were going back to New York—?" David began, then closed his mouth when Will shook his head.

"I didn't mean permanently. My sister told me to expect to be back here within a week. Her kids will be out of school soon and she'll be busy making sure they have a great summer instead of sitting around watching their grandfather try not to die."

"Jesus, Will." David gritted his teeth. He truly had no idea how to deal with this guy. "So what are you suggesting? A truce?"

"Yes, exactly."

David rested his hands on his hips while Will watched him. "Fine, I can do that. But I'm not the only one who needs to work at keeping the peace." He fixed Will with a glare and didn't waver when his cheeks reddened again.

"I know. And I'll do my best to make it work." He rolled his eyes when David didn't reply. "Come on, man. At least give me some credit for trying here."

David pressed his lips thin, his reserve of patience gone. Will was flat-out delusional if he thought David had forgotten about his behavior of the other night. As David moved to push past him, Will grasped his arm, and only the regret flashing in his eyes stopped David from lashing out.

"I shouldn't have said that. I didn't even mean it," Will said. "I'm not sure why, but every time I'm around you, I seem to say exactly the wrong thing."

"I think that's because you're a douchebag," David muttered. He allowed himself a smile when Will bit out a laugh.

"Ouch. I won't pretend that's the first time I've heard that."

"Then you'll forgive me when I say I believe you."

Will stepped back, his expression amused, and lifted his hand as if to straighten David's collar before dropping it to his side. "So, let me buy you a drink," he offered, "or better yet dinner. We can break bread and keep working on the whole peacekeeping thing over some lobsters or steaks."

Seriously?

David shook his head. "I'm gonna pass," he said. "I'm beat and not up for going out. Maybe we can try the next time you're in town, if you're still in a peacekeeping mood."

"Oh, come on—are you sure? How about I pick up some takeout and meet you at your place instead? What's good to eat around here?"

David worried his bottom lip with his teeth. He hardly recognized this earnest, charming stranger. But did Will honestly think he could gloss over how badly their last meeting had gone? More importantly, could David let him? *No, you can't,* he told himself. Still, he was curious to hear what Will had to say next, and whether he truly wanted a truce between them. Besides, David had urged Will to give his father another chance—he'd be a hypocrite not to do the same for Will.

"There's a place a couple of blocks down the street," he said at last. "They serve a mix of Cuban and Italian if you like that kind of food."

"Right now, I like any kind of full-fat food—I'd sell a piece of my soul for some steak, to be honest." Will pulled his car keys from his pocket. "Why don't you call in an order and I'll pick it up and circle back to your house?"

"You don't know where I live," David pointed out, and this time he did push past Will. "Meet me at Tony Cuban in an hour and you can follow me from there," he called over his shoulder.

"An hour? But where are you going?"

David glanced back with an almost smile. "To walk my dog and pick up some beer — see you in a bit."

* * * *

"Well, you weren't wrong about the view. This is beautiful, David."

David smiled and popped the top off a bottle of ale. They'd brought their food out to the sun deck and sat at the patio table, a cluster of citronella candles burning between them as evening fell and Mabel snoozed at David's feet.

"The house is a bit big for Mabel and me, but I wanted someplace to call home." David handed Will the bottle of beer. "I used some of my inheritance for the down payment and I think my parents would have liked that. Isabel thinks it's weird the houses on the street are so close together, but who cares when you can come out here?"

Will cocked his head. "Wait, doesn't your sister live in the city?"

"Yes, she does." David chuckled. "But you know how warped your perception gets when you're living with neighbors stacked on top, beneath and on both sides. Isabel comes out here for lunch and acts like it's supposed to be farm country.

"How's your food by the way?" he asked.

"It's fantastic." Will speared more steak onto his fork. "The marinade on the meat is amazing but I think I may actually be in love with the sweet plantains on the side."

"So good, right? That place is far and away my favorite restaurant in town."

"Mabel's too, huh?" Will grinned when David put down his fork and laughed. "I'm not sure I've ever known someone who orders a separate entrée for their dog."

"Well, then you don't know many dog owners," David insisted. "I only do it once in a while, and besides, my girl deserved a treat after being in Albany with me all week."

"So, you take her up there with you?" Will hummed at David's nod. "And where do you stay? My parents bought a second house in Saratoga Springs before I was born, but that doesn't seem like your speed."

"I rent a loft in Shaker Park. All I need is a place where Mabel can hang out while I'm working and a bed to crash in at the end of the day."

As the quiet conversation continued, David wondered again at the change in Will. Though he suspected the peace wouldn't last, he definitely enjoyed glimpsing another side of him.

At nine p.m., David finally rose to clear the table. The two beers he'd had with dinner had left him warm and pleasantly drowsy, and he was very aware of Will as they carried everything inside. Even so, a thrill of surprise went through him when Will took the empty beer bottles from his hands, backed him up against the kitchen counter and kissed him.

David's breath caught. Will's mouth was soft and warm on his, his grip firm on David's shoulders. That touch broke through David's daze. He grasped Will's waist with both hands and closed his eyes as he opened his mouth to Will's. Heat zinged over his skin. Will's tongue slipped into David's mouth, and he tasted beer and spices. A hum rolled through Will's chest.

Oh, God.

Will nipped at David's upper lip, the coarse hairs of his stubble deliciously rough against David's mouth. A shiver ran through David when Will's fingers slid beneath the collar of his shirt, and he pulled Will closer. They stood in the kitchen's low light for a long time, kissing and groping until David's head spun. Their groins brushed through their jeans, and David's knees went weak at the rough movement over his own half-hard cock.

He was breathless when he finally pulled back. A flush colored Will's face and his eyes shone. He licked his lips through a smile.

"What would you say to taking this somewhere more comfortable?" he asked, and smoothed a lock of David's hair back from his forehead with one hand. He lowered his head slightly when David hesitated, his gaze terribly appealing. "I'd like to pick up where we left off the last time we saw each other."

A chill raced down David's spine at the mention of that last time. He dropped his hands and carefully pushed Will back. "Not...not tonight. Ask me again sometime, and I promise I'll think about it."

Will crossed his arms over his chest, his expression wry. "What makes you think I'll want to ask you again?"

"Nothing." David shrugged through a sharp pang of disappointment. "Still, I think we both know this is the right thing to do tonight."

"So, this is payback for what happened in my parents' wine cellar?" Will scoffed. "That's a shitty thing to hold over my head considering I apologized already."

"No, that's not what's going on here. Or not all of it, anyway." David scrubbed his hands over his face. God damn it, this man infuriated him. "The fact you think so tells me it's time to call it a night."

Will rolled his eyes. "Fine. I'd still like to know why you suddenly seem so pissed off."

Nodding, David turned to the sink and washed his hands. He took his time about it, but needed those moments to get his frayed nerves under control. He dried his hands on the roll of paper towels before speaking again.

"When Isabel and I were kids, she had a friend named Carlie Johnson. Carlie and her family lived down the block and we all went to school together. Sometimes my parents would walk with us, sometimes Carlie's dad, and my sister and Carlie saw each other almost every day.

"When Carlie turned eight, she invited Isabel to her birthday party. I wasn't tight with Carlie so I didn't get an invite, but I was always hanging out with my buddy Tommy, so I was good." David smiled and passed his fingers over his lips.

"Tommy and I went out to the playground behind Tommy's building with some other kids. Tommy's building was next to Carlie's and that's why I saw Isabel. She was sitting on the swings and none of the other kids from Carlie's party were around.

"Of course, I went over and asked her why she wasn't upstairs at the party. Turns out Carlie's mom told Isabel to wait outside while the rest of the kids ate cake and ice cream. See, Mrs. Johnson didn't want Isabel in the house because our dad wasn't white. And that's when I realized for the first time *all* of Carlie's friends outside of school were white except Isabel — the only person of color in the group."

David drew in a breath and held it for a moment before exhaling slowly through his nose. Over twenty years and his stomach still curled in anger over the memory. "Carlie was a nice girl, even if her mother was a bigoted asshole. Even so, Isabel and I both knew then Carlie's friendship wasn't good for my sister because she'd always feel less than worthy in the Johnsons' world."

Will's jaw had dropped when David raised his head. "David, I—"

David cut him off. "I know what you're going to say—nothing that happened last week between us was about the color of my skin or the shape of my eyes. Are you sure that's true? Because you basically left me with a bad case of blue balls in your parents' basement after I wouldn't let you blow me one floor down from where my colleague was sleeping. And I have no idea why. You made me feel like shit, Will. Small and used and...*less* than you and your family. But you obviously don't care. The only reason we're even talking about it now is because I shut you down again and that made you mad. I don't even know if you wanted to be with me that night or if getting it on with the mixed-race guy was a convenient way to say 'fuck you' to your father."

"Oh, my God, no." Will's face had paled, and David's anger softened at his obvious dismay. "I'm so sorry. The idea you'd think that about me... Jesus, I am *not* that person."

David nodded. "Fine. I think you mean it when you say you'd like for us to be on better terms for Bill's sake. But, after the other night, I'm not sure being your friend would be good for me. I don't think we're particularly compatible. I don't even know where you're coming from with this overture, to be honest. Plus, there's so much fucked-up shit going on between you and your parents and I end up in the middle, like some kind of chew toy you're all fighting over. I don't like being put in that position." He held up a hand when Will opened his mouth to speak. "And I know you don't want to hear it, but I *work* with Bill. My job is important to me and so is the respect of my colleagues, including your father. The last thing I should be doing is getting my dick out in the man's basement because you've got an itch you want scratched."

Will's Adam's apple bobbed. "You're right. I wasn't thinking straight. I put you in an untenable situation, and I am truly sorry."

Slowly, as if fearful David would bolt, he captured one of David's hands. "And yes, things *are* fucked up between my parents and me. I'm... I don't know what to do about that yet, but I'm working on figuring it out."

"Good." David squeezed Will's fingers lightly. "If you ever want to talk about it, I'll lend you an ear. No judgments, I promise," he added.

"Thank you." Will cleared his throat and drew his brows together. "And this...whatever this is between you and me?"

"I don't know what this is." David shrugged. "But I told you I'd think about it. For now, let's work on getting along. If you still think you want something more once we're there, ask me again and we'll see how it goes."

Chapter Seven

"Will!" Riley stood and offered Will a wide grin as he stepped into the speakeasy. "I'm so glad you could make it tonight."

"Me too," Will said sincerely and hugged his friend.

He'd messaged Riley after returning to Manhattan the day before, and learned his trip coincided with the guys meeting up at Under. The speakeasy had officially opened the week before, and Will was glad to make the trek to Morningside Heights. He caught sight of the familiar faces around the bar area and raised a hand in greeting. Jesse, Carter and Kyle returned it. God, it felt good to be back home where he belonged. The strange fog of discontentment he'd been trudging through on Long Island had finally lifted. He dreaded going back, but Olivia had her hands full with her kids now that they were out of school for the summer.

"How's your father?" Riley's concern was palpable.

Will glanced around. Despite the fact no one else was close by, he lowered his voice anyway. "He's doing as well as can be expected, but we'll know more after the next round of testing and appointments with his doctor. The idiot insisted on going to Albany to work this week, but the surgery was hard on him."

Riley squeezed his upper arm. "I'm sorry."

"Thank you."

"How's it been living there? You seemed pretty rattled in the texts you sent."

"Rattled is a good word for it," Will agreed. "It's this perpetual feeling of déjà vu coupled with a sense of being off-kilter. Everything's the same and yet it's not. I don't know. I can't seem to get a handle on it. It's partly why I've been an absolute jackass to David—" He stopped abruptly, unsure of how much Riley would want to hear.

"Ahh, yes, the mysterious *David*." Riley raised an eyebrow at him. "I understand if you aren't comfortable going into depth about this guy, but I'm dying of curiosity."

"I could use some input." Will chuckled ruefully. "I wasn't sure if it would be too weird since we dated…"

"Don't worry about it. You're my friend." Riley's tone held a touch of reproach, but his smile softened it. "That's the important part. If you need a sounding board, I'm here to listen."

"Thanks." Will shot him a grateful smile. "I think we both need drinks before I get into that."

"I'll go grab some while you find us a table. What would you like?"

"Kyle can surprise me again."

"I'll tell the guys we'll be over once we're done talking."

Will nodded his agreement and found a table in a quiet corner, far from anyone's ears. Although his father's staff and those close to him had been notified, the press hadn't gotten wind of the specifics of his father's illness yet. Only that the senator had taken some personal time for health reasons. He watched Riley cross the room to the bar and when Carter slid a hand along Riley's back, was surprised to feel none of the lingering wistfulness he'd experienced before. Was Will actually starting to get over Riley?

He was lost in thought when Riley returned with two tumblers, one holding a clear cocktail with citrus peel and a star anise pod, the other holding a beautiful orange-hued drink with a sprig of rosemary. Riley handed the second cocktail to Will.

"Kyle made you a Spiced Orange Bourbon with fresh rosemary."

Will took a cautious sip. The bright citrus and warm spices were balanced by the hint of herbal astringency of the rosemary and Will savored the taste. The spiciness made him think of David's preference in wine and for a moment he wondered if David would enjoy the drink. "Damn, Kyle's good."

Riley took a seat across the small table from him and chuckled. "He and Jesse have done an amazing job with this place. I could get addicted to their gin and tonics." He gestured toward his glass. "They make the tonic water themselves and get the gin from an artisanal distillery in Brooklyn."

"I've never liked gin, but that almost makes it sound good," Will said.

"It's a love it or hate it kind of liquor, I think." Riley sobered quickly. "So, no more stalling. We have our drinks. It's time for you to tell me about this David guy. I got the impression he was on your father's staff?"

Will took a fortifying sip of his cocktail before he answered. "It's complicated. Obviously, I need you to be discreet, because David's not my father's employee but a colleague whom my father is mentoring. Senator David Mori to be precise."

Riley blinked at him for a moment before he fished his phone out of his pocket. Will could only guess he was googling David, as Will had done after their first encounter.

"Damn," Riley whistled quietly. "I'm curious about the name Mori. That doesn't sound Asian, but…"

"David's Japanese-American, Japanese on his dad's side."

"You have stellar taste in men, my friend."

"How self-congratulatory of you," Will joked.

Riley shot him a brief grin before looking down at his phone again. "I meant your senatorial fuck buddy. He's *gorgeous*."

"You're telling me. And we're not fuck buddies. We're not…anything. We've made out a few times, but I made a mess of things with him and probably shot any chance of anything else." His tone held a bitter edge. "Besides, his relationship with my father makes things horribly complicated, not to mention the—"

"Wait, I just realized he's a *Republican*." Riley's disbelief was clear as he stared at Will. "You're lusting after a conservative colleague of your father's? Jesus, complicated doesn't begin to cover it."

"He claims he's a moderate, actually," Will said. "I did some digging on his voting history and he's one of a very few Republican senators crossing the aisle." He winced. Oh Christ, he sounded defensive. David's passionate appeal about his political stance had apparently stuck and now Will was arguing on his behalf.

"Still…" Riley set his phone down and sat back.

Will laughed hollowly. "Oh, believe me, I've tormented myself with the same thoughts. Hell, David and I can't seem to have a conversation without arguing. I detest the idea of gay Republicans but damn, he makes some good points," Will said. "And the arguing is kind of hot, which is why it turns into kissing."

Riley shot him a grin. "Well, I can see the appeal then."

Will drummed his fingers on the table. "I was a complete ass, and when we had dinner at his place the other night, he rebuffed any advances."

"Because he doesn't want you or…?"

Will shrugged. "I don't think either of us can deny our attraction to each other. But he basically said he wanted to work on getting along first. He left the door a bit open by saying once we got along I could ask him out and he'd let me know, but…"

"I can understand that." Riley took a sip of his drink. "Hell, from a privacy perspective alone, I'm sure he has to be cautious about the people he gets involved with. He's out at least, I hope."

Will nodded. He'd learned that from his online searching too. "He's had several public relationships with men, but not since being elected."

"Well that's something at least. I can't imagine you'd want to get involved with a closeted senator."

Will grimaced. "No. Jesus, that sounds like a nightmare."

"So, do you want to get involved with David?"

"I…I…yeah, maybe?"

Riley smirked. "You don't sound very sure about that."

"That's because I'm not. It's so fucking complicated."

"Why are you interested in him? I mean, is it that you want to get naked with the guy? Because I completely understand. Or is there some element of getting back at your father mixed in there?"

Will immediately shook his head. "No. David accused me of the same thing and I've thought long and hard about it since. It's definitely not a conscious way to get back at my father. I'd be attracted to David even if we'd met under completely different circumstances and he was a fellow professor or something."

Riley flashed him a small smile. "Well, that's good."

Will struggled to explain himself. "There's this...chemistry there. I get around him and I can't think straight. Of course, when I'm not around him, I think it's totally insane to even try to make something work, but when we're together, I lose my head. It's like I'm reacting rather than thinking things through."

"Tell me how it all went down between you. You can leave out the dirty details—I'm not Jesse, for God's sake—but I feel like I've only gotten part of the story."

Will chuckled. Jesse *would* ask for the dirty details. "Sure. It started a couple of days after my dad got home from having surgery."

As Will talked, he watched a range of responses flicker over Riley's face. When Will had finished, he sat back and focused on his cocktail, silent as Riley observed him.

"Okay, I see your dilemma," Riley finally offered. "Frankly, I feel like you're being hard on David. You have to admit, he's in a tough position with your father."

"I know he is," Will agreed. "And I'm not blaming him for what happened. I was a total asshole. I tried to blow the guy and when he said no, I lost my shit."

Will cringed as the words left his mouth. It sounded so much worse when he laid it out like that and the look on Riley's face signaled he didn't think highly of Will's behavior, either. "It's like these horrible things keep coming out of my mouth before I can stop them."

Riley frowned at him. "You have a bit of a temper, but that doesn't sound like the Will I know."

"It's not. Or at least it didn't used to be." Will ran a hand through his hair. "I'm in a shitty place right now and it's all tied in with the crap with my family."

"How so?"

"My father...he's very black and white about things. And I suppose I am, too. So, we spent a good chunk of my adolescence butting heads. We argued about politics, about religion, about every possible current event that came up. I resented the scrutiny of being the child of a public figure. I hated being in my own family, to be honest. I never fit. And there was so much pressure to present the perfect façade. Appearances above all else, right?"

Will's memory flashed back to what he'd seen in the family photo albums. "Now I'm starting to wonder how much of that was my own doing. I mean, not all of it. We both had our parts to play in the estrangement. But once I realized I was attracted to guys I pushed them away because I was terrified about how they might react. It just kept getting worse and it was almost a relief once my father knew and told me not to come home anymore."

Riley gave him a sympathetic smile. "Hey, believe me, I'm familiar with the demanding father, public scrutiny and keeping-closeted thing."

"I know you are."

"So I understand why you're in a rough place over the relationship with your dad. But why are you taking that out on David?"

Will swirled the alcohol in his glass as he took some time to think about Riley's question. "To be honest, I resent the hell out of him having such a good relationship with my father," he blurted out.

Riley's eyes widened. "Oh, shit. Well, I get that."

"Here's this out, gay man whom my father respects and has a close working relationship with. Hell, someone he invites to his house. To whom he never once mentioned having a gay son. It's not David's fault, but all this shit under the surface seems to boil up and I find these horrible things coming out of my mouth that I later regret saying."

"So maybe you should deal with the family stuff first."

"David keeps pushing me to give my father another chance, but I don't know if I can."

"Why?"

Will glared at him. "You of *all* people should understand some people are too toxic to have in your life."

"I do understand," Riley said gently. "But it sounds like maybe things with your father aren't as simple as they were before. Maybe time or his illness has changed things."

Will sighed.

"I'm saying maybe you should talk to him. You don't have to forgive your father, but you should consider having a conversation and seeing if you two can find some common ground. This may be the *last* chance you have, Will."

Will sighed again. "David said that, too."

Riley sat back in his chair with a smirk. "Well, it sounds like you have good taste in men. They're gorgeous *and* smart."

Will chuckled, but quickly grew more serious. "So, if your father softened toward you and your relationship with Carter, you'd give him another chance?"

"I'd be very, very suspicious until I felt sure he was sincere, but yeah, I think I would."

"Hmm. It seemed like you'd totally written him off."

"I've stopped *hoping* for it. Stopped wishing it'll happen. But I'd love to be proven wrong." Bitterness colored Riley's smile. "Damn it, you're being so stubborn here, you're cutting off your nose to spite your face! Why don't you start simply with your father? Start with your writing career. You said he owns your books and complimented them. Find a way to discuss your upcoming book with him and go from there. You were so sure he hated that you didn't go into politics, but it's clear he's proud of what you've done. Use that common ground to build…whatever you can with him. I'm not saying he's going to turn into the dad you've always wanted, but it's possible you could put some old hurts to rest. You may not have much time left. I don't think you'll want to live with those regrets for the rest of *your* life."

Riley's words rolled over Will and sank in. He had a hard time letting go of the resentment that had built fortified walls around his heart. It was even harder to let go of the anger that fueled the building of those protections. But Riley and David were both right. Will had no idea how much time he and his father had left and he'd be the one living with regrets when his father was gone.

"Yeah, okay," he said slowly. "I can do that. I'll give it a try anyway."

Riley's smile was brilliant. "Now, what are you going to do about David?"

"I have no idea."

"Jesus, do you need me to solve everything in your life right now?"

Will managed a wry grin. "Could you? Because I'm doing a terrible job at it myself."

"I'd have to agree with that." Riley leaned forward. "Okay, do you have a way of contacting him without going through your father or anything related to his work?"

"Yes. We exchanged numbers the last time we talked."

"And have you talked to him?"

"Uh, no," Will admitted.

"Not even a text?" Will shook his head. "Jesus, I've never seen you this indecisive about anything."

"What can I say? Being in Long Island brings out the worst in me."

"I can see that. Okay, here's what you're going to do. While you're still in Manhattan and before you turn back into douche-y Long Island Will Martin, text David. It doesn't have to be anything elaborate. Just a 'hey, I was thinking about you and wanted to say hi' would do."

"I can do that."

"And if he seems like he's willing to talk, have a conversation. Ask how his dog is doing or talk about the weather. Whatever it is, find some neutral ground. Forget the fucked-up back and forth you've done until now and that he's your father's colleague. Treat him like a *man*. Not a senator or an adversary, but a man you want to be friends with and maybe more. You're charming as hell, Will. I know you can show him what a great guy you are."

"I definitely haven't up until now," Will said.

"Well, fix that!" Riley swallowed the last of his drink and stood. "Okay, I'm getting another drink."

"Has the 'lecture Will Martin' portion of the evening concluded then?" Will joked before he stood too.

"Unless you think you need more."

Will snorted. "No, I think you've given me plenty to think about and do."

"Good." Riley turned toward the bar but when Will caught his elbow, he looked back with a quizzical smile.

"I wanted to say thank you. I appreciate your help with this."

"Of course. I'm happy I could help."

* * * *

Will excused himself a little early and with reluctance. "I had a great time tonight, guys. Thanks for inviting me."

"Leaving already?" Jesse asked. "Do you have an early bedtime, Will?"

He grinned and winked. "Not when I'm going to bed alone."

"Oohooh. I haven't seen much of this side of you. I think I like it," Jesse teased.

"In all seriousness, I am heading home, alone, but that's because I need to text a guy." He shot a glance at Riley who smiled encouragingly. "Now that I've gotten my head out of my ass." He glanced over at Carter. "I know, I know, impossible task, right, Carter?"

Carter's laugh was a short bark of surprise. "Hey, I didn't say it!"

"Nah, but I know you were thinking it. Actually, I think you and this guy would be in complete agreement about me." Will made a face.

"Oh, so he dislikes you because he's too chicken shit to admit he's in love with his best friend?" Carter asked with a grin.

"No. Thankfully I haven't made that mistake again." Will's tone was fervent.

Riley crossed his arms and pretended to scowl. "Calling dating me a mistake, huh?"

Will laughed. "No. In fact, I think it was one of the best choices I've ever made."

Twenty minutes later and in the back of the Lyft car, Will agonized over what message to send David. In the end he went with what Riley had suggested.

Hey, I was thinking about you and wanted to say hi.

A reply appeared almost immediately.

Hey! I was starting to think I wouldn't hear from you after all.

Sorry. A friend informed me I need to get my head out of my ass and I fully intend to do so.

Delighted to hear it. I think I'd like this friend of yours.

Will smiled.

I think you would too. He's an ex, actually. And I know you'd get along with his new boyfriend. He's in complete agreement I can be an asshole.

LOL. I think you just need to figure out what you want.

What I want is to apologize for putting you in some very uncomfortable situations and getting pissed at you when you didn't react like I thought you should. Then I want to prove I'm actually fun to be around.

Apology accepted. I look forward to getting to know the guy I've caught some glimpses of. The funny, charming one.

I'll try to make sure he's the only one you're dealing with from now on, Will replied.

You're human, Will. I don't expect perfection. Just to be treated with respect.

He winced.

I can definitely do that.

How's Manhattan?

Like heaven after Long Island. How's Albany?

Tiring. Lots of long days right now. There are a couple of bills coming up for a vote that I'm reading up on.

A photo appeared of a desk stacked high with file folders and legal pads filled with scribbled notes. A couple of framed photos sat in the corner. One was of Mabel with her tongue lolling out of her mouth. The other showed a younger David with his arms around a woman in a wedding dress who strongly resembled him, and a couple Will guessed were David's parents. David's family. David had inherited his mother's smile, but his father's coloring and features. They looked close. Happy together. Will thought wistfully of his own family and the rift there. Maybe David and Riley were right that he needed to mend that rift.

He glanced at the timestamp on the message. 10:27 p.m.

Please don't tell you're STILL there?

A moment later, another photo appeared. It showed David in a big leather chair, jacket off, tie loosened, top shirt button undone. He looked exhausted but still so handsome it hurt to look at him. *'Fraid I am* was the accompanying message.

Want me to leave you to it?

Nope. I'm glad you messaged me actually. I didn't realize how late it was. My stomach is growling and Mabel is probably pouting at my absence.

Aww, poor thing.

Me or the dog?

Definitely the dog. How is the beautiful girl?

Other than unhappy with me for my long hours? She's great. I've promised her a nice long walk this weekend.

Give her a pat from me.

Should I start worrying you're only interested in me for my dog?

I wasn't thinking of your dog when I saw the picture of you looking all rumpled at your desk.

Do tell.

I shouldn't. Not if I'm going to be on my best behavior and focus on our friendship.

Damn it! Good point. I appreciate that.

Another message arrived before Will could respond.

I'm packing up and driving to my apartment. Can I message you after I get Mabel walked and some food in me?

Of course. I'll be up for a while.

Thanks. Catch you later.

The Lyft arrived at his apartment a short while later and Will thanked the driver. Once in the apartment, he hastily showered and threw on sleep pants and a T-shirt, hoping he wouldn't miss David's text. He was reading on the couch when his phone buzzed with an incoming call.

"Hey," he answered.

"Hey, Will. You don't mind me calling, do you?" David replied. "I figured we could talk while I walk Mabel."

"Not at all. Did you eat?"

"Jesus, you sound like Agnes." Will chuckled as David continued. "Yes, I ate. I scarfed down leftover chicken nachos from last night's dinner."

"Yum."

"Your father gave them a rather wistful glance last night when we were having our dinner."

The idea of his father working long hours alarmed Will. "Please don't tell me he's been staying late. I thought he was crazy for going to Albany at all, but..."

"No, no, he keeps shorter hours. I brought him up to speed on a few issues last night over dinner. I ate the takeout and he had a meal Agnes packed while we talked."

"Good. How does he seem?"

"Tired." David paused for a moment. "Honestly, I think being here is taking a lot out of him, but he seems less..."

"Like a grumpy old bastard?" Will supplied.

They both laughed. "I was going to say malcontent, but that fits too."

"He's always lived for his work."

"Are you so different?" David asked gently. "You're clearly passionate about your teaching and writing."

"That's a fair point," Will conceded. He heard the sound of a door opening then closing and wondered if David was back home.

"So, what have you been up to the last few days?"

"Packing for a few more weeks in Long Island for one. Oh, and I went to a speakeasy tonight with friends."

"A speakeasy? How roaring twenties of you."

Will chuckled. "Friends of my ex, Riley, own it. It's a great place. I'd love to take you there sometime if you're ever in Manhattan." The invitation rolled from

Will's lips before he could think twice, and a small pause followed on David's end.

"I'd like that. Although I can see the headlines now, *Republican Senator Caught at Sleazy Manhattan Speakeasy.*"

"It's far from sleazy. Very upscale with amazing cocktails."

"I'm teasing." David's tone was warm. "Besides, it would hardly make news unless a sex scandal were attached."

"Well, one of the owners is Jesse Murtagh, so a sex scandal is certainly possible if you're interested," Will said drily. "Are you familiar with him?"

"Vaguely. And only by reputation—which is provocative, I'll give you that."

"Oh, he lives up to the reputation. The man is practically a real-life Tony Stark."

"Billionaire, playboy, philanthropist?"

"*Exactly.* I hesitate to ever tell him that because I'm afraid of what it'll do to his ego," Will joked.

David laughed. "So which Avenger does that make you?"

Will considered the question, then groaned. "Unfortunately, I'm pretty sure I'm Bruce Banner."

David snickered. "Next time you go into Hulk Smash mode, I'm going to call you out on that."

"Here's hoping that'll be enough of a reminder so I don't do it again."

"What you don't understand is this conversation is *right* up my alley. I'm a huge comic book nerd."

"I was under the impression comic book nerds weren't usually so good-looking."

"We tend to fly under the radar a bit better. Get us talking, though…"

"How did you get into comics in the first place?"

"My dad." David's voice went soft. "He took me to Comic-Con in San Diego for the first time when I was eight. And we went every year after until he died. They're some of my favorite memories of him."

"Do you think you'll ever go back?"

"I don't know. I still go to Cons here on the East Coast, but I haven't gone back to San Diego. I keep saying I will, but every year I find an excuse not to. Maybe when I have a child of my own."

"That would be a nice family tradition."

David yawned. "Sorry, but I think I'm going to have to cut this short. I have an early day tomorrow."

"Of course."

"I enjoyed this a lot. I'm glad we talked."

"Me too," Will admitted. "I'm sorry *this* wasn't the first impression you got of me."

David chuckled. "I'll text you tomorrow when I have time."

"I'd like that." Will hesitated. "Could you pass a message along? Tell my dad...tell him I hope he's feeling well. And that I'll see him in a few days."

"I'd be happy to." David's voice was warm. "G'night, Will."

"Night, David."

* * * *

Will awoke the following morning to a text notification. He expected it to be from David and was surprised to see a message from his sister instead.

I'm taking the train in because I have an appointment in Manhattan today. Would you like to grab a late lunch before I head back?

Sure. What time?

"We need to talk about Dad," Olivia said later that afternoon when they were seated across the table from each other on a shady patio at a bistro.

"Good afternoon to you too, sis," Will said drily. "How are you?"

"Sorry." She flushed and twisted the large emerald ring on her right hand. "I'm having a hard time with this."

"I'm sorry I haven't done more to be sure you're doing okay. Tell me what you need."

Her narrow shoulders hunched a little. "I don't know, Will. I'm overwhelmed. Between Dad's illness, and the kids, and Phillip's work…"

"What's happening with your husband?" Will asked with a frown.

Olivia sighed. "Of course, Phil had nothing to do with it, but one of the other partners in the office is being sued for sexual harassment by a paralegal. It's a mess and Phil's had to take on some of his partner's caseload."

"Ugh. That's messy."

"Very." Olivia smoothed the crisp white tablecloth. "It has to be done. The clients need to be kept happy, but Phil's never home now and the kids *are* and they're missing their father and taking it out on me. On top of everything going on with Dad, I'm worn out. I had to get a part-time nanny. I hated to do it, but Mom can't help like usual."

Will shot his sister a sympathetic smile. "I'm sorry."

"I know you are and I'm so grateful you came home to help. It's a load off my mind. But I'm concerned about what we're going to do for the rest of the summer."

They were interrupted by a waiter before he could respond. Will ordered the first thing he spotted on the menu and the moment they were alone again, he spoke. "I packed for another few weeks. I'm heading back to Long Island tomorrow."

Her large brown eyes shimmered with tears. "I appreciate that. I need to know when things get rough, I'm not going to be left dealing with this all on my own."

"You won't," Will promised. "I mean that."

"What do you think about staying through to the end of the summer? Or until..." She cleared her throat. "Until we don't need you there."

Until Dad's dead, Will finished in his head. The sudden pang in his chest took him by surprise. And he had to take a few deep breaths to steady himself. "Let's take it a little bit at a time, Liv."

But she shook her head. "Please, Will." Tears spilled down her cheeks. "I know Mom is trying to be optimistic but I was there when the surgeon came out after the operation. They didn't get all of the cancer. It's going to keep spreading and they won't be able to do much more than buy him time. He's dying and we all need you. You're the strong one."

Will sat forward and placed a hand on hers, squeezing tightly. "I don't feel like the strong one, Liv. Being back there is hard. I don't even know Dad anymore and I'm *trying*, but it's hard to forgive a man who implied I was dead to him when he caught me with my boyfriend. I know none of you support me being gay, but you have to understand how that felt."

Olivia pulled her hand away and wiped at her eyes. "I support you. I don't care who you live with. But don't you get Dad was more pissed that you lied to him than that you were gay?"

"And all the homophobic legislation in the past ten years doesn't matter?"

She leaned forward and skewered him with a look. "I'm not saying he's always been supportive of the LGBT community, but have you even *looked* at his voting record in the past few years? Or are you so convinced he's exactly the same man he was a decade ago that you can't see what's right in front of your face?"

Will swallowed hard. "I admit I made some mistakes, Liv. I've been carrying around a chip on my shoulder, but I'm *trying*."

Her expression softened. "I know. But try harder. Because I don't think we have much time left."

Another pang shot through Will's chest. "How long are they talking?"

"I don't know." She shrugged. "Three or four months, maybe. If we're lucky. That's why you need to stay through until the end of the summer."

"What if...what if it's longer than that? I have a life here in Manhattan, you know," he said gently. "My career is important to me."

"I understand, and I'm sorry to drag you away."

"That's a lot to ask when none of you have made any effort to be supportive of my life in the past," Will said quietly.

Hurt flashed across Olivia's face, but quickly melted into understanding. "I know."

"I can't just trash everything I've worked so hard to build. I have a mortgage and a career here that I love."

"What if you sublet your place and went on sabbatical? You're a tenured professor — I'm sure NYU would agree to that, given the circumstances. Maybe you could do some guest lecturing at one of the schools on Long Island. I'm sure SUNY or Briarcliffe would be thrilled to have a writer of your caliber there."

Will smiled faintly. "I'm not so famous I can get hired anywhere, Liv."

"But you are well-respected, Will. We're all proud of you for what you've accomplished. Even Dad."

He nodded. "I saw my books on his shelves. I had no idea he'd even read them."

Olivia leaned forward, her expression earnest. "Give him a chance. I know Daddy's not perfect, but he's a good man. He loves you, even if it's not easy for him to say."

"Give me time to think about things. I promise I'll seriously consider your suggestions, okay?" She nodded. "And we'll know more after his scans and doctor's appointment in the next couple of weeks, right?"

"Yes." Her lips trembled. "They should have a clearer idea of what to expect then."

Olivia composed herself when the waiter arrived with her salade Niçoise and Will's grilled chicken club with rosemary aioli.

"So, are you seeing anyone right now?" she asked after the waiter had gone, a falsely cheerful note in her voice.

Will blinked. "Uh, no. Not at the moment. I was seeing someone last year, but I got my heart broken so I took time off dating."

Her smile was sincere. "I'm sorry."

"Thank you. We stayed friends, so that's good." Will cleared his throat. "Actually, he's pushing me to mend fences with Dad, too."

"Aside from not seeing what a catch you are, he's clearly a smart man."

"It's okay. He's in love with his best friend. Has been for years. They're good together. I can see now it's way better for him than what we had." Will smiled. The thought was freeing.

"Well, maybe you'll meet someone on Long Island," Olivia said philosophically. "I think one of the guys in Phil's office is gay."

"No. You are *not* setting me up on blind dates, Liv." He wondered what she'd think of his interactions with David but decided the less they discussed that subject the better.

"I want you to be happy."

"I appreciate that." He changed the subject. "So, tell me more about Jocelyn and Adam. If I'm sticking around this summer, I want to get to know my niece and nephew."

Chapter Eight

David pulled into the Martins' driveway and cut his car's ignition, then smothered a yawn behind one hand. He noted the Zipcar parked in front of him and smiled, sure it belonged to Will.

They'd exchanged messages and phone calls during David's five days in Albany and he'd enjoyed each exchange more than the last. They'd stuck to lighter subjects, often joking and teasing, and he'd gotten to know Will bit by bit.

David's phone chimed, and he picked it up from where it lay on the passenger seat between his briefcase and a pale green bakery box. The incoming message from Will made him grin.

How long are you going to sit in the driveway like a creeper?

I've got French cookies and a six-pack of ale, David replied. *You got a better offer?*

No, but I'll be your designated driver if you bring both inside and hand the cookies over to me.

David chuckled. He picked up his briefcase and the box before opening the car door and sighed as the warm late-afternoon air hit him. A dizzy sensation swept through him when he stood, but he shook it off and headed for the house.

He didn't have time to press the doorbell before Will opened the front door, his eyes twinkling.

"Senator Mori—nice to see you. Great suit, by the way."

David stepped inside and played along, though he failed to keep a straight face. "Hello, Will, and thanks. I wasn't sure you'd be here tonight."

"I'm on my way out, actually, but saw you pull up and wanted to say hello."

Will closed the door and turned toward David with a tiny smile. He looked particularly handsome in his blue-striped mariner shirt and jeans, but David could read tension in Will's posture and the fine lines around his eyes.

Being here is hard on him, David reminded himself, *especially now, when things are so unsettled.* Without thinking about it, he put a hand out to clasp Will's shoulder, squeezing lightly when Will raised his brows.

"It's nice to see you," David said. He let his hand drop and smiled wider as Will's cheeks flushed pink.

"Mom and Dad are on the patio," Will said with a nod toward the far end of the foyer. "Come on and I'll get you a drink since you clearly ignored my instructions to bring the beer inside."

"Hey, I brought the cookies," David protested. He handed the box to Will as they headed for kitchen. "Just promise you'll share them with Agnes and Greta."

"I'll certainly try," Will returned, and now tension crept into his voice, too. "Mom hasn't had much of an appetite recently and I'm not sure who's lost more weight, my father or her."

Once in the kitchen, Will led David to the counter and set down the box. "What would you like?" he asked. "There's iced tea, or I can mix you a drink if you're in the mood for something stronger."

"Iced tea is fine—I've got to drive home, anyway."

Will nodded and opened a nearby cabinet, then pulled out two glasses. "What are you doing here, anyway? And where's your better half?"

"Mabel's at home, no doubt pulling the sheets off my bed because I'm running late." David leaned against the counter and watched Will set the glasses down, then move to the refrigerator. "I'm here because I have some proposals Bill is interested in reviewing. He mentioned being home the next few days before his next appointment in Philly, so I brought them by."

Will extracted an ice bucket from the freezer with one hand, then opened the refrigerator with the other and brought out a tall pitcher of tea.

"My parents aren't leaving until Sunday, so he'll have plenty of time to read over…whatever the hell it is that can't wait." Will carried everything back to the counter. He frowned and dropped ice into the tumblers. "Or you could not give the proposals to him and hope he forgets about them."

David said nothing until Will had filled the glasses. "I don't think this can wait," he said at last, and his stomach sank at Will's scowl.

"Oh? Why not?"

"You may have heard the Senate was to vote this past week on two LGBTQ-focused bills," David began and paused when Will made an exasperated noise.

"I missed that." He ran a hand through his hair. "I'm too distracted to focus on much of anything these days, unfortunately."

"You've had a lot going on," David reasoned. He sipped his tea before continuing. "GENDA prohibits discrimination against transgender persons in areas like employment, housing and education. Bill A6983, in the meantime, protects minors from conversion therapy efforts."

"Conversion therapy." Will pressed his lips together into a tight line. "Jesus Christ, that we even need these laws is disgusting."

"I agree." David shook his head at Will's skeptical expression. "Bills like GENDA and A6983 are necessary to protect the interests of the LGBTQ community, Will, which is also *my* community."

Will's expression shifted, turning slightly abashed, and David's gut twisted. Will still underestimated his commitment to LGBTQ rights. He rubbed a hand over his face and drew in a deep breath.

"Anyway. Both bills were passed by the State Assembly earlier this year — in fact, GENDA has passed the Assembly the last seven years."

Will's frown deepened. "Why would it need to pass more than once? And what happened with the bill banning conversion therapy?" The words were hardly out of his mouth before his face went hard. Will set his glass on the counter. "Let me guess — the Senate voted against both bills."

"Not quite—neither bill reached a vote. The GOP ignored them until this year's Session ended. Now the bills have to be re-sponsored and the process toward passing them begun all over again—"

"So my father and his cronies let the bills die out of spite," Will cut in, his voice flat but his anger unmistakable.

"No," David bit out past his own flare of irritation. "It's true many of my colleagues purposely dragged their feet, but not every member of the GOP agreed with their tactics. I was ready to vote and so were Bill and many others."

Will glanced away with a disbelieving sound and once again, David reached out to grasp his shoulder. He waited for Will to glance back before continuing. "Why do you think he traveled up there this week? We both know your father shouldn't have made the trip, but he did. He wanted to vote on GENDA and A6983, Will. And this may have been his last chance to do so."

Will's throat worked before he cut his gaze away. "Do I want to know how he planned to vote?"

"I couldn't tell you—Bill didn't share that information with me, and I'd never expect him to. He and I discussed the details of both bills at length, particularly A6983. Bill wanted to understand the ramifications their passage would have on the community. *Our* community."

David dropped his hand. "I don't take my job lightly. As a lawmaker, I have the power to literally affect people's lives, and my intention isn't to harm people but make their existence better if I can. I firmly believe Bill has been committed to the same ideals throughout his career, too."

"Oh, I know he has." Will crossed his arms over his chest. "The problem is, my father's notions about bettering people's lives are frequently at odds with bettering *my* life."

"Understood. However, you should know Bill's alluded to regretting those conflicts. So, I think you need to ask yourself — have your father's ideals changed over time?"

Will drew breath to respond, but the patio door at the far end of the kitchen opened then and Agnes stepped inside, with Bill close behind.

"Hello, David!" Agnes exclaimed with a quick smile. "Bill said you'd be stopping by, but I picked up a book after lunch and I'm afraid I lost track of time. Why are you two cooped up in the kitchen instead of coming outside?" She turned a chiding glance on Will who rolled his eyes.

"I just got here, Agnes," David said.

"And he brought you cookies," Will added.

"Oh, thank you, dear — I'm sure they'll be wonderful." Agnes stepped up to join them and David bent to give her a brief hug.

"Will answered the door and offered me a glass of tea," he explained. "We were about to move outside when you came in."

"I'm surprised he's still here." Bill shook David's outstretched hand. "Will's been muttering to himself since yesterday about getting out for something battered and fried." He smiled at Will's aggrieved noise. "I certainly don't blame you, son. I'd happily sell my soul for a nice porterhouse right now."

David remembered Will's similar declaration the last time they'd seen each other and smiled.

"Hush," Agnes scolded. "I know you miss eating what you like, but there's no reason to condemn yourself to eternal damnation in the name of red meat!"

"Then allow me to live vicariously through you." Bill's expression warmed. "Why don't you let Will take you out tonight? I'll bet David can suggest a place you'd like, and you and Will can enjoy fried and battered things together."

Will nodded. "I think that's a great idea, Mom — what do you say?"

Agnes blinked, obviously taken off guard. "But what about you?" She furrowed her brow when Bill waved her off.

"Oh, I'll be all right. Greta's here and I'm more than capable of entertaining myself for the evening. David's brought me some materials I want to review anyway, so go on and treat yourself to a night out."

"I don't think so." Agnes shook her head.

David cleared his throat and gave Agnes a small smile when the Martins glanced his way. "I can stay and keep Bill company, if you'd like. We'll go over the docs I brought and Greta's got everything covered in the kitchen — we'll be fine." Mabel would be super pissed at him, but David experienced a flush of warmth when Will caught his eye and nodded.

Agnes frowned. "Thank you, dear, but no."

This time, Will stepped forward and took Agnes' hand. "Why not, Mom? It'll do you good to get out of the house."

Agnes brought her other hand up to rest on top of Will's. "I know you mean well, darling, and I appreciate it, but it's better I stay home. I'd spend the entire time worrying about what might go wrong here anyway, and that's not fair to you. Honestly, you're all acting as if *I'm* the one who's sick and needs taking care of," she added, her laugh so brittle David felt a wave of pity.

A heavy silence fell over the group. David glimpsed a storm of fear, anger and guilt in Bill's gaze, though his face remained impassive. Will's disappointment was more evident, and his father's emotions were reflected in his blue-gray eyes.

"No one's forgotten I'm the one who's ill, Agnes," Bill said, his voice kind. "You can't blame us for wanting to keep it that way, either. It's my job to make sure you take as good care of yourself as you do everyone else."

Agnes' cheeks flushed but she managed a wry smile. "Point taken," she replied quietly, then turned to her son. "I'm still staying home tonight, but I promise to be more aware of my own well-being. And I'd appreciate you not ganging up on me again," she added with a scowl so fierce David bit back a laugh.

Will didn't bother to stop his own and pressed a quick kiss to his mother's cheek. "Okay, Mom. We didn't plan this, by the way—it just sort of happened."

"As this is the first time you and your father have agreed on anything in a very long while, I'll consider it a win."

Will stuck out his tongue. "I'm sorry you won't come to dinner with me, but I'm definitely going out—I need unhealthy food before my body goes into shock."

The group spent the next few minutes bidding each other good night, but David was conscious of Bill's gaze on Will and himself as they drifted out of the kitchen. He waited for a lull in the conversation and nodded at Will.

"I'm parked behind you—give me a minute to back out of the driveway and you can be on your way."

Will gestured toward the front door with a grin. "Thanks, I appreciate that."

Five minutes later, David's phone chimed with an incoming call while he sat idling in his car at a traffic light. He used the car's Bluetooth to connect, and smiled as Will's voice rang out.

"Are you hungry?"

"What, no hello?"

"*Hello*, David, are you hungry?"

David checked the rearview mirror and saw empty street behind him. "Where are you?"

"A couple of blocks over. You didn't answer my question."

"I could eat," David allowed.

"Join me for dinner?"

"Why, so we can pick up where we left off at your parents' house?" David smiled at Will's snort of laughter.

"No, thanks. I'm done talking politics with you for tonight."

David stepped on the gas as the light changed. "I say that very thing to myself at least three times a week and politics is my job."

"So, come out with me. We'll go eat a bunch of meat and drink wine at the Colombian place you like."

"It's Cuban-Italian," David corrected with a smile. His mouth watered at the idea of a good meal, but he didn't feel up to it. He was still trying to figure out a graceful way to back out when Will cleared his throat.

"I'm guessing this awkward silence is a no, huh? Damn, first Mom and now you."

"It's not a no," David said hastily. "I mean, it is, but not because I don't want to have dinner with you."

"O-o-kay…you want to have dinner but you're still saying no?"

"Afraid so. I can't, Will. I need to get home, walk Mabel then sleep for about ten hours. If we can do this another time —"

"Of course we can," Will cut in. "Are you okay?"

"I'm fine," David assured him. "Tired after a lot of long hours this week, but there's nothing wrong with me that can't be fixed with some sleep."

Will sounded dubious when he replied. "All right, raincheck then. But if I ask you to meet me at Hempstead Lake Park tomorrow at two, you'll be there? It's supposed to be beautiful and the park is ten minutes from your house, if you haven't been there already."

"I have, actually. Is Mabel invited?"

"Well, of course she is, Senator." Will's tone of exaggerated patience made David laugh. "What kind of guy would I be not to invite your girl along, too?"

David made a right. "Despite your overwhelming sarcasm, I think that's a fine idea. We'll meet you at two and I'll park in lot three, near Shodack Pond."

An hour later, he turned Mabel back onto 4th Street and she made a yowly noise that meant she'd spotted something exciting. He followed her gaze, and couldn't hold back a smile when he saw Will, leaning against the side of the Zipcar, a smile on his face and holding a big paper bag.

"Fancy meeting you here," David called as he and Mabel drew closer.

"I was not really in your neighborhood," Will tossed back. "I brought you a care package." He handed the bag to David and squatted down to pet Mabel, who greeted him with pricked ears and wagging tail. "Hello, gorgeous," Will said, his voice fond. He dug his fingers into her scruff and Mabel grumbled happily.

David stared at the bag in his hands, struck almost speechless with surprise. "What—"

"I found a crab shack on Woodcleft Ave.," Will said over Mabel's head. "You know I'm craving fried foods and the menu is a seafood lover's idea of paradise. I brought you an order of crab cakes and coleslaw. There's a burger for Miss Mabel, too, along with some fries, but I'm sure she won't tell if they magically disappear into your mouth instead of hers."

"Whoa, thank you." David laughed. Delight zinged through him as Will got to his feet again. "This is so thoughtful."

"I'm capable of a thoughtful notion or two when not in Hulk mode." Will winked. "Anyway, enjoy your dinner and I'll see you both tomorrow."

David nodded and caught himself wishing Will would stick around. "Where are you off to now?"

"Back to the crab shack, of course." Will opened his car door. "I have a date with a Fisherman's Platter and a tall glass of beer—if that doesn't satisfy the craving, I'll grab a bucket of chicken from KFC and hope for the best!"

* * * *

"Thanks again for dinner last night," David told Will the next afternoon as they walked Mabel along the shore of South Pond in the park. "And for suggesting this, too. It's nice to get out in the sun for a change."

"You were looking a bit peaked," Will said. He opened the flap of his messenger bag and pulled out two bottled waters, offering one to David. "I noticed after that blue suit of yours stopped grabbing all my attention."

David cracked open his bottle with a smile of genuine pleasure. "Thanks. It's Dunhill and one of my favorites, actually. It's getting a bit too warm in the season to keep wearing it, unfortunately."

"You must cut quite a figure in chambers." Will ran his gaze up and down David's body with frank appreciation, despite David's plain white T-shirt and khaki cargo shorts. "I mean, even dressed down, you're camera-ready."

"You're one to talk," David replied, keeping his tone light. Will also wore a T-shirt and shorts, and, as always, was impeccably put together.

"Yes, but I don't work with a bunch of old white guys who probably wouldn't know a Dunhill suit if they fell over it in Neiman Marcus."

"Oh, come on. Not all my colleagues are old or white, or even men, and there's a Dunhill counter in Garden City's Neiman Marcus."

"I can't believe you know that." Will laughed. "But seriously, how do you stand it? You've got to be the youngest member of the Senate, not to mention the gayest."

"There are a couple of members around my age," David protested. "And while I'm not *the* gayest man in the chamber, I am currently the only openly gay member of the GOP."

Will leveled a stare at him. "Meaning…?"

"Meaning some of my colleagues are closeted," David finished. "A few of them have made a point of approaching me about it, and they know I won't out them." He frowned as Will shook his head, and his voice was much quieter when he spoke again.

"Again, I have to ask, how do you stand it?"

"Will, no one should be forced come out before they're ready. Besides, there are closeted Democrats in the Senate, too, and we both know your party isn't without its own flaws." David paused his steps when Mabel stopped to nose at a tree trunk. "To answer your question, I focus on doing my job. I conduct a ton of research and make a lot of phone calls. I listen to my constituents when they have something to say and talk to my colleagues when it's my turn to share information. I write bills, I vote and at the end of the day, I try to be there for the people who need me and keep their best interests at heart."

"Even when you have to cross the aisle and vote with the other party?"

"Especially then." David focused on the pond for a long moment. "Did you know that three of the four Republicans who voted for marriage equality in 2011 are no longer in office? Despite the Governor's and Mayor's promises to protect them from political retribution, one senator chose not to run for re-election and two others were voted out of office. Every time I weigh siding with 'the opposition', I have to remember those votes may come back to haunt me."

Will uttered a low oath, outrage obvious in his expression. "But you do it, anyway."

"Of course, when I feel it's the right thing to do. Democrats vote against party lines on occasion, too. I didn't get into politics to help myself — I got into it to help others."

"You're a better man than I." The conviction in Will's tone made David smile.

"A time may come when I'll need to remind you of that comment," he teased, and tugged at Mabel's leash.

They spent a couple of hours ambling along the dog-walking areas of the park, talking the entire time. Neither shied away from difficult topics — including their opposing politics — but while Will's temper surfaced now and again, each took care not to get personal and stayed civil even when their debates grew heated.

David cocked his head at Will as they approached their cars in the parking lot and Will mimicked the gesture with a playful expression.

"What's that face for?"

"Don't take this the wrong way, Will, but you are ten thousand times easier to talk to when you're away from Garden City."

Will tipped back his head and laughed. "Oh, man, that's not news. *Everyone* likes me better away from Garden City, especially me."

"Well, we need to get you out of that village on a regular basis if we're going to keep being friends."

"I'd like that. Being friends and getting out of Garden City. As much as I bug my mother to get away from the house, I need the timeouts even more."

Will looked pleased and a bit shy in that moment, and David found his soft expression very, very appealing. He drew a steadying breath before he spoke.

"If you don't have any plans tonight, I'm happy to help extend today's timeout."

"What did you have in mind?"

David shrugged through the nervous tumbling in his stomach. "Drinks and dinner at my place. I bought fresh orata from the fishmonger today and I'm not bragging when I say I make a mean fish taco."

"I'm still trying to wrap my head around your claim to have a fishmonger," Will said. He seemed bemused. "But I like that idea."

"You sure your parents won't miss you?"

"Like I said, my mom's been bugging me to get out of the house." His expression sobered suddenly. "I didn't tell them I'd be seeing you today."

David frowned. "Okay. Can I ask why not?"

"Because they don't need to know. I don't like my parents sticking their noses into my private life—I never have." Will shrugged. "The last time they got too close, things got ugly, and I'd rather not have a repeat."

"Understood." Sadness for Will and his parents washed through David. They were on speaking terms again, but the estrangement still ran deep.

"How about I pick up some beer or wine, and meet you back at your place?" Will asked.

David smiled and unlocked his car's doors. "I've got beer, but wine sounds great. I'll see you in a bit."

This time as they sat on David's deck, David felt entirely comfortable beside Will. They sipped Sauvignon Blanc while the sun dropped steadily lower, staining the sky scarlet and orange. Any tension between them was purely physical in nature. It was evident in the way Will stared at David's mouth, and David's touch when he laid a hand on Will's forearm while telling a story.

David's initial attraction to Will had deepened as they got to know each other. Whether either of them should act on it—and how that might affect their burgeoning friendship—was another matter altogether. Starting up with Will screamed *bad idea*, but David didn't want to stop himself.

"I should get started on the food," he said at last. Mabel rolled up to stand as David pushed back his chair, and both eyed Will when he got to his feet, too.

He picked up the bottle of wine in its steel chiller. "Can I help?"

"I don't know...can you?" David grinned. "Are you useful in the kitchen?"

"Not very," Will said with a laugh. He stepped out of Mabel's way as she headed for the door. "But I can be your gopher and get things from the cabinets or wash dishes."

David smiled fondly and opened the door. "Why don't you keep me company?" he suggested. "I'll talk you through the recipe and if you feel like helping, you can."

Once inside, he fed Mabel, then made an earnest attempt at preparing to cook. He gathered a cutting board and his knives, and directed Will to the appropriate cabinets and drawers for plates and flatware. But after going to the pantry for a paper bag of tomatoes, he found Will waiting for him in the doorway when he turned back. Will smiled and rested his hands on David's waist.

In an instant, David's misgivings about acting on his attraction for Will evaporated. Tonight, he just wanted to feel. He leaned in and kissed Will, humming low in his chest when Will gripped his waist tighter. David quickly shifted the bag to one hand so he could take hold of the back of Will's neck with the other and deepen the kiss. Will crowded him back against the doorframe, the heat of his body seeping through David's shirt and into his skin.

He made a noise of complaint when David finally pulled away. "What?"

"I need to put this bag down before I drop it."

"Oh!" Will chuckled and kept one hand on David's waist as he leaned to set the bag on the counter. "Will whatever's in it keep for a while?"

"Definitely," David replied, then paused. "You're okay with this, right?" He slid his fingers into Will's short hair and bit back a smile when Will flared his nostrils.

"Are you kidding? I've wanted to kiss you since yesterday."

Neither spoke as David led the way out of the kitchen and upstairs, but once they were in David's room, Will was on him again. He threaded his arms around David's neck and David pulled him close. He spread his hands wide on Will's back and licked his way into Will's mouth. Will groaned when David dropped one hand to squeeze his ass.

"Jesus, David."

David moved to nip at Will's throat with his lips. "Mmm. Definitely an indication this is okay."

Will huffed out a laugh. "Stop fussing. If you do anything I have a problem with, believe me, you'll know." He ducked his head to catch David's lips again, and when they separated a minute later, they shared a smile.

David led Will to the bed, and swallowed at the heat he saw in Will's gaze. He reached for Will's belt buckle while Will pulled his T-shirt off. Will grabbed the hem of David's shirt and David's skin pebbled in the cool air as they stripped. He couldn't resist another kiss before he guided Will down to sit. David opened the nightstand drawer and plucked out lube and condoms. He set them beside the lamp and stretched out beside Will, stroking his torso while they exchanged kisses.

They ground against each other until David was breathless.

With a grunt, he pulled back and rolled up onto his hands and knees. He worked his way down Will's torso, licking and sucking his skin and relishing his hungry sounds. Will brought his hands up to rest on David's head, and swore loudly when David bit the soft skin of his groin. David chased the sting with his tongue.

"I want you," he murmured. He spread Will's legs with his hands and rubbed his palm over Will's right hip before he settled between his thighs.

Will trembled as David nosed at his groin, and David sighed with pleasure. He breathed in the smell of clean, warm skin and cock and licked Will's shaft. Will gasped and fisted the sheets when David kissed the head of his dick.

"You taste fucking good," David said, and bent to lick Will's inner thigh.

Will whined. "Come up here," he urged, his voice rough, one hand tugging gently at David's hair.

"Uh-uh." David stroked Will's thigh with his palm. "I want to make you feel good."

After a moment, Will dropped his hands, framing David's face for a moment before he nodded. David smiled, and waited for Will to move his hands onto his own thighs. David opened his mouth, slowly sliding his lips over Will's cock, his own twitching at Will's hiss. Will's face transformed as David sucked. His breaths grew ragged and his quiet moans made David's balls ache. Closing his eyes, David dropped a hand to palm his own erection.

He took his time, working Will over and gradually unraveling his control. Will's thighs were trembling on either side of David's face by the time he pulled off to tongue Will's sac.

"Oh, God," Will muttered. "I…ah, that feels so good."

David lavished attention on his balls while bringing both hands up to stroke his cock. Will's pupils were blown when David opened his eyes, the heat in his gaze intense enough to make David roll his hips into the mattress. Desire coiled in his belly.

"David," Will bit out when David shifted and took him deep. Whatever Will planned to say next got lost in a strangled noise, and he brought his hands back up to twine his fingers in David's hair.

David closed his eyes again, reveling in the sting along his scalp and the ache between his legs. He swallowed around Will and used his hands and forearms to hold Will down when he bucked his hips forward.

"Shit," Will ground out, his grip on David's hair tightening to the point of pain. "Gonna come."

David wrapped one hand around the base of Will's cock and swallowed again, feeling Will's body go rigid. He pulled off in time to watch Will come, and bit his lip as the orgasm racked his body. Will called out and pressed his head back hard into the pillows, his skin flushed and damp with sweat as his cock pulsed over David's fist.

He was still panting when David shifted back up onto his hands and knees, but opened his eyes immediately and let go of David's hair, his expression dazed.

"Watch me," David murmured. He leaned forward, maneuvering himself to straddle Will's waist, then took himself in hand, using Will's cum as lube.

Will let out a deep groan as David pumped himself. "Oh, yeah," he breathed out, and ran his hands up

David's thighs, his touch raising goosebumps all over David's skin.

"Fuck," David rasped. He tipped his head back as the sensations rushed through him, winding around his hips and down his spine. "*Fuck.*"

"Come on, David."

Will cupped David's balls and he shuddered. He forced himself to straighten again, and peeled his eyes open to catch Will's hungry, awed expression before he got lost in the white noise of his own orgasm. He came hard, curling forward and streaking Will's torso with his cum, and gasped when Will pulled at him.

Will guided him onto the mattress, his touch anchoring David through his aftershocks. David closed his eyes and waited for his breathing to even out, and enjoyed the simple delight of lying boneless and satisfied beside a man he desired. He roused again when Will shifted beside him, and smiled at the simple delight in Will's expression.

"You know, I never would have pegged you for dirty talk," Will observed. He hummed when David reached up and ran a finger through the mess marking Will's skin. "Then again, you're a Republican senator from *Queens*, for God's sake. I suppose I shouldn't be surprised you're an undercover freak."

David poked Will in the side and made him squawk, and Will tried in vain to wriggle out of his grasp. David simply hooked his other arm around Will's neck and dragged him closer, poking him without mercy until Will fell against him, laughing and breathless.

"You're a mess." David ran his fingers along Will's belly, enjoying the jump he noticed in Will's breathing.

"Says the guy who's shining like a glazed donut." Will smiled when David burst out laughing, then moved to sit up. "Okay if I take a shower?"

Real regret ran through David at the idea of their night ending, but he quickly schooled his expression. "Sure. Okay if I join you?"

Will turned to cock a brow at him. "Sitting out isn't an option, big guy," he chided, then patted David's thigh. "C'mon. Get that excellent ass up before you fall asleep on me."

"Fine. Are you still hungry?"

"I could eat," Will replied with a smile.

"Good." David sat up and swung his legs off the bed with an answering grin. "Let's get cleaned up and I'll make you dinner before you head out."

Chapter Nine

"Thank you for coming with us, Will." His mother smiled softly at him. His father nodded at him, then looked out of the window of the car. Will glimpsed the gratitude in Bill's eyes and his throat tightened.

"You're welcome," he managed.

With Olivia taking the kids to summer camp in upstate New York, Will had volunteered to travel to Philadelphia with his parents for the meeting with his father's oncologist. The relief on his mother's face in that moment and the surprise on his father's had made Will feel like even more of an asshole.

Since coming back from Manhattan, he'd made a sincere — if awkward — effort to connect with his father. Conversations at the dinner table had shifted from combative to politely stilted. They'd steered clear of politics, which proved harder than Will had anticipated, but the effort had paid off and the tension between them was slowly dissipating.

"Struggling with your book?" his father said a short while later.

Lost in thought, Will looked up from the laptop screen he'd been staring at. The Town Car taking them to Philadelphia was roomy enough for him to work in, but he hadn't counted on not being able to focus.

He raked a hand through his hair. "A bit. My editor isn't happy with the pacing in the middle and I'm not sure how to fix it without losing some parts I feel are pretty crucial. I'm sure I'll figure it out." He paused when a thought occurred to him. "Actually, do you mind taking a look?"

Bill looked at him, surprise clearly written on his face. "I'm no author, Will."

"I know. But you said you've read my books and you're familiar with Bernard Schwartz's life. Maybe you can see what I'm not seeing," he offered. Initially, he'd meant the gesture as a way of making peace with his father rather than a solution to his editing issues, but the more he talked, the more he warmed to the idea. "And you're no slouch in the writing department. I remember that from when I was a kid. Your speeches were always very impressive."

Bill's expression softened slightly. "I always had help with my speeches."

"And I'm asking for your help now," Will said quietly.

Bill nodded. "I'll see what I can do."

Will handed the laptop over to his father. Bill pulled a pair of reading glasses out of his jacket pocket and settled them onto his nose before he focused on the screen.

"Let's change seats," Agnes said, and before Will could argue, she'd gathered her purse and carefully moved to take the seat next to Will. The Town Car was designed with two comfortable leather seats in the middle, facing the back, and two in the rear. Will had been seated across from his parents but now he took the spot his mother had vacated.

"There." She smiled at them both. "You two work while I get back to *my* book."

"Vikings or lords?" Will asked. His mother read widely across fiction and non-fiction. He had — in fact — gotten his love of reading from her. But for as long as he could remember she'd read romance novels for escapism. He felt sure whatever was on her tablet at the moment was something she could get lost in. Goodness knows, she deserved every moment of relief she could get.

"Scotsmen," she said primly and looked down at her screen.

"Why are they never about Irishmen?" his father grumbled. But there was fondness in his gaze as he looked at his wife.

She met his gaze. "They *are*. But Irishmen are always the rogues."

Will chuckled. The Martin surname could be found in Ireland, Scotland and England, but Bill had always focused on their Irish heritage. The family had even taken a trip to Ireland the summer before Olivia went off to college.

Bill's smile deepened before a wistful expression crossed his face. He looked down at Will's laptop and cleared his throat. "Show me the part you're having trouble with."

For once, Will didn't bristle at his demanding tone.

"The top of the chapter here." Will pointed at one of the comments he'd gotten back during edits. "My editor feels like it bogs down here."

"Hmm." Bill stared intently at the screen. "Let me back up a few chapters and I'll read through the whole section before I give you my thoughts."

"Take your time," Will said. He brought out his phone and played with it. He thought of messaging David to let him know how things were going, but David had gone to Manhattan for a meeting and Will was afraid his father might oversee their chat. David's meeting was with a potential donor who held staunch opinions against socialized health care and he and Will had managed to keep discussion about the topic civil instead of arguing, which seemed like progress to Will.

Since he couldn't message David, he brought up a news site. He had read a few articles before his father cleared his throat.

"I've taken the liberty of highlighting a few places you can cut. I think I kept the bulk of it, but it should streamline it some." He handed the laptop to Will, who scanned through the chapters.

His father had suggested cutting some extraneous wording and repetitive passages while retaining the rest. "Thank you," Will said. "I think that may have fixed it."

"You're welcome. It's a solid foundation. Sometimes a fresh pair of eyes are needed to see how to refine it."

"I appreciate it."

"I assume I'll be credited in the acknowledgments?" Bill removed his reading glasses and tucked them in the pocket of his jacket. His tone was stern, but his eyes twinkled. Will's father had always been formidable, but an undercurrent of dry humor snuck into his conversations.

Will chuckled. "That seems fair. I might even sign a copy for you if you play your cards right."

"Duly noted." A shadow crossed Bill's face. No doubt he wondered if he'd live long enough to see that. The book wouldn't be released until November. By then, it could be too late.

* * * *

"Good to see you again, Senator and Mrs. Martin," the handsome, bespectacled doctor said with a kind smile. He held out a hand to Will. "And you must be William Jr."

Either Dr. Milbank had done his research, or Will's parents had mentioned him.

"Will, please." He shook the doctor's hand.

"Right this way." They followed Dr. Milbank through the contemporary, light-filled building and into his personal office.

"Have a seat." Dr. Milbank took a seat behind his desk and the Martin family followed suit in the guest chairs. "Senator, I know you prefer I get right to the point, so I won't delay any longer."

Bill nodded and Agnes took his hand.

"As you know, we weren't able to get all of the cancer during the surgery. After seeing the most recent scans, we know the cancer *has* spread to your lymph nodes. Unfortunately, that diminishes the likelihood of a favorable prognosis. That being said, there are some options. I'd like to begin you on an aggressive adjuvant chemotherapy regimen. It's showed promising results in extending the lifespan of pancreatic cancer patients."

"What does this mean for my work?"

"Senator." Dr. Milbank's voice softened and he folded his hands on the desk and leaned forward. "It is ultimately your decision, of course, but I'd highly suggest this is the time for you to step down. The chemotherapy treatment will be quite grueling. You likely won't have the energy for work. Focus on your family and the time you'll have with them."

Bill pressed his lips together tightly. "What kind of time are we talking?"

Dr. Milbank took a deep breath. "The combination of surgery and the chemotherapy I'm suggesting gives an estimated twenty-nine percent survival rate of five years for the type of pancreatic cancer you have. However, the extent and rate to which your cancer has spread are concerning. Realistically, I think four to six months is most likely."

Agnes made a strangled sound and blood rushed in Will's ears. Olivia, Riley, David...they'd all been right. His father was dying. He might not even make it to the holidays.

Will listened numbly as the doctor outlined a treatment plan at a facility on Long Island and gave them reading material about it. He shook Dr. Milbank's hand and responded to his kind platitudes with a strange, detached feeling.

By the time they left the oncologist's office, Agnes appeared gray and grim. If anything, she looked worse than the patient himself. Bill remained silent as they returned to the car for the nearly four-hour drive home.

They were humming along I-95 North before Agnes spoke.

"I know that wasn't the news you were hoping for." Her voice held a false, cheery note. "But there are always second opinions."

"Dr. Milbank is the leading expert in the Northeast, Agnes." Bill sounded wrung out. "We've done the research. This was always a possibility. Pancreatic cancer has a high mortality rate."

Agnes' face fell. She dug in her handbag and brought out a tissue to dab at the corner of her eyes. "Well, I'm not giving up hope."

Bill took her hand and brought its back to his lips. Will looked away, touched but uncomfortable with the intimacy of the gesture. He remembered a conversation he'd had with Riley when they'd taken a trip to Provincetown to celebrate Gabe and Charles' engagement. Riley had asked if his parents loved each other. Will had maintained their relationship had been politically expedient but that they cared about each other. He saw now how wrong he'd been. Perhaps his parents hadn't been wildly, passionately in love when they'd married, but they'd obviously developed a deep relationship over the years. They cared for and supported each other. If that wasn't love, what was?

The three of them spent the remainder of the ride home in silence. Agnes read, but based on how infrequently she flicked her finger across the screen, Will guessed she wasn't truly seeing the words. Bill stared out of the window in stony silence. Will brought out his laptop and tried to work, but the words swam in front of his eyes.

Throughout the trip, his parents' hands remained connected on the seat between them and a sudden, deep longing for someone to hold his hand as tightly seized Will.

No, not *someone*. David.

* * * *

Back on Long Island, Will helped Agnes settle Bill into his favorite chair. He sat in it with a heavy sigh. The day—or maybe the prognosis—seemed to have drained him.

"Is there anything I can get you?" Agnes asked.

"No. You go on and have a cup of tea. You look like you could use it."

She gave him a fond look and nodded. "Only if you promise you'll rest."

"I wasn't planning on a round of golf."

Agnes cracked a smile and placed a kiss on Bill's cheek before she walked toward the door.

Will followed, and surprised himself by reaching out to pat his father on the shoulder as he passed. Bill didn't hide his shock either, but gripped Will's hand with a quick, hard squeeze.

Will closed the French doors behind him and followed his mother into the kitchen. "Want me to make you the tea?"

"I need to call Olivia first with the news."

"I can do it if it would be easier," Will offered, but Agnes shook her head.

"I told her I'd call, but you're sweet to offer. And you have no idea how much I appreciate you coming today."

Will leaned a hip against the island. "I feel like I should apologize, Mom."

"Whatever for?" Agnes looked perplexed. "You've gone well above what we expected."

"I'm sorry I was so stubborn all those years. I'm starting to see it's not nearly as black and white as I thought."

"You and your father. I know you don't want to hear it, but you're so much alike sometimes."

"I suppose we are," Will admitted. A part of him wondered if perhaps his father's softening had more to do with the painkillers he was taking than true regret about their past relationship. Will wanted to believe it was genuine but it was almost too much to hope for.

"I saw what you did with your book. It meant more to him than you know." She placed a cool hand on his cheek. "You go relax now. I'll call Olivia and fix myself some tea. Greta left food in the refrigerator if you're hungry."

Will glanced at the clock. Nearly eight-thirty p.m. Thursday night traffic had been a nightmare on the way back from Philly. He probably *should* eat, but he couldn't muster up the energy.

"No, I'm not that hungry. Do you want me to heat you up something?"

"I'll have a bite after I call your sister."

"Okay. I think I'll go upstairs and read or work. Night, Mom."

Will collected his laptop bag from the foyer and trudged up the stairs to his room. He fell back on the bed, and sprawled out to stare up at the ceiling. He felt strange, exhausted and restless all at once. Like he needed an outlet for all the feelings inside him. He briefly contemplated using the pool in the backyard — he'd swum almost daily since coming to Long Island — but it was right outside his father's room and Will didn't want to disturb him. He'd been meaning to find a gym or sports complex with a racquetball court, but he wasn't sure he had the energy for it.

He brought out his phone and thumbed through his text messages. His first instinct was to message David, but he wanted his parents to tell David the news before he did. Besides, Will had no idea if David had returned from Manhattan yet.

Will hesitated when he got to Charles Barrett. He hadn't spoken to Charles in a while. Funny, their friendship had petered out ever since his relationship with Riley had ended. Charles hadn't understood why he'd stayed friends with Riley, despite the fact Charles and Will had dated years ago and still remained friends.

Natalie Curtis perhaps—there was no question his friend was always a good listener—but she was out of town with her boyfriend.

Will contemplated calling Riley, but the news of his father's diagnosis seemed too personal to share with his ex.

With a sigh, he turned off the screen and dropped his phone onto his chest. He must have dozed, because at some point his phone buzzed, startling him awake. *David.*

Your mother called me with the news. Are you okay? Call if you want to talk.

The message was simple but Will's relief at the gesture wasn't. He didn't hesitate to call.

"How are you doing?" David's tone sounded warm and concerned.

"I don't know," Will admitted. He hadn't slept long according to the clock on the nightstand, and he'd fallen asleep on his back so his neck ached. He shifted so he was propped against the pillows. "Tired. Restless. Completely mixed up about this shit with my father."

"What can I do to help?"

Unexpected tears gathered behind Will's eyelids. "Are you home?"

"I was pulling into the driveway when your mom called."

Will hesitated. He badly needed David's presence and reassurance, no matter how difficult it was to admit. "I know you just got there, but I...I could use some company right now."

"I'm about to take Mabel for a walk now. Come straight over. I'll leave the door off the deck unlocked, in case you get here before we make it back. I'll make it brief."

"Thank you," Will choked out. He got out of bed, changed his wrinkled shirt for a fresh one and brushed his teeth.

Will met his mother on his way down the stairs. She'd wrapped herself in a thick robe and carried a mug of something—likely chamomile tea. "Are you heading out?" she asked with a puzzled frown.

Will nodded. "I'm meeting a friend. I need to get out for a bit."

She pursed her lips, but merely nodded. "Will you be home tonight? Not that it's any of my business as you're an adult, but I still worry."

"I'll be home," Will promised. "Try to get some sleep, Mom."

"I'll do my best. You be careful."

"I will." He leaned in and kissed her cheek. "Night."

When he reached David's house, Will circled around to the back, unsure if he and Mabel had returned from their walk. The patio door off the kitchen was brightly lit and Will could see David filling Mabel's food dish. He knocked softly and opened the door without waiting for a reply.

"Hey." David's face lit up when they made eye contact, and a fraction of Will's tension eased.

"You made it back, I see," Will managed. He closed the door behind him.

"I did. Mabel's not entirely happy with me for cutting it short, but she'll forgive me." David returned the dog food container to the pantry. "You sounded like you needed me."

"I did—I *do*." Will felt *so* strange. Almost shaky and sick.

David crossed the room to him and Will didn't argue when he wrapped his arms around Will. "Do you want to talk about it?"

He did. Or at least that's why he'd come over. To talk and not be alone, but with David holding him close, that need was quickly replaced by another. He needed the feel of David's firm body against his and the smell of his cologne.

He kissed David, frantic all of a sudden, needing to be closer.

"Easy," David murmured against his mouth, but he kissed Will back and took control. Will gripped the back of his shirt and pulled him closer. David framed Will's face with his large hands, and delved deeper to taste Will's mouth.

Will shuddered and softened against him. David broke the kiss and moved to Will's neck and throat, licking and biting gently.

"Please," Will said with a whimper. "Please."

Please make this easier, he thought. His throat constricted. *Please make it stop hurting.*

It did grow easier as David guided him toward the bedroom and his hands never left Will's body. Will hurt less as David stripped him and pushed him on the bed.

The frantic feeling and the awful ache inside of him eased as David lowered his nude body over Will's. And when he wrapped a hand around Will's aching cock, the turmoil in Will's mind settled to a low, background hum.

Then there was only David and the feel of his mouth on Will's dick, and a slick finger sliding into him.

"Do you want me to fuck you?" David asked a while later, when Will was strung so tightly he thought he'd snap at the smallest provocation.

"Please," Will whispered again, reaching for him.

David rolled on the condom and settled between Will's thighs. The intimacy between them was almost painful as David looked him in the eye and pushed inside, but the burn eased a little more of the ache in Will's chest. He pulled David close and guided him deeper. The pleasure on David's face obliterated everything but the desperate rhythm and sweet slide of David fucking him.

Will cried out when David wrapped a hand around his cock and he came in thick spurts that coated his belly and chest. David followed a few moments later, his grip on Will's hair tight as he shuddered with a hard, gasping cry of Will's name.

David collapsed on him, but when he moved to pull out, Will held him in place. He could feel David's harsh short exhalations against his cheek and the frantic pounding of both their hearts.

He felt wrung out and drained in the best of ways.

David shifted to the side and pulled Will with him, their bodies still intertwined.

"Thank you," Will said quietly.

"You seemed like you needed it." David combed his fingers through Will's hair, which made him smile.

"I did. Honestly, I could get used to this." Will froze and wondered if he'd crossed a line. When he opened his eyes, he caught David staring at him with a soft, unguarded expression.

"Me too." David trailed a hand down Will's back before he dropped a hand to hold the condom and pull out. "You know, I am starting to like this version of you."

Will smiled faintly. David tossed the condom in the trash and reached for the tissues. "The Bruce Banner version is far more agreeable, isn't he?"

"I take it things didn't go well today?" David wiped the bulk of the cum from their bodies. "Your mother didn't go into details, but she said Bill would want to discuss it with me in the next few days."

Will swallowed hard. "It's pretty grim. I'll — I'll let my father tell you the specifics himself but it's only a matter of time."

"I'm sorry, Will," David said softly. He settled back on the bed next to Will and pulled him closer.

Will shifted onto his side so he could wrap himself more fully around David. "It's your loss too. I know you're close to him and…" His throat tightened and for a moment he couldn't speak. He finally managed, "We'll both be losing someone."

"You seem like you're feeling differently about your relationship with him."

"I am. I've been trying since I came back from the city. We had a bit of a breakthrough on the way to Philly, actually."

"Good. I'm glad. Tell me about it."

"I did what you and Riley suggested. I found some common ground with Bill."

"What was it?"

"My books. I'm in the middle of editing one and I asked for his advice."

"Appealing to the man's ego. Nicely done."

Will managed a small smile. "It helped. We spent most of the ride to Philly talking political history and the law while my mother smiled at us and pretended to read."

David hesitated. "I think the estrangement has been hard on her."

"I know it has. If she'd been there when he disowned me she might have felt differently."

"What happened, exactly?"

Will closed his eyes. The day was etched into his memory. "He caught me with my boyfriend."

"What's for dinner?" Toby asked as he hopped onto the bar stool. Toby wore only the towel he'd wrapped around his waist after their post-sex shower and the motion made it fall open.

Will eyed him, then glanced at the clock. Was there time for him to suck Toby off?

"Pizza. It's on its way. I called before I jumped in the shower," Will said.

"Well planned," Toby said with a grin. "How long do we have?"

Will glanced at the clock again. "Not long enough." But he dragged his hands up Toby's bare thighs anyway.

"I'm getting sick of pizza," Toby said and leaned back so his elbows rested on the counter.

"Me too." Will nuzzled Toby's neck. "But neither of us has learned to cook, so..."

"I know." Toby tilted his head to give Will better access. "And you know the rule."

Will straightened. "You'll learn to cook once you move in officially," he said flatly.

Toby shrugged. "Seems fair."

It was fair. That was the worst part. For all intents and purposes, Will and Toby did live together. They slept in the same bed nearly every night—usually here at Will's apartment—but he wasn't quite ready to put Toby's name on the lease. Not on a one-bedroom apartment. There was too much of a risk of someone discovering it and surprising his father with the news at a press conference.

"*I know.*"

Toby's expression turned sad. "*You know I love you and I'm trying to be patient, but I don't want to be your secret forever, Will.*"

"*I know. I don't want you to be either, but my family…*"

"*Senator Fucking Martin and his perfect family,*" *Toby snarled.* "*What did you say? Appearances above all else?*"

Will nodded. "*I'm sorry,*" *he offered lamely, already worn down by an argument that hadn't even started. Or maybe the problem was it never ended. They went around and around in circles and every time, Toby pulled away a little further.*

And who could blame him? Will kept stuffing their relationship deeper and deeper into the closet. He didn't want to, but he couldn't think of a single good way out.

"*It's not a great time, Toby,*" *he said.* "*I had that fight with my dad a couple of weeks ago. He blew up at me about me taking the NYU position. He's livid I'm teaching instead of practicing law. And pissed I wasn't following in his footsteps with a political career. I can't hit him with this at the same time.*"

"*You can do whatever you want,*" *Toby retorted.* "*Only you* won't. *Because you're as bad as they are. You're hung up on what people think and how they'll treat you if you come out.*"

"*It's not my fucking fault my father's a New York State senator! You think I want this? That I like hiding my relationship with my boyfriend and weighing every move*

based on what my father's going to say? I'm trying, Toby,
but cut me some slack. I'm under a lot of fucking pressure."

"Sometimes I think you do like it. I think you like the fact
you don't have to be out except for in our little corner of the
world here at NYU. I think you like — " The ding of the
doorbell interrupted his fury. "Fuck. We'll finish this later,"
Toby muttered.

"Damn it, I'll get the door." Will dragged jeans on over his
briefs and walked toward the door. He patted his pocket and
pulled open the door. "Would you grab my wallet, babe? I
think I left it on the dresser or the nightstand before we got
in bed..."

He looked up at the person on the other side of the door. The
blood drained from his face as he saw the man he'd grown up
with. The man staring at him with a disapproving frown.
"Dad?" he said faintly.

Will froze, unable to stop the train he could see bearing
down on him and Toby. He couldn't even warn Toby of what
was coming or soften the blow in any way.

William Martin Sr.'s gaze flicked between him and some
point behind him, no doubt the half-naked Toby.

"What are you doing just standing there, Will?" Toby
asked with a laugh. "Give me the damn pizza and pay the
man. I hope you ordered extra breadsticks. I don't know about
you, but I'm going to smoke tonight. I don't have to be at
work until late tomorrow. Forget the fight we had about your
asshole father. I vote we go back to bed and eat."

Gay sex, recreational drug use, and insulting my
father, *Will thought wildly.* Of course, this is how it will
all go down.

"I'd like an explanation for this, son." Ice hardened his
father's tone.

Numb, Will swung the door open. "Toby, I'd like you to
meet my father, Senator William Martin. Some people call

him Bill, but I'd suggest you don't. Dad, this is my boyfriend, Toby."

His father's wintry expression matched his voice. "I'm afraid I can't say it's nice to meet you, young man. I neither knew you existed, nor can I say I condone any of this."

Will sighed and stepped back. "Toby, why don't you get dressed and go home? I'll deal with my father."

Toby looked between Will and his father, and apparently whatever he saw convinced him to flee. He disappeared into the bedroom and returned a few moments later, fully dressed. He hesitated, then kissed Will on the cheek and left without a word.

Once they were alone, Will turned to his father. "Well, now you know."

"Know what?" he said coldly. "Know that you flout every single value you your mother and I have tried to instill in you? First the teaching job and NYU and now this? She would be heartbroken to find out you've been lying to us."

Will laughed hollowly. "In some families being a college professor and in a loving relationship would be a good thing. Not something to be ashamed of."

"You are the one who kept your life a secret, Will. And may I remind you we are not any family. We have expectations for you and a life of secrecy and deceit is not one of them, not to mention the drug use."

"You drove me to this," Will shot back, his voice suddenly loud. "You're the reason I couldn't be truthful about my relationship with Toby or my career. God, the pressure you put on me is —"

"We raised you to handle pressure better than this," Bill snapped. "This discussion is over. You will end this relationship, come home to Long Island and get your life in order."

Will crossed his arms. "And if I don't?"

"If you don't, don't bother coming home at all. I will not condone this lifestyle. It's your family or this...Toby person."

"Toby it is then," Will said thickly.

"Then I will no longer acknowledge you as my son. Don't come home begging for money or anything else if you screw your life up even further. You're on your own."

Will couldn't manage a single response and Bill walked to the door without another word. He opened it, and looked back at Will. The set of his face was hard, flinty, and he'd never looked more like a senator and less like Will's father.

The door shut behind him, leaving Will alone in the apartment.

"Oh, Will." David's voice was filled with compassion. Will blinked and looked at the man beside him. The man he'd spilled his heart out to. He'd never told anyone the complete story, not even Riley. "I see why you two didn't speak for years."

Will rubbed his forehead. "I should have bent some and gone to talk to him. He should have contacted me again. We were both stubborn."

"You're making up for lost time now." David cupped Will's cheek in his hand and looked him in the eye.

"But there's so little time left," Will said sadly.

"I know."

David gathered him close and with a shuddering sigh, Will sank into the embrace. He'd get up in a while and go home, but for now, the arms around him were the only things keeping him together.

Chapter Ten

"Have you heard anything yet from the photographers we contacted?" David glanced up as his campaign manager sat down in one of his visitor chairs. "I loathe the idea of posing for photos again, but we should get them shot before the end of the month."

Jerry Andov cocked his head. "August begins a week from today, David — what's the rush?"

"Well, for one, I'd like to have them taken before we're crushed by the heat."

"You mean before you get too tan." Jerry's lips twitched into a small smile. "Don't deny it."

David shrugged. "I'm not. We both know it's better for me to be paler in campaign photos — let's keep the number of voters I alienate with my Asian-ness to a minimum."

"You could hide inside for the month."

"No thanks. Also, you've clearly never owned a dog."

"I'm more of a cat person," Jerry said, "but I'm too busy to own any kind of pet."

David smiled. "I think there's a crass joke about hot babes in lingerie there, but Kerri is just outside the door, so I'll leave it alone."

"You're smarter than your pretty face would lead one to expect," Jerry replied, "which brings me to my next point. No one's going to care how ethnic you look in the campaign literature because they'll be too busy staring at that dreamy mug of yours to notice. Besides, you're running unopposed for your own seat."

"No one in the major parties is running against me, but the deadline for independent nominations isn't until mid-August." David cocked a brow. "I may end up running against someone who thinks it's a good idea to remind voters Mori is a Japanese surname and not Italian."

"Mori *is* an Italian surname and you know it." Jerry grinned at David's laugh. "In answer to your original question, we've got quotes from three photographers — all we need to do is choose one, hire some extras to pose with you and let the magic happen. I'm not saying we'll be done by next Friday, but I think the second or third week of August is feasible. Where do you want to shoot these photos?"

"Around town." David ran his fingers over his mouth while Jerry took notes on his tablet. "We need a few in a work setting — say here in the office — and some with the constituents, obviously."

"Plus, casual shots of you being, you know, a regular human."

"Nothing stuffy or fake."

"What, so nothing in a swimsuit?"

David grimaced. "Please, shut up."

"Okay, fine. We definitely need some of you in a suit and tie." Jerry grinned. "What about some dramatic shots of you in chambers in Albany?"

"Oh, God, no."

Jerry held out his arms to frame David's face in the air with his hands. "Come on, people eat that kind of stuff up—everybody loves a well-dressed man! Plus, serious shots reassure the retirees that whippersnappers like you can do the job."

"Dude, I'm thirty-four years old. I'm pretty sure that makes me too old to be a whippersnapper in anyone's eyes."

"You called me 'dude', so don't count on it. Regardless, we also need shots to show your personal side." Jerry's expression turned apologetic. "Don't take this the wrong way, but it's moments like these where I wish you were more of a traditional candidate. Or at least one with a husband and some cute surrogate kids. You don't have any stashed away, do you?"

David's eyes went wide and he barked out a laugh. "Sorry, no."

"Damn." Jerry pursed his lips. "How can you still be single? Is there a dearth of single gay men out here?"

"Oh, there are definitely available men—Kerri and some of the other staff are always scheming to set me up with some likely candidates."

"So, what's the problem?"

"What makes you say there is one?"

"Your continued lack of a relationship status."

David shrugged and propped his elbows on his desk. "I don't have a lot of time to devote to building a relationship right now. I travel at weird times of the year and don't keep a traditional schedule, and it can be hard to socialize outside of work."

Jerry's gaze turned appraising. "I don't buy it. You've got friends in town, and not everyone has coupled up."

"Gay men are capable of sustaining platonic friendships, Jerry."

"Duh, I know that. So, if the problem isn't meeting single men, I must conclude you simply haven't found the *right* man."

"I suppose that's true." David smiled, but his thoughts immediately turned to Will.

The Martin family's workings had been profoundly changed by Bill's second diagnosis. David noticed it most in Will's behavior around his family. The angry, resentful person David had first met had been replaced by Will's 'Bruce Banner persona', who was measured and even stoic.

Will's sister, Olivia, often turned to him for emotional support, but Agnes relied on him too, and Will ensured both women took care of themselves. His efforts to reconnect with Bill had been paying off, and the awkwardness between the two men lessened each day. Will would never forget his father's initial rejection of his sexuality, but he'd finally moved on, drawing strength from the experience rather than letting it hobble him.

Will had sought out David's company regularly over the passing weeks. Their times together were low-key, usually spent walking Mabel in the dog-parks and spending time in David's house on 4th Street. They cooked meals and watched movies, and even explored David's comic book collection, which had fascinated Will beyond David's expectations. They started many evenings chilling out on the sun deck, and always ended in David's bed, where they sought the easy pleasure of touch.

David had no illusions about what drew Will to him. Their encounters supplied Will with creature comforts and sorely needed emotional and sexual outlets. For all his reserve around his family, Will was tactile and open when in the Freeport house, as if simply being under its roof gave him permission to put aside his stoic front.

Looking objectively at the time they spent together, they were friends with benefits. Will had never stayed the night in David's bed. They spent limited time together away from David's home and neither of them put a name to their unusual friendship. No one knew David and Will were acquainted beyond their individual relationships with Senator William Martin.

So why did claiming he couldn't find the right man feel like a lie in David's head and heart?

Shaking off the errant thoughts, he pushed back his office chair and stood. "Sorry, I can't magic up a perfect man. However, I do have a spectacularly charming dog and she will pose for any photo in exchange for dog treats."

Jerry rubbed his hands together before getting to his feet. "Now you're talking. Hell, more people prefer dogs over children anyway, so that's perfect."

* * * *

David spent the next day doing chores and errands. While he paid a housekeeper to come in weekly to keep his home tolerably neat, he preferred to wash his own laundry and worked through three loads while organizing his bills and mail.

With the last load folded and put away, he went to the grocery store to replenish his refrigerator and pantry, which had grown bare now that he cooked for two so often. He caught himself planning dishes for Will and rolled his eyes at the heat that crept up under the neck of his gray T-shirt. He nearly laughed when his phone chimed with a call from Will.

David placed a bag of avocados into his cart and accepted the call. "Hello, Professor. I was just thinking about you."

"Hello yourself." Will sounded friendly, but that he'd skipped over David's name meant other people were within earshot. "Did I catch you at a bad time?"

"Not at all. I'm actually at the supermarket and Earth, Wind and Fire is playing over the PA system, which is pretty excellent."

Will chuckled. "I see. What've you been up to the last few days? My parents are inviting friends round and it's like old home week here."

"I caught up with friends, too." David moved on to a display of summer berries. "I had dinner at Dario's with my campaign manager last night — the gnocchi were so good I nearly cried."

"I think I've been there, though not for years!"

"You should take your parents." David smiled to himself. "I'm sure they could do something for Bill if you called ahead. Oh, and I'm pretty sure I went to that crab shack of yours on Tuesday night."

"Woodcleft Crab Shack?"

"That's the one. Between trips upstate and hanging out with you, I went MIA too long and some of my buddies got worried. They staged an intervention and showed up to my office insisting we go out. So, we gorged on seafood and made plans to meet up again next weekend."

David considered extending the invitation to Will to join them, but pressed his lips together. He wanted to see Will's face when he jumped the script they'd followed for the last month and a half.

"What about you?" he asked instead, leaning to examine heads of Boston lettuce. "What's going on with Will?"

"In between writing and helping out here, I went into the city on Wednesday for dinner with my friend Gabe and some other guys. Then I had drinks at Under on Thursday night with Riley and his stupidly hot friends."

David heard the smile in Will's voice and grinned. The noises on Will's end suggested he'd moved, presumably to get some privacy. "How are they?"

"A little crazy and a lot hilarious, as usual. They're a lot of fun, actually, and I enjoy hanging out with them."

"You sound surprised."

"I am, a bit! I never dreamed I'd get friendly with Riley's boyfriend, Carter, never mind Carter's buddies, but they make it easy. Kyle mixed up a drink called a Kentucky Buck which involves bourbon, ginger beer, lemon juice and strawberries — they were unbelievably delicious. Jesse actually said 'fuck a duck' on two occasions. He also had a girl with him who tried to talk Carter into dyeing his hair blue and I thought Riley might sprain something laughing."

"Isn't Carter a corporate guy?" David asked, mystified by Will's story but pleased to hear his obvious amusement.

"He was before he quit his job," Will replied. "They're all corporate guys, except for Kyle. But even if Carter never works again, he doesn't seem the type to wear technicolor hair. I'm sure his kids would like it." Will hummed. "Riley said he's spending some quality time with Carter's kids. Sounds like he's enjoying being domesticated again."

David licked his lips, his skin prickling at an off tone he heard in Will's voice. "How do you feel about that?"

"I'm not sure, really," Will said. "Riley's not the first of my friends to settle down in the last few years — far from it. He's the first man *I* thought about in that regard, meaning going long-term.

"I'm sure it's because my own situation is so unsettled this summer, but it's weird to see Riley already so immersed in a new life. We only split up in December and he talks about Sadie and Dylan like he's their dad, too." He huffed out a tight little laugh. "You know, last year at this time Riley and I were watching my friends, Gabe and Charles, get married. We got into a nasty fight about Carter that night, and I actually considered ending things. I should have known it was never going to work out."

"I'm sorry, Will." David frowned. He'd assumed Will was at peace with the way things had ended with Riley, but now he wasn't so sure. And that didn't sit well with David at all. "That sounds all kinds of shitty."

"Meh. I'm whining," Will replied, obviously trying to shake off his mood. "Anyway, it was great to see them, and Gabe too. I needed a change of scene, you know? If it weren't for you and those get-togethers at Under, I'd have lost my shit weeks ago."

David glanced around to make sure no one stood nearby. "Well…if that's your way of asking to come over tonight so I can feed you then fuck you into the mattress, you should know I'm totally on board with that."

Will let out a low groan. "Jesus. I'll be here till at least six reviewing some legal docs with my parents—see you after that?"

"Sounds good," David said easily. He saw a neighbor walking toward him then and smiled. "I'll see you later tonight."

An hour later, David had nearly finished putting away groceries when he heard his front door open and Isabel call his name.

"In the kitchen," David shouted over the noise of Mabel scrambling to her feet. "I'll be right out!"

"No rush, dude," Isabel replied.

He grinned. He hadn't expected to see his sister, but it wasn't unusual for her to turn up without calling first. He carried boxes of grains and pasta into the pantry to put away while Isabel and Mabel fawned over each other.

"I swear that dog of yours gets sweeter every time I see her," Isabel announced after finally walking into the kitchen. "I wish I'd listened to you and adopted one of her littermates."

"That's what's you get for listening to Allen over me," David said. "But he's your husband, so I suppose that's understandable. You could always go back to the guy I bought Mabel from, you know—I probably still have his number," he added and stepped out of the pantry, but his words trailed off as he laid eyes on his sister.

Isabel stood at the kitchen island in a peasant blouse and denim shorts, her head bowed and hands on the counter, arms braced as though she were holding herself up.

David went to her side at once, hesitating at the last moment to touch her. Isabel hadn't been able to meet for dinner since their birthday, but they'd spoken on the phone at least twice a week without fail—what the hell had gone on in the past six weeks to make her appear like the weight of the world rested on her shoulders?

"Is? Are you okay?"

Isabel said nothing for a moment, though a muscle in her jaw tightened. When she raised her eyes, they were red-rimmed but dry, and David held his breath at the emotion he saw in them.

"Can I stay here tonight, Davey? I don't want to go home and I…I need you." She furrowed her brow when David laid a hand over one of hers. "I should have called first, but—"

David shook his head. "Hey," he murmured, and carefully peeled Isabel's hand up from where it gripped the counter. He pulled her into a hug, and his throat tightened at the tension in her body. "Of course you can stay and you don't need to ask. I'm here for you no matter what, okay?"

Isabel went pliant in David's embrace, as though a string had been cut. She brought her arms up to wrap around his shoulders. "Thanks," she whispered.

He rubbed circles between her shoulder blades with one hand. "What can I do?"

"You're doing it," Isabel replied, and when she held on tight, David squeezed her back just as hard.

They stood silent for a long time in the kitchen, in front of the groceries still waiting to be put away. When Isabel finally loosened her grip and pulled back, she gave David a small smile that didn't reach her eyes.

"I'll, ah, go grab my overnight bag from the car."

David cocked his head at her. "Need any help?"

"I'm good." She waved at the groceries on the counter. "Finish putting your stuff away and pretend I'm not here."

"Uh-uh." He brought his hands to rest on her shoulders. "Get settled so we can talk. You can tell me as much or as little as you need to, but I need to know if you're okay."

Isabel exhaled through her nose. "All right."

"Do you want a glass of wine? I made sangria this morning before I went out."

"God, yes. I promise you can have some too," Isabel joked, and the warmth in her grin lessened the chill in David's stomach.

He turned back to the task of putting things away after she'd walked out, Mabel at her heels. He took the pitcher of punch from the refrigerator and washed some berries he'd bought, and had gotten two glasses out of the cabinet when he noticed it was already four p.m. David remembered he'd made plans with Will and his stomach fell.

"Shit." He set the glasses on the counter and pulled his phone from his pocket. He brought Will's number up to call, but stopped himself. Though he badly wanted to hear Will's voice, he counted backward from five and sent a message instead.

Change of plans. Isabel's here.

Will replied as David was pouring the drinks. *Everything okay?*

I'm not sure. She's upstairs, but we'll be talking soon.

Can I do anything?

David hadn't yet figured out how to reply when Isabel walked back into the kitchen.

"What's with the face?"

"Um. Well, I invited a friend over for dinner tonight and I'm trying to figure out when to reschedule."

"Don't." Isabel shook her head. "I'll help you cook and head out while you and your friend have dinner."

"Absolutely not." David leveled a glare at Isabel when she lifted a brow in challenge. "You show up here out of the blue, ask to spend the night and now you're offering to fuck off for a few hours so I can have dinner with a guy?"

Isabel grinned. "What guy? Is he hot?"

"A guy named Will. And don't get any ideas — we're only friends." David cursed inwardly as heat splashed across his cheeks.

Isabel made an 'ooh' kind of noise. "Where did you meet him?"

"He's Senator Martin's son. We've gotten to know each other through his family. Stop changing the subject!"

"Oh, stop with the melodrama." Isabel flapped a hand at him. "If it makes you feel better, I'll stay and have dinner with you both. *Then* I'll take Mabel for a long walk. I see your pink cheeks, Davey — you'll want me gone for a bit so you can spend time with your mentor's son while no one is watching."

David stared at his sister for a moment before he laughed. "You know what? Fine, I'll introduce you. But only if you tell me what the fuck is going on with you first."

"Of course I'm going to tell you," she retorted. "I drove out here to see you, didn't I? Now call your friend and invite him over so I can finish garnishing those drinks before all the fucking ice melts."

David snorted, but his sister's bitching reassured him immensely. He stepped away from the counter and checked his phone, which showed another message from Will.

You still there? Call me back when you can.

Though tempted to make that call, David decided against it. Introducing Will to Isabel definitely jumped their script, and David wanted to give him the chance to decline without feeling pressured.

Sorry — negotiating some things with Isabel. She wants to meet you, if you're okay with that.

David glanced up when Isabel nudged him and accepted a glass of punch. Will replied a moment later.

You told Isabel about me?

David worried his bottom lip with his teeth. *Nothing specific. That you're a friend and invited to dinner. And your general identity.* He winced and kept tapping. *It's okay if you'd rather pass.*

No, no — I'd like to meet her. Just realized you know almost my whole family, and I haven't met anyone in yours except Mabel.

David hated himself a little for feeling way too pleased by the idea of Will and Isabel at his table. *So come for dinner and meet my sister.*

I'll be there around 6:30, Will replied, capping off his message with a thumbs-up emoji that made David chuckle.

"All set?"

He glanced up to find Isabel watching him with a smirk and made a face at her. "Yeah. He'll be here after six. I'm making Cobb salad with shrimp, by the way."

"Yummy." Isabel's expression sobered and she held out a hand to David, which he immediately took in his own. "Come outside with me and we'll talk."

True to his word, Will arrived at the house shortly after six-thirty p.m. David and Isabel had finishing prepping, so David poured Will a glass of sangria then put him to work making a fresh batch. Isabel and Will got on immediately, and David laughed when Will made a point of announcing he was a registered Democrat. They chatted while David brought dishes and flatware out onto the deck, and had fallen into a conversation about NYU by the time the meal was ready.

David listened more than he spoke, more because he was still digesting the conversation he'd had with his sister than anything else. He was also unsure how or even if he could talk about it with Will. They were both accustomed to talking about Will's family dramas — they'd met through the aftermath of Bill's cancer, after all. David wasn't sure if Will wanted to know more about his own family, other than the few specifics David had shared with him as they'd gotten to know each other.

David needed to talk about Isabel tonight, though. And, if he were honest, he liked watching her with Will. Isabel spoke about her work and lit up with enthusiasm at Will's interest, despite his claims not to understand most of what she said. Talk turned to Will's book and Bernard Schwartz, which neatly dovetailed into politics and David's re-election campaign, until David almost begged them to lay off the anti-GOP ranting for the night. All three of them steadfastly ignored the two very large elephants in the room—William Martin Sr. and Isabel's unexpected appearance.

Warmth filled David at the knowledge Isabel liked Will, even if it didn't matter in the long run—he had no idea how long this thing between him and Will was meant to last.

After Isabel excused herself for the evening, David and Will took Mabel for a walk. They were picking their way along Main Street when Will finally broached the subject of David's sister's appearance.

"I understand if you can't tell me what brought Isabel here, but you don't seem yourself tonight." Will's tone and expression were uncharacteristically tentative when David met his gaze. "Are you okay?"

"Not really," David admitted. He guided Mabel and Will left toward the entrance to Cow Meadow Park. "Isabel and her husband, Allen, are trying to have a baby. I know that's not exactly earth-shattering news, but Isabel's never been interested in having children until recently." Even in the lower light of the streetlights, he saw Will furrow his brow.

"Not at all?"

"No. She likes kids fine, but having a baby isn't something she ever wanted to do. She's always leaned more toward adopting children than bearing them.

"When she and Allen started getting serious, they talked a lot about having kids, because Allen *does* want them. Isabel weighed the options she had available to her, because she wanted to make sure they could make it work, given their different philosophies."

"I get it—that's a major decision for lots of couples," Will replied. "You don't exactly have a lot of control over what happens after you get started, either."

David's heart squeezed in his chest, but he forced a smile. "You're exactly right. Isabel decided she was okay with the idea. She did things you're supposed to do, like eat well and get fit. She's a scientist, so she read everything she could lay her hands on about pregnancy and childbearing. They didn't get pregnant right away, or after three months, then six months, then a year. It didn't happen."

"That must be hard for them, and you too," Will said.

"I had a hard time watching their disappointment," David agreed. "Knowing what they wanted and being unable to help."

He paused by a streetlight so Mabel could do her business on a stretch of grass. "They tried for a year and half before Isabel's OB prescribed an estrogen modulator called Clomid. They hoped the meds would stimulate Isabel's ovulation so she and Allen would have better luck."

"I don't know anything about Clomid," Will confessed. He looked amused when David snorted out a hard laugh.

"I didn't either, until today when Isabel sat me down and told me she'd been taking it."

Will raised both brows and let out a low whistle. "Shit. Were you pissed off?"

"I don't know how to answer that." David heard the hurt so clearly in his own voice. "I hate that they kept it from me, but I understand why. My sister is an adult and entitled to her privacy. How can I give her a hard time about this?"

He glanced down as Mabel bumped against his knee, clearly sensing his distress, and he ran a hand over her head. "It's okay, girl." He waited until Mabel moved to nose against his palm before he squatted down to clean up after her.

"We should get back," he said after he'd straightened. Now that he'd started to process his feelings, David didn't want to lose his shit on the street.

A thoughtful expression crossed Will's face as they turned around. He stayed quiet until after David disposed of the bag in a waste bin on the other side of Main Street.

"Is this thing with the Clomid the reason you're so quiet tonight?"

"Yes and no. My problem isn't so much with the Clomid as with what it's doing to Isabel. She experienced some of the rarer side effects, specifically visual disturbances, like flashes of light and dragging motions."

They turned onto 4th Street and David swallowed down a wave of nausea. "Those types of vision issues can lead to seizure in some people and...well, Isabel had a tonic-clonic seizure two weeks ago." He stared at the ground, conscious of Will's sharp intake of breath, and tried to hide his fear. He could still hear the strain in his sister's voice as she'd described falling into a black hole she feared would eat her alive.

"Oh, my God."

"Luckily, she was at home with Allen and not, you know, out on the street," David pressed on. "They went to the emergency room so she could get checked out and she seized again while they were there." He shook his head, still dumbfounded, and stopped walking when Will grasped his arm.

"Let's go inside."

The concern in Will's low voice curled around David like an embrace and his breath caught in his throat. God, he *was* going to lose it here on the street. He nodded and allowed Will to steer him along the sidewalk, then over the flagstones to the house, his touch featherlight at David's elbow. Once inside, David let Mabel off her leash and Will immediately crowded him up against the front door and wrapped him in a tight hug.

"I'm sorry," Will murmured. "You must be terrified."

Looping his arms around Will's waist, David closed his eyes. He buried his face in the join between Will's neck and shoulder. A tremor shook his whole body. "I am. Isabel and Allen are the only family I have, Will. I haven't been afraid like this since my parents died."

Will made a soft noise of sympathy. "Is she okay?"

"Physically, she should be. She stopped taking the Clomid and hasn't experienced any more symptoms — that's the only reason she's been cleared to drive again. The problem now is Allen."

David fisted Will's shirt in his hands. A wave of grief and anger swept over him, making his voice tight. "He thinks Isabel should take anti-seizure medication so they can try the Clomid for another cycle. Isabel refused. She doesn't want to fuck around with her brain chemistry and I don't blame her. Allen isn't listening."

"Is that why she's here?"

"Yeah. They've been fighting for over a week. She wants a break from it so she can get her head on straight and decide what she wants to do next. I said she can stay as long as she needs."

"What about Allen?"

David blew a noisy breath out through his nose. "I promised I'd stay out of it for now. But Jesus, I want to kick his ass so hard. Isabel's freaked out enough by what's happened. The last thing she needs is Allen guilting her into something she's afraid to do."

A lump rose in his throat when Will pressed a kiss to his cheek. God damn, David wanted some TLC tonight. Not so much sex as gentle touches and affection.

"I don't blame you for being angry," Will said. "But you're doing the right thing by staying out of it. Isabel will tell you if she needs you to do more."

"I hope so."

"She did today, right? She knows you're there for her." Will kissed him again. "C'mon, I'm taking you upstairs."

Will kept a steady arm around his shoulders as they headed for David's bedroom. Once inside, Will urged him to wash up while he turned down the bed. When David emerged, Will approached him, his touch wonderfully warm as he laid his hands on either side of David's neck. For the first time in hours, the knot of tension in David's chest loosened a bit.

"What are you up to?" he asked as Will tugged at the collar of his shirt. David raised his arms, and heat pulsed deep in his groin as the shirt slid over his head.

"I'm putting a sleepy little senator to bed," Will replied, and they shared a smile.

"Don't be weird," David chided.

"And you hush. I know we're not alone in the house tonight, so I'll promise to be quiet if you do."

Will stripped David down to his boxers, then skimmed a hand over his belly. David closed his eyes.

Will pressed against him, his breath warm against David's lips when he spoke again.

"Is this okay?"

"Feels good." David brought his hands to Will's waist. He kept his eyes closed and Will guided him back a few steps until the backs of David's knees met the bed.

Will laid him down. David peeled his eyes open to watch him undress, and was vaguely relieved when Will kept his boxers on. The afternoon's intense emotions had left him drained, and he wasn't sure he had the energy for sex. However, his desire to touch Will was intense, almost overwhelming. He reached for Will as soon as he drew near.

I need this, he realized. *I need it with Will.*

They exchanged few words as they kissed and touched. Will ran his hands over David's body for a long time, almost petting him, while David simply held on, his body responding through his fatigue. He bit his lip when Will finally leaned back. David hadn't made out with someone like this in years, with no real end goal but to feel and give pleasure.

Will leaned in for another sweet kiss, and slid his fingers under the waistband of David's boxers. "I want to make you feel good," he whispered, echoing David's own words from the first time they'd come together in this bed.

Will slid David's boxers down his thighs, and David shifted his weight so Will could pull them off. Heat built in David's gut as Will kissed along his belly and pelvis, but he stopped Will before he could take David in his mouth. He tugged Will back up the bed, needing him closer, needing to feel and hear his breath.

Will smiled and changed his position, then leaned toward the nightstand. The sound of the drawer scraping open sent a frisson of anticipation through David. He folded one arm behind his head and grasped Will's waist with the other hand. He hummed low in his chest at the sight of Will slicking his fingers. Will's eyes shone when he finally reached for David again.

David sucked in a breath as Will wrapped a warm, wet hand around him.

Will slid his free arm under David and drew him close. He pumped David's cock, his touch tender-rough and perfect, and David closed his eyes again.

"I wish you could see yourself," Will said, his voice hoarse. "So warm and relaxed under my hands."

David made a hungry noise that Will covered with a kiss, and pressed David into the bed with the weight of his body. David was floating on a haze of desire and need, and he used both hands to draw Will closer. Will's cock was hot and hard against his thigh.

When Will broke away again, David gasped. Sweat dampened his skin and a familiar, sweet ache pooled low in his groin.

"Will," he rasped. David pressed his head back into the pillow, his gaze locked with Will's. Will tightened his grip and pumped David with long strokes that made him fist the sheets. David tried to speak again but couldn't form the words.

"Gorgeous," Will murmured, his expression rapt.

David managed a soft grunt before Will leaned in to lick David's lips with the tip of his tongue, and the simple action broke David apart. The orgasm barreled through him, drawing every part of him almost painfully taut before leaving him limp and panting under the waves of bliss. He glimpsed triumph in

Will's face before he had to close his eyes, his breaths loud in his own ears and his limbs heavy as Will stroked him through the aftershocks. David peeled his eyes open, but Will shook his head at David's clumsy move to touch him.

"I, uh, sort of took care of that myself." Will grinned, and only then did David notice Will's boxers were wet where they pressed against his thigh. Will laughed at his arched brow and pulled back, extricating himself enough to remove them.

"It's been a long time since I came in my pants," he said, and used the boxers to clean them both up. "Watching you come, though...god damn. So hot. I suppose I should be used to the unexpected when it comes to you by now, so don't let it go to your head," he added with a mock glare.

Too late. David cleared his throat and closed his eyes again. "I'll try. No promises."

Once they were clean, Will stretched out beside David and they lay quietly for a time. David drifted, almost dozing off until Will shifted against him. David drew in a long breath. Watching Will leave got harder every time, and tonight the idea made him ache.

"There's a package of boxer briefs in the top drawer of the bureau in the closet," he murmured, "unless you want to walk around commando."

Will smiled against David's temple. "Thanks—I appreciate that."

"If I fall asleep, wake me up before you go." David turned onto his side and hummed against Will's collarbone when Will dragged him in closer.

"Don't be silly." Will ran a hand over David's hair. "Get some sleep, David. I'll lock up when I head out."

For a moment, David wanted to argue, but he was so comfortable and enjoyed the feeling of Will holding him far too much to spoil the moment with bickering. So instead he gave in and drifted off in Will's arms.

Chapter Eleven

"I'm slightly perplexed by the housewarming happening *before* you move in," Will said as Riley finished the tour of the townhouse he and Carter would be moving into in a few weeks.

"Well, Carter and I never have done anything in the proper order." Riley chuckled. "In this case, it mostly has to do with the kids' schedules. They're starting school in a few weeks—right after Labor Day—and we'll be moving in sometime around mid-September. We figured by the time we got the kids settled and the house ready, it would be late fall and things would start getting crazy with the holidays."

"That makes sense." Will smiled and changed the subject. "It seems like you're settling into the parental role well."

Riley shrugged and leaned a hip against the kitchen counter. "I'm *trying*. Sadie and Dylan seem pretty comfortable with me and they're excited about the move. They've always liked Audrey and Max's place, it's closer to their school, and—best of all—they get their own bedrooms now."

"Yeah, it's a great place." Will looked out of the wall of windows in the kitchen at the back of the house. It overlooked a private garden—a rare thing in Manhattan. "Four bedrooms, plus the top floor you could finish if you want—thinking about more kids?"

"No. I don't think so. Carter and I are pretty content with where we are. I think Sadie and Dylan will keep us plenty busy." Riley's face softened every time he mentioned the kids. His happiness was palpable.

"Where are they tonight? Is Carter's ex bringing them by?"

"No, Kate and Robert took them on vacation. We have them Labor Day weekend and we'll be making a trip to the beach house."

"That'll be fun. You guys are welcome to stop by Garden City on the way to or from there. It's on the way from Manhattan."

Riley raised an eyebrow. "You sure you want to subject yourself to that?"

"Well, I wasn't suggesting you all move in or anything. Just stop and grab an ice-cream cone." Will chuckled. "And I do like kids, you know. In fact, now that they're back from summer camp, I'm getting to know Adam and Jocelyn, my sister's kids. They're weirded out by having an uncle they'd never met before, but they're starting to get used to the idea. Buying presents in apology hasn't hurt, either. Olivia had to gently remind me I don't need to buy their love."

"I'm glad to hear things are improving with your family. How's your dad doing?"

"Not well. I went with him to his appointment with the oncologist in Philly and the prognosis is pretty grim."

"I'm sorry." Riley covered Will's hand with his own.

Will smiled thinly. "Thank you. I think my mom is still somewhat in denial."

"I take it things are going better with you and your father?"

"They are. I took the suggestions you and David gave me and found some common ground. I wouldn't say it's undone all the issues we have, but we're making progress."

"I'm glad to hear that." Riley smiled. "Speaking of the hot senator...how is that going?"

Will chuckled. "I'll have to tell him you called him that. He'll be amused. And to answer your question, it's going well. We're...well, to be honest, I don't know *what* we're doing. But we definitely have stopped deliberately antagonizing each other."

Riley grinned. "From that smile on your face, I'd say it's more than that."

Will cleared his throat. "Let's say I discovered how good Senator Mori looks with his suit *off*. And his way with words is not reserved for the Senate floor."

"Well done, Will," Riley murmured, his blue eyes twinkling with amusement. He sobered quickly. "Is this casual or is it leading to something else?"

"We haven't discussed it, to be honest. I-I don't know. Hell. I'm not sure what I want." Will raked a hand through his hair. "I enjoy the time we spend together — in *and* out of the bedroom. But there's the vastly differing political opinions and situation with my father..."

"What do you mean? The fact that David and your father work together?"

"That's part of it, yeah." Will licked his lips. "David and I are keeping it all a secret. Well, from my family, anyway. My relationship with my father is so tentative right now and I have no idea how he'd feel about my involvement with David. There's so much to lose, you know? It could derail all the progress we've made, strain his relationship with David, and to do all that while he's so ill? I can't bring myself to do it."

Riley nodded. "That makes sense."

"So, I don't know where things with David can realistically go. Or if it *should* go anywhere."

"Fair enough." Riley hummed thoughtfully. "I assume it's more than 'wham, bam, thank you, Senator', right?"

Will laughed. "It is. We go out to dinner occasionally and take his dog for walks and stuff like that. Friends with benefits, I guess."

Riley frowned. "Feel free to tell me if I'm out of place, but are you — I don't want to say capable, but *suited* to that kind of thing? You and I started out pretty casual, but it didn't stay that way."

"You're right." Will nodded, surprised that Riley's observation didn't sting more. "I'm not great at casual."

Then again, are things with David really casual anymore? he asked himself. His father's illness and the situation with Isabel had brought them closer and led to them emotionally supporting each other. They couldn't go back now. Even if they could, he wasn't sure he wanted to. But where did that leave them?

"I don't want to see you get hurt." Riley glanced down. "I know that's probably hypocritical coming from the guy who hurt you but…"

"Hey, it's okay," Will reassured him. "I don't know if it's the thing with David or time and distance, hell, maybe it's seeing you and Carter together, but I'm feeling good about things. We were never right together and I'm okay with that."

Riley flashed him a bright smile. "I'm glad to hear it. And I don't want you to think I'm not supportive of what you have going on with David. I think you need someone while you're there."

Will nodded. "Thanks. I—"

"I thought you were throwing a party tonight, Riley. What are you doing standing around talking?" a female voice interrupted them.

Will turned to see Carter's sister Audrey, arms laden with market bags. She flashed him a grin when he moved to take them from her.

"I waited for you to get here so I could put you to work," Riley teased. He pointed to the counter to indicate Will could set the bags there.

"For that, I may charge you and my brother extra to buy this place." Audrey patted Will's arm as she went past. "Hey, Will. Nice to see you."

"Nice to see you too, Audrey." Will nodded at Audrey's husband who'd walked in. "Hey, Max."

"Hey, glad you could be here, Will." They shook hands, then exchanged pleasantries for a few minutes before Riley cleared his throat.

"All teasing aside, Audrey is right. I have a few things to prep before the party. That was part of the deal, Will. You get here early and I put you to work. I know you're useless in the kitchen but I figure you can schlep stuff and help set up."

"I'm getting better," he protested with a laugh. "I've helped my, ah, friend, David, in the kitchen a few times now."

Riley snorted at Will's lame attempt at subterfuge. "Oh, I bet you have," he muttered under his breath.

Will grinned and elbowed him playfully. "That's definitely not what I meant."

* * * *

Several hours later, Will surveyed the party. Music played on a set of speakers, drinks flowed, food was being devoured and the yard — lit with string lights and torches — looked festive as people milled around, talking and laughing.

Carter had made a grand announcement about his new career path with Corporate Equality Campaign and when he walked over to the food table, Will approached him to congratulate him on the house and job. Their exchange seemed slightly forced and Will felt guilty that Carter was still so uncomfortable around him. He needed to work on that, because he really had turned the page on the relationship with Riley.

"Riley's been telling me a bit about Corporate Equality Campaign," Will said, "and the work they do to ensure the rights of LGBTQ employees in the corporate workplace. It sounds pretty fascinating."

Carter nodded. "It is. It's very necessary work, too. They're one of the only advocacy groups in the country that focuses on corporate policies and practices pertinent to people like us. Being out in the workplace isn't something that should kill a person's career."

"Like it did yours?" Carter's coming out had torched both his relationship with his parents and his career. It hadn't helped that Carter's family had established the advertising firm where he and his father worked.

Carter dipped his head. "Yes, though coming out wasn't the only reason my career at Hamilton Ad ended. I could have fought to keep my position at the firm, maybe even won, especially if I'd had someone at the CEC helping me. It didn't seem worth it, though. I wasn't content there, for many reasons. By the time I felt ready to come out, I was also ready to leave the firm. Being disowned by my parents made it a hell of a lot easier to leave, too."

Will nodded. He had more in common with Carter than he'd realized. "That takes some kind of balls," he said sincerely. "Good to hear that you'll be loaning yours out to other people in the same position who need them."

Carter huffed a laugh, and his expression lightened. "You've certainly got a way with words, Will. I may just add that to the skill set on my résumé."

"Feel free." Will relaxed, glad he and Carter were finally finding some ease in their conversations.

"How are you doing?" Carter asked more seriously. "Riley mentioned someone in your family was ill and you were spending a lot of time on Long Island."

Will nodded and pitched his voice lower. "Please don't repeat this to anyone, but my father has cancer. The prognosis is...not good. His staff are trying to keep it from the media until he's ready to make a formal announcement."

Carter frowned. "I'm sorry, I feel like I should know who your father is, but Riley's never mentioned him. Or if he did, it's slipped my mind."

Will waved off his apology, surprised Riley hadn't told his boyfriend more. "My father is New York State Senator William Martin."

Carter opened his mouth in a small 'o' of surprise. "I understand the discretion, then. Nothing you tell me will travel any further than this conversation."

"I appreciate that." Will sighed and raked a hand through his hair. "It's been a difficult summer. My father and I have been estranged for years, you see. I went to Long Island to support my mother and sister, but my father seems like he's softening a little. Or maybe it's just the painkillers." His laugh held a touch of bitterness. Will hadn't admitted that to anyone before but the thought had definitely crossed his mind. Was his father's change of heart real or a byproduct of the opioids?

"I really am sorry you're going through this," Carter said. "I can't imagine how difficult this has been for you all. I know we've had our differences, but please, if there's anything Riley or I can do…"

"Thank you. I appreciate that. I'll be fine, though. Believe it or not, seeing you all at the bar every couple of weeks has been a real sanity saver. David's also been a huge help and—" Will cut himself off and grimaced.

"David?"

"David Mori." Will wondered if he'd made a misstep. "This is also off the record. David's a first-term senator who works with my father. He's a great guy, but on the other end of the political spectrum from me. It's…complicated."

"I would imagine." Carter looked over at where Riley and Audrey were chatting. "But, hey, some people are worth the complications."

Will nodded, surprised but appreciative of Carter's support. "I'll keep that in mind."

The line at the table finally moved forward. After Will and Carter filled their plates, they went their separate ways.

He found an open seat on a chair next to his friend Natalie in a relatively quiet corner of the yard. "Mind if I sit?" he asked. Natalie had been the one to introduce him to Riley in the first place, more than a year and a half ago.

She gave him a wide smile. "Not at all. I was hoping we could catch up!" Their schedules hadn't allowed them to do much more than email or text lately. He had done his best to keep her abreast of the situation with his family and progress with David, but there had been little time for anything else.

"I know." Will made a face and reached for a mini vegetable tart. "I've been so busy I feel like we've lost touch."

She patted his knee. "You've had a lot going on. Besides, I can't take it personally when you're hardly keeping up with Gabe and Charles, either."

"Charles doesn't seem to understand my continued friendship with Riley and it leaves us at kind of an impasse."

She shifted in her chair to face him. "I think he and Gabe are having trouble."

"Already? They've barely been married for a year."

"I know. But they had a rough start to the relationship, remember?"

"Yeah, I know they did, but I thought things had settled down." Will pushed a peapod through the chive and dill dip.

Natalie shrugged. "Jealousy issues have cropped up again. Charles is on a tear about Gabe's new sous chef at the restaurant. I guess he's *very* good-looking."

Will frowned. "Why the hell didn't Gabe mention this when we had lunch the other day?"

"I'm sure he didn't want to bother you with everything that's going on in your life," Natalie said gently before she lifted a bite of food to her lips.

"I feel like a shitty friend," Will said.

"Will, you've moved back in with your estranged family and are trying to rebuild those relationships while coming to terms with your father dying. I think you can cut yourself a little bit of slack."

He huffed a laugh. "Well, when you put it that way..." He grew serious. "The thing is, dealing with my father and meeting David highlighted the fact that there are some things about myself I don't like. My temper is way too short, I steamroll over other people and don't listen to them, and I'm way too quick to make snap judgments. It's not pretty, Nat."

"Well, admitting the problem is the first step, right? Just keep working at it." Natalie gave him a soft, sympathetic smile and nodded toward Riley and Carter who sat on a bench across the yard and appeared to be in their own world. "Am I right in assuming David's also making it a lot easier for you to be comfortable with *that?*"

Will watched Riley play with the hair at the nape of Carter's neck then lean in to kiss him. Longing thrummed through Will, but not for Riley. For David. Funny, when had that happened?

"You may be right," he said to Natalie. He jolted slightly as he remembered Riley's comment about his tendency to fall for his bed partners. David was having a much bigger impact on his life than he ever would have anticipated. And, it felt good to talk about David with someone. At home — on Long Island, he corrected himself — he had to watch what he said so carefully around his family. But he trusted his friends to keep the information under wraps and it felt nice to relax and talk about the person he'd spent so much time with lately.

In fact, he'd like to introduce David to the speakeasy guys and Natalie. He thought they would actually get along quite well.

An outburst of laughter came from the corner where Riley and Carter were now talking with Jesse and Ingrid, his date. As Will watched, Riley and Ingrid, a striking blonde, stood and disappeared into the house while Carter and Jesse settled into conversation.

"They're an interesting group, aren't they?" Natalie said, drawing his attention back to her.

"They are," Will agreed. "I've been to Kyle and Jesse's speakeasy a few times and I've gotten to know them some."

"Wait, which one's Kyle?"

Will nodded toward the dark-haired Kyle, who was talking to Audrey and Max. "The hot hipster. Well, I guess both he and Max could be described that way, but I meant the one on the left."

"Mmm, yummy," Natalie murmured.

Will elbowed her. "Don't you have a man of your own?"

"Yes, but Julian certainly doesn't mind if I enjoy a little eye candy."

"Where *is* he tonight?"

"Dinner meeting with a producer about a new show." Natalie's boyfriend was a choreographer for the New York City Ballet. "He's sorry to miss you, by the way."

"Tell him I said hi. Hopefully we can all catch up when I'm here next time."

"Absolutely."

"How are things going with him?"

Will liked Julian a lot and he seemed to be the perfect foil for Natalie. Other than a few relatively minor bumps along the way, they seemed to be doing well.

"It's going great." Natalie's face lit up. "We're taking a trip to Italy in a few weeks to visit my family."

"Umbria in the early fall? That sounds amazing."

"We planned it so we'd be there for the grape harvest." Natalie shifted in her seat and settled the fashionable floral skirt she wore around her knees.

"I'm envious. I can't think of the last time I traveled *anywhere*. I didn't even make it to P-town with the guys this year."

Natalie offered a sympathetic smile. "I'm sure your family appreciates the sacrifices you've made."

"I didn't mean it like that," he muttered. "A missed trip is nothing compared to what my parents are dealing with."

Natalie reached out and squeezed his thigh. "Of course not. And I didn't intend it as criticism. I meant I'm amazed by how willing you've been to put your life on hold while you help out. I can't believe you're taking a sabbatical from NYU!"

"I'm not sure I can believe it either," Will admitted. "A few months ago, if someone had said I'd be trying to line up a guest lecturer position at another university in order to spend more time with my father, I'd have told them they should see a shrink."

Natalie snorted delicately, but quickly turned serious. "I think it's pretty incredible, to be honest."

Will waved off her praise. "As everyone keeps reminding me, this may be the last opportunity I have to make peace with my father. I didn't want to live with any regrets." He sighed. "Which is why I'm packing up a good share of my personal belongings this weekend and either putting them in storage or taking them to Long Island."

"You're subletting your place, right?"

"Yeah, I figured it was the best way to make up the loss of income from teaching. Book sales help, and so do my investments, but not enough to justify paying for a one bedroom in Tribeca I'm not even living in."

"Makes sense. I bet you never imagined living with your parents again at this age, did you?" Natalie joked.

"Ugh, don't remind me."

She chuckled, then stood gracefully and gestured for him to stand. "C'mon, I think we both need another drink. And you need to re-introduce me to some of the pretty men around here."

Will stood, laughing, and offered her his arm. "I'll see what I can do."

Hours later, Will collapsed on the bed in his apartment, his head spinning slightly from the excellent booze that had flowed at the party. He couldn't resist the urge to message David, despite the late hour.

Still up?

Will nearly dozed off waiting for David's reply. He assumed David had gone to bed and shut off his personal cell, like he usually did. He forced himself to get up so he could brush his teeth and prepare for bed. He'd stripped down and put on a clean pair of pajama pants when his phone pinged with a message.

Just got home, actually. I had dinner with Isabel and Allen and she and I stayed up talking.

How's she doing? Will asked.

Ugh. Not great. Mind if I call? It's a bit long to type out.

Not at all. Call whenever you're ready.

A few moments later, the phone rang. "Hey there," Will answered.

"Hey, Will." David's smile was audible.

"So what's going on with Isabel?"

"Nothing new, per se. More of the same fights with Allen about fertility treatments. He and I got into it a bit, which wasn't my plan, but it's hard to see her upset and not want to go off on him for being willing to endanger her health."

"I'm sorry."

"Thanks. I'm just frustrated. And she's frustrated and it's a whole huge mess, unfortunately," David continued. Will listened and put in the appropriate responses when he could.

After he'd filled Will in on the conversation, David let out a soft laugh. "God, sorry about that. I didn't mean to dump that all on you."

"Hey, no need to apologize," Will said gently. He didn't mind listening to David vent—he'd certainly listened to Will complain often enough, but he wished he could do more to help. "I'm happy to listen."

"How was your night?"

"Really good."

"You went to a housewarming party, right?"

"Yeah, for Riley and Carter."

"It's impressive you've managed to build such a good friendship, under the circumstances."

Will laughed. "Oh, believe me, I was bitter as hell at first. But they're appallingly good together in a way Riley and I never were. And now that I'm getting to know him, I genuinely like Carter. Plus, being friends with the other guys makes it all a lot easier."

"The speakeasy crew, as you refer to them, right?"

"Yes."

"You definitely have some interesting friends, Will."

"I try. I mean, I am da — sleeping with a Republican senator. I have to keep things balanced." He winced at his near slip of the tongue. He'd almost said he was dating David. But they'd certainly never discussed *that*.

"Mmm. A bisexual libertine does make for a nice contrast."

"I'd like for you to meet him," Will blurted out.

"Jesse?" David sounded amused.

"Well, Jesse and the whole group," Will explained. "You know. You've met my family and I've met your sister. It would be nice for you to meet my friends."

"I'd like that."

"I thought about it at the party," Will confessed. He wasn't about to admit he'd missed David, but that was close enough, right? "That you'd fit in with the guys. Uh, politics aside."

David snorted. "Well, as long as they're not afraid of a rousing debate, we'll do fine."

"I think they'll be able to hold their own," Will said. "And I *know* you can."

David yawned. "Ugh, you know, if I weren't so tired I'd think about driving into Manhattan tonight."

"Yeah? Why would you do that?" Will asked with a smile.

"Oh, I don't know. Maybe there's a hot law professor I'm thinking about getting naked with."

"You're awfully sure I'd welcome the company," Will teased.

"Good point."

"I'd leave the door unlocked. And I might even wake up if you crawled into my bed."

"Tired or not, I'm tempted. Unfortunately, I'm meeting a friend from college for brunch. An *early* brunch."

An irrational stab of jealousy went through Will. "Sounds like fun," he said aloud.

"Yeah, it'll be nice catching up with her." A female friend then. Interesting. Had David heard something in his voice? Before Will could respond, David continued. "When are you going to be back?"

"Monday night at the earliest. I have to get my apartment packed up to either bring to Garden City or put in storage."

"You decided to sublet then?"

"Yeah. It makes the most sense with what's going on."

"Well, I can't say I'm sorry you'll be spending the fall on Long Island."

"I never expected to say this, but me either," Will said. "Now, I guess I'd better let you get to sleep, huh?"

"That would be good." David yawned, this time loud enough that Will could hear his jaw crack. "Glad we got to talk."

"Yeah," Will said with a smile. "Me too."

Chapter Twelve

Contrary to Will's plans, David didn't see him for almost a week after the trip to Manhattan to attend Riley and Carter's housewarming party. David missed him, and couldn't help hating himself for it, especially as the days passed with no sign of him. David had started to doubt Will would come back at all as the first week of September drew to a close, and genuine happiness spiked through him on Thursday afternoon when his phone lit up and Will's number flashed across the screen.

"Hello, Professor. Long time, no speak."

"David! I'm glad I caught you. Good time to talk?"

"Fine time. I'm going through some paperwork." David furrowed his brow and listened to the noises on the other end of the line. "Are you in a car?"

"Driving back to Long Island as we speak, actually. I just made it over the Queensboro Bridge and I'm sitting in a whole lot of traffic."

"Lucky you."

"Eh, it's not like I'm in a rush," Will replied, sounding amused. "I need to catch up with my parents and stash some things I brought from my apartment first, but do you have plans for dinner?"

David straightened in his seat. He couldn't help feeling very, very pleased Will wanted to see him so soon after coming back to Long Island. "I don't, actually."

"So, you'd be okay with me inviting myself over?"

David smiled at his sly tone. "I don't recall the last time I had a problem with it."

"Neither do I." Will laughed. "I can help cook, if you're feeling extra patient, or we can go out."

"I think you're due for another lesson, so let's cook in." As much as David enjoyed going out to eat in Freeport's restaurants, he wasn't in the mood to share Will's company. He frowned at the idea Bill and Agnes might feel the same. "Are you sure you can get away tonight? Your parents might want to see you, too."

"My parents had time with me over the weekend when they came into the city to check out my apartment and office over at NYU."

"What was the occasion?"

"There wasn't one," Will replied. "They'd never seen where I've lived and worked since leaving home, and decided it was time. They came in and I showed them around. We had a nice, slightly strange time," he added and, through his laughter, David heard a note of sorrow. Will's voice nearly always gave him away when he was thinking about his father's illness.

"I'll be home by six," David said. "If I don't answer the door when you get there, it's because I'm out with Mabel."

"Can I bring anything?"

"I'm out of beer, actually." He smiled when Will whistled.

"Oh? There's a story there, and I hope it's sordid."

"I'll be happy to tell you all about it."

"See you after six, Senator."

David shook his head. "Points off for gratuitous alliteration, Professor — see you later."

Once home, he walked Mabel and started prepping to cook. He'd gone to the sink with some carrots and a red bell pepper when a knock sounded at the door leading to the deck. Will let himself in and his face lit up when he spied David. His smile made David's heart do a funny flip.

Even in a plain white T-shirt and rust-colored shorts, Will looked so good David nearly rolled his eyes. He put the vegetables on the counter and walked around the island. "Hey, stranger. It's good to see you again."

"If I didn't miss the city so much, I'd say it's good to be back." Will closed the door with a grin. "Since I can't say that, I'll say I am glad to see you." He handed David the beer then pulled him in for a kiss, all while trying to pet Mabel, too.

David kissed him back with enthusiasm. He couldn't resist going in for a second kiss and a third, then both of them were chuckling and trying to get their arms around each other, in spite of the six-pack and Mabel grumbling for attention.

"Come on," David murmured, pulling back enough to smile. "Let's put these on ice. And thanks for picking them up."

Will slipped his free arm around David's waist as they walked to the counter. "Hey, you're feeding me after working all day — it's the least I could do. The guy

I talked to at the liquor store said this beer goes with almost any kind of food. Can I pour you one?"

David held up the pack of Zombie Dust Pale Ale for closer inspection. "Yeah, that'd be great. You know where the bar glasses are." He held the pack still so Will could grab two bottles.

"Why don't you go get changed?" Will's expression turned impish as he checked David out, head to toe. "Not that I mind ogling you in what's left of your suit, but you must be dying under all those clothes in this humid weather. Christ, you're still wearing your tie!"

"I was getting to it." David slipped the rest of the beer into the refrigerator and turned to face Will. "Is this the part where I excuse myself to slip into something more comfortable?"

"It is if you're a giant cheeseball named David Mori." Will grinned before squatting down to stroke Mabel. "Go on, I'll set the table while you make yourself somehow even hotter."

David barked out a laugh and got moving, working on his tie and the buttons of his shirt. Upstairs, he peeled off his clothes and sighed as the slightly cooler air hit the perspiration on his skin. He quickly changed into an olive-green T-shirt and dark cargo shorts. He was both relieved and disappointed Will didn't turn up to watch and tease and maybe more.

There were two glasses of beer on the counter when he walked into his kitchen, and Will stood at the sink, rinsing the carrots and bell pepper David had set out. He glanced at David over his shoulder.

"My mom said she invited you to dinner tomorrow night."

"She did, yeah. I haven't had a chance to get over there much lately because of work, and I had plans last weekend." David stepped up beside Will with a dishtowel to dry the vegetables he'd placed in the strainer.

"Would these be the plans that resulted in the disappearance of your beer?" Will asked.

"Yes. I went out with friends on Saturday."

"The ones who dragged you out to the crab shack?"

"Uh-huh. We went to a bar."

Will hummed. "I see. So, there was pre-bar drinking then post-bar drinking?"

"Oh, yes." David carried the vegetables to the island while Will turned off the water. "We have no business even trying to put away alcohol like that."

Will joined him at the counter, shaking his head in mock disappointment. "You got hammered, huh?"

"No, not exactly — it wouldn't do for the senator from District 8 to be falling down drunk. But, I definitely felt very relaxed."

"Where'd you go?"

"A gay bar over in Farmingdale." David laughed at Will's incredulous expression. "It's a twenty-minute drive, Will — not exactly a hardship. Besides, I prefer to be away from the Nautical Mile when I get my drink on, which isn't very often. Fewer opportunities to run into my neighbors, voters and, most awkwardly, employees." He went to the refrigerator for a rotisserie chicken he'd bought on his way home.

"Anyway, I hate being hungover," he added, placing the plastic container on the counter. "Especially when I have house guests."

Will raised his brows. "Aren't you a little old to be hosting sleepovers?"

"Better that than let anyone drive drunk." David licked his lips — did Will think he'd brought someone home with him? They'd talked about relationship statuses once early on, but Will had never mentioned seeing anyone else. David hadn't been seeing anyone else, but Will had no way of knowing.

"I don't mind putting my friends up for the night," he clarified. "I've crashed on their couches and beds plenty of times over the years."

They worked together to prepare a cold noodle salad with chicken and sesame sauce, with David guiding Will through the recipe while they chatted. They'd transferred everything into a serving bowl when Will circled back to the topic of David's friends.

"Do you all have plans to get together again?"

"Well, Nik will be working in Munich for the next several months, but I'm having dinner with Walter and Dana in a couple of weeks. We're good at touching base a couple of times a month, but it's gotten harder with my schedule and Nik traveling." David smiled. "We make it work."

He imagined Will mixing in with his friends and smiled. "You could join us, if you like. For dinner, I mean, when Walter and Dana come over. I think you'd like them and I trust them not to gossip about meeting you."

"Sounds fun," Will replied. His expression turned droll. "Is it a requirement I drink my face off?"

"That's optional, and besides, we usually eat in." David tossed the noodles with the dressing they'd mixed. "Dana and I share the cooking while Walter stands around and issues orders even though he can't boil water to save his life."

"What about Nik? Does he cook too?"

"Yes. He makes a few dishes, very well, and that's the extent of it. Says he doesn't feel the need to improve upon perfection. That actually tells you a lot about his personality." He grinned at Will's laugh.

They took the food out to the deck and talked as they ate, catching each other up over the last week and a half. Warmth settled into David's chest. He'd expected Will to be slightly down, maybe even resentful over having to pack up and put his life on indefinite hold. But Will's gaze was clear and his shoulders unbowed, and he was very tactile, frequently brushing his fingers along David's forearm and hand. Those brief touches were heady for David, who'd looked forward to seeing him for days.

I love him, David thought in a rush. His breath caught in his chest and he froze, thrilled to his core. Then, the impossibility of the situation slammed through him and he swallowed hard. He couldn't tell Will about his feelings — he couldn't tell anyone. As far as most of the world and their families were concerned, David and Will were only friends, and Will had made no secret he considered his time on Long Island temporary.

But by the time they'd finished eating, Will was holding David's hand and David's brain and body were buzzing. Will didn't show affection in public, and the fact they were sitting on David's deck in near darkness did nothing to diminish David's contentment. Their bodies were angled toward each other, their knees touching, and any neighbor glancing out of their window could see them. David shivered at the thought.

Will frowned. "What was that? You can't possibly be cold, can you?"

"I'm fine," David said. His cheeks heated as another shiver ran through him. Jesus, he was covered in goosebumps, all because the man beside him was holding his hand — how much more ridiculous could he make himself?

Will, wholly ignorant of his struggle for composure, moved in closer, concern evident in his expression. "No, you're not," he murmured, and brought his free hand up to cup David's jaw, his touch so tender David's chest ached. "Do you want to go inside?"

David closed his eyes and tipped his head forward to rest his temple against Will's. "I'm all right," he insisted. "Just enjoying the evening and seeing you again, that's all."

Will dropped his hand from David's jaw and uttered a soft laugh. "If I didn't know better, I'd say you missed me, Senator."

David opened his eyes to find Will watching him, his gaze amused, and something in him balked at pretending he didn't care one way or another about Will being by his side. He sat back slightly and squeezed Will's hand a little tighter.

"I did miss you." He was saying more than he should, but pushed on anyway. "I've gotten used to having you around here and when you don't show up, I notice."

"I had to pack up my place, David," Will countered gently. "I couldn't exactly accomplish that in a couple of days."

David nodded. "I know that. But we both know you didn't have to come back here, either. You could have changed your mind and decided against the sublet and the sabbatical, and driven up here to see your parents every other weekend."

Will pursed his lips, as if he wanted to deny David's words. After a moment, he nodded.

"You're right. I thought about changing my plans the whole time I stayed in the city." Will licked his lips.

"Staying out here is the right thing for my family, and I know that. It might even be the right thing for me, too, but I miss my real life. The longer I stay out here, the more it feels like that life is slipping away from me."

David nodded. Will's words weren't surprising — he was homesick. Still, knowing Will's 'real life' didn't include David hurt more than he wanted to admit. Worse was his guilt at hoping Will stayed on Long Island when he clearly wanted out.

"I'm sorry, Will."

"It's okay." Will gave him a small smile. "Like I said, it's for the best I stay here right now. Besides, I got to know you, and I'm not complaining about that."

David's heart did that funny flip again. Taking hold of Will's other hand, he leaned in to kiss him, keeping his movements slow to give Will time to back off. Will didn't stop him, though. He opened his mouth to David instead, and though the kiss stayed chaste, David bit back a groan.

Will's gaze was heated when David pulled back. "Let's go inside," David urged, and both of them grinned as they stood.

They let Mabel back into the house, then carried the dishes inside and stacked them in the sink, neither speaking a word about cleaning up further. David took Will upstairs, and he'd barely turned on the nightstand lamp before Will was at his side, sliding his hands under the hem of David's T-shirt to rest on his waist.

David turned to face him and raised his hands to Will's shoulders. The air between them became charged as they stared at each other, and the hunger he glimpsed in Will's face made his heart pound.

Will broke the stalemate first, moving in to press his chest to David's. He wound his long arms around

David's waist and this time, there was nothing chaste in the meeting of their lips. David licked his way into Will's mouth with a hum. He slid the fingers of one hand into Will's hair and moved the other behind his head, spreading his fingers wide across the nape of Will's neck. He relished the rumbling moan that rolled through Will's chest.

They broke apart to undress one another, and David wanted to touch every inch of Will's fair skin as the clothes fell away. He pulled Will toward the bed and pushed him down to sit. As Will stared up at him, David read trust and desire in his eyes, and something more intense he couldn't interpret.

David's heart clenched. God help him, but he loved this.

Will lay back when he moved in for a kiss and pulled David with him. David settled between his legs, delight and lust shooting through him as their erections brushed together. He couldn't hold back a low whine of pleasure.

"Jesus, Will." His dick throbbed at Will's wanton expression.

"I need to feel you," Will said, his voice rough.

David leaned over Will to grab a condom and lubricant from the nightstand. He met Will's burning gaze as he slicked his fingers from the little bottle. Will dropped a hand to touch himself and licked his lips as David tore open the foil wrapper. Wrapping his wet fingers around his cock, David pumped himself, hissing at the burst of intense pleasure before he forced himself to stop. He rolled the condom on, and smiled when Will held out a hand.

"Come here."

"Not so fast," David chided. He laughed at Will's scoff.

"I don't want prep."

David's stomach clenched. "That's nice," he replied, keeping his voice low. "But you're going to get some anyway."

He spread Will's thighs wide and worked him open, and nearly growled when Will reached down to slide a finger in beside David's. They both groaned. At last, Will raised his hands over his head to grip the pillow.

"David, please."

David pulled his fingers clear and shushed Will when he made a desperate, needy noise. Moving quickly, David braced himself over Will's body.

"If I didn't know better, I'd say you missed me," David teased, throwing Will's words back at him with a smile. His smile faded when Will simply nodded in return and brought his hands to rest along David's ribs.

"I did," he said. "I didn't expect to, you know, but it's true. I missed you, too."

David held his breath, his chest almost bursting with the things he couldn't say. He pressed his forehead to Will's and guided himself forward, exhaling slowly as he pushed inside. Will moaned as David slid home, and brought his legs up to encircle David's waist. David bottomed out and closed his eyes. He held still, clinging to what little remained of his control, then rolled his hips. Will let out another moan.

Reaching down, David hooked Will's right leg up, tucking the knee under his arm as they found their rhythm. The movement opened Will up more, and he cursed when David's cock brushed his prostate. He pressed his head back into the pillow and closed his eyes, pulling at David roughly with his hands.

David could feel Will thick and hard between them as they moved, and finally took him in hand. He covered Will's desperate noise with his own lips, pumping him in time with his own thrusts. A familiar tingling started low in David's groin and quickly wound up his spine. He grit his teeth and struggled to hold on, intent on watching Will's face as he soared.

"God, you feel so good," he got out, his voice hoarse. "So good, baby, every fucking time."

Will went rigid with a cry. His arms were like iron around David and his cock pulsed between them, smearing their skins with cum. David thrust hard and fast, erasing the space between Will and himself until the room tilted around him and he came.

David rolled onto his side and pulled Will with him as he floated slowly back down to earth. Panting, Will snuggled in, his head on David's shoulder. Instead of getting up to clean them off, David lingered, greedily savoring the feeling of Will's body pressed against his.

"Wh'time is it?" Will asked after a few minutes. David had to smile at his sleep-slurred words, even though they meant Will would leave soon.

"It's just past nine," he replied. When he moved to sit up, Will quickly sprawled over him, effectively pinning him back down. David laughed, pushing gently at Will's shoulder and coaxing him to move until Will rolled onto his back with a grumble to let David up.

He expected Will to be out cold when he returned a few minutes later with a damp washcloth, but found him awake and watching David instead. They were both quiet as David wiped Will down, and again David sensed the tension thrumming between them. In a flash, he understood that silence was filled with words they weren't saying to one another.

Only one way around that, he told himself, and Jesus, he needed to watch himself from saying too much. He brushed Will's hair back from his forehead with his free hand. "Got time for another drink? There's bottled water if you don't want beer."

Will smiled. "Actually, I'd love another beer if you're having one, too."

"I did plan on it." David got to his feet, taking a moment to pull on his boxer briefs before heading downstairs.

Padding quietly around the house, David turned down most of the lights. He left the washcloth in the laundry room, then went to the kitchen for the beers and a slim purple box he'd picked up earlier in the day. He didn't know what Will would make of his gesture, and he hoped—really hoped—he wasn't tipping his hand. Will didn't want anything serious here on Long Island, no matter what David's feelings were.

He found Will sitting up in bed, the sheets arranged over his lap and paging through a comic book he'd set aside from David's collection. The sight made David melt a little inside. Will met his gaze and smiled, then carefully closed the comic and put it back on the nightstand's shelf.

David handed him a beer. "I'd never have pegged you for a *Fantastic Four* junkie."

"I'm kind of fascinated by Johnny Storm." Will shifted to make room as he climbed back into the bed. "His insouciance appeals to me."

"Are you sure the appeal isn't based on Chris Evans playing him in a couple of the movie adaptations?"

"Certainly doesn't hurt," Will agreed with a laugh. "Michael B. Jordan made a badass Human Torch, too. Maybe the appeal is about being able to talk to you about comics." He shrugged, but his smile warmed David through and through.

David set the purple box on the bed beside him. "We got a bit sidetracked earlier, but I did buy dessert."

Will arched a brow and handed David his beer. "Beer *and* dessert in bed? What on Earth has gotten into you tonight?"

"Jeeze, open it already," David muttered, and he smiled smugly when Will opened the box and made an excited noise at the sight of a dozen beautifully colored macaron cookies.

"Your mother told me you were irate after she and Olivia ate the last box I brought to their house," David explained. "I bought this box for you, and hoped you'd let me have at least one." He laughed outright when Will clutched the box to his chest with a glare. "Only if you want to, of course."

"I suppose I can part with a couple, but only for you."

They took turns tasting the cookies and feeding each other and David insisted Will eat the lion's share. David was partial to the Earl Grey, but Will declared he couldn't decide until they bought another box with more flavors so he could make an informed decision.

"You're like my friend Nik," David said. He leaned back against the headboard while Will decided between another pair of cookies. "He loves to try anything and everything."

"That's how you see me?"

"I do, yeah. It's sort of odd you don't cook, though."

"Maybe that's why I appreciate everything." Will smiled. "You can't exactly turn your nose up when other people are feeding you. Where did you and Nik meet, by the way?"

"At school," David replied. "We were neighbors in our first-year dorm at NYU. Nik was a poli sci major like me and we had a lot of the same classes. We got along, even when we didn't see eye-to-eye. We just fit." He glanced down and drew in a breath, aware of Will watching him. "Nik was also my first serious boyfriend out of high school. We were together until after graduation."

Will stayed quiet for a beat, and his tone was neutral when he spoke again. "What happened?"

David bit back a sigh. It occurred to him Will might wonder if he was fooling around with another man still hung up on an old friend. "We wanted different things," he replied. "I'd been accepted to law school and Nik decided to travel. His family is originally from Macedonia, and relatives of his emigrated all over Europe. Nik stayed mostly overseas for almost three years before coming back to the US."

"And you remained friends," Will prompted, his expression curious when David met his gaze.

"Yeah, we did. We tried dating again after Nik moved back, but he didn't agree with my career choice. Nik is a progressive and almost redundantly liberal." David smiled at Will's grimace. "He couldn't respect my conservative opinions, especially given I'm a minority. He thought I should 'know' better than to side with people who hated us for how we were born."

David cleared his throat. He still had trouble talking about Nik, even after so many years. "The tension between us took a toll on our friendship. I'd always enjoyed debating views and policy with Nik, but things were different after he came back and I started working. We fought all the time. Things got really bad when I took a job with my local senator at his office in

Queens. Nik considered my boss, Jack Percy, a homophobe and an asshole."

"And was he?"

"Yes and no." David sipped his beer and swallowed before answering. "Percy was ignorant of a lot of LGBTQ issues and not always willing to educate himself, but he always listened when I brought him my concerns. He also held a lot of moderate views, particularly on other social issues, that lined up with mine. Percy taught me how his job worked. He also introduced me to your father. When the senator from District 8 decided not to run for re-election, Percy and Bill were the first to suggest I run for his seat."

Will hummed. "Nik must have loved that."

"He stopped speaking to me for a while, actually." David shrugged as Will's eyes went wide. "Nik wasn't the only friend who backed off when I started in politics—I've lost other friends over time. People who thought I wasn't capable of seeing or voting past party lines. I missed Nik the most. He and I didn't have anything like a grand romance, but we love each other very much and it hurt when it seemed I'd lost that. The other guys worked on him, and eventually he came around. We figured out how to…well, how to work our friendship around my job, mostly by ignoring it."

"And you're okay with that?"

"It works for us." David shrugged again. "You and I do a similar kind of dance, don't we? I know we're able to debate my positions without making it personal, but I doubt you've made an effort to truly understand why I've stuck with the Republican Party." Will's face fell and David swallowed his guilt. "And I shouldn't have to remind you that Democrats are far from perfect."

"I know that, but I simply can't understand how *you* can be comfortable as a member of the GOP," Will replied. "Especially now that I've gotten to know you better. You're a decent man, David, and I know how determined you are to make your constituents' lives better. All too often, your party seems intent on doing the opposite."

David took Will's hand. The obvious regret in Will's expression only made him feel worse. He hated that he couldn't speak to the people in his life about his job, and the work he found so important. But debate was the last thing he wanted right now with the man he'd come to love in his bed.

"Time to change the subject." He smiled. "I'm happy Nik's back in my life, even though staying friends with an ex can be a pain in the ass. You probably know something about that."

Will grinned in return. "Why yes, I do."

"You and your ex *did* have a grand romance."

"I don't know if it was grand, but I certainly wanted it to be." Will rubbed his thumb over David's fingers. "I'd been single for a while when I met Riley and he...well, he was everything I wanted in a man. Attractive and intelligent, and he even liked opera. He'd started up a division in his family's company and recently come out as bi. Riley seemed to know exactly what he wanted out of life. He was the first man I dated who felt like a real partner and I liked that."

David stayed silent a moment, trying not to wonder if Will could ever feel the same about him. "I'm sorry he hurt you."

"Me too," Will replied with a shrug. "I wasn't in a good place about it for a while — you know that. But now I can see I was a substitute for what Riley wanted.

I don't doubt he enjoyed being with me when we were together and he is a great partner, but not for me."

"You definitely enjoy being around him now."

"It's true." Will smirked. "I'm lucky too, in that none of his friends has tried to set me up with anyone or expected me to pick anyone up. Not even Jesse's tried and he, I am *very* sure, knows a multitude of beautiful people he'd like to pair up with each other."

"Maybe Jesse wants you for himself," David pointed out, smiling past a pang of jealousy when Will laughed.

"Jesse would probably be into that, sure, but he flirts with everyone. If he wanted me, he'd make an overture, and if he wanted to set me up with someone, he'd bring them to the speakeasy and wait for me to show up."

David nodded and drank some more of his beer. He smiled when Will held a purple macaron to his lips. "What's this one?"

"Cassis. Seems more your speed."

David held Will's gaze and took the cookie into his mouth. "Mmm...oh God, that's delicious," he murmured as the earthy blackcurrant flavors exploded on his tongue, then quickly ducked his head to kiss Will's fingertips. "I changed my mind about my favorite flavor."

Will rolled his eyes and dropped his hand. "You're cute even when you're talking with your mouth full. And I still can't believe you bought me cookies. Pretty sure no one's ever done that for me."

"Pretty sure I've never done it for anyone else," David replied, ignoring the heat that flashed across his cheeks. Oh, Lord, he was in trouble. Will gave him a sweet smile.

"Really? Not even Nik?"

"Nope. Nik's more of an ice-cream kind of guy."

"What about the men you've dated since?"

"There were a couple who might have enjoyed cookies in bed," David allowed. "Neither of them would have appreciated them the way you do."

"Clearly, you have been dating morons," Will mused. He put the lid back on the cookie box and gazed at David for a long moment. "I'd like to stay tonight if that's all right with you."

David grinned. Inside, however, he was doing a private victory dance. Maybe he was wrong about what Will wanted. "I'd like that. I should warn you I get up early to run."

Will brought a hand up to rest on David's bare chest. "I need to be back at my parents' house for breakfast tomorrow morning so that's perfect."

"Will they wonder where you spent the night?" David furrowed his brows.

"Probably," Will agreed. "They don't ask, and I wouldn't answer if they did."

"All right, then." David leaned in to run the tip of his nose along Will's cheek, then slid his free hand along his lower belly. "How about a shower?"

"Oh-h-h, I don't know." Will turned his head and when he spoke, his breath warmed David's lips. "I'm not sure I'm dirty enough for a shower yet. I wouldn't want to waste water."

With a dark chuckle, David slid his hand underneath the sheet and palmed Will's cock, lust pooling in his belly when Will's breath hitched. "All right then," he murmured. "We'll see how ready you are to be clean after I make you come all over yourself again."

* * * *

Waking up the next day beside Will put a smile on David's face, despite the pre-dawn hour and Will not being a morning person. His mood improved dramatically after David blew him, however, and by the time they were ready to leave the house forty minutes later, both of them were smiling.

"I'll see you at dinner tonight," Will said as they stood in the kitchen exchanging some more kisses. "Why don't you bring some more confections?"

"No way," David mumbled in between kisses. "Watching you eat them would be fucking torture after last night, and I don't think anyone wants me bending you over the patio table."

Several times that day, he remembered the way Will had laughed, and it made him grin every time. He put on a straight face as he rang the Martins' bell that evening, but knew his good spirits were showing when Agnes opened the door and immediately grinned.

"I'd say someone had a nice day. What's got you smiling?"

"Nothing in particular." David bent to kiss her cheek. "It's Friday and I'm looking forward to the long weekend."

"I see." Agnes gave David an indulgent smile, but her eyes lit up when he handed her an orange box from her favorite chocolatier. "Oh, thank you, dear."

"Thank you for inviting me to dinner."

"You know we love having you," Agnes said. "It's been a while since we've seen you, what with Will being out of town and all."

David frowned. "What do you mean?"

"I know you two have become friendly, David. He hasn't said anything about you directly, of course, but I couldn't help noticing how well the two of you hit it off. I imagine you both enjoy the time you spend together far more than the time you spend with Bill or me, particularly outside of this house."

David swallowed hard as Agnes smiled at him. Oh, God, he hated lying to this woman, and it pained him to pretend he and Will weren't more than friends. Lying about love not only made him feel guilty, it made him feel like shit. Yet here he was, pasting on a smile and acting like Will was nobody special.

"Agnes, I've been working crazy hours on my re-election campaign with my staff — that's what's kept me away." At least that was true. "Will and I are definitely friendly, but that's the extent of it. We, um, haven't gotten to know each other much outside of the time we spend here with you."

"Oh." Agnes' smiled faded. "I'm sorry. I've obviously misunderstood some things."

The disappointment in her expression only added to David's unhappiness. "No, I didn't mean to — "

"You haven't done anything at all," Agnes cut in gently. "It was all me. Seeing Will again this summer has been so wonderful, you see. You and he are close in age and always thrown together here...honestly, I think my imagination simply got away from me. I suppose it doesn't hurt that I *want* you to like each other."

David pressed his lips into a thin line at Agnes' soft, self-deprecating tone, and tried to shake it off when she took his arm. He'd come to know Agnes well enough to understand she'd quietly worry she'd offended him with her assumptions. That she *wasn't* wrong about Will and David's connection made the sting even sharper.

"Come on out back," she urged. "The others are on the patio already. Will made some kind of white sangria punch with fresh berries and mint and I've had to move the pitcher away from Bill twice already."

"I didn't know he'd gotten the okay to drink alcohol," David said.

"Oh, he hasn't, dear. The silly man thinks we've all forgotten he's not allowed to have anything stronger than tomato juice."

David didn't have to pretend to smile when Agnes rolled her eyes. He did, however, take a deep breath and brace himself to pretend the man who'd been his lover for over two months meant nothing to him.

Chapter Thirteen

Will carried the last of the dishes in from the patio after dinner and glanced at his mother. "Is there anything else I can do?"

She smiled and waved him off. "I'll help Greta load the dishwasher, then your father and I will relax. You and David should do the same."

Across the granite counter, David stiffened. Will gave him a quick, searching glance, but he looked away. Hmm, David had seemed off since he arrived and during dinner he'd been cooler toward Will than usual. Obviously, they were trying to avoid the appearance of being overly familiar with each other, but Will had no idea where the sudden tension had come from. The night they'd spent together had been more than pleasant and he hoped they'd do it again. Soon.

"What do you say, David? Want to find a bottle of wine in the cellar and share a drink with me?" Will had every intention of getting to the root of whatever the issue was.

David cleared his throat. "Uh, sure. I won't be able to stay too long, though. Mabel will be waiting."

Will kissed his mother's cheek, then called "Good night" to his father as he and David passed the door to his room. Bill looked wan and tired in the armchair where he was reading, but he lifted a hand to greet them.

"The treatment's really taking its toll on him, isn't it?" David said when they reached the bottom of the basement stairs.

Will sighed. "It is. And he's so angry at having to go easy on himself."

"I'm not sure I blame him." David's tone was sympathetic. "I can't imagine how hard it must be."

"No, me neither."

Will held the door to the wine cellar open and David followed. Rather than pick out a bottle, Will turned to face him. "What's wrong, David? I noticed you seemed off."

David winced. "I had a lot on my mind. Agnes has picked up on our closeness and asked me about it. I led her to believe we were only friends and had nothing beyond our encounters here, but I'm not sure how long that will cover it. And I have no idea whether or not she's picked up on the sexual tension between us."

"I shouldn't underestimate my mother," Will muttered. "She's every bit as shrewd as Bill. Hopefully more so, because I don't want to think what his reaction would be."

"Aren't you being a little hard on them, Will? They've opened up to the idea of you being gay and welcomed you back into their lives. For all you know they'd be fine knowing we're dating."

"Is that what we're doing?" Will asked. He felt wary all of a sudden. He'd wondered the same things lately, but still wasn't sure it was worth the risk. "I mean, we haven't talked about it."

"No, we haven't." David's expression was intense. "But I guess it's time."

"I'll grab some wine then."

"Sure." David stepped out of the way and Will focused on the wine rack in front of him. Delaying the conversation was stupid, but was it because Will feared David wanted more? Or that David didn't?

By the time they sat at the bar with a glass of wine in front of them, David looked tense and agitated — unusual for someone normally so even-keeled.

"Look, Will," he blurted out, "I..."

Will glanced up from the ruby-colored wine he'd been scrutinizing in an effort to gather his thoughts. "Yes?"

"I'm going to be candid here. I care about you. And while we went into this expecting things to be casual, I think we're at a point where it's naturally transitioning to something more. And I'd like to explore that."

Will froze, staring at David while his head whirled with the possibilities. David really had laid his feelings out there. "What are you suggesting?"

"Telling your parents and going public."

He swallowed hard. "Like press release kind of public?"

David nodded. "There's going to be increased scrutiny on me with the election in November and I'd hate for it to get out before we can get ahead of it."

"Wait." He held up a hand to stop him. "This is a *political* move for you?"

"No, that's not what I meant." David grabbed his hand. "I think we have the potential for a great relationship and it'll be a lot easier if we're not worrying about your family picking up on the vibes or the press accidentally getting wind of it."

Will felt vaguely queasy and pulled his hand away. "I don't know that I can do the political partner thing, David. That's a huge commitment. It's not only us having the relationship, it's the press and the public too. Worrying about reporters' scrutiny and how our decisions impact your constituents...that's asking a lot of me."

"I know." David's tone was calm, but a worried edge lurked under the surface. "But you have experience with this. You know how to handle it. And I can always put you in contact with Jerry, my campaign manager. He could find someone who specializes in this sort of thing and can help us navigate it."

Will's queasiness turned into a full-blown stomachache at the thought of campaign managers and political handlers. "Did you ever wonder why I stayed away from my family for so long? It wasn't *only* the rejection. I *detested* the scrutiny. It was exhausting being the son of a politician. The press dissected every single move Olivia and I made. It drove me crazy."

David gave him a sympathetic smile. "I do understand."

"I'm sure you saw the various rainbow shades I dyed my hair as a teenager. Do you know *why* I did that?"

"Rebellion? To piss off your father?"

"Oh, sure, that was definitely part of it," Will admitted. "But I also did it so the press never knew the real me. They just saw the weird Martin kid. They could focus on my hair and the way I dressed but not *me*. I didn't know who the hell I was and I didn't want reporters speculating about it either. So, I used a distraction technique."

"I know you had a hard time, but that was years ago. You're not a seventeen-year-old kid now. You're a charming, successful man. I think you are more than capable of handling this."

He shook his head. "Being the teenaged son of someone in office was hellish — I can't imagine what it would be like now as the partner of a gay Republican senator. That's got to be a thousand times worse in this political climate. Someone scrutinizing the way we interact in public, the way I dress." He gestured down at his pale blue chinos and blue and white gingham shirt. "Just thinking about it makes me feel claustrophobic. Like I'm being suffocated."

Hurt flickered across David's face. "What we could potentially have together could never be worth it to you?"

"I-I don't know." Will's heart lurched painfully. "I do care about you, David, and if this weren't so fraught with difficulties, I'd seriously consider it. I'm more than willing to see if we have the potential for more, but not in a public forum."

"So, you're suggesting what? A relationship on the down-low?"

"At least until we're sure we work. I don't think I can handle having our breakup discussed in the papers and on the TV. Not to mention all over social media."

David crossed his arms over his chest. "You're awfully sure a breakup is inevitable."

Will closed his eyes for a moment and took a deep breath. "We're coming from such different places, David. We're on opposite sides of the political aisle. It

may work for James Carville and Mary Matalin but..."
He ran a hand through his hair in agitation. "I've
already uprooted my life and quit my job. I'm working
on my relationships with my family, my father is dying,
I...I have so much on my plate right now I can't even
think straight. A relationship in the public eye is more
than I can handle."

"I've already lied to your mother about our
relationship, *and* my sister. I'm not willing to risk my
relationships with them, or your father. The longer we
keep this under wraps, the worse it'll be when it comes
out. And I don't want to think about the repercussions
there will be if we're found out by the press!"

"Well, it sounds like there's your answer, then," Will
snapped.

David knocked back the rest of his wine in one gulp.
"And there's the famous Will Martin temper. I was
waiting for it to rear its ugly head."

"Good thing we're not having this argument in
public, then," Will said, the snarky response rising to
the surface before he could stop it. He'd tried so hard
to rein in his temper, but there was only so much he
could take. "See? I'm too volatile to be the partner of a
politician. Every goddamn day of my childhood we
were drilled to remember 'appearances above all else'.
I'm not about to spend my adult life living under a
microscope too. Even for you."

"I would *never* ask you to be someone you're not. And
if you can't see that, maybe you're right. Maybe we
aren't ready for anything else."

"So that's it, then?" Will asked. "Goodbye and good
luck and, oh, nice fucking you?"

"I didn't say that either," David snarled. "I don't
know *what* this means. But I'm going home tonight.

Hopefully in a day or two, once we've both cooled down, we can have a more productive conversation."

David took the steps two at a time and though he didn't slam the basement door shut, he closed it firmly enough for the sound to ring in Will's ear for minutes after. Or maybe that was just his aching heart, filled with fear of losing the man he'd grown closer to every day. His response hadn't been the one David was looking for. Will had hurt David, and he hated that. But he had no idea what the solution was.

* * * *

Will awoke with a groan the following morning, feeling as if he'd been run over by a truck. He'd finished off the remainder of the bottle of the wine after David left, and fallen asleep quite drunk. Now his tongue was dry and furry and his head pounded. He picked up the glass of water he normally kept on the nightstand and found it empty. He cursed and threw back the covers before staggering to the bathroom.

Will gulped down two glasses of water and emptied his bladder. He stared at himself in the mirror while he washed his hands, feeling like a complete and utter asshole. God, what had he done? Not the overindulgence of wine — that had been stupid but forgivable. Fighting with David had been a mistake, though. He hadn't meant to escalate their argument but the thought of being in the spotlight made him panic.

He'd gotten out of the political life as quickly as he could and couldn't imagine voluntarily jumping back in. Especially with everything else he had going on. Even for David.

But Will hated losing a chance to be with David. Despite the rocky moments, David was someone he cared about. And he'd hurt David last night. That was the worst of it.

Will groaned and turned on the water in the shower. Resolved to at least talk to David about the issue again, now that tempers weren't so high, Will decided to make himself semi-human again, pick up breakfast and knock on David's door, hoping for the best.

An hour later, he stood on David's front steps with a bag in his hand and his heart in his throat. The sound of excited barks greeted his ringing of the doorbell, and a few moments later, David and Mabel appeared in the doorway.

Mabel's tail wagged frantically, but David looked exhausted.

"I come bearing breakfast," Will said softly. "If you'd rather eat it alone, I'll leave what I brought and go. But I was hoping we could talk."

"Come in." David pushed open the door and took the offered bag. "You didn't have to bring peace offerings. I would have let you in either way."

"I wouldn't have blamed you if you hadn't." Will crouched down to pat Mabel. She'd clearly picked up on the tension between them and her wagging tail had slowed, but she leaned into his touch. "Hi, pretty girl," he crooned and ruffled her thick fur. "Don't worry. I brought you breakfast, too."

"You're good to her. To us."

Will stood. "I acted like an ass to you last night."

"I wasn't at my best, either," David said. "So, uh, where would you like to eat?"

"The deck?" Will offered. "You'll need to grab a sweater. It's cooled down." September on the island was often unpredictable.

"Yeah, I just got back from taking Mabel for her walk. It's chillier outside than I expected." He moved toward the kitchen and Will followed. "Coffee should be ready in a few. I was contemplating what to eat, so your timing is perfect."

"Good," Will murmured, but he wondered if timing was the problem between him and David. If they'd met at a less chaotic time in Will's life, would it have helped?

They fixed their mugs of coffee in silence and carried them out to the deck. The sun was rising above the tree line, there was steam coming off the canal and dew sparkled on the grass. The morning was absolutely breathtaking and Will wished he could simply relax and enjoy the company of the man beside him and the dog at their feet. He ached to be a part of this quiet slice of domestic life, and it felt more like home than his parents' house ever had.

But there was no changing the public nature of David's life, and thus, his relationships.

They ate in relative silence. When they'd finished the breakfast sandwiches, Will broached the subject of their future again.

"I'm sorry about last night," he said quietly. "I tried to keep my temper in check, but I got frustrated and I shouldn't have taken it out on you."

David crumpled the foil from his sandwich. "I shouldn't have pushed you so hard and stormed off."

"I thought about it a lot after you left and again this morning," Will admitted. "And I'm still not sure how I feel. I care about you, David. If I didn't say that last night, I should have. I care about you and under different circumstances, I'd want to build a relationship with you. The last few months have been so good."

David took Will's hand in his own. "I'm sorry I dismissed what you're going through. I know you have a lot on your plate and I'm asking you to take on something that's difficult for you."

Will nodded. "Thinking about it made me feel sick to my stomach. What you're proposing is everything I've tried so hard to get away from. I can't imagine how stressful it would be to dive back into that."

David tightened his grip on Will's hand. "I know. And I respect that. But you have to understand how hard this is for me, Will. Political repercussions aside, if your parents find out about our relationship, they will be hurt. My sister doesn't know about us, nor my friends. I've never closeted any part of myself, and it doesn't feel right."

"Whoa, I never asked you to keep it a secret from everyone," Will protested. "Only my parents."

"Can you blame me for extrapolating and coming to that conclusion?"

"No." Will swallowed hard. "But I don't want to cause my parents any additional stress right now. They have enough to deal with."

David frowned and let go, sitting back in his chair. "Your father would never trust me again if he learned about it from the press."

Will nodded. That was certainly true.

"And Bill means a lot to me. He's my mentor and colleague and I wouldn't be where I am without him. I respect him too much to keep hiding this. Maybe it was okay when you and I were just getting off together but

I've developed feelings for you and...that's a whole different thing."

Will jolted at David's description of what they'd been doing together. It bothered him for some reason. He did understand David's feelings about his relationship with Will's father, though. "I know," he said softly.

"And I wish I could tell you politics has nothing to do with what I'm asking, but this is my career. I know how much you love teaching and writing. If hiding our relationship would jeopardize that, would it be so easy for you to dismiss?"

Will shook his head and looked out over the canal, unable to meet David's eyes. A pair of ducks lazily floated down it and out of view before he spoke. "I understand," he said hoarsely. "But I don't know what else to say."

He looked back at David and found him staring, his expression stricken. "I don't, either."

Will swallowed hard. "I want a relationship with you, David, but I'm not ready to go public."

"And I can't keep it secret." David looked and sounded anguished.

Will closed his eyes and took a breath before he could reply. Walking away from David felt utterly wrong, but he didn't see any way for them to compromise. "Then I guess we have to put the idea of a relationship on the back burner and focus on our own lives for right now. Maybe...maybe someday when I have less on my plate and elections aren't looming over you it'll be different."

David nodded slowly and stood. Will followed suit.

"We'll still see each other at the house," he offered, knowing it was nowhere near enough.

Will leaned in and impulsively pressed his lips against David's. His breathing hitched as David responded with a savage but tender kiss that ended all too soon. They stood there for several long moments after, staring at each other in silence with David's hand still wrapped around the back of his neck while Will clutched the back of his shirt. David's dark eyes looked as damp as Will's felt.

Eventually, Will forced himself to let go and step back. He left David and Mabel on the deck, his heart aching with every step away from them he took.

Chapter Fourteen

David said nothing as Will walked away, but pain knifed through David's chest when he moved out of sight, so sharp he brought a hand up to press over his sternum. He sat down again, eyes burning, and drew in a long breath. Mabel crowded up against him, shoving her way in between his knees in an effort to get close. David slid his fingers into her ruff when she sat down, and leaned forward to press his face into the soft fur. He took care not to grip her too hard so she wouldn't feel trapped, but Mabel rested her muzzle against his shoulder. He closed his eyes and worked at calming himself enough so he didn't feel like he was falling apart.

A while later, his phone chimed on the kitchen island. The ringtone told David his campaign manager wanted to speak to him, but he let it go through to voicemail. He didn't feel ready for a conversation with a fellow human, and Jerry would call back.

David waited for the voicemail chime before he straightened up again. Mabel lifted her head too and he stroked her fur, smoothing it with his hands while she watched him, her gaze dark and steady. He knew from the thump-thump of her tail he'd made her anxious, and he scritched behind Mabel's ears to reassure her, even managing something like a smile at her rumbled appreciation.

"Good girl," he murmured, then bent to press a quick kiss to her muzzle when his phone chimed again, this time with a text message. David was pitifully grateful for Mabel's comfort as he gathered up the plates and coffee cups and went inside.

I'll be in Freeport in thirty — sandwiches okay for later? Jerry wanted to know.

David's stomach lurched at the mention of food, but he swallowed and replied without hesitation.

Sounds good. I'm here.

After sending the message, he headed upstairs to the bathroom to wash his hands. David caught sight of himself in the mirror and pressed his lips tightly together while he studied his reflection. His skin was pale and his eyes red-rimmed, and all he could do as he stood there in front of the sink was wonder how everything had gone so fucking wrong.

The morning prior, he'd shared this same bathroom with someone he loved. He and Will had gotten ready together, both of them joking and laughing while David crowded Will up against the sink to kiss him. Today, David was alone and coming to grips with the knowledge Will didn't want him if it meant being part of his public life. That Will wanted to keep hiding this thing between them from the people they loved.

Never mind the anguish in Will's expression when he'd turned David down.

And never mind that David had fallen in love with him.

Getting involved with Will was a bad idea, he reminded himself. It didn't make his heart ache any less.

Gripping the edges of the sink, he blew out a long breath and stared at his reflection for a minute. He made himself stand straight, then ran both hands through his hair. He had a job to do, and however broken he might be now, he could deal with his feelings another time.

David's life took on a bland, gray quality as the weeks passed. Not much held his interest outside of work. Food was mostly tasteless and he didn't see the point in spending time with people for purely social interaction. The only spots of color were his dog, of course, and Isabel. Now that things with Will were over, David stopped hiding the relationship from his sister and told her everything. It hurt to acknowledge Will had turned him down, but simply telling Isabel had been freeing, even if the ache didn't lessen one bit.

He filled most of his days with furthering his career. He went into the office early and took meetings with constituents and special interest groups eager to influence his votes. He spent all the hours he could with Jerry and the small army of people who'd volunteered to staff David's re-election effort. He made hundreds of phone calls and went door-to-door, shaking hands and talking to voters.

"You know, this is starting to feel like overkill," Jerry mused one Friday after they'd lunched with members of a local teachers' union in a West Babylon diner. "Your opponent is an Independent no one's ever heard of."

"Doesn't mean he's unelectable," David reasoned. "No one knows Steve Hunchard right now, but nobody knew me two years ago either. And I was both brown and gay, two things Hunchard is not." He smiled when Jerry rolled his eyes.

"You'd also worked for a member of the State Senate for four years, and had both his and Bill Martin's endorsements."

David said nothing as they walked up to Jerry's Toyota Highlander. He met Jerry's gaze over the vehicle's roof and nodded. "I know — I had a lot going for me back then."

"You have a lot going for you right now, David. You've served the voters in this county well and your approval ratings are consistently high. The constituents like you."

"That's all well and good." David opened the car door and slid into the seat. "Doesn't mean we should assume people will vote for me simply because they did two years ago."

"I didn't say we should assume anything," Jerry replied as they buckled their seatbelts. "I think it would be perfectly okay for you to scale back a little, however."

David frowned. "What do you mean?"

"I think you're working too hard." Jerry turned in his seat to regard him, his expression sober. "Between time at the office and campaign headquarters, you're spending some crazy hours being Senator Mori right now. Don't think I didn't notice you hardly touched the sandwich you ordered, either."

David chuckled. "More room for coffee," he replied, holding up the iced Americano he'd ordered to go. "Besides, it's hard to eat when people are asking you questions, and my mama didn't raise me to talk with my mouth full."

"Okay, fine, but tell me this — when's the last time you had a day off? And I don't mean not coming into the office or campaign HQ because you took a meeting with someone from the Corporate Equality Campaign in the city."

"I haven't taken any meetings with Corporate Equality," David replied with a frown. But didn't he know someone at CEC?

"Well, you should — they're an advocacy group you could get behind. My point is you need some time off."

David shook his head as if waking himself up. "I'm in the middle of a re-election. People need to know I'm serious about being re-elected and that's not going to happen with me sitting on my ass."

"Point taken, but I'm not changing my mind." Jerry held up a hand when David drew breath to protest. "I understand why you're working so hard on this campaign. Your commitment to things you believe in is a big reason people vote for you. But I also know you're beat, man, and I don't want you to burn out before the election even happens."

David tried not to bristle. He loved his job. The work was tough and heartbreaking and inspiring and fulfilling, all at the same time. He didn't want time off to sit in his house with Mabel and think about why they were alone there. Especially since his career was the reason he'd grown apart from friends and nearly lost Nik. It had cost him something special with Will, too, yet he continued breaking his back to hang on to it. And why?

Because this job is bigger than you, David told himself. And his heart ached to know it would keep driving away people he loved.

Pursing his lips, he turned his head to stare blindly through the passenger-side window, hoping Jerry wouldn't notice the flush heating his cheeks. After a long moment, Jerry cleared his throat, and David winced at his careful, even tone.

"David, is something going on? You've seemed — I don't know — off for a couple of weeks. And by off, I mean down. I thought you were overworked, but now I'm not so sure. I doubt you're eating or sleeping well, or taking time to recharge. Are you okay?"

"I'm...not totally okay." David rubbed his chest where it hurt. Isabel had said almost the same things the last time they'd seen each other. She understood his dark mood, though, and why he'd been working like hell to distract himself.

He sighed. This was why he didn't want to think about his messed-up life — it made him feel like shit. Guilt raced through him when he turned to face Jerry and saw honest concern on his friend's face.

"Is this about the election?" Jerry asked. "Because if you've changed your mind about keeping your seat, we can —"

"No. God, no." David's stomach tumbled. "I'd have told you if I had decided against running again."

"Then what is it?"

"Can we talk while you drive?" David suggested. He was stalling, but he needed a minute to gather his thoughts. Besides, the people of West Babylon didn't need to watch them have a heart-to-heart while parked outside *Pancake Magic*. "I'd rather not give people ideas you and I do anything but work together," he added with a smile.

Jerry blinked. He snorted out a laugh, then started the ignition and they sat in silence for a couple of minutes while he guided the car east toward Freeport. They'd merged onto the Southern State Parkway when David spoke again.

"I know we don't discuss my dating and personal life except on a need-to-know basis, but I'm sure you know this job often takes a toll on relationships."

Jerry frowned. "Sure, I can understand that. Is that what's going on with you?"

"Long story short, yes. I was pursuing a relationship with someone and…it didn't work out. It's taking me some work to put the whole thing behind me, but I'll be okay. I just need some time." David smiled a little as Jerry raised his brows. "And not time off — working is actually helping me get my head back on straight. That and some space will help me process the whole thing."

Jerry worried his bottom lip between his teeth. "Okay, fine. I still want you to cut your hours. It's obvious you're burning the candle at both ends and that's no good. One day a week is all I'm asking, okay? One day where you don't do anything campaign- or work-related."

David murmured some kind of agreement. Jerry had a point — he needed to cut back on his work hours or, with his luck, he'd end up getting sick and he didn't have time for that. His mood tanked even further at the idea of dealing with his feelings over the split with Will, however, and he glanced up in surprise when Jerry put a hand out and squeezed his shoulder.

"You know you can talk to me about this shit, right?" he asked David. "Obviously, I don't understand what it's like to be you in a conservative's world, but you and I have been through a lot in the last couple of years. I know a bit about the guy under all that perfection."

A lump rose in David's throat. He was a shell of himself these days, and as far away from perfect as he could get.

"Thanks," he got out and patted Jerry's hand. "You're a good friend. If I need to talk to someone about what's going on, you will absolutely be on the list."

"Okay. And in the spirit of being a good friend, I propose we not see each on Sunday, okay?" He gave David a smile that bordered on impish. "Sunday is the day of rest, dude! Oh, wait, you're having lunch with Bill Martin, right? That means you won't be taking the day off anyway."

"Oh, shut up," David chided. Jerry's laugh made him smile. "It's brunch, and Bill's introducing me to Neil Seward, who's running for his seat. So, yes, we'll talk a lot of shop."

"Mmm, I've heard a little about Seward. What do you know about him?"

"Only what's in the public record. Born and raised on Long Island, and a member of the Levittown Board of Education for twenty-five years. He took the job of Nassau County's Director of Risk Management five years ago, and he and Bill have known each other for at least twenty years." David furrowed his brow. "I'm guessing what you're referring to is the stuff you wouldn't find on Seward's résumé."

Jerry shrugged. "He's got a reputation for being a hardass. He serves on a couple of boards at private schools in Manhattan, including Newhouse Day

School, and has a record for not supporting diversity in the student bodies — that was true when he served on the Board of Education in Levittown, too. I'm guessing he's tough the way Bill Martin was back in the day when he wanted to set the world on fire."

"Why don't you ever say such dramatic things about me?" David teased.

"Because you're always trying to build the world back up." Jerry grinned. "And that's another reason I'm glad you decided to run for re-election — your party needs leaders like you looking out for the people's best interests rather than their own."

* * * *

A familiar melancholy settled over David as he parked his car in the Martins' driveway a few days later. It hurt to be around this family, and for reasons he'd never have imagined.

He'd spoken to Agnes and Bill regularly and visited the white Colonial a handful of times since Will had called things off between them. Bill's continued decline in health evidenced itself in his dwindling frame and jaundiced skin, and while his will remained strong, he was obviously spent and in pain. As always, Agnes was patient and serene, but sorrow tinted her every move. David glimpsed resignation in her gaze when she watched her husband.

Then there was Will, beyond his reach but present in the very fabric of the Garden City house. David had taken steps to avoid seeing or hearing from Will since he'd walked off David's deck. It hurt too much to think about being near him, and, though David considered contacting him many times, he couldn't bring himself to reach out. He avoided places Will might frequent, and only visited the Martin home when Will would be out or holed up on the second floor working on his book.

David climbed out of his car now, a small box of fudge for Agnes in his hand and dully aware Will's Zipcar was nowhere in sight. He crossed the driveway to the door, his navy blazer and dress shirt crisp and his dark jeans immaculate, despite the hollow feeling running through him.

As usual, Agnes and Greta put on a delicious brunch. They'd made the whole-wheat pancakes he liked and a vegetarian strata Bill ate without bemoaning the absence of his beloved pork products.

Unfortunately, David had difficulty enjoying his meal. His appetite had suffered over the last month, but his inability to stomach food that day was a direct result of sharing the table with Neil Seward.

The man running for Bill's seat in the Senate embodied everything David strove not to be as both a Republican and a policy maker. Slim and striking, with angular features and a stylish cut that set off his salt and pepper hair, Seward personified the studied charm of a politician. He was cynical and cool, and frequently dismissive in both demeanor and speech, though he always addressed Agnes politely. With a calculated smile, Seward disparaged many of the hot button issues raised during brunch such as gun control, education reform and environmental law and David could only imagine he had little good to say on LGBTQ issues or, hell, David himself.

Unsurprisingly, he didn't have to wait long to find out.

"Bill's a tough old bird," Seward said after Bill and Agnes excused themselves to attend to Bill's medication. "He always has been, since our first meeting. Interesting he took you under his wing and helped you toughen up."

David nodded. "I met Bill and Jack Percy early on in my career. They gave me advice and counsel and helped me understand what kind of lawmaker I wanted to be."

"But neither of them ever got you to go to church?" Seward narrowed his green eyes slightly. "Constituents value the role of religion in their government officials, David. Surely Bill and Jack advised you to find God?"

"I'm unaffiliated with any particular church, but I'm not an atheist." Dread bubbled in David's gut. "My parents were Presbyterians, as were my sister and I growing up."

Seward drew his brows together. "I'm surprised you didn't stay affiliated. Presbyterians are tolerant of your people, what with allowing gay ministers and weddings."

"Congregations are allowed to ordain openly gay and lesbian clergy, yes, and recently voted to allow same-sex marriage."

"And you left anyway?"

"Moving away from organized religion was unrelated to my sexual orientation," David replied.

"You'll forgive me if I find that hard to believe," Seward scoffed. "It seems to me most gays give up religion in pretty short order once they figure out they're not cut from the same cloth as the rest of us." He shook his head. "Still...you're obviously sharp. Well educated, well groomed, a state senator before the age of thirty-five. It's puzzling you'd stack the deck against yourself even slightly given you started out behind and still managed to make people forget."

David folded his hands on top of the table, an icy calm spreading through him. "Started out behind in what way?"

Seward showed him a cold smile. "You mean besides being queer, which, frankly, is problem enough? Well, you're, what's the PC term these days...mixed? Granted, your parents' story wasn't the usual cliché with a serviceman bringing home some girl from overseas. Your parents met here. Your father was a second-generation citizen and well educated, not some busboy in a tiki restaurant. I understand he had relatives in the internment camps in the Pacific Northwest. Maybe that's where you inherited your tenacity."

"Probably. It takes a lot of discipline to stay the course when the world throws fools and petty obstacles in your way." David showed Seward a slow smile in return, and held his stare until discomfort registered on Seward's face. Clearly, the man was angling to get an idea of exactly how tough David had become. And while he'd finish the meal out of respect for Agnes and Bill, he was definitely done playing games with Neil Seward.

"I wouldn't discount my mother's family," David added. "They're from Ireland, and everyone knows the Celts are stubborn bastards."

"Crazy, too," Bill called. He and Agnes made their way back into the room, both of them smiling. "There's Irish all over my family tree and I've never met a more lunatic people in my life."

Bill's eyes shone with amusement and he leveled a look at Seward. "You want my advice, Neil, you'll avoid crossing them altogether. You'll have a fight on your hands you won't soon forget and chances are, you won't win."

Agnes laughed softly as she and Bill resumed their seats, and the smile she showed David melted the ice in his chest.

He walked Bill back to his room after brunch was over and Seward had gone back home.

"You handled yourself well," Bill said. "I don't know what Neil said to you when I was away from the table, but I could tell from your expression it wasn't pleasant."

"Nothing I haven't heard before." Bill squinted and David gave him a lopsided smile. "I've had worse from much tougher opponents with a hell of a lot more style, Bill. I'm not sure what Seward expected, but it's safe to say we each know where the other stands."

Bill chuckled. "I'd never have imagined otherwise."

They paused talking and Bill slid onto the now familiar hospital bed. "Is that why you invited us here today?" David asked. He couldn't help being curious as to Bill's motivation—he'd clearly anticipated David and Seward to be diametrically opposed on many issues. "To size each other up?"

"In part, yes. Today was for you, however." Bill sighed, his face slack with fatigue. "I wanted you to know who may be filling my seat, David, because you'll be in a position to regroup after the election and form new alliances. I don't doubt you'll do well, even with Jack and me out of the picture—you're ready to assume a leadership role in the party, if that's what you want."

David managed a small smile. "I appreciate your faith in me."

"You don't have to thank me, son—you're a much stronger man and more focused than I was at your age. However, don't forget that sometimes you'll have to put aside the petty bullshit a man like Neil Seward will peddle in order to work together on issues that mean something to you both."

"You're assuming a time will come when Seward and I agree on any issue."

Bill cocked a brow at him. "I'm sure you'll find common ground at some point," he chided before his expression turned sly. "That or you'll finally jump ship and go Independent."

They talked a while longer, mostly about David's re-election campaign. The subject provided a distraction for Bill, and a way for him to make amends for being too sick to be involved. David finally got to his feet when it became obvious Bill couldn't fight sleep any longer, and he stooped to pat his friend's hand where it lay on the bed. It hurt to see Bill so wrung out.

"I'll see you soon, Bill. You call me if you or Agnes need anything."

"Feel free to bring me a butterscotch milkshake anytime," Bill murmured and sniffed at David's soft laughter.

"I'm not so sure your doctors or Agnes would approve."

"Well, bring a milkshake for Agnes, then—she likes chocolate, like Olivia. Will, naturally, is never interested in chocolate."

David's smile faded. He met Bill's gaze, sharp under his half-mast lids, and it left him feeling suddenly shaky and exposed. "What flavor does Will like?" he asked when he was sure he could trust his voice.

Bill's eyes twinkled. Despite the sickroom around them and his haggard appearance, in that moment, he appeared for all the world like an indulgent father.

"Will always enjoyed pushing boundaries. He used to order black raspberry macadamia fudge, which just sounded confusing to me. He had a certain flair, even at a very young age." Bill paused, his expression thoughtful. "It took me a while to get him to try the butterscotch. He kept insisting it was better suited to cookies than milkshakes. He came around eventually, of course. He always does, when he decides he wants something."

Chapter Fifteen

"Is something on your mind, son?"

Will glanced up from his laptop to see his father frowning at him. Since things with David had ended, he'd thrown himself into spending time with his father. When Bill wasn't receiving chemo, Will spent most days keeping him company in his room and working on his new book.

Bill hated anyone fussing over him, but he'd accepted Will's assertion he found it convenient to work where he had easy access to Bill's extensive collection of law books. Will often worked for hours at a stretch, with Bill reading or napping in the recliner nearby. He'd devoted the past few days more to napping than reading.

"Will?"

Will snapped out of his stupor and shook his head to clear it. "Sorry. Something on my mind? Yeah, you could say that."

Bill tucked a bookmark into the open book on his lap and set it on the table beside him. "Do you want to tell me about it?"

Will hesitated. "I'm not sure."

Being apart from David hadn't become any easier. If anything, the draw to him had grown stronger. Will felt shaken after he saw the first campaign photo of David. He'd nearly been sent into a tailspin by a television spot showing David playing in a nearby park with Mabel, looking handsome and distinguished while still appearing approachable. It seemed everywhere Will turned he spotted campaign signs in yards emblazoned with *David Mori for State Senate*. Each one was like a small stab to the heart that his worries about David's career had gotten in the way of a relationship. With every day that passed, Will grew less sure he'd made the right decision.

The urge to tell his parents — particularly his father — about his feelings for David had been growing.

Bill cleared his throat. "I know this is difficult to believe, given our history, but you *can* talk to me about what's bothering you." Will nodded and met his father's gaze. Bill looked spent, but his blue eyes were steely. "There was a time when we used to talk."

Will had to admit the truth in his father's words. Bill Martin had always been a busy, rather stern man, but he'd been there for his children when Will was growing up.

Not until Will had begun to suspect he was gay had they stopped talking. Terrified of how his father would treat him, Will had retreated to a safer distance. The rebellion against the media scrutiny had widened that divide with the final straw being Bill's discovery of Will's relationship with Toby. But looking at their relationship through the eyes of an adult made Will realize *he'd* been the one to pull away first.

After looking through the photo albums and spending time with his parents in his childhood home, memories had come flooding back. Over the years, his hurt feelings led him to focus on only the negative thoughts. Now, he could see it from a more balanced perspective. Yes, his father had been busy, and later, their relationship had fractured, but he'd been there when it counted in Will's youth.

"Dad, I—" He cleared his throat. "I haven't been honest with you about something."

Bill raised an eyebrow, but didn't respond verbally.

Will sucked in a deep breath. "David and I...we...well, for a while we were seeing each other."

"Romantically?" Bill sounded surprisingly neutral.

Will nodded. "Yeah."

Bill regarded him impassively. "Did you expect me to be shocked?"

Will shrugged. "Maybe slightly?"

"You've never given me any credit, Will. Do you think I couldn't read your body language when he was around or put together the pieces?"

Honestly, Will thought they'd done a better job of hiding it, but maybe he *hadn't* given his father enough credit. "I wasn't sure you'd want to see it," he admitted aloud.

Bill folded his hands. "I'd be lying if I said this would be my ideal choice for you. But I am well aware I have no choice in the matter." Will opened his mouth to comment but his father held up a hand. "Let me finish, son. I don't want you to misconstrue my words. That happens too often with us.

"While you being gay wouldn't be my first choice, my views on homosexuality have changed in the last decade. At first, I truly believed it was a sin, but that line of reasoning no longer holds weight. I am too rational a man to believe the Bible is infallible. However, there is more than that."

"I don't understand what your objection is then," Will said softly. For the first time, he truly wanted to know why his father was against him being gay.

"I simply don't *understand* it. I can't comprehend why same-sex attraction exists. Biologically, societally, it's so much more difficult. It doesn't make sense to me."

Once more, Will made to speak, and once more, Bill held up a hand.

"I need you to understand. Being without my *son* for years changed my views. Seeing what a success you've become — in no way because of me but *in spite* of me — changed me. Getting to know a man like David and seeing what I missed out on with you changed me. I now know it doesn't matter what I think or whether or not I understand. As your father, it is merely my job to support you."

Flabbergasted, Will sat silent. He had no idea how to respond.

Bill continued, "I'm not thrilled by your insistence on keeping your relationships secret. But if you need or want my blessing to be with David, you have it. You are both good men. If you make each other happy, I have no intention of standing in the way."

"You have no idea how much that means to me." Will's throat tightened. "David was very uncomfortable with us keeping this a secret from you. In fact, that's one reason we stopped seeing each other recently."

"I did notice you seemed to be avoiding being around him. Do you intend to change that now you know where I stand?"

Will exhaled through his nose. "Unfortunately, that's not our only problematic issue."

"Is it his politics?"

"I can't say I love them," Will admitted, "I'm definitely more liberal" — Bill made a sound that resembled a smothered snort — "but if that was the only thing we could work around it." Will sighed. "I'm not sure I'm cut out for the role he needs me to fill."

"As the, er, partner of a politician?"

"Yes. Especially the scrutiny I'd be under as the gay and liberal partner of a Republican Senator. Not to mention the connection to you."

Bill winced. "Yes, I see where that complicates the situation."

Will leaned forward. "I struggled *so much* with the scrutiny growing up, Dad."

"I know you did." Bill's voice turned slightly gruff. "And I'm afraid your mother and I weren't as understanding as we should have been. I think at the time we thought you and Olivia were being a bit overdramatic."

Will cracked a smile. "Well, I'm sure we were."

"Fair enough. But neither of you had any say in the matter or agreed to be scrutinized that way. I feel we did a disservice to you and your sister."

Jesus, his father *had* been doing a lot of soul-searching. It made Will's head spin. "I appreciate that."

"Do you think you and David are compatible in other ways?" Bill asked. "Do you respect each other, challenge each other, inspire each other to be better men?"

"Without question. If it weren't for his career, I wouldn't hesitate."

Bill hummed thoughtfully. "Relationships often require sacrifice. I hope your mother would say it was worth it." A shadow crossed his face. "I gave so much to the people of New York, and I don't regret that. But sometimes I wish I'd given her more of my energy and attention over the years. I thought we'd have more time. I thought I'd have more time with you and Olivia, too. And with the grandkids."

Swallowing hard, Will stared at his father. He'd never seen him so vulnerable. His father's diagnosis and Will's return to Long Island had put the first cracks in the wall between them. This conversation had reduced them to a heap of rubble. Will's occasional doubts that the medication had made his father soften were gone. His father had fundamentally changed.

"I'm sorry you don't, Dad," he said. Will meant it. He wished he'd have more time with the man his father had become.

"I have so many regrets, Will. I never should have disowned you. At that moment, I meant what I said, but the anger didn't last long. And after, I regretted my words so much, but I didn't know how to take them back."

"I have regrets too," Will said. "I could have come to you and Mom and tried to work things out."

"But you were so young. And you are my *son* and the responsibility laid with me. You'll never know how sorry I am that I didn't come to you."

For a while, Will had put aside his differences with his father enough to let go of the past and connect. Now, for the first time, he felt like he could truly forgive him.

"It doesn't matter anymore, Dad," Will said, his voice slightly thick. "I'm home and we got this chance before it was too late."

"Now I need you to do one thing for me." Bill fixed him with a piercing stare. "No man should die with regrets. So, think long and hard about what *you'll* regret, Will. Would it be sacrificing some of your privacy to be with David? Or losing him?"

* * * *

That evening, Will was still thinking about his father's words. He headed out into the crisp October air and the leaves made a pleasant crunching sound under his feet as he walked the sidewalks of his parents' neighborhood, deep in thought. He'd hoped the exercise would clear his head, but after an hour, he was nearly home again and was no closer to reaching a conclusion than when he'd left.

A part of him desperately wanted to run to David and tell him he'd been wrong and made a mistake ending their relationship. But Will had to be sure he was ready to handle what lay ahead for him if they did move forward. His father had given him plenty to think about and solid advice. But Will was afraid if he rushed into it, he'd wind up in over his head. His relationship being discussed in the media seemed like a gross invasion of his privacy and the idea still sent a shudder of revulsion through him. But could a relationship with David be worth it? He had to be sure.

He let himself into the house and ran into his mother who stood at the foot of the stairs.

"You startled me, Will." She pressed a hand to her chest. "Were you out for a walk?"

"I was trying to clear my head."

An expression of concern crossed her face and she stepped closer to him. "Thinking about the situation with David?"

Will managed a half-smile. "Dad told you?"

"Yes and I'd figured out some of it already. He's worried about you. We both are."

Five months ago, Will wouldn't have believed it. "I appreciate it. I just need some time to think about things."

She cupped his cheek, her hand warm against his chilled skin. "We want you to be happy."

"I think I could be happy with David. If it weren't for his career, I wouldn't have any doubts," he admitted.

"I know. But would he be the same man if he weren't a politician?" Agnes gave him a wistful smile. "I don't regret it, you know."

"Marrying a politician?"

"Any of it. Building a life with your father, having you and Olivia. We all made sacrifices. But he truly believed he was doing good for his community, and so did I. In the end, it was worth it."

"I know," Will replied. "But some of those choices weren't good for *my* community. For me, personally."

"Your father has wrestled with that. I believe he'd choose differently now."

"I know. But unlike you and Dad, I *don't* agree with all of David's political views. And I can't imagine standing quietly by his side when he makes decisions I disagree with. I'm not sure I'm cut out for that."

"Has David asked you to be?"

"No," Will said. "We didn't make it that far. We didn't discuss what would be expected of me as his partner because I freaked out at the thought of every moment of our lives being public."

His mother offered him a sympathetic smile. "I won't pretend that it's easy. And it's only gotten worse with the advent of cell phones and social media. But do you remember the car accident I was in?"

Will nodded. How could he forget? His mother had nearly died.

"A reporter called nine-one-one and held his jacket to the wound on my leg. He saved my life."

"I had forgotten that part."

"They're not all monsters. Sometimes you're so black and white, my darling. Someone hurts you and you lose all sense of the good in them."

"I didn't with my last boyfriend. We stayed friends," Will argued. "And I'm here and having a relationship with Dad again. Look how far we've come."

She gave him a brilliant smile. "Nothing makes me happier. Keep that in mind when it comes to dealing with the press. There are a few rotten reporters out there, but most of them are only doing their job. If you think you can live a life that's above board, you can manage it."

"Other than having the occasional drink with one of Manhattan's most notorious playboys, I'm squeaky clean," Will said. "I've never cheated on a partner, I pay my taxes and I've even paid my parking tickets."

"Yes, you've always had your father's sense of morality and duty."

Will paused. His mother was right. "They'll still go digging, trying to find something."

"Yes, likely they will. But if there's nothing to find, what do you have to worry about? You give them a taste of your life with David, enough to satisfy them, then shut the doors firmly behind you. You're a brilliant, charming man. You'll figure out how to manage it, if you want it bad enough."

"You approve then?"

"Of David?" She sounded astonished. "We care for him very much."

"Of David and *me*."

"Yes, Will." She gave him a soft look. "I can't think of a man more worthy of my son than David Mori. And vice versa."

* * * *

Although the drive was pleasant, Will breathed a sigh of relief when he pulled up at the address his GPS had directed him to. A little more than an hour alone in the car had given him far too much time to think.

When the door opened, an unfamiliar wet nose and wagging tail greeted him first, and Riley appeared a moment later.

"Did you guys get a dog?" Will leaned in to hug Riley.

"Nah, we got temporary custody of Leo," Riley explained, and pulled back to offer Will a dazzling smile. Riley was dressed in a pair of faded jeans and a crimson Harvard sweatshirt. He was still painfully beautiful, but he didn't send Will's heart into overdrive anymore. David was the one who did that, as Will had discovered when he'd stopped to get coffee and breakfast on his way out of Garden City and come across David's picture in the newspaper.

Riley stepped back to let Will in and continued speaking. "Leo usually lives with Kate, but the kids wanted to bring him to the beach house for one final weekend while we close everything up."

"That's right. You warned me you'd put me to work," Will joked. He leaned down to pat the border collie thumping his tail against Will's leg. "Hi, Leo."

"How was your drive?" Riley turned away and Will followed him down a short hall into the spacious main area of the house. Leo padded quietly after them and settled on the thick dog bed beside the leather sofa.

"Uneventful, if a bit tedious. Too much time to think. I have a lot on my mind."

"Mmm. You seemed a bit off last night when we texted." Riley strode toward the large, open kitchen. "Coffee? I'll show you around after."

"Perfect, thank you." Will took a seat at the large, concrete-topped island.

Riley reached for a mug hanging from an open shelf near the coffee pot. "Should I assume this is why you didn't bring the delicious senator like I suggested? Or why you responded with 'it's complicated', at least? Because complicated is a given in your situation, right?"

He watched Riley add milk and sugar to the steaming cup of coffee. "Complicated is a given. But David and I...we ended things a little while ago."

"Oh. Shit, I didn't see that coming." Riley set the mug in front of him. "What happened? Did your father find out and throw a shit fit?"

"No. I'll get around to him in a minute, but surprisingly, my father is *not* the problem."

While Riley topped off his own mug of coffee, Will told him the story of his discussion with David about their relationship, the subsequent decision that they couldn't move forward, and Will's discussion with both of his parents.

Riley stared at him, open-mouthed, for a moment when he finished. "I'll get to things with David in a minute, but holy shit. Your father is *supportive* of you and David?"

"Apparently." Will took a sip of the coffee.

"Is it terrible of me to say I kinda wish my father would be diagnosed with cancer?" Riley muttered. Will nearly sprayed his coffee across the room. "I'm kidding," Riley said. "Well, mostly."

"No, I get it," Will said with a chuckle. "Honestly, anything less earth-shattering would never have moved either of us enough to get to this point. We're both stubborn."

"Exactly."

Will grew serious again. "It's odd, but nice that we're slowly repairing our relationship. I don't know that I can forgive him for everything, but I think I can move past it. And now I can see some of it was my fault."

Riley leaned against the counter and scrutinized him. "If your parents are on board with your relationship with David now, why haven't you run to that man and told him you want him?"

Will frowned and wrapped his hands around the warm mug. "Because I'm scared shitless about jumping into a relationship with a politician."

"Because—" The sound of the door opening and the shouts of excited children filled the kitchen and cut Riley off. "Sorry. We'll have to continue this later."

* * * *

Later that evening, Will stared drowsily into the flame of the fire pit on the deck. "I'm glad Riley talked me into this."

Carter chuckled softly from the lounge chair a few feet away. "It is nice, isn't it?" Carter and Riley had both put the kids to bed, but Dylan had requested Riley be the one to read him a bedtime story. "This is one of my favorite spots."

Will stretched and sat up, trying to shake off the stupor. "I needed the break."

"I would imagine." Carter's tone was sympathetic. "How's your dad?"

"Truthfully, he's dying," Will said. "He's undergoing treatment, but it's just to prolong things."

"Oh God, Will. I'm sorry."

"Thank you."

"Should I ask how things are going with David? I know Riley invited you to bring him along and…"

"At the moment, we're not seeing each other, but I'm starting to have second thoughts about it."

Carter listened attentively as Will brought him up to date on what had happened with David. By the time he'd finished, Carter nodded his agreement. "I totally get that. I'd have a hell of a time being in the public eye like that. It's bad enough when Riley and I end up on the society pages because of our families."

"God, that's even worse, isn't it? You haven't even done anything except be born to a family with money and they're still hounding you." Will cringed. "Shit. I didn't mean it like that. I'm sorry."

But Carter waved off the apology. "No, you're completely right. Riley and I *never* did anything to earn it. But our families are wealthy and influential and that makes us fair game. It's complete bullshit."

Will sat up and stared into the flames again. "I don't know that I can voluntarily subject myself to that, you know? I mean, I occasionally make the society column, but it's rare. This would guarantee everything I did was scrutinized."

Carter nodded. "It's a tough choice. I don't envy you right now."

"You don't think I'm crazy for being hesitant?"

"Hell, no! That's a huge decision." Carter paused. "On the other hand, I think your mom had some good points about what David would expect of you in the relationship. I don't think it would hurt to talk to him."

"Yeah, I agree." For a moment they were both silent, listening to the crackle of the fire and the sound of the waves on the shore. The silence was companionable and it felt good to have all the enmity behind them. "If it were Riley, could you do it?" he finally asked.

"For Riley? Yeah, I'd do anything."

Half an hour later, Will said goodbye to his friends and drove back to Garden City. The advice his family and friends had given him echoed through his mind. He didn't consciously point the car toward David's place, but he wasn't surprised when he found himself pulling into the driveway of his home.

It was late, but not too late, and he didn't hesitate to knock on the door.

A minute later it swung open. For a moment, all Will could do was stare at David, drinking in the sight of his face. God he'd missed him.

"Will," David said finally.

"I think I've made a mistake," Will said. "Can we talk?"

Without a word, David swung the door open and Will stepped inside.

Chapter Sixteen

David closed the front door and listened to Will greet Mabel, but paused with his hand on the knob for a moment to gather his wits. He'd taken Mabel to the campaign headquarters that day and they'd only been home about an hour when he'd heard the knock at his door. He'd expected to see his friends Dana and Walter on his doorstep, or maybe his neighbor Mrs. Cohen — she sometimes popped by if she didn't spot him and Mabel on their evening walk.

The last person he'd expected was Will and nothing prepared him for the emotions that crashed over him. He'd diligently shoved his feelings for Will into a little box at the bottom of his heart, certain he could deal with that box when he was ready. Now, with Will only a few feet away, everything David had worked to control threatened to blow up in his face.

He hauled in a deep breath and balled his hands into fists, only loosening them when he forced himself to turn back around. Of course, laying eyes on Will again did nothing to calm David's rattled nerves. Will had knelt down to pat Mabel, who was being particularly vocal, behavior she displayed when either very excited or upset. Knowing Mabel liked Will and had no doubt noticed his absence, David suspected it might be a mixture of both. He grimaced. He'd projected his own feelings onto his dog. He *really* needed to get a life.

"I know, girl, I know," Will murmured to Mabel. "I'm happy to see you, too." He met David's stare over the dog's head and David swallowed at the deep ache that ran through him.

Will looked...incredible, of course. He always did, even dressed down in jeans and a thick cable-knit sweater, his hair wind-blown and messy. But tonight, there were stress lines around his eyes, and the corners of his mouth were downturned. He'd practically radiated dejection when he'd straightened up to stand. He trailed one hand over Mabel's head.

"Thanks for inviting me in."

David stepped away from the door. "Of course. Is everything all right?" He frowned, struck by a sudden thought. "Are things okay with Bill and Agnes?"

Will brought a hand up and ran it through his hair. "Shit, I didn't think what my turning up here without calling might look like. My parents are fine. Or, you know, as fine as they can be right now. I'm not here for them," he added, his tone softening. "I'm here for me. Can we talk?"

"Of course." David gestured in the direction of his kitchen. "I can fix some drinks if you'd like, or there's coffee..."

Will gave him a small smile. "I'd love a drink, thanks. Whatever you have is fine."

David nodded and led the way, his insides tight. "I have some red wine you might like," he said, waving

Will toward the bar stools at the island. "Isabel hosted dinner last Sunday and someone brought a delicious Barbera. I picked up a couple of bottles for myself."

"How's your sister?"

David picked out a bottle from the wine rack in the corner and found his bottle opener. "She's okay, thanks. No more incidents since she stopped taking the Clomid. She and Allen decided to separate for a while," he added, aware he was babbling but knowing Will would ask anyway.

"Oh, David, I'm sorry." Will sounded sincerely saddened by the news and David paused to glance over his shoulder at him.

"Thanks. It's for the best until they decide if they can make it work." He turned back to the bottle and cut away the foil. "I've spent time with Allen, and heard his side of things and I know they love each other very much. I'm optimistic they'll work things out. They need some time to understand what comes next." Something David needed to do, too.

Will stayed quiet as he popped the bottle's cork. He poured two glasses and carried the drinks to the island, but instead of walking around to take the seat beside Will's, he slid a glass over its top toward him.

"Thank you." Will folded his hands around the base of his glass, his expression somber. "How have you been?"

David's throat tightened. Quickly, he brought his drink to his lips and used a mouthful of wine to swallow down the words that immediately jumped to his mind. *Lonely. Miserable. Stupid and in love.*

"Not great," he admitted once he'd swallowed. "I hadn't been with anyone for a while before meeting you. I didn't expect things to end so abruptly when I thought we were...well. The whole thing took me off guard." He shook his head at Will's frown.

"It's okay. I've had a lot of work to do with the election coming up, and it's kept me busy and focused. I'm always better when I've got an occupation," he joked. But the words fell flat and David sort of wanted to kick his own ass. He couldn't keep pretending everything was okay and he didn't have the energy to try.

Moving his hands away from his glass, David leaned forward slightly and propped himself up on his hands. "Will, what did you mean earlier when you said you'd made a mistake?"

"I've been thinking about you a lot. About us." Will blew out a long breath. "I haven't been able to get away from you, no matter how hard I've tried. We haven't seen each other in over a month, but your face is everywhere. Hell, my parents are more invested in your campaign than in Neil Seward's and his is the one that'll fill my father's seat."

David fixed his eyes on his wine and his stomach sank as he processed Will's complaints. He'd actually thought the same thing. Despite not having spoken in weeks, he and Will had remained stuck with each other in a strange way.

"That's not going to be the case forever," he replied at last. "Things will quiet down again after the elections. If I win back my seat, I'll go back to being mostly under the radar for the next two years and if I don't, I'll have to find a new job anyway. Just be patient, Will, and it'll get better."

"If by 'get better' you mean to disappear completely from my life, then you're wrong. That won't make anything better."

David went still. He glanced up to meet Will's intense gaze. "I don't understand."

In a flash, Will had gotten to his feet and rounded the counter to stand at his side. David straightened up to face him but jammed his hands in his back pockets to hide the fact they weren't steady.

Will licked his lips and stepped closer. "I don't want you to disappear from my life, David. I've *missed* you. I thought I'd be able to get away clean when we ended it because…well, because in the beginning we were more friends with benefits than real friends, but I was wrong. I miss my friend."

"I miss you, too," David rasped out, though he didn't dare move.

"I wanted to call you so many times, but I didn't know if you'd want to hear from me." Will furrowed his brow in a deep frown. "And I haven't seen you because you've been coming to my parents' house when I'm not around."

David nodded. "It seemed easier. I didn't want to make life awkward for you or them."

"You've been avoiding me because I hurt you." Will's expression was grim. "I know I did when I asked you to choose between me and your career. That wasn't fair and I'm so sorry."

"It's… It's fine. I understand why you did it."

"I'm not sure you do," Will returned. "I've thought about my reactions a lot. The idea of living under a microscope again made me angry, but also afraid. Afraid of living like my parents—like my mother, really—and getting wrapped up in duty and self-sacrifice and always wearing my game face. I was never good at any of that as a kid and my parents' world seems even more alien to me now." He grimaced. "I mean, take you and I. We avoid talking about politics and policy to keep things civil. But policy is your job. You can't stay silent around me forever, and I'll never be able to keep my mouth shut when I disagree."

"So, don't." David frowned. "I won't ask you to withhold your opinion. It's not like we *never* argue about politics, we've simply learned not to be nasty about it. Part of who I want to be in this career is a person who listens to dissenting views. The last thing I expect the people in my life to do is ignore their own feelings and opinions out of deference to me." He bit out a hard laugh that nearly broke when Will put a hand up and squeezed his shoulder.

"I believe you. I'm also scared shitless by what it would mean to be with you, and not at all sure you grasp that I could easily be a liability." A smile lit Will's face, small and hopeful, and it sent a thrill through David. "But I definitely made a mistake walking away from you. I'd rather be in your life and fight with you every day than lose you for good."

The balloon of tension that had sat in his gut since Will walked into the house deflated all at once. David tipped his head forward and closed his eyes, then leaned his hip against the island, equal parts relieved Will still wanted him and regretful in his certainty his career would continue to haunt them.

"It's my fault, too," he muttered. "This isn't the first time politics has fucked up my personal life and it won't be the last. It hurt to hear your reasons for wanting to call it off, but I understood why you had them. I don't blame you for wanting something different for yourself. I'd—shit, Will, I'd never want you to be unhappy, even if it meant losing you."

David drew a breath to say more, but the words caught in his throat when Will wrapped him up in a hug. David pulled his hands from his pockets, then wound his arms around Will. He pressed his face into Will's shoulder, fighting to keep his composure while his heart thundered and his eyes burned.

He had no idea how long they stood there together, but Will's eyes and cheeks were red when David pulled back. He kept his hands on David's shoulders, his expression sad.

"Are you okay?"

"No," David replied, his voice hoarse, "but I will be. What about you?" He cocked his head, but Will surprised him with a sheepish smile.

"Honestly, I feel a hundred times lighter than I did an hour ago. I was bothered by the way we parted...by the things I said out of fear. It all felt so wrong."

He ran his hands along Will's ribs. "So, what changed?"

"I talked to my parents," Will said. "I told them we were seeing each other and that I called it off because I freaked out over the idea of going public." He gave David's shoulders a shake when he didn't respond. "Did you hear me?"

"I heard you," David replied, blinking slowly. "I'm parsing out your words so I understand them. Your parents know about us?"

Will chuckled. "Yes. I can't say they were particularly surprised, either."

David groaned. "I knew your mother suspected more than she let on, but Bill, too?"

"My father seemed offended by my assumption he hadn't 'put the pieces together' for himself."

"Oh, my God. Is that a direct quote?"

"It is. They also made clear how much they like and admire you," Will said with a smile. "And that I'd be a fool to walk away from you out of fear."

David cocked a brow. "Really?"

"Well, not in those words, no." Will chuckled. "But they think you're good for me, and vice versa. My father also reminded me that living with regrets isn't something anyone should want. And I'd definitely regret not trying to make it work with you, if you'll have me."

"Wow." David blinked, feeling short of breath and dangerously pleased all at once, especially when Will leaned in to kiss him.

It took several heartbeats for his brain to get with the program enough to return the kiss, but even as his heart clenched almost painfully tight, he held back, giving Will room to pull away if he chose. Will didn't pull away. His hold on David tightened and he deepened the kiss, and nearly obliterated what remained of David's control. He and Will were breathing heavier when David forced himself to pull away, and he only moved far enough so he could rest his forehead against Will's. He was having trouble believing this was happening.

"It's never been a question of whether I'd have you," he murmured. "But there are some things we need to talk about before you decide whether being with me is what you want."

Will grumbled. "David."

David shook his head. "I'm serious. Avoiding topics of conversation to keep the peace may have worked for us short-term, but you said it yourself—we can't keep that up forever, especially if we plan to be together outside this house."

"Okay, that's fair. But you know I've been through this before and I already have a good idea of what it's like to live with people watching my every move."

"You're right—you're better prepared for life around someone like me than most people."

"Stop that." Will scowled. "'Someone like you' is a man I like very much."

"Sorry, bad joke," David muttered. He ignored the heat flashing across his cheeks and let go of Will so he could pick up his drink. "Can we sit down and talk some more?"

Will leaned across the island for his own glass. "Of course. What's on your mind?"

"Well, the last time we talked about this, I considered getting my campaign manager involved." David took hold of Will's hand and guided him around the island, heading for the living area. "I still think it's worth talking with him about a strategy to help us get over that first hump of people knowing and what happens afterward.

"Things have changed from when you were young and dealing with being Bill Martin's son," David said as they sat together on his couch. "The political climate is different and the immediacy of social media increases the levels of exposure a thousand times."

Will nodded. "My mother said some similar things to me the other day, actually."

David set his glass on the side table and steeled himself before he spoke again. "Your name would also be linked from now into the future with mine, regardless of how things turn out between us. I have good relationships with the voters and colleagues on both sides of the aisle. I can't hide my race and I've never hidden the fact I'm a gay man from anyone. But

I'm a person of color in a pretty white field of work *and* I've never identified a romantic partner while in office. People will be interested in us, especially given who your parents are."

"I'm starting to warm up to the idea of getting your campaign manager involved," Will replied with a weak smile. "I may be a writer but I'm sure he'd be better at putting together a press release than I."

"Maybe we don't need anything as formal as a press release," David said, trying to soothe Will's obvious discomfort. "We could go out and not act any different. We could just be us." A shiver went through him at Will's smile.

"I like the sound of that. I don't want to be anyone but us."

"Good." David took Will's free hand in his own. "One positive thing about being unattached for the last several years is my opponents have never had opportunity to leverage my partners against me or me against them. With that in mind, I think we should wait until after the election to go public."

Will drew his brows together in a frown. "What? But why?"

"I don't want anyone making assumptions about why I'm with you. That by associating myself with you I'd be leveraging Bill's reputation and career in an appeal to voters. Neil Seward is already doing so with your father's blessing, but I don't want people thinking the same about me." He swallowed as Will's face fell. "I'm sorry, I know you hate hearing this, but—"

Will shook his head. "No, don't apologize. What you're saying makes sense. I never considered how our being together would appear to someone on the outside. To strangers." Pain filtered through his expression. "And here I thought I knew so much about your life in the public eye."

David squeezed Will's hand. He needed to get this right. "What I'm asking isn't about my career, Will, it's about you. About us. I don't want to give people the opportunity to use you to get at me, and with the election literally around the corner, that could happen. Sure, my opponent seems like a decent guy who doesn't give a damn who I go out with, but who knows?"

Will let go of his hand and set his glass aside. "Are you sure that's what you want? To wait and hope no one figures out we're more than acquaintances?"

"Yes. Your parents already know, and I told my sister, too. Not hiding from them is more important to me than other people finding out."

Genuine alarm crossed Will's face. "Oh, hell. Does Isabel hate me?"

"No." David smiled. "She was sort of pissed at first, but I made her understand we were both to blame. You had good reasons for what you did and I should have known better than to push so hard. Waiting will mean changing our behavior," he added, hoping Will could read his regret in his gaze. "You probably shouldn't be around me for a while, unless we're at your parents' house."

"Ugh, really?"

"There are a lot of eyes on me at the moment, but in two weeks, people won't be paying half as much attention. I'd rather wait those two weeks than rush and turn what we have into a circus."

"I hate to break it to you, but I don't think people are going to ignore the fact you're sleeping with Bill

Martin's Prodigal Son," Will muttered, and though he was mostly joking, there was truth in his words, too.

"Probably not," he replied. "But I'm okay with putting off having to deal with all of that for a while longer." David licked his lips, the urge to tell Will he loved him so intense it stole his breath. "I've already watched you walk away once — I don't want to have to go through it again."

Will pulled David into a fierce embrace, and he closed his eyes, allowing himself to be soothed even as he forced himself to ask the question he dreaded hearing the answer to.

"Are you *sure* you want to do this?"

Will's breath was warm against his cheek. "Yes. I don't want to be without you anymore."

Will drew back to kiss him, his movements slow and so sweet David's heart ached, and he relaxed fully for the first time since seeing Will on his doorstep. He brought his hands up to frame Will's face as they kissed, and Will eased him backward until they were both lying down.

David reveled in the press of Will's body against his own. God, he'd missed this. His skin pebbled in the cool air as Will slowly unbuttoned his shirt, and he slid his hands under the hem of Will's sweater and T-shirt beneath, delighting in the heat of his skin.

"Can we go upstairs?" Will spread his palms wide across David's bare chest, his expression shy. "I know we need to be careful about being seen together for a while but I need more of you tonight."

Neither spoke as they climbed the stairs to the second floor, but they shared a smile once they were standing by David's bed. They took special care to touch and kiss each other, rediscovering each other's bodies as the clothes fell away. Heat pooled in David's groin. He stared at the hard lines of Will's torso, and he hummed when Will pulled him close to kiss him. The wet slide of Will's tongue made his heart race.

Will pulled back, his gaze burning. "I need you."

David nodded, his throat too tight to speak. He slid a hand between them to palm Will's cock. Will was already hard. The low rumble that rolled through his chest made David gasp. Jesus, he might lose it before they even got started.

He forced himself to turn Will loose, then climbed into the bed. He shivered as Will lay down beside him and stroked David's flank with his hand.

"I missed you, David," Will whispered.

David brought a hand up to touch Will's lips. "I missed you, too."

Will surged forward to settle over his body. He braced himself up on his elbows and forearms and nuzzled David's skin, licking and sucking while David touched Will anywhere he could reach. Desire coiled tight in David's belly. He shuddered when Will grazed his nipple with his teeth, and brought his hands up to slide his fingers into Will's soft hair, urging him back up through touch.

"Come here," he begged. His breath caught at the light in Will's eyes.

Will reached between David's legs to take him in hand, then shifted to align their bodies. David groaned. Will lined up their cocks, and the feeling of his long fingers closing around their erections made David's head spin. He arched up into Will and kissed him, unable to stifle his noises as Will frotted them and too overcome to feel embarrassed. He just wanted more.

"Want you in me," he murmured against Will's lips. His body buzzed with need. "Now, Will."

Will pulled back to stare at him, eyes wide and pupils blown. It had been years since David had wanted anyone to top, and he and Will had never discussed switching. He *needed* this, though. He needed to know Will wanted him. That the connection between them was still whole before everything changed again, this time with no way to turn back.

Will kissed him, another slow, sweet kiss that bruised David's heart, and David dropped his hands to fist the sheets, fighting the urge to say too much. He sighed as Will broke away, then turned onto his stomach and curled his arms around his pillow. The rustle of the condom wrapper seemed very loud, and he buried his face when Will hissed. Will nudged David's thighs wide with his knees. A cool, wet finger slid along his perineum, making him jump, and he exhaled hard as Will slowly pushed a finger inside him.

Will used his body weight to hold David down as he opened him up, and hummed appreciatively when David pushed back. "I've got you," Will promised, his breath hot against the side of David's face. He slid a second finger home.

David cursed. He turned his head on the pillow toward Will and flexed his hips, rutting against the sheets and only dimly aware of Will's appreciative noises. He couldn't stay quiet when Will slipped his fingers away and replaced them with the head of his cock.

"Baby, *please*," David whispered.

He inhaled sharply as Will pressed forward, breaching the tight ring of muscle in a single, slow push. Sweat sprang out over David's skin and he clenched his eyes shut against the too-hot stretch. Will curled over him and wrapped his left arm around David's shoulders. He found David's right hand with his own and twined their fingers tightly together.

Slowly, Will rolled his hips forward. He drove David's cock into the sheets as he fucked him and the dual sensations wiped all rational thought from David's mind. His world became heat and the crackle of nerves, and his mouth fell open as the pain began to bloom into a deep, aching pleasure.

Will rested his forehead against David's temple, and murmured nonsense into his ear. David gasped Will's name and Will drove deep, each thrust unwinding David a little further. The angle of Will's cock was enough to sometimes punch his prostate and the ecstasy jolting through David's body was so intense he sobbed.

David's orgasm overtook him without warning. He arched back hard into Will and his eyes flew open wide. His nerves sang as his untouched cock emptied onto the sheets, the world around him tunneling down into the roar in his ears. He closed his eyes and floated in a haze while Will continued to thrust, his hold on David tight when he finally came.

They lay quiet for a while, curled together as the sweat and cum cooled against their skins. David buried his face in the pillow again when Will finally pulled out, the loss of sensation making him ache for a whole different reason. His heart twisted as Will climbed out of bed, but then Will's hands were on him again and turning him onto his back.

Will used a washcloth to wipe David down and muttered playfully, "You're a mess."

"I blame you," David replied, and he blinked at the dry hand towel Will carefully placed over the wet spot.

"You look too comfortable to change sheets and I'm too lazy to leave right now." Will climbed back into bed, his expression fond.

David had to agree—his whole being was more than ready for rest—and he frowned as it dawned on him how worn out Will must be, too. Catching hold of Will's hand, he brought it to his chest. "Are you okay to drive?"

"Yes." Will's smile was bright and only slightly melancholy. "Are you working tomorrow?"

"Not if Jerry has anything to say about it." He smiled when Will cocked his head. "He's always after me to work less, so I took tomorrow off. Figured I'd take Mabel out if it's nice, considering she's come to work with me the last few days. Why?"

"I feel like picking up breakfast for my parents tomorrow." Will leaned down to pull the bedding back up over their bodies. "The Martins haven't had a proper bagel spread in a while and my dad can have small portions of everything." He raised a brow at David. "You think you're up for a round of twenty deeply awkward questions with Bill and Agnes?"

An easy happiness lapped through David, warming him as thoroughly as Will could with his touch. He brought Will's hand up to his lips with a smile. "Yeah, I'd like that."

Chapter Seventeen

"Thank you for joining me here this evening to celebrate my re-election to the New York State Senate representing the Eighth District!"

The crowd erupted with cheers and Will tried not to fidget as he stared out at the sea of excited faces. He lingered a few steps behind and to the right of David, who stood tall behind the podium in a charcoal Dunhill suit. Watching him put the suit on had led Will to all sorts of inappropriate thoughts.

The room felt uncomfortably warm to Will and made his own dark blue suit suddenly constricting. The blood pounding in his ears made it hard to hear David's carefully constructed acceptance speech. He'd listened to David practice it at least half a dozen times, but the familiar words weren't registering, so Will focused on the crowd—particularly David's sister seated in the front row—and used their cues to know when to clap and smile. The last thing he wanted was to look like a robot in front of the press.

"You okay, Will?" Jerry Andov murmured during the next round of applause.

Will smiled and spoke through his teeth. "Hanging in there."

David's campaign manager had been a godsend. Will had expected grudging tolerance of his presence in David's life, but Jerry had been enthusiastic and happy to meet Will. He'd listened thoughtfully to Will's concerns and assured him they'd find a way to navigate his need to be himself and still support David's career. He'd also persuaded them to make a more formal announcement, and though Will was anxious about how it would go, Jerry's arguments had been compelling.

"You're up next."

Will took a deep breath and shifted minutely, bringing his shoulders down and his chin up a fraction.

"...and last but not least I'd like to thank two extremely important people in my life. Former Senator William Martin mentored me and helped shape my career. His dedication to his constituents has inspired me for years and I am deeply saddened by his illness and early retirement. However, I owe Senator Martin for much more than influencing my career, because he has also brought a great deal of joy to my personal life. He has become a friend in the past year and, more recently, he introduced me to his son, Will."

David gestured toward him and Will stepped forward to stand by David's side.

"Without further ado, I'd like to introduce William Martin Jr. — a dedicated law professor at NYU, a published author of legal political history, and a man I'm extremely proud to call my partner." David paused as the crowd erupted with noise. Once they'd calmed down, he continued, "Will has been a rock to his family in these difficult times and I am deeply grateful for his support during my re-election."

Will waved and tried not to flinch at the crowd's sudden noisy uproar and the camera flashes.

David took hold of Will's hand. When he squeezed Will's fingers, Will relaxed a little. He was out of his element, but he cared for David and wanted to support him. Even in the midst of a victory speech, David was thinking of Will and that was a balm to his frayed nerves.

In the past few days, they'd thoroughly discussed the issue of public displays of affection. David had been all for a brief kiss, but Will and Jerry had agreed that hand holding during the acceptance speech was enough for now. It had nothing to do with hiding and more to do with Will hating a staged show of affection. If they were out walking Mabel and he wanted to kiss David, he wouldn't hesitate, but Will wasn't about to do it for a photo op.

David wrapped up his speech and after more cheering, he moved on to answering press questions. Will half-listened as David deftly fielded them, knowing they'd soon turn to their relationship.

"Mr. Martin, is it true you and your father were estranged for years?" a reporter queried.

David stepped back and allowed Will to take his place at the microphone. Will took a deep breath before he answered. "Yes. Unfortunately, we had a falling out after I graduated from college and we didn't reconcile until this past spring after his cancer diagnosis."

"Does Former Senator Martin know about your relationship with Senator Mori?" another reporter called out.

"He does. In fact, I think he may have figured out my feelings before I did." That got a laugh from the crowd. "He deeply respects David and has given us his blessing."

"You're a registered Democrat. Do you find that causes conflict in your relationship with Senator Mori?"

"Yes," Will answered bluntly. The crowd laughed again. "David and I have disagreed on *a lot* of issues. But we respect each other's beliefs and I also deeply admire David's willingness to vote across party lines and his openness to hearing other points of view. We may disagree about some of his policies, but in the end, I know David sincerely wants to do his best for the people of New York and I value that about him."

"Do you and Senator Mori have plans to move in together? You are a resident of Manhattan, are you not?"

Will tried not to blink in surprise. That was a question none of them had anticipated and he scrambled for an answer. "Currently, I'm living with my family here on Long Island while we deal with my father's illness. I will stay there as long as I'm needed."

By the time he'd finished fielding questions and the press conference ended, Will was drained. As soon as they were away from the crowd, he sighed in relief.

Jerry grabbed his hand and shook it heartily. "Well done, Will! You handled that like a pro!"

Will gave him a relieved smile. "I tried."

David wrapped an arm around him and pressed a kiss to his cheek. "Jerry's right. You handled yourself beautifully. Thank you."

"It wasn't so bad," Will admitted. "I can't say it was easy, but I think I'll be able to handle it."

"I *know* you can," David said. "And if it gets to be too much, talk to me. We'll figure out a way to take some of the pressure off, I promise. You come first to me."

"Thank you." Will pressed a brief but heartfelt kiss to David's lips. "If I haven't said it enough already, congratulations on your re-election, Senator."

David smiled and tightened his grip around Will's waist. "Thank you, Will. I'm glad I'll be serving this term with you by my side."

* * * *

Will woke up the next morning to a wet nose nudging his hand. David was still sound asleep beside him, sprawled on his stomach and snoring lightly. Though tempted to press a kiss to David's muscled shoulder, Will let him sleep — David had been working himself to death lately and Will wanted him to rest.

Mabel nudged Will's hand again and he glanced over to find her staring at him expectantly, her tail wagging.

"Hey, girl," he whispered. "Give me a minute and I'll take you out."

Will slid out of bed and tucked the covers around David. It didn't take him long to dress and make himself semi-presentable, and David was still asleep when Mabel followed Will out of the bedroom.

He yawned as he laced his shoes, put on a warm jacket, and clipped a leash onto Mabel's collar. "I might actually love that man," Will joked, half to himself, half to the dog. "Getting up early to walk you so he can sleep…"

When his hand hit the doorknob, it occurred to Will that reporters could be camped outside and he froze. It had happened a few times at his parents' house in

Will's youth, particularly after his mother's car accident. Now, he peered through the glass and was relieved to see the street and lawn were clear.

A few cars passed as they walked and no one gave him a second glance. Maybe he was being overly paranoid about things. Sure, he and David would be news, but there were other gay politicians out there. Will and David would be old news fast.

The bite in the air held the promise of winter and the frost-covered grass crunched under his feet as Will and Mabel walked. He'd taken her out with David many times and knew their usual route.

He was chilled but invigorated by the time he let Mabel and himself back into David's house. David greeted them with a sleepy smile in the kitchen, dressed in a pair of low-slung pajama pants and a soft, heather gray long-sleeved T-shirt that showed off his lean, hard body.

Will's mouth watered and his fingers were clumsy with desire as he unclipped Mabel's leash.

"I thought maybe you kidnapped my dog," David said with a smile. He cradled a mug of coffee in his hands.

"Just to get some exercise. I wanted to let you sleep." Will shrugged out of his jacket and hung it on a hook by the door.

"Mmm, thanks." David ran a hand over Mabel's head and leaned in to give Will a quick kiss. "I feel pretty well-rested. I was disappointed to wake up hard and find my bed empty."

"Sorry." Will kicked off his shoes. "I'm not opposed to going *back* to bed now that the beast is satisfied, however."

David chuckled. "There's several ways I could take that..."

"I meant your dog. But we can definitely see about satisfying some other animal needs." Will slid a hand along David's waist and when he tucked his fingers under David's shirt, David yelped.

"We definitely need to warm you up. You're *freezing*."

"Well, there's an obvious solution to that," Will said cheerfully. "Lots of vigorous exercise and a hot shower."

David set his mug on the counter. "That's a brilliant plan."

Forty-five minutes later as they stepped into the steamy shower, David asked, "Well, now that we're out to the whole world, do you think sex has lost its thrill? I mean, we were sneaking around behind people's backs before."

Will snorted and closed the glass door behind them. His thighs were still shaky from the orgasm that made him feel like he was being turned inside out. "Hardly."

"Same here." David leaned in to give Will a lingering kiss. "Oh, and remind me to give you a key to my place. I think it's about time, don't you?"

"I think so," Will said with a smile. "Now, Senator, one of your constituents is in desperate need of getting his back washed. Do you have strong feelings about that?"

"Very strong feelings," David joked. "In fact, I think you're going to need to turn around so I can thoroughly examine the issue in question."

* * * *

Will let himself into his parents' house a few hours later and came face-to-face with his mother, who had stepped out of the den.

"How is Dad doing?" he asked.

"He's tired but okay." Agnes patted his arm. "You can see him later, but he should sleep for a while. He needs all he can get."

"Of course. I'll run my bag upstairs and we can catch up for a few minutes."

"I'll be in the kitchen. Coffee?"

"Please."

Will quickly deposited his overnight bag in his room as his keys jingled in his pocket. He pulled the ring out and set it on his dresser, the shiny silver key David had given him earlier gleaming in the sunlight that spilled through the window.

The sight made him smile. David's place felt like home and Will liked knowing he could come and go as he pleased.

When he returned to the kitchen, his mother slid a mug of coffee toward him, already doctored with cream and sugar.

"How are *you*? We saw David's acceptance speech and your Q & A with the press last night."

Will groaned and took a seat on the stool near the island. "Of course."

"I know it isn't easy, but you and David make a handsome couple and you handled the press beautifully."

"Thanks, Mom." Will sipped his coffee. "Any tips? Jerry's advice is helpful, but there's no one more qualified to advise me than you."

She gave him a pleased smile. "Oh, I'm not sure you need my help, but let me think about it."

"Sure."

"Have you changed your phone number? I'm afraid it'll only take a day or so before it's ringing off the hook with requests for interviews."

He made a face. "Ugh. Yeah, I can do that later today."

"You'll want two phones. One for your friends to contact you and the rest for anyone you don't know and trust."

"I feel like I should be taking notes," Will joked, but Agnes slid a notepad and pen across the counter to him. She used it for making grocery lists, but it would do the trick.

"I'd suggest hiring someone to field interview requests and manage your schedule," she said, "even if it's only part-time, or temporary until things settle down."

Will scribbled as Agnes continued.

"Until then, keep track of names, numbers and who someone is working for. Politely tell them you'll get back to them as soon as you can, but don't agree to any until you have a good selection and can pick the ones you'd like to do. "

"Okay." Will began to feel slightly panicked. He'd thought he was prepared, but this was overwhelming.

Later that afternoon, Will's phone buzzed with a call from David.

"Senator Mori, you *are* thorough."

David chuckled. "Hey, I just wanted to touch base with you."

"Sure," Will said. "Is everything okay?"

"Yes." David hesitated. "You should know there are some reporters camped out in front of my office."

Will grumbled. "Damn it."

"No, it's fine. I wanted you to be prepared if you drop by in the near future."

"Duly noted," Will said with a sigh. "They're not at your house or my parents' house, so that's something."

"It could be much worse," David said. "Be glad I'm in the state senate and not federal. The pressure is less intense."

"Very true," Will agreed.

"And trust me, if Mrs. Cohen saw reporters camped out, she'd be calling the police. I don't think she'd be the only one, either."

"Oh, that reminds me. My mother suggested I change my phone number and hire an assistant to field interview requests."

"Great suggestions." David chuckled. "We may have to hire your mother as a consultant."

It occurred to Will then he had no idea what his mother would do after his father died. Agnes had spent a huge part of her life supporting Bill's career and now managing his illness. Will made a mental note to figure out how to help her. Losing her husband would be hard enough, but Will suspected she'd be losing a good portion of her identity, too.

"You still there?"

"Yeah, sorry. Got lost in thought."

"That's okay. I have a meeting in about twenty minutes that I should prepare for. I wanted to warn you about the reporters and say hi."

"Thanks. And hi."

"Have a good day." David sounded like he was smiling and Will realized he had a grin on his face too. It was amazing how good simply talking to David could make him feel.

"You too. I'll talk to you later?"

"Definitely."

"Will Martin!" a familiar voice said in an annoyed stage-whisper several hours later. Will looked up from his laptop screen to find Olivia glaring at him. "Why on earth didn't you tell me about your boyfriend?"

He shrugged at his sister. "It's new-ish?"

"I don't care how new! I shouldn't have to find out in the newspaper about my brother dating a Republican senator!"

"I'm sorry, Liv," he said, trying to keep his voice down so they didn't wake their father. Will felt guilty, but he wasn't used to being close enough to his family to warrant sharing his personal life with them. "It's been a long time since we spilled everything to each other and I'm out of practice. I'll try to be more forthcoming in the future, but can you cut me a little slack?"

"Would you two stop whispering?" Bill grumbled from across the room. "I'm awake."

"Sorry, Daddy." Olivia sounded contrite. She crossed the room and kissed their father on the cheek. "How are you doing?"

"Glad to see you," he said gruffly. "What made you stop by today?"

"I wanted to see you. And I wanted to be sure you didn't kill Will for dating one of your colleagues."

Will snorted. "I appreciate that, but Dad's very supportive."

Olivia's eyes widened. "Oh! Well, that changes things."

"Have I really been such a monster?" Bill jabbed a button on the bed control.

Olivia shot Will a slightly alarmed glance and mouthed, *"Don't answer that."* Will stifled a chuckle.

She turned to face their father and patted him on the arm. "You weren't very flexible about some things, that's all."

"Well, not only did I give Will my blessing to get involved with David, I encouraged him to get his head out of his ass about it. Is that flexible enough for you?" The bed had raised so Bill could sit semi-upright and he glared at both of them with all the imperiousness of a Roman senator.

"That's impressively flexible," Olivia said with a laugh.

"I've said it before and I'll say it again, David is a good man. He's good for Will. And I have him to thank for giving you reason to stick around here, son."

Will stood with a frown. He crossed the room to his father and Olivia. "I didn't stay here because of David, Dad. Sure, he helped, but I would have stayed regardless once I realized how much you and Mom needed me. And once you and I started to—" Will flailed for a few moments, trying to find the right words. "—mend fences, I didn't want to waste what time we might have."

Bill cleared his throat and took hold of Will's hand. His hand felt bony in Will's grasp, but his grip was still strong "That means a lot."

Olivia blinked rapidly a few times, clearly on the verge of tears. Will wasn't too far behind.

"I still don't know why I had to be the last one to find out," she grumbled as she wiped at the corner of her eye. "Next you'll tell me you and David secretly got married and adopted a family of orphan children."

Will laughed. "I am unmarried and childless still, though David does have a dog whom I adore. I promise, if we ever decide to go the marriage and family route, you'll be the first to know, Liv."

A ghost of a frown passed across Bill's face. In the past, Will would have assumed his father disapproved of him marrying a man or having children through a surrogate. But now, Will suspected his father was thinking he wouldn't be there to see those things happen. It made Will's heart squeeze painfully. How little time did they have left?

"Promise me you'll consider a biological child," Bill said. "Not that adoption isn't noble, but it would be nice if both you and Olivia passed on the family genes."

Will blinked at him. "Uh, well, if or when it's time for that, I'll take it under consideration."

"Good," Bill said. He closed his eyes as if tired.

Truthfully, Will hadn't spent a lot of time thinking about whether or not he wanted kids. And he'd never had a partner he'd wanted to raise kids with. He could certainly see David as an excellent father and Will wasn't opposed to the idea, but they'd barely started a relationship. That wasn't a bridge they needed to cross at the moment. Thinking about a future with David was pleasant, however.

"Speaking of grandkids," Bill said, opening his eyes again. "When can I see Adam and Jocelyn again?"

"Are you sure you're up to it, Daddy?" Olivia asked, doubt lacing her tone.

"They probably can't stay long, but I'd like to see them."

"How about Saturday?"

"Saturday is good. And you're all coming on Thanksgiving?" His tone left no room for argument.

"Are you sure you're up for that?"

"I'm sure." Bill was firm. "I won't be able to eat much and I may not even be able to sit at the table for long, but it's going to be my last Thanksgiving. I want my family around me." He leveled a look at Will. "And you'll bring David."

Tear pricked Will's eyes. "He may have plans with his sister already," he said gently.

"She and her family can come too."

"I'll talk to him about it tonight."

"Good." Bill's eyes closed and opened a few times, and in a few moments, he dropped off to sleep with a gentle snore. Will gestured toward his sister, who pressed a soft kiss to their father's cheek before she followed Will out of the room.

Will closed the French doors behind him and they walked quietly into the kitchen.

"It won't be much longer, will it?" she asked, wiping at her eyes.

"I don't think so," Will said. "Maybe a few weeks, but Dad's already held on longer than they expected."

"I know." She fished a tissue out of her bag and blew her nose. "I'm so glad you two had the time to make up."

"Me too," Will said, his tone heavy. "You and Mom and David were right. I would have regretted it if I'd missed the chance."

Olivia's sad smile brightened after a moment. "Speaking of, I need to hear more about the delicious Senator Mori! Who would have thought you'd end up back in politics?"

"Don't remind me," Will muttered.

"Well, you may not be the only one. Phillip is considering running for office."

"But he enjoys his career at the law firm." Will frowned.

"He did, until the lawsuit. He's sick of dealing with the other partners' fuckups and he's thinking about letting them buy him out."

"Huh. Well, good luck to him."

"Thanks. I'll pass that along." Olivia nudged him with her elbow. "So, wanna make a bet on which Martin sibling makes it to the White House first? You'd make a stunning First Lady."

Will mock-glared at her. "I believe the term would be 'First Gentleman'. And for my sake, I hope it never comes to that." He shuddered at the thought.

"You could always dye your hair wild colors again," Olivia said cheerfully.

"Only if you promise to shave your head," Will teased.

A soft noise of distress came from the doorway and Will turned to see his mother standing there. "Please, not this again. It's beyond me why two people with such beautiful hair would ever want to desecrate it that way."

"Just to drive you crazy, Mom," Olivia said.

"That I believe," Agnes said with a laugh. "Will either of you be staying for dinner?"

"I'll be here," Will said.

"I can't stay." Olivia glanced at her watch. "In fact, I should leave to go pick up the kids soon. But I want to talk to you about Thanksgiving. Dad seems to be inviting half the neighborhood. What can I do to help you get ready?"

Chapter Eighteen

"Are you ready for this?"

"Sure. Or...well, I think I am." David rolled his eyes when Will smirked, but inwardly he was pleased by Will's rare playful mood.

Outside of time spent with David, Will had few opportunities to unplug and simply be. Instead, he was caught up in helping care for his dying father and supporting the members of the Martin clan as each came to terms with the idea of losing Bill. Add to that coming out as David's partner and it was no wonder Will seemed constantly wrapped up in everyone else's affairs.

David understood why he spent so little time on himself — a part of him even approved of the energy Will devoted to his father. Still, David worried Will was taking on too much and ignoring his own emotional needs. Many times, David had seen him brush off his own feelings so his family had a shoulder to lean on. Will would have to face his compartmentalized emotions sooner rather than later. David suspected that would be a rough road for Will, and he planned to be there for him when the time came.

For now, he simply tried to make Will's life easier. Typically, that meant offering up his home and bed as a kind of safe haven where both of them could drop the fronts they were forced to assume around others. Today, it meant heading for a speakeasy in Morningside Heights to meet the group of men who had become Will's friends over the last year.

Will talked often about the private parties at Under, but hadn't invited David along until after the election. David immediately agreed, and also insisted they extend their weekend by staying over in the city for a few days. Privately, he'd questioned how on earth he'd get along with a bunch of men who lived like celebrities. They were even staying with Will's friend, Riley, because Will's sublet apartment was unavailable and neither he nor David wanted to rent a hotel room. Now, riding a Lyft along the 97th Street Transverse through Central Park, David stared at his overnight bag and wondered if maybe he'd bitten off more than he could chew.

"You're nervous, aren't you?" Will asked, his eyes growing a fraction wider when David shrugged.

"Maybe a little. It's not every day a guy like me gets invited to an exclusive boy's club." He narrowed his eyes at Will. "And you can stop being so pleased with yourself."

"It's a bar, not a club, David, and I can't help it." Will laid a hand on his knee. "You're always such a cool customer, it's kind of cute to see you out of your element for once. Especially since you're exactly the kind of man who'd get along with this group."

David shook his head — he'd been out of his element around Will almost since the moment they'd met. "I'm not sure what to expect. You talk about Riley and Jesse all the time, so in a way I feel like I know them, but we both know that's not true. I've never known people who were born into families regularly featured on society pages, Will — none of this is in my element."

Will's expression softened with sympathy. "I think you've formed the wrong impression of my friends with your googling." He smiled when David let out a wry laugh.

"Okay, I'm busted." David had googled the shit out of every one of the speakeasy guys.

"It's true Riley and Carter and Jesse were born into money, but they all work for a living, like you and I," Will said. "In fact, they're freakishly ambitious workaholics which is sort of annoying because they could each literally live out the rest of their lives on their trust funds. And Kyle's as far from a trust fund baby as you can get. He moved to New York from Vermont with almost nothing and spent a year sleeping on people's couches until he could afford to rent a room for himself. He owns a successful business, but his background is nothing like the others'."

Will moved his hand to grasp David's. "You'll get along fine, not only because they're easy-going and charming, but because you are, too."

David twined their fingers together. "Thanks for that. And I'm fine."

"Good." Will gave David a smile. "You should know I'm enjoying tonight as payback for that time I showed up to your place for dinner while your sister was staying over."

"*So* not the same thing," David scoffed, though his words lacked heat.

Despite Will's assurances, nervous energy swooped through him as the car pulled up in front of the unassuming establishment known as Lock & Key. Will had told him about the speakeasy's front, so he expected the pub's utter ordinariness, from its bland decor to the jukebox playing Smashmouth's *All Star*. However, David hadn't expected to see Riley Porter-Wright and Carter Hamilton seated at a rundown table with pints of beer. They were dressed in dark suits but were tieless and dashing as they turned to greet David and Will. Judging from Will's wide eyes, he was surprised to see them in Lock & Key, too.

"Well, hello. What are you two doing up here?"

Riley arched a brow and stood. "We're the welcoming committee, William."

Will groaned and dropped his bag on the table before hugging his ex. "I've asked you never to call me that," he chided.

"And you know I never listen to you," Riley shot back gently, his arms tight around Will's shoulders.

Riley closed his eyes for a moment, then gave Will an extra squeeze and turned him loose. The emotion that streaked across Will's face when he stepped back left David aching, but Will shook it off in an instant. He turned a genuine smile on Riley's partner, along with an outstretched hand.

"Carter, hey. It's good to see you again."

Carter shook hands with Will, a grin on his face. "Same. Glad you could get out here tonight—we missed you last month."

"My schedule's crazier than usual, lately." Will dropped Carter's hand and turned to David. "David's been flat out with the election, and I'm busy with more family business than I ever dreamed possible." He let out a soft laugh and shrugged. "Anyway, this is David. He knows who you all are, of course, because none of you can keep your faces out of the newspapers for long."

"Look who's talking," Riley muttered, and stepped forward immediately to shake David's hand. His blue eyes were striking, and not for the first time, David wished Will's former boyfriend wasn't quite so attractive.

"It's great to finally meet you and congratulations on your senate win! We'd give Will shit for hiding you away for so long, but he's had kind of a weird year, so we're letting it go."

Will made an aggrieved noise, but Riley flashed an open, friendly grin that David couldn't help returning. "Thank you. It's great to finally put faces to names, and in real time, too."

"Same here," Carter called out and peered over Riley's head, making them all laugh.

Riley turned and gestured to Carter, who stepped up with a smile and congratulations of his own. Carter actually stood taller than David by an inch or two, and his hazel eyes and voice were warm as he captured his hand. Good grief, he was even more handsome in person.

"We don't spend a lot of time up here, but we wanted to catch you before you went down." Carter dropped David's hand and cut his gaze toward Riley, and their shared smirk caught Will's attention.

"Is that code for something?"

"That's Carter-speak for 'we don't want to freak out the new guy'," Riley put in. He turned to David. "Jesse and Kyle are *really* excited to meet you."

"Oh, God," Will muttered. "What did they do?"

"Nothing too wild, I promise. They spent some time researching political-themed cocktails in honor of David's election win," Carter explained, his voice wavering with amusement at Riley's laugh. "You know how much fun they have with drink recipes."

"We had dinner at Kyle's last Saturday and I swear the things they were mixing up could peel paint." Riley shuddered. "I thought we were going to die."

Will snickered. "Did they come up with anything potable?"

"Eventually, yes, but it took a few tries," Carter replied. "First, they made the Bipartisan Compromise and none of us liked them—Everclear and egg whites do not appeal." He grimaced. "They mixed up some Democrats next, which I'm pretty sure were a nod to you, Will."

"They're fantastically delicious," Riley declared. "Political affiliations aside, I'm planning to ask Kyle to mix up a round."

Will grinned. "I'm sure David won't be offended, but is there a cocktail to honor his party, too?"

"Not that they could find, but Kyle made a drink called the Darkside Iced Tea and Jesse decided it's 'the one'."

David furrowed his brows. "Never heard of it."

"It's a tribute to the Long Island Iced Tea," Carter said. "In place of the clear liquors and Coke, there's dark liquors—rye whiskey, rum, orange liqueur, an herbal liqueur I'd never heard of—"

"And again, delicious." Riley exchanged another grin with his partner. "They were pretty pleased to find a cocktail they consider not only a hat tip to your new hometown but also something we'd all want to drink."

"Have you two eaten?" Carter asked. "If not, we can order some plates from the kitchen here before we go down."

"We had dinner with my sister before coming here," David replied. "Will even invited Isabel along tonight, but she already had plans."

"Next time then," Riley suggested. He picked Will's bag up from the table. "Come on, let's get downstairs before Jesse's limited patience is exhausted and he comes prowling to find you himself."

Despite knowing what to expect, David found the experience of finding and being admitted to the secret bar in the pub's basement utterly charming. The unmarked doors and hidden staircase appealed to the comic reader in him, and he bit back a laugh when Will picked up the handset of the old-fashioned wall mounted phone to utter the evening's special passphrase— "I'm out of Grandpa's cough medicine."

Once downstairs, Riley and Carter took their bags to store in Jesse and Kyle's office, leaving Will to show him around a bit. Under had an elegant, masculine vibe while remaining welcoming. Low lighting set off the sleek furnishings, and the house music piping in through unseen speakers throbbed at levels low enough not to discourage the conversation of the roughly fifteen people scattered around the room.

"I can see why you like spending time here," he said. "This place is gorgeous."

"Not nearly as gorgeous as you, Senator."

Jesse Murtagh's velvety voice was like a physical touch. David turned to meet their host's gaze and found Jesse standing behind the bar with a wild smile, cocktail shaker in hand and styled as if he'd stepped out of a magazine ad.

"That's unbelievably cheesy, Jesse, even for you," Will shot back, his expression amused. "You disappoint me."

Jesse gasped and placed a hand over his heart with dramatic flair that made both David and Will laugh. "You wound me, Professor—I see your sharp tongue hasn't dulled at all." He sniffed. "That said, come over here so I can pour and talk to you without shouting."

They seated themselves at the bar as Jesse raised the metal container with both hands and shook it briskly, making its contents rattle. He'd dressed simply in dark trousers and a navy pullover that set off his fair complexion, and his blue eyes sparkled merrily. He set the shaker down and pulled off its top.

"I'm sure Carter and Riley told you all about the mixing Kyle and I did the other night." Placing the strainer on top of the shaker, Jesse poured its contents into two highball glasses filled with ice. "We did get carried away, but the odd hangover is justified in the name of research. Carter always stops at two because of his medication anyway, and he's happy to act as official taster."

Jesse garnished the glasses with lemon slices, and set them down in front of David and Will with a flourish. "Drink up in the name of science, gentlemen—whence these came, there will surely be more." Jesse paused then and furrowed his thick brows at David. "Shit, I should have asked—you believe in science, don't you?"

"With the entirety of my brain," David replied with a laugh. "My sister is a scientist, actually, and she likes to think she keeps me on the straight and narrow."

Jesse stared him up and down, a slow grin curving his full lips. "You look anything but straight to me, Senator, but you let your sister keep thinking that." He extended a hand. "Jesse, rogue and amateur mixologist."

"Also professional cheeseball," Will muttered and Jesse stuck out his tongue.

David shook Jesse's hand. "David. You already know what I do for a living, so I won't bore you with the details. Besides, Will and I came out tonight to relax and there's no way in hell that'll happen if we start talking politics. We've already talked ad nauseum today about a bill to provide public employee retirees with permanent partial cost-of-living increases in New York State."

"That's because I still can't believe it even needs to be discussed," Will sniped. Jesse immediately held up a hand and laughed.

"Time out. For the record, I agree—God knows, Will's never needed any help being tense."

"I'm sitting right here you know," Will chided, his brow creased. "Don't be an asshole."

"Yes, dear."

"Where's your better half?" Will asked as Jesse rinsed out the shaker. "Don't tell me he's not here after the way Carter and Riley built him up."

"Will's speaking figuratively when he says 'better half'," Jesse said to David, then nodded toward the far end of the room. "Your friendly neighborhood bartender is right over there with Carter and Riley, probably hatching an evil plot to take over the world."

David turned his attention to the trio approaching the bar, all talking and laughing with one another. In contrast to Jesse's warm gold-and-blue coloring, Kyle McKee's was dramatic, all pale skin and dark eyes and hair, emphasized by his clean shave and black button-down shirt and trousers. He greeted David with a genuine smile and grasped his hand between his before walking around the bar to Jesse's side.

"I hope one of those is for me," Kyle said pointedly as Jesse garnished another pair of Iced Teas with lemon slices.

"Sure, darlin'," Jesse drawled. "Though Carter and Riley appear to have left their beers upstairs."

"It's true," Riley said. "We got to talking with Will and David and totally forgot about them."

Kyle slid one drink toward Riley and the other toward Carter. "No worries. It's not like I can't make more. Now, how about you make some room, babe, and let a professional help with the mixin'?"

The group spent the evening talking and joking over cocktails while David got to know Will's friends. They were excellent company, all smart, likeable and welcoming. He talked books with Riley and travel with Jesse and Kyle, and was genuinely excited to discuss Carter's work for the Corporate Equality Campaign. They tabled their discussion after Will chided them for talking too much business, however, so Kyle introduced David and Will to the bar's other patrons, many of whom were friends or lovers of both Jesse and Kyle. It wasn't easy to tell, given Jesse flirted openly with everyone, including David and Will.

David didn't know what to make of Jesse, when it came right down to it, and he'd never known anyone so completely forthright about sex. An air of unpredictability surrounded Jesse, perhaps rooted in his apparent disregard for people's relationships. He made his feelings of attraction to people known, regardless of pairings. David didn't think Jesse was actually pursuing Will or himself, but he made it clear he wasn't averse to getting one if not both of them into bed.

David watched Jesse with Will and Riley. They'd seated themselves on one of the low couches scattered throughout the room and while Will wasn't smashed, the drinks were affecting him. He was loose-limbed and pink-cheeked, his eyes bright as he and Riley laughed at Jesse's storytelling. David wasn't sure he'd ever seen Will more handsome.

"Don't take Jesse's flirting seriously."

David's eyes went wide at the quiet words. He turned to Carter and was arrested by his earnest expression. "I'm not," he replied with a smile. "Will told me all about Jesse before he ever asked me to come here."

Carter shrugged, but David saw the line of his shoulders relax fractionally. "Flirting is a kind of second language for Jesse. I'm not sure he even knows he's doing it a lot of the time. Most people find it easy to write him off as a total libertine, but he does respect other people's boundaries."

David cocked his head, intrigued by Carter's unknowing echo of his own thoughts.

"He'd never actually go through with anything you weren't sure about, despite what people think, and he's not into couples unless they're into him." Carter glanced up as Kyle sent down a tall glass filled with a deep crimson cocktail and garnished with silver-green leaves.

"Blackberry Sage Spritzer," he said and grinned when Carter smiled.

"Thanks, babe."

"So the jokey comments about wanting to get Will and me into bed?" David hedged.

"Oh, Jesse's definitely serious about wanting to get you into bed," Kyle agreed. "But the comments are simply that—joking unless both of you wanted to make it happen. Everyone needs to be on board before he'd ever agree to anything."

"That happens far less often than you'd think," Carter added. "I won't say Jesse's all show—he's not. But he'd never pursue someone who didn't want him, too. Will's not interested in Jesse and Jesse knows it, but they both play along."

Kyle chuckled. "Jesse was beside himself when he got a gander at your photo in the paper. He couldn't believe Will met you first. He and Will haven't always gotten along either, so this," he said with a wave at the group on the couch, "is one hell of an improvement."

"Really?" David shook his head, nonplussed. "Will said he'd had trouble reconciling himself to Riley's relationship with you, Carter, but I didn't know that awkwardness extended out further."

"I wouldn't call it awkwardness so much as outright hostility." Carter grinned at Kyle's low laugh. "Will didn't much care for anyone close to me for a long time, which put Kyle on the shit list alongside Jesse. That all changed once we started hanging out here at Under and Will got to know us better."

"I've been on the receiving end of that hostility myself—I understand how unpleasant it can be," David confided. "But Will has nothing but warm things to say when he speaks of you. He's very fond of this place and coming here has been a lifeline for him this past year."

The impact of his words on Carter and Kyle was clear in their faces.

"We're his friends, David," Carter said quietly, "whether Will knows that or not. If he needs us, we'll be there."

David simply nodded. The obvious loyalty these men had toward one another made him glad Will had them in his corner.

"I don't see him with friends much, you know," he said. "Outside of family friends and neighbors, anyway, and a few people he knew back in high school who still live around Long Island. We've both had so much to do, we tend to retreat a bit when we have free time and hunker down together." David shrugged. "Will's different with you all than he is with people back in Garden City. Less burdened and more relaxed. It's nice to see that side of him with someone other than me."

"How is he?" Carter wanted to know. "Riley worries about him, especially since he skipped out on the party last month."

"He's managing," David replied. "He compartmentalizes a lot of his pain, because the family expects him to be the strong one. It's incredibly fortunate he and his father mended fences. I think they're both struggling with regret for not reaching out before Bill's health put a timeline on their relationship." He blew out a long breath, weighed down by the Martin family's fractured history. "I know Will's grateful they had the opportunity to change each other's lives for the better after so many years of letting the past drag them down."

Kyle regarded him solemnly, while Carter's handsome face took on an expression of true sadness.

"Call us if he needs us," Kyle said. "No questions asked."

David had time to nod before Jesse slid in beside Carter, his smile wide. "Gentlemen, I must protest at these long faces," he chided and curled one arm around Carter's waist. "Clearly, you're having conversations that are much too serious and should stop immediately."

Carter chuckled. "Sorry, babe."

"That's better." Jesse pressed a loud, smacking kiss on Carter's cheek before turning to Kyle. "Will has requested a round of Democrats, my good man, and I wondered if you'd be so kind as to help me mix them?"

Kyle cocked a brow. "Do you remember the recipe?"

"It's a bit fuzzy," Jesse admitted. He gave Carter another squeeze then made his way around the bar. "That's why without you and your freaky memory, this place and I would truly be lost."

Kyle gave an enormous eye roll. "Girl, please with the dramatics. Have you been reading Shakespeare again?"

"I'm being serious! And no!"

Laughing, David and Carter got to their feet. David caught Will's eye as they crossed the room to the couch, and his smile made David's heart seemed to skip a beat. This weekend away had been a very good idea and David was determined to enjoy each minute.

Chapter Nineteen

"And I am thankful today to have all of my family surrounding me." Will's father squeezed his hand. "This has been a difficult year but I am grateful for what it's allowed me to do. I am deeply appreciative to all of you for being here to support me and each other."

Bill looked gray and tired already in the chair at the head of the table. He'd needed a wheelchair to get from his bedroom to the dining room. The house was large, but not *that* large. He grew weaker by the day. He'd spent the past few days sleeping a lot, and on fairly high doses of medication. He had eased off them in order to enjoy dinner with the family, but Will knew his father had to be hurting.

Will glanced around the Thanksgiving table at the people assembled. Everyone his father had hoped would be there had made it. His mother sat across the table from Will, and David beside him. Liv and Phillip sat next to David, plus their kids, Adam and Jocelyn. Isabel and Allen were both there as well. Will had been surprised when Isabel had R.S.V.P.'d for two, but

David had told him she and Allen were making progress with their relationship.

Will looked at David and shared the bittersweet moment. Liv had started crying halfway through everyone sharing what they were grateful for. Listening had been difficult for Will, too, but he'd reconciled with his family and had David, and that was all that mattered.

"Happy Thanksgiving," Bill said. "Now, let's eat! Well, you eat. I'll enjoy my delicious meal replacement shake." He tried to joke, but it fell a little flat. Will gave his father a sympathetic look. Thanksgiving had always been his favorite holiday and it had to be torturing him not to partake.

"Will, I'd like you to carve."

Will blinked. Carving was one of Bill's favorite traditions and now he was clearly passing the torch.

He cleared his throat. "Sure, Dad. I could use some instructions, though. Think you can walk me through it?"

"Of course."

Will stood and took the offered knife and fork from his father. They'd given Greta the day off to be with her family. Rather than make it all herself, his mother had hired a personal chef to come in and make dinner, using her recipes and under her supervision.

It had taken the bulk of the work off her and the food looked wonderful.

"Now, this is how you want to begin..." His father instructed.

Will listened attentively as his father walked him through it, his heart aching at the thought that every family celebration would be different from here on out. Will doubted his father would even make it to

Christmas. And to think of all the holidays he'd missed over the years. All that time lost. And wasted.

He struggled to maintain his composure as he finished carving and sat back down again.

"You okay?" David leaned in and spoke quietly, his voice disguised by the babble of sound around them as people passed dishes and filled their plates.

Will shrugged. "I'm hanging in there. It's just..."

"I know." David gave Will's shoulder a squeeze.

"So, Will, how is your new role treating you?" Phillip asked a few minutes later.

Will glanced up from his forkful of mashed potatoes. "As a full-time writer?"

"As partner to a politician."

"Oh." Will chuckled. "It's not as bad as I expected. I could do without the interviews, but Mom was right, giving in to a few seems to be working. That way I'm not giving the impression I'm blowing them off completely, but it gives me some bargaining power about what I will and won't talk about. And, while I resisted the idea at first, having a consultant – along with David's campaign manager and Mom – has helped."

"I heard women in the checkout line at the store gushing about how adorable you two are – it was so gross," Isabel said with a smile. "And Mabel is the icing on the cake. I loved the photo shoot of the three of you in the park."

David chuckled. "I'll have to give Mabel an extra treat when I get home."

"I love dogs!" Jocelyn piped up from the other end of the table. "Can I meet her? Mom won't get one because Dad's allergic."

Phillip chuckled. "I know. We ruin all your fun, don't we?"

David smiled at Will's ten-year-old niece. "I'd love to have you meet Mabel. She's very friendly and I'm sure you two would have a lot of fun. If your parents say it's okay, maybe we can figure out a time when you can come over and hang out with her for an afternoon."

"Me too!" Adam piped up. "I wanna come!"

"Thank you, David," Olivia said with a smile. "That's very generous of you. If you're sure you're feeling brave enough to take them both off my hands for an afternoon *and* give them their dog fix, that would be wonderful."

Will nodded and scooped up some cranberry sauce. "Of course. Maybe they could come over during Christmas break." He glanced at David who nodded.

"If we're lucky, we'll have snow. You should see her play in it! She acts like a puppy. In fact, after dinner I can show you some videos of her playing in the first snowfall we had last winter."

Jocelyn and Adam were wide-eyed with excitement at the idea and enthusiastically agreed.

Will caught his mother looking at him from across the table with a small smile. His father had been right to get everyone together. David was getting to know his extended family and he had an opportunity to get to know David's.

He really did have a lot to be grateful for.

* * * *

Bill made it halfway through the meal before excusing himself. The part-time nurse the family had hired was there and she and Agnes helped him to bed and gave him more pain medication.

After dinner, everyone but Bill gathered in the living room to play board games. They ate pumpkin and pecan pies, and some excellent pumpkin cheesecake bars Isabel had made. On top of dinner and wine, Will felt stuffed but content.

Isabel kissed his cheek as everyone gathered in the foyer, saying their goodbyes. "Happy Thanksgiving. Thank you for inviting us."

He smiled at David's sister. "We're glad you could make it. I know my father was a bit demanding about David coming, and we appreciate you being so accommodating."

She offered him a sympathetic smile. "Under the circumstances, it's the least we could do."

Isabel and Allen had appeared comfortable around one another during dinner and there was little sign of strain between them. Will was relieved, not only because the meal had gone smoothly, but because he wanted David and his sister to be happy.

Truthfully, he liked Allen. He was a warm, engaging man and Will had enjoyed having two more liberals in his corner during the spirited but friendly debate around the Thanksgiving table.

"We appreciate that," Will said, including his parents in the statement. "It's been a rough year, but my father was determined we all come together today."

"It was lovely, truly." Isabel squeezed Will's arm. "And I'm so pleased you and David worked things out. He's incredibly happy."

Will smiled. "I am too."

He shook Allen's hand, and a few minutes later, the guests cleared out leaving only Will, Agnes and David standing there.

"I'm going to check on your father," Agnes said. "David, if I don't see you before you go, thank you for coming."

She said her goodbyes and disappeared down the hall.

David slipped his arms around Will, who went into his embrace gratefully. "How are you feeling?"

"Dead-tired," Will said. "But glad we did this."

"Yeah, me too." David dropped a kiss to his temple. "Do you plan to stay here or do you want to come over?"

Will debated for a moment. "I think I'll stay here tonight. I'm beat and I should be here in case my parents need anything. Dad looked pretty wiped out by the time he excused himself."

David nodded. "Of course."

"See you tomorrow?"

"Absolutely." David leaned in to press a lingering kiss on Will's lips. "Sleep well," he said when he finally drew back.

"You too." Will spent a moment savoring the feel of David's arms around him. "G'night."

"Night." David let himself out and shut the door with a quiet click.

Will sighed and locked up behind him. He hated seeing David go. He'd briefly considered asking him to stay, but it didn't quite feel right when Will wasn't sure about how his parents would feel about it. Now wasn't the time to push their comfort levels.

Will headed down the hall as Agnes slipped out of the den, but before she could close the French doors, he stopped her. "Wait, I'm going to say goodnight."

Agnes looked up at Will with a small frown. "He's exhausted."

"I know. I'll keep it brief. I don't want to miss any opportunities."

A pained expression crossed her face, but she nodded and stepped back.

The room was dim save for a small light beside the bed and one in the corner as Will entered, and he could hear his father's strained breathing. So far Bill had refused oxygen, but Will wasn't sure how much longer he could do that.

"Hey, Dad," Will said quietly. The nurse had left for the evening, and his father looked pale and gaunt. "I know you're tired but I wanted to say goodnight."

"Come here, son." Bill held a frail hand out to him. Will moved closer and took it, grasping the cool skin gently.

"I'm glad you insisted on the full family Thanksgiving. It was nice."

"Yes, it was." His father drew in a shallow breath. "I want you to know I'm happy for you. For you and David. You make each other happy." The last part sounded like an order as opposed to a statement, so Will nodded. "And I want you to know how proud of you I am."

"I know." Tears gathered in Will's eyes and he blinked them back. "Thank you."

"You take care of your mother and sister when I'm gone." There was a slight slur to his words.

"I will," Will choked out. Time was slipping through his fingers so fast. How long did his father have left? A week? A few days, maybe? It seemed so bitterly unfair.

For the first time in many, many years, Will pressed his lips to his father's skin. His cheek was slightly rough and whiskery, though Agnes still dutifully shaved him every morning. "G'night, Dad." Will gently squeezed his father's hand and let go, afraid anything more vigorous would be too much. "I love you."

"I love you, too, son." Bill's eyelids dipped, opened once, and closed.

Will turned out the light beside the bed, leaving the lamp in the far corner on.

He closed the doors behind him and leaned against the wall, squeezing his eyes tightly shut. Will bitterly resented the fact he had so little time left with the man who was finally his father again. A man Will was desperate to get to know now.

It seemed so pointless and cruel for them to have reunited nearly too late.

Eventually, Will pulled himself together and walked slowly down the hall. He turned off lights as he moved, but left one burning in the hall for Agnes. Most nights she spent by Bill's side, sometimes dozing in the recliner by his bed. She slept for a few more hours after the nurse arrived each morning, but she got far less sleep than she should.

In the past, Will hadn't understood his mother's unwavering devotion to her husband, but he'd finally begun to grasp it. The weeks without David had been excruciating and their relationship had barely begun. What must it be like to be with the same person for over fifty years? And how impossible would it be to say goodbye?

Will ran into his mother on the stairs. She'd gathered her hair in a braid and wrapped herself in her robe. Her face, stripped of makeup, looked tired.

Will hugged her when she reached the foot and pressed his lips to her forehead. "Love you, Mom."

"I love you too, my darling. Sleep well."

Will didn't respond in kind. His mother wouldn't. But what did it matter at this point? There was so little time left. He'd keep an eye on her to be sure she wasn't getting too close to exhaustion but he wouldn't intervene otherwise.

He walked up the stairs slowly, debating if he had the energy to shower or not. The sight of his bed seemed far more tempting. He did the bare minimum and brushed his teeth before stripping down to his boxers then collapsed onto the bed with a grateful groan and burrowed under the covers. Will had a fleeting thought of missing the feel of David's body against his before he succumbed to sleep.

Will awoke to a quiet house. He'd slept later than usual and was struck by how still everything seemed as he came downstairs. Greta wasn't humming as she dusted the table in the hallway or laughing in the kitchen with Agnes, and it was a moment before he remembered the family had given Greta time off for the holiday.

Agnes was nowhere to be seen when Will poked his head into the kitchen. He frowned and gently rapped his knuckles on the door to the den, wondering if maybe she was helping the nurse.

When no answer came, he opened the door and peered in. His breath caught as he met his mother's gaze. Agnes sat in the chair beside his father and her expression set the first stirrings of uneasiness in Will.

He cast his eyes over Bill's form in the hospital bed and his heart sank.

Will crossed the room, taking in the sight of his father lying motionless, his eyes closed. Although Will strained to see the rise and fall of his breath, there was nothing. *No. Please no.* Will's brain rebelled at what he saw. He'd hoped for a few more weeks. Or at least a few more days.

"Mom?" he said quietly. His voice cracked.

She shook her head and reached for Will to grasp his hand. Her expression was serene, despite the deep sorrow in her eyes. "He's gone," she said.

Will crouched down, his heart aching. "When?"

"Last night. We talked for a short time, then he drifted off to sleep. I dozed for a while too, but woke when he started breathing hard. He was gone shortly after. He didn't wake up."

"Oh, Mom." Will's heart clenched.

Tears spilled down her cheeks. She fell forward onto Will's shoulder and made a quiet, whimpering sound. He held her close for a long time, long after his leg had gone numb and she'd loosed a last shuddering sob.

His whole chest throbbed and eyes burned, but they were dry. He would cry later. For now, he needed to take care of his mother. He gently let her go and climbed to his feet, wincing as blood began to flow again.

"What do you need me to do?" he asked softly.

Agnes dabbed at her eyes with a tissue. "Call your sister. I know I should but I...I don't know if I can get the words out."

"Hey, it's okay," he said soothingly. "I'll call Liv."

"Thank you. Oh, and Greta, too, please. She's like family."

"Of course. What about…other arrangements?" Everything had been discussed and all of Bill's affairs were in order, but Will wasn't sure what happened next. He'd avoided thinking about it.

"The nurse has been here. She's called the coroner, and they'll come shortly and release him to the funeral home. Your father wanted everything in order, of course." She smiled tremulously. "He was always looking out for me. Even at the end."

"I know." Will squeezed his mother's hand. "I'd better call Liv now, then. In case she wants to say goodbye before — before they take him."

Agnes squeezed back. "Thank you."

Will walked slowly into the sunroom. His whole body felt leaden and he had to force himself to put one foot in front of the other. He hesitated before he tapped his sister's number on his phone.

"Hey, what's up, little brother?" Olivia asked, her voice bright. She sounded like she'd been laughing and it hurt to deliver such horrible news.

"Liv." He cleared his throat. "It's…"

He heard her breath catch. "No, Will…"

"I'm sorry, Livvie. Dad's gone," he finally managed.

For a moment he heard only silence, then the sound of muffled crying.

"I'm sorry," he said softly. "Mom was with him. And he went peacefully."

"No! He wasn't supposed to go!" she cried out, startling him. "He was supposed to stay and fight! Dad was a fighter and…" A fresh wave of sobs overcame her. "I wanted…"

"I know. I wanted more time too." His voice was thick. "Do you want to come say goodbye before they take him to the funeral home?"

"Yes." Olivia sniffled. "I'll be right there. I-I have to tell the kids and see if the neighbor will keep an eye on them while I come over. Phil went into the office and I'm not sure how long it will take him to get home."

"Are you okay to drive? Or do you need me to come pick you up?"

"I'm okay." She drew in a deep, shuddering breath and blew it out slowly. "See you in a little bit."

"Be safe," Will said quietly. After he ended the call, he walked into the kitchen and found his mother by the coffeemaker. She lifted the pot, but her hands shook as she moved to fill the mug.

"Let me get that," Will said gently and took it from her. "I called Liv. She'll be on her way over shortly."

Agnes sighed. "Thank you. I don't know what I'd do without you here."

After Liv came to say her goodbyes, Will spoke with the funeral director who'd come to take Bill to the funeral home. He called the medical supply company to come pick up the supplies and equipment and he and his mother spent a good portion of the day making phone calls to a few relatives, colleagues and friends. Bill's former staff members were also notified, and his father's assistant handled the media announcement.

Will also left a choked message for David, who called an hour later, after leaving a meeting. Will's voice broke when he told David the news and David promised to be there as soon as possible.

By early evening, Will was completely wrung out. Agnes had gone upstairs to rest, and he sat sprawled in an armchair in the living room waiting for David. No doubt there were other things Will should be doing, but he was too numb to manage a coherent thought.

A knock on the door brought a sense of relief. He let David in and the sight of his face made Will's heart ache. David stepped inside and closed the door behind him. He gave Will a long, searching look.

"Oh, Will. C'mere," David said softly. Will nearly fell into David's arms. Something in his chest cracked wide open, threatening to spill out the bottled-up emotions from the day as David pulled him close. "I've got you."

Will broke.

He muffled a wordless sound of grief in David's thick wool jacket. The tears he'd held in check all day streamed down his cheeks, soaking into the fabric. His chest heaved and he struggled to pull himself back together, but in the shelter of David's arms he couldn't seem to stop them.

David stroked his hair and murmured quiet words of reassurance and support that overwhelmed Will even as they soothed him. It was all too much, and exactly what he needed.

When Will finally pulled back, he wiped at his eyes and David pressed a tissue into his hand. He blew his nose and looked at David.

"I'm sorry I couldn't get here earlier." David appeared anguished.

"No, no, it's fine," he reassured David. "I know you came as soon as you could. I feel so fucking lost. How do I deal with this?"

He was met with a glance filled with tender understanding. David had been in his shoes. Worse, because he had lost both his father and his mother at the same time and there had been no time for goodbyes. Will couldn't imagine it.

"Take it one day at a time," David said. "One hour at a time if you need to. I'll be here. I told Jerry to clear my schedule of everything for the next few days."

"Thank you," Will said gratefully. "I just…"

"Hey, it's okay." David pulled him in for another hug and for a while they simply stood there holding each other.

"Will?" A soft hand touched his elbow.

He pulled back, startled. He hadn't even heard his mother come down the stairs. "Sorry, Mom, I…"

She shushed him. "No, don't apologize. You were strong for Olivia and me earlier, now let David be strong for you."

Will managed a faint smile. "I'm trying."

"Why don't you two go upstairs? Take a nap, talk, whatever you need."

"Are you sure? Is there anything else we need to do?"

Agnes gave him a small smile. "Tomorrow will be soon enough. Rest. I'm going to try to do the same."

"Okay," Will agreed.

"And if David wants to spend the night that's fine by me."

Will didn't argue. "Thanks, Mom."

He took David's hand and led him up the stairs to his childhood bedroom.

"How are you feeling?" David asked quietly when Will had shut the door after him.

Will sighed. "Drained. Sometimes numb."

"That's natural." David smoothed Will's hair off his forehead. "What can I do for you? Are you hungry?"

Will thought for a moment, then shook his head. "Not particularly."

"What do you need right now?"

"You." Will swallowed past the lump in his throat. "I want to lie down with you."

David reached to unknot his tie before Will had finished speaking. They both stripped down to their underwear and Will allowed David to maneuver him under the covers.

The moment he was horizontal, a bone-deep sense of exhaustion settled over him. He yawned. "Shit, I knew I was tired, but I didn't realize *how* tired until now."

"So, sleep." David ran his fingers through Will's hair. "I'm not going anywhere."

"But my Mom," Will protested feebly. "She says she's fine, but…"

"Shh," David soothed him. "I'll go downstairs and check on her in a while. You rest."

"Okay." Will nodded sleepily, too weary to argue. It felt good to have someone else take over and make the decisions.

Sometime later, he woke to a dark room illuminated by the light of David's phone. For a moment, Will forgot where they were and why, but when he remembered, grief settled over him like a sodden blanket.

"Hey," he managed. His voice sounded hoarse and scratchy.

"Hey." David set down his phone. "How'd you sleep?"

"Good, I think. How long was I out?"

"Mmm, almost two hours."

"How's my mom?"

"She's okay. I found her curled up with a book and some tea. She told me to stop fussing and take care of you." Will could hear the smile in David's voice. "You two are so much alike. Always worried about each other, not yourselves. But she said she'd take a sleeping pill and go to bed."

"Good." Will stretched and his stomach rumbled. Had he had anything but coffee that day? "God, I'm starving."

"I have the solution for that." David clicked on the light and once Will stopped blinking and his eyes adjusted, he spotted a plate on the nightstand. "I ate and brought food up for you a while ago."

"You wonderful, wonderful man." Will sat upright and propped himself against the headboard.

David chuckled and handed the plate to him. "Turkey, provolone and pesto sandwich."

"Where did you get that from?" Will asked, his voice slightly muffled by his first bite.

"Someone from Bill's office brought a platter by."

"Oh God, it's so good." Will relaxed once he'd gotten half of the sandwich into him. "Thank you for the food. And for being here. I…" He shook his head. "I couldn't have done this alone."

David squeezed his thigh. "And you're not going to have to."

* * * *

"Thank you for coming today," Will greeted the next person in line and shook her hand. How many times had he said that in the past two days? A public viewing had been held yesterday at the funeral home and today's viewing was for close friends and family.

Agnes, Olivia, and Phillip stood to Will's left and David to his right. David looked handsome in his black suit and subtle charcoal-and-black striped tie, but most importantly, he acted as Will's anchor. Will was sure he wouldn't have made it through this without him.

David had done so much for all of them. If Will had ever doubted he was the kind of partner he needed, his doubts were gone now.

Will extended a hand to the next person. "Thank you for coming today."

"How are you holding up?"

Will looked at the man in front of him and did a double take when his brilliant blue eyes and high cheekbones finally registered. "Oh, God. Riley. I didn't even..." He shook his head. "I'm sorry. I'm kinda on automatic pilot."

"Of course." Riley grasped his upper arm and squeezed. "That's understandable."

"Thank you for coming," Will said, and really meant it. "You have no idea how grateful I am you're here."

"Of course. We all wanted to be." Will glanced down the line of guests and saw Carter talking to Liv, and Kyle standing in front of Agnes. Past Kyle was Jesse.

"You all came?"

Riley looked incredulous. "Of course we did, Will."

"That—that means a lot." Gabe and Charles had called Will and sent their condolences with a bouquet of flowers. Will wasn't upset not to see them today, but their absence drove home the knowledge the speakeasy guys had become some of Will's closest friends. He was deeply grateful for their presence. Natalie and Julian had come too and Will was humbled by the support he'd gotten from all of them. "Please come back to the house after the funeral, if you can. We're holding a luncheon."

"Of course." Riley tipped his head toward the line forming. "I'd better move along. I'm holding things up."

"Thanks again." Will hugged him and let him go.

He hugged and thanked the rest of the guys as they moved past, and invited them back to the house after the funeral. The line eventually dwindled, and Will mingled with the guests. He listened to them speak about Bill and reminisce about times they'd spent with him. So many of the stories made Will's heart ache for the time he'd missed with his father, but they helped too, and gave him a clearer picture of the man Bill had become in the years they were estranged.

"I'm glad your friends made it," David murmured later that afternoon as a limo whisked them toward the Protestant church the Martin family had attended for generations.

Will nodded. "So am I. Those guys are pretty amazing."

"I'm glad you have them in your life," David said.

"Me too," Will said. "And I'm so grateful for you, David. I..." He choked up, unable to finish.

I love you, he thought.

The truth of his feelings settled over Will with a sudden, intense clarity. He loved David Mori. A quiet contentment filled Will in the midst of his grief. His mother glanced over at them, and a soft smile lightened the heavy grief she'd carried for days.

When David squeezed his hand, Will leaned his shoulder against David's. This wasn't the time or the place to express his feelings, but the certainty of his feelings gave Will strength.

With David by his side, he could make it through the funeral service, interment at the cemetery and luncheon.

Will recalled his father's words instructing him and David to take care of each other. He wanted nothing more. He would always be sorry he'd lost so much time with his father, but in the end, they'd mended the rift between them and that was all that mattered.

The limo pulled up in front of the church, and Will helped his mother out. They climbed the stairs of the church and David joined the funeral director and the other pallbearers. Will glanced back at the man he loved, and felt a profound sense of gratitude toward his father.

Thank you, Dad, he thought. *Thank you for bringing David into my life.*

Chapter Twenty

Following Bill's interment, many of the mourners returned to the Martin family home, where the late senator's family and friends mixed with his colleagues over luncheon. David kept an eye on Will throughout the afternoon, and enlisted Isabel's help to make sure Will took time to eat and drink and even sit down once in a while, rather than being constantly on the go taking care of everyone else.

Watching over Will distracted David from his own sadness. He'd lost a mentor and friend, and eventually he'd need to process his grief, but he'd put it off starting that first evening after Bill's death. He'd held Will while he cried, and his sorrow and regret had cracked David's own heart.

Now, as they chatted with some of Bill's staff in the dining room, a flash of movement by the doorway leading to the foyer caught David's eye. Glancing around, he spotted Jocelyn and Adam peering at him around the door's frame. He smiled as both children waved him over, and nearly laughed when Adam smacked Jocelyn with one of his wild gestures.

"Ow!"

David turned back to Will and the others. "Would you excuse me? It appears I'm needed in the other room," he explained, then inclined his head toward the door. The children froze under the scrutiny of several sets of eyes, and quickly disappeared back around the doorframe, creating an only slightly muffled racket.

Will bit his lip and smiled at David. "I'd say it's pretty urgent," he replied over the others' chuckles. "You'd better go, but don't be afraid to send up a flare if you need help."

David squeezed Will's arm and held his gaze, simply because he could. Will hadn't appeared anything but crushed for days, and seeing a spark of light in his eyes now lifted David's own low spirits.

"Wish me luck," he joked quietly before making his way to the foyer.

He found Jocelyn and Adam engaged in a furious wrestling match that stopped the moment they spotted him. Both children were towheads like their father but had inherited their mother's soft corkscrew curls and lively brown eyes, which they turned on David like a pair of dolls.

"Hi, guys." He smiled and kept his voice low. "What's up?"

Jocelyn smoothed down the soft gray skirt of her dress. With her pink ribbon sash, she resembled a sweet, slightly somber ballerina. "Um. Adam and I were upstairs and we heard a noise in Uncle Will's room."

Adam nodded. "It sounded like a...doggy kind of noise."

David hummed and glanced between them. "Well, that was Mabel. I brought her with me this morning because I knew I'd be busy all day helping people remember your grandpa."

His heart sank as he recognized how subdued Jocelyn and Adam were acting compared to their first meeting. He squatted down to put himself at the kids' level.

"You know, Mabel hasn't been out of that room since this morning and this would be a good time for me to bring her outside to do her business." Carefully, he reached out to straighten Adam's tiny blue tie then dropped his hand again. "If your mom and dad say it's okay, I'd bet Mabel would love to meet you. After she finishes peeing by the bushes near the neighbor's yard, anyway." He smiled and Jocelyn covered a laugh with both hands and Adam giggled outright.

"Go on and ask your parents and make sure they don't mind, and meet us outside if you can," David urged, then straightened up as they took off down the hall in search of Olivia and Phillip. He nearly jumped when Agnes cleared her throat behind him.

"That was very nice of you," she said when he turned to face her. "We've all been so busy the last few days taking care of the arrangements, I'm sure the children are wondering when things will go back to normal."

"Maybe," David allowed. "They seem okay, if quiet. Maybe some time outside will give them a chance to unwind, and God knows Mabel will love the attention."

Agnes stepped forward to squeeze his arm. A smile graced her careworn face. "Thank you for taking care of us, and of Will in particular. I hope you know you've come to mean a great deal to him."

The emotions rushing through David took him off guard and he quickly laid his hand over Agnes' to keep himself in check. He did know Will cared. Will's every touch and word and glance spoke of his affection. Even in the midst of these dark days, when he met Will's gaze, he found acceptance and tenderness. Someday, he hoped, he'd find love, too.

"Will means a lot to me, too, Agnes. He and I... We took the long way around to figuring out what we are to each other but I think we're on the same path now."

"I'm sure of it." Agnes patted David's hand. "Now, go on and take a break for yourself, dear — you deserve it. I'll let Will know you stepped outside with your girl."

As promised, David had Mabel out by the neighbor's bushes when Jocelyn and Adam emerged from the house through the patio doors, and both of them made a beeline across the yard. Quickly, David tightened Mabel's lead and gave her the command to sit, then waited for the children to get closer before he held up a hand in what Isabel called his 'slow your roll' gesture. Typically, Mabel behaved very well with children, but he didn't want today to be the first time she spurned someone's advances.

"Hi again, guys," he said and smiled as Jocelyn and Adam came to a stop a short distance away. "So-o-o, this is Mabel. She likes to sniff people when she first meets them. I'll walk her over to you and you just keep your hands at your sides while she figures out who you are with her nose, okay?"

"Does Mabel like kids?" Adam asked, and David smiled even wider. He gave Mabel the command to stand.

"That is a very good question, Adam, thanks for asking," he said. "Mabel likes kids a lot. She gets to know new people in her own way, which is why she smells everybody and checks them out, sort of the way humans shake hands when they meet."

Jocelyn and Adam giggled as the dog sniffed and huffed at their hands, and in under a minute, her movements were easy and her mouth and ears relaxed. David knew she was happy when her tail started wagging.

He showed the kids how Mabel liked to be petted and let her off the lead, and only then noticed Will's friends from the speakeasy had also come outside. Jesse, Carter, Riley and Kyle were crossing the yard toward him, carrying glasses of wine.

"I had no idea you were a dog whisperer," Jesse said with a grin. He held out an extra wine glass to David who accepted it gratefully.

"Mabel's with me sometimes when I'm working," he replied. "I like to make sure she behaves."

"I guess it'd be kind of a downer if she mauled potential voters. Pretty badass way to take out your opponents, though." Jesse winked when David laughed.

"Stop being weird," Carter chided, and turned to admire Mabel. "She's beautiful, David. You didn't buy her through a breeder, did you?"

David shook his head. "You can probably tell Mabel's mixed breed — kind of like her owner." He preened a little at Jesse's cackling.

Carter groaned. "Dude."

"Sorry, that was in poor taste, but I trust you guys to keep it a secret." David sipped from his glass as Riley and Kyle stepped up to the group. "I found Mabel on

Craigslist. My sister wanted a dog, but somehow I walked away with a puppy and Isabel escaped scot-free. But Mabel's great, so I feel like I'm the one who lucked out."

"I'd say so." Riley gestured toward the far end of the yard with his glass. "I'm pretty sure those kids would agree with you, too."

As David watched Jocelyn and Adam play with Mabel, his emotions reared up to surprising him again. He blew a long breath out through his nose and the world went out of focus. He was aware of the November air that chilled his cheeks and hands, and of movement around him and the pleasant hum of deep voices. When he blinked and came back to himself, Carter, Jesse and Kyle had moved to join Mabel and the kids, leaving only Riley by his side.

David managed a smile. "Sorry — spaced out there for a second."

"Don't apologize," Riley replied. He smiled kindly, but his gaze was almost too intense. "Thank you for letting us know about Will's dad."

David swallowed. "Kyle and Carter pulled me aside at the speakeasy a couple of weeks ago...told me to reach out if Will needed anything."

Riley nodded, then glanced back at the house. "How is he?" he asked, a frown marring his handsome face when he turned back to David. "I've talked to him several times since his dad died and he seems a little frazzled. He said today he's mostly running on autopilot."

David ran the fingers of his free hand over his lips and considered how to answer. Riley deserved the truth — he and Will had been more than friends at one time, and Riley clearly still cared for Will.

"He's hurting," David said at last. "He's worn out, too, and trying to be there for Agnes. I think living here was harder on Will than he likes to admit—he gave up a lot of himself to get close to his family again. But I know that, deep down, he's grateful he and Bill had the opportunity to get to know each other again. They put a lot of ghosts to rest."

He ran a hand over his head. "Right now, though, he's beating himself up for not coming back sooner...for not having had more time with Bill. And there's nothing anyone can do about that."

Pain flashed across Riley's face. He glanced across the yard to Carter, who'd gone down on one knee alongside Adam to pet Mabel. David knew from Will that Riley and Carter's relationship had thrown their respective families into disarray and estranged them from their parents. His heart hurt with sorrow for them both, and he silently thanked the universe Will's family hadn't given up on him, despite all appearances.

He cleared his throat. "Will's going to be okay, Riley. He's going to be sad for a long while, and there are still things he needs to figure out, but he needs time."

"We can all give him that." Sympathy tinged Riley's expression. "You should take him away for a weekend. I know Will's technically on sabbatical, but he probably needs time off from his time off, and I'll bet you do, too."

"That's a great idea. I don't think he'd leave Agnes alone right now, though."

"So, come into the city in a week or two." Riley shrugged. "I know we tend to wait for Jesse and Kyle's Thursday parties, but it's not like we can't all get together whenever we want. And you'd only be an hour's drive away from Garden City...or two hours, depending on traffic."

David chuckled, then furrowed his brow as an idea struck him. "Are you all staying overnight?"

"Yeah—we'd planned to head back to the house in Southampton and find someplace for dinner. You and Will should join us," Riley began, but trailed off when David shook his head.

"Honestly, I think we're both too worn out to make that trip—I know I am," he said with a grimace. "But if you don't mind sticking around this side of the island for a while longer, there's plenty of places here we could eat. It'd do Will good to get out for a couple of hours."

"Get out of where for a couple of hours?" Will asked. He came to stand in between David and Riley, his face pale over his black wool coat, and his eyes slightly bloodshot, but he gave David a sweet smile. "What are you two plotting over here?"

"Dinner with your crew," David replied. "Riley mentioned they're all staying over in Southampton tonight. Why don't we have dinner together? You haven't had much time to unwind over the last few days, Will. You need to recharge."

"I suggested we all go back to the beach house," Riley added, then cocked a brow. "But I think David's worried about what might happen if we let Jesse and Kyle near the bar. Can't say I blame him, either. Carter restocked the booze after Labor Day and God knows what kind of potions those two could mix up given the chance."

Will leaned into David's side. "I'm not up for speakeasy levels of revelry," he said, "but dinner sounds great. Liv and Phillip and the kids are staying here tonight, so Mom's got plenty of people to look after her if she needs it. Plus, she spent ten minutes telling me to get you out of the house tonight." He smiled at David. "I came out here to ask if you wanted to hit the crab shack in Freeport."

"Um, yes, please." David turned to Riley who immediately nodded, rubbing his hands with obvious delight.

"I second that crab motion. I'm speaking for them too," he said, and lifted a hand to wave Carter, Kyle and Jesse over.

"How many cars did you all come in?" Will asked as the others jogged across the yard, Jocelyn perched on Jesse's shoulders and Adam riding Kyle piggy-back.

"Just one," Riley replied. "Carter said he'd take over driving after dinner. He doesn't drink much because he takes medication for anxiety," he added quietly for David's and Will's benefit. "But Jesse's got a new Range Rover and keeps volunteering to drive, so we left the other cars at the beach house and rode over with him."

"Are you guys talking about my car?" Jesse asked, his eyes wide and eager. He stopped short in front of them while Jocelyn smiled down at everyone.

"No." Riley rolled his eyes. "We're talking about dinner at some crab shack in Freeport."

"Oh, yes," Kyle said. "I like me some crabs." He glanced over his shoulder at Adam, who gave him a thumbs-up. "Whaddya say, kid—think we can beat Jesse and your sister back to the house?"

Adam didn't even have time to respond before both Kyle and Jesse took off running with Mabel at their heels. The others followed behind at a slower pace, their quiet laughter audible over the kids' excited squeals.

Much later that night, David lay awake, staring into the darkness while Will slumbered at his side.

They'd shared a truly excellent dinner with their friends before parting ways with promises to get together again at the speakeasy, then gone back to David's. Will had checked in with his mom while David walked the dog, and they were too fatigued to do more than strip down and snuggle up together in David's bed. But while Will had fallen asleep almost instantly, David had not.

He blew out a long breath. He rarely had trouble sleeping, and though he tried to relax, his thoughts filled not only with memories of Bill, but of his own parents, too. A sense of restless frustration seized him every time his eyes snapped open again to stare into nothing, and when the clock on his phone read two a.m., he finally gave up.

Moving carefully to avoid waking Will, David climbed out of bed and drew on a pair of sleep pants. He made his way downstairs to his office, where he went to the walk-in closet. With Mabel curled up on her bed nearby, he pulled out the banker's boxes that housed his father's comic collection, along with a smaller lockbox where he kept his mother's family photo album. He spread out on the closet floor and flipped through the album and the books in their protective plastic sleeves, losing himself in the vivid colors and aging ink and paper smells he'd come to associate with his father's hobby from a very young age.

David missed his parents every day. Losing them so suddenly had been a shock, and while he'd moved on from their loss, he wasn't sure his heart had ever fully recovered. Even now, years later, he sometimes thought to call his mom with an idea or funny story, or to get his father's opinion on a piece of news, only to remember with a sharp, sinking ache that he couldn't call them, ever again.

Watching Bill's long decline had been terrible in its own way, but David was thankful he'd had the chance to say goodbye. Despite the imaginings of some of their colleagues, he'd never regarded Bill as a father figure. He'd valued Bill's comradeship and loyalty, though, and was grateful for the time Bill spent helping David shape his career.

Like Jack Percy, David's first boss on the political scene, Bill had recognized David's raw potential. Unasked, he'd taken on the task of guiding David without overwhelming David's ambitions with his own. David had admired Bill's conviction in his beliefs, but even more, his compassion and willingness to grow. Unlike many politicians his age and in their party, Bill had been unafraid of self-reflection. He'd shown remarkable willingness and capacity to change, and tried until the very end to understand the needs of the people he represented.

Now, as he faced his second term in the Senate, the loss of his friend cut deep.

Mabel's stirring caught his attention before Will appeared in the doorframe, wearing one of David's old law school T-shirts and an expression of concern. "Are you okay?"

David nodded and cleared his throat, unsurprised by the moisture that blurred his vision. "I'm fine. I didn't wake you, did I?"

"No." Will stepped carefully over the piles of books until he found an empty space where he could sink down to sit at his side. "I woke up and you weren't there."

"I'm sorry." David put down his comic book. "I couldn't sleep. I came down here to let you get some rest, but that didn't work out very well."

Will patted his arm and stared at the comics and boxes. "This is your dad's collection, right? The one you showed me back when we were first getting to know each other?"

"Yeah." David ran a hand over a pile of *Judge Dredd* books. "My dad and mom were in my head a lot tonight...and so was Bill." He swallowed hard around the lump that rose in his throat. "I'm sorry he's gone."

Will sighed and slid his arms around David's shoulders. "Oh, David. I'm sorry, too. I've been so caught up in everything, I haven't even asked you how you're doing."

David shook his head and leaned into Will's touch. "I'm okay. I'm sad, but watching you go through these last few days was much harder to bear. I wish I'd done more." He gulped as Will closed his eyes and pressed their foreheads together.

"You're the only reason I even got through the last few days. I'm not sure how I'd have done it without you, to be honest, and, God, I'm so grateful to you for keeping me together."

"Jesus, you don't have to be grateful." David leaned back and waited for Will to open his eyes before he spoke again. "I love you, Will. There's nowhere else I'd choose to be but with you, *especially* when you need me."

Will caught his lip between his teeth and squeezed his eyes shut again, his grip around David's shoulders almost painfully tight. His eyes were wet when he opened them again, but David read happiness in them, too.

"I love you, too," he whispered, smiling so David thought his heart would burst. "And I don't care what you say, I'm grateful you're in my life."

He kissed David, soothing the edges of his pain with his sweet touch, then pulled back with a shaky laugh. "I'm not sure I ever told you, but my father was the first person to tell me you were worth getting to know."

David choked out a laugh through his own tears. "I'm kind of surprised you listened to him." He gathered Will close. "But damn, I'm glad you did."

Chapter Twenty-One

"Where do you want this box? I think it's the last of them for this room."

"Somewhere over there with the rest of them." Will waved in the general direction of the far wall, which was lined with a somewhat precarious-looking stack of boxes. He'd been sitting on the floor, sorting books into piles for the better part of an hour, and David was just now bringing in the second, and final, load.

"Should have known better than to ask a writer and professor to move into my place," David grumbled and set the box down. But he smiled and walked over to kiss Will.

"Probably should have!" Will said cheerfully when David pulled back. "But it's too late now. You're stuck with me."

David's grin widened. "I like that thought."

Will leaned back on his palms. "No last-minute regrets we're combining households?"

David snorted and dropped into Will's office chair. "None whatsoever. You?"

"The only regret I'm having is the decision not to cull more things." Will contemplated the stacks of books scattered around the room and the well-crafted maple floor-to-ceiling bookshelves that lined three walls. "I think the books may have multiplied on the trip from Manhattan to Long Island. I'm not sure they're going to fit."

"You donated a ton," David pointed out. "And the man with an extensive comic book collection can hardly complain about the number of hardcover books his partner owns."

"Yes, true."

After word got out they'd moved in together, Will suspected there were would be tongues wagging about the speed at which their relationship was progressing, but neither of them were concerned. Bill's death had put things in perspective for Will.

He had remained on Long Island after the funeral to help his mother. With Christmas approaching, Will hadn't wanted to leave Agnes there alone. But as he contemplated the idea of moving back to Manhattan, he found he was no longer sure that was what he wanted.

David, his mother and his sister and her family were all on Long Island. Will had a life there. He missed teaching, but Liv's reminder that there were schools in the area that would be thrilled to have him led him to research job opportunities. He'd found a position at SUNY after the previous professor had resigned her post for health issues and put in his notice at NYU with far less regret than he would have expected.

It had been a scramble to pick up the reins of the classes he'd be teaching, especially since they were already two weeks into the semester, but thankfully a very efficient and helpful TA had helped smooth Will's transition.

He and David had decided to move in together and now all the pieces had finally come together. Unlike previous points in his life where he'd contemplated living with a partner, Will and David both had established careers, solid finances, and — best of all — a truly great relationship. David had been his rock through one of the most difficult times he could imagine and Will had no doubts he'd made the right choice. He'd put his condo up for sale and, as of today, was officially a resident of Long Island. He smiled. Seven months before, when Agnes called about his father's diagnosis, Will never would have believed it.

"What are you smiling about?" David asked as he stood.

"Oh, contemplating how much my life has changed," Will said. "I never imagined moving back to Long Island, but I am so happy here."

"I'm glad," David said. "I'll go downstairs and throw together some lunch for both of us, unless there's something more I can do to help?"

"No, I've got this," Will said. He rose to his feet. "One thing before you go, though…"

Will closed the distance between them and leaned in to kiss David. He slid his hands into the pockets of Will's jeans and pulled him closer. They kissed for several long minutes before Will drew back with a contented sigh.

"I bet I could get unpacking done a lot more quickly if you promised to reward me with a kiss like that after every box I get done."

David grinned and dropped another peck on Will's lips. "I think that could be arranged." He gave Will's ass a squeeze.

"Excellent. I bet I'll have the next one done before lunch."

"You're on."

With a final, brief kiss, David left him to his work.

Will surveyed the disaster of a room for a minute, then walked over to his computer to bring up a podcast he'd enjoyed lately.

David had bought the four-bedroom house with a future partner and possibly children in mind, so when they'd decided to move in together, Will had his pick of the two unused bedrooms. The smaller one overlooking the canal had spoken to him immediately. He'd set his desk up by the window and he looked forward to writing with Mabel sprawled at his feet.

A glance out of the window showed a gorgeous, wintry vista. A late-January cold snap and snowfall almost immediately after had left everything but the sea water coated in icy white. Despite the chill, Will enjoyed the daily walks with Mabel, who delighted in the snow. He'd sent a number of videos of her to Adam and Jocelyn, and they'd come over once already to play with her in the snow.

The sound of David's movements downstairs reminded Will to get back to work and he turned back to the wall of bookcases and the stack of books awaiting him. "I can do this," he muttered.

Several hours later, after a delicious lunch, more kisses from David and a hell of a lot of work, Will's office was more or less under control. The bulk of the books were on the shelves in some semblance of order. There were still a few boxes to tackle, but they were primarily files and paperwork that needed to go into the filing cabinet.

Will broke down another empty box with a feeling of satisfaction and added it to the ever-growing stack to be recycled. He might actually finish the office today if he kept going.

Will kept working after the doorbell chimed, and the sound of voices wafting up from the first floor made him wonder if a neighbor had stopped by. He paused, both hands filled with folders, when David called up a moment later.

"Will, can you come down?"

"Sure," Will called back. He stood, dusted the back of his jeans, and ran a hand through his hair. Hopefully he didn't look too much of a mess.

He jogged down the stairs and saw two familiar faces and Mabel's wagging tail as she greeted his family. "Mom, Liv, what are you doing here?"

Agnes smiled and handed him a basket. "We popped by to drop off a few housewarming gifts. I made some muffins and scones, and there's coffee beans from that place downtown you like so much. Oh, and Greta sent a jar of her peach jam."

"Yum, thanks, Mom." Will hugged her and pressed a kiss to her cheek. "I'll send Greta a thank-you note."

Olivia stood from where she'd crouched to pet Mabel. "And I brought wine!" She handed the bag to David. "I hope you don't mind us dropping by unannounced."

"Not at all," David said with a smile. "It's nice to see you both."

"We're not intruding? I know moving can be hectic," Agnes said.

"Of course not. I love seeing you. Besides, you can bribe me with baked goods and wine anytime," Will teased.

Olivia lightly smacked his arm and, laughing, Will pulled his sister in for a hug. "I'm glad you came, too."

She smiled at him. "Mom and I had lunch together and wanted to see you for a bit."

"I've been getting settled into my new office. It'll be nice to have a break. Come on in and let me get your coats."

Will helped his sister with her short cream-colored wool jacket, while David took Agnes' long, camel car coat. Will took his family on a quick tour of the house before they settled in the living room.

"It's a lovely house," Agnes said. "I know you'll be very happy here together."

"Thank you." Will leaned back against David's arm, which he'd draped over the top of the sofa. David squeezed Will's shoulder. "I'm sure we will."

Agnes' answering smile was warm and genuine. She'd admitted she struggled to sleep alone in the big house and though she looked thin and tired, there was more color in her face than in the past few weeks.

Christmas had been fairly subdued for all of them, but Adam and Jocelyn, helped by Mabel's presence, had injected some joy into the otherwise difficult day.

After the first of the year, Will had approached his mother about coming on as his media consultant. She'd asked him if he was doing her a favor, but he'd assured her that, if anything, Agnes was doing Will the favor. She knew the ins and outs of everything he had to deal with and was tremendously helpful to him. After Will explained he'd have hired her even if she hadn't been his mother and in need of something new to do with

Bill gone, she'd readily—and gratefully, from what Will could tell—agreed, and things were working out well for them both.

Agnes cleared her throat. "I know we met with the lawyer about your father's will a few weeks ago, but Liv and I want to talk to you about the house."

"Sure," Will said slowly, unsure of where they were going with this.

David shifted in his seat. "Would you like me to give you three some privacy?"

Olivia and Agnes both shook their heads.

"Of course not," Agnes said. "You're family."

"This potentially impacts you, too, David," Olivia added quietly. "Please stay."

Will looked between his mother and sister. "Is everything okay?"

"Yes." His mother's face was serene. "I've thought a great deal in the past two months. The house was left to me with the idea it would pass to both you and Olivia someday, but as you know, it's difficult for me living there alone. I want to offer it to you and Olivia *now*. I'll move somewhere a bit smaller and more manageable. I love the home, but it's impractical for me and, honestly, wasteful for just one person. I would prefer it stay in the family, of course. I know this is a strange time, given you've moved in here with David, but I wanted to see how you felt about it."

Will glanced at David. "Obviously, David and I will talk more, but I don't think either of us have any interest in the house. It's beautiful and I know it's an important part of our family history, but I don't think it suits either of us."

David nodded his agreement.

"I suspected that," Agnes said. "And that's perfectly understandable. I don't want you to be burdened with a place you won't love."

Olivia leaned forward. "Phillip and I discussed it, too, and we are interested. We love the house. It would be a nice place for Adam and Jocelyn—especially with the pool—and it's close enough they wouldn't have to switch schools."

"I think that's a great solution," Will said. "If you and Phillip are happy with it, why not?"

"I wanted to be sure I didn't step on your toes," Olivia said earnestly. "If you wanted it or…"

He shook his head. "I love *this* house. It's perfect for our tastes. If you want Mom and Dad's house, go for it." He paused. "Oh, there is one condition."

"We'll figure out market value and pay you your half of the inheritance, of course," Olivia said.

Will waved off her comment. "No rush. Dad was more than generous already. We can figure it all out at some point in the future."

Between what he'd been left in his father's will, the inheritance from his grandmother, the pending sale of his condo and his book royalties, Will would never have to work another day in his life. The department chair at SUNY had been apologetic about not being able to offer Will a larger salary, but unless the market completely crashed and he lost all his investments, money wasn't a concern for him. He was extraordinarily privileged to be in that position and perhaps he could find a way to put the money from the family home to good use.

"My condition involves the pool. Any chance I could have a free season pass to use it in the summer?" Will asked.

Olivia grinned back. "I think that could be arranged. I'm sure Adam and Jocelyn would be delighted to swim with their Uncle Will."

"Perfect." Will grinned back at his sister. "Then the house is all yours."

Agnes smiled at Olivia and Will. "Oh, this is wonderful. Your father" — her breath caught — "your father would be so happy for all of us."

Tears stung Will's eyes and David rubbed his shoulder. "Yeah, I think he would."

* * * *

"How are you feeling about the arrangement with your sister?" David asked later that evening as they drove toward the grocery store.

Will shrugged. "Relieved. I didn't want the house anyway and if their family will be happy there, I think that's the perfect solution. You don't mind I made the decision then and there, do you? I said we'd talk and everything kind of fell into place..."

David shook his head. "Not at all. If you'd *wanted* to move to the house, we'd have had a different discussion, obviously, but in this case, it didn't matter. And I'd have spoken up if I thought you were leaving me out of the decision-making process too much."

"Good," Will said firmly.

"Frankly, I'm glad you didn't want the house." David slid into a parking spot. "It's a beautiful old home, but..."

"But it's not *us*," Will finished.

"Exactly."

"How do you feel about Brussels sprouts?" David asked a short while later. "I thought I'd make them for Sunday dinner. Your mom said she's doing roast pork."

Will made a face. "I'm not a big fan and I have no idea how my sister or the kids feel about them."

David gave him a contemplative look. "Have you ever had them roasted with bacon?"

"I haven't."

"Okay. Then I'll make them Sunday and test them out on all of you. I'm pretty sure you'll change your mind after eating them, but I'll also make potato gratin in case they don't go over well."

"Sounds good. You don't mind the weekly family dinners, do you?" After Bill's death, the regular dinner had come together. It made Will happy, but he didn't want David to feel like he had to come.

David paused. "I enjoy them. Having lost all my family except Isabel, it means a lot to be included by yours now."

Will squeezed his hand. "I lost my family for a while, so on some level, I can relate."

"And I appreciate your mother extending the invitation to Isabel and Allen, by the way. That was unexpected but very kind."

"Of course." Will fought back the urge to lean in and kiss David.

David gave him a lopsided smile as if he'd thought the same. "Before we do something that'll get us in all the papers, I'd better go get the Brussel sprouts and potatoes."

"Tell me what kind of cheese and bacon and I'll get those," Will said.

After David handed him the shopping list with the information, Will wandered toward the dairy and meat departments. He was waiting in line to get the bacon when he overheard two older women talking.

"What is with the Asian Invasion in this town?" the one closest to him muttered. "I swear, it's all nail salons and restaurants now."

"Oh, I know what you mean," the other agreed. "And have you seen the number of them in the store today? It didn't used to be that way."

The first woman sniffed. "I don't mind the doctors — they're quite smart, you know — but the rest? Ugh."

"That tall man over there must be a doctor. He's well-dressed." Will followed the direction of her nod and saw David perusing the wine section. "And I know they're smart, but I'd still rather have an *American* doctor. The accents are so impossible."

Will scowled. What would they think of the news David was both an American citizen and one of their elected officials? Of course, these two women were probably in the group that hadn't voted for David.

Will was grateful when the man at the butcher counter called the next number and one of the women stepped forward. Engaging the general public and calling them on their racism wasn't prudent, but Will doubted he could stay quiet much longer.

He was still steaming when he met David in the wine aisle. "How do you *stand* it?"

David gave him a bewildered look. "Did bacon prices go up? I try not to spend too much on food, but I don't think either of us is in a position where we have to worry about economizing our bacon purchases…"

Despite his anger, Will chuckled. "Not that. I'll pay more for organic and humanely raised pork. I was talking about racist assholes."

David raised an eyebrow. "Babe, I can see you're upset, but I'm going to need a little more context."

Will took a deep breath and relayed the conversation he'd overheard. When he finished, David nodded. "I'd like to say I hadn't heard similar things myself, but…"

"How do you tolerate it? You're so *calm*."

David laid a hand on his forearm. "Look, I'm not going to pretend I don't find it disgusting, and I definitely get angry. But even more so, I feel sorry for people like that. They're out of touch with reality, Will. Out of touch with the world and the way it changes and moves."

"I just…" Will sighed. "I had a hard time not telling them they were insulting an elected official."

"I understand that. I'm more inclined to roll my eyes at those women, honestly, because deep down I know what they're saying isn't so much about me as it is about them and the sad, fearful way they see the world around them. This isn't going to be the last time you have to deal with this. You have to develop a thicker skin to protect yourself."

"I know. And I know I shouldn't respond. That'll blow up in our faces."

"It could," David agreed. "But will you feel better if you don't speak up? You're allowed to have your own opinions and call people out on their attitudes when you don't agree. I've always admired that about you — your willingness to stand up for your beliefs."

David's expression grew grave and he paused before speaking again. "Desmond Tutu once said, 'If you are neutral in situations of injustice, you have chosen the side of the oppressor.' So, don't play the neutral party. Step up as an ally, but because you want to, not because you think it's expected of you. It's wonderful if you want to stand up for me, but in doing so, remember you're not speaking up *only* for me. You're also speaking up for others who may lack a voice to do so themselves."

Will's breath caught in his chest as he stared at David. "You're right," he said quietly. "I never thought about it that way."

"That's understandable," David replied. "And heavy topics aside, I want to make sure your blood pressure doesn't get the best of you."

Will chuckled and the remainder of tension leaked out of him. "Was I Hulk-ing out again?"

David gave him a small smile. "Maybe a little."

"It's going to take me a while to adjust to dealing with attitudes like that," Will admitted. "I know I'm disgustingly privileged when it comes to just about everything but being a gay man. But I heard what you said and you've given me a lot to think about. I'd...I'd like to talk about this more with you."

"Of course," David said. "You're an aware sort of person, and a lot of new things are being thrown at you right now. I know you'll learn how to best deal with the shit that gets thrown at us because of my race."

"I will definitely do my best," Will promised.

"Good," David said. "Now what are your thoughts on the wine we're bringing?"

Chapter Twenty-Two

A pleasant feeling of familiarity settled over David as he walked into Under with Will, Isabel and Allen. The amber lighting cast a cozy glow over the place and the low thump of the house music surrounded them like a heartbeat. Kyle stood at the far end of the bar, dressed in his customary black and pouring drinks for a pair of men David didn't recognize. He smiled at David and Will when they caught his eye.

"Hello, boys — I'll be right with you."

"Take your time," Will called back with a smile. He turned to David and their guests to take their coats. "You already know Kyle's one of the owners. His cocktails are amazing, and I'll warn you now to pace yourselves."

Allen chuckled. "Because they're potent?"

"Potent and delicious," David clarified. "The drinks taste so good it's easy to forget they contain alcohol and suddenly, oops, you're tipsy."

"Tipsy already, David? I'd say this speakeasy is rubbing off on you."

Jesse's deep voice curled around David and made him smile. He quickly turned to include Jesse in their circle.

"Hello, all." Jesse was still dressed for the office in a beautiful brown check suit, and he shook Will's hand before extending it to David with a smile. "Should you be worried your constituents will take issue with their senator frequenting a blind pig?"

"They'd tell me it's about time I relaxed and enjoyed myself," David said. He gestured toward Isabel. "Jes, you remember my sister, Isabel, and her husband, Allen. Jesse is Kyle's business partner and helps run the place when he's not playing corporate mastermind," he added for Isabel's and Allen's benefit.

Jesse smiled, and David could almost see the wheels turning behind his merry blue gaze. He extended his hand to Isabel. "Of course, hello again. I don't do much to help Kyle around here other than blunder through drink recipes when he's busy. I'm glad David finally saw fit to bring you round. That's a great color on you, by the way."

David's jaw dropped slightly as his sister's cheeks flushed pink.

"Thank you. David invited us last month, actually." Isabel brushed a stray curl back away from her face while Jesse and Allen shook hands. "I was working at the lab and couldn't get away."

Jesse slipped past David and Will to escort Isabel and Allen toward the bar, a hand on each of their elbows. "That's right — you're a scientist."

David exchange a glanced with Will as they moved to the coat room. "My sister is wearing black — technically that's not even a color." He wrinkled his nose at Will's laughter. "Remind me why I agreed to bring them here?"

Will handed David two of the coats. "Isabel's been pestering us since the New Year. I certainly wasn't going to be the one to tell her no."

David laughed. "You don't have any problem telling me no."

"That's because Isabel is a lot scarier than you." Will chanced a glance back into the bar. "Don't tell her I said that."

They settled in after hanging the coats and joined the conversation with Isabel, Allen and Jesse, who was busy filling rocks glasses with roughly chunked ice.

"Who's Kyle talking to over there?" Will asked.

"Oh, you mean Hot and Hotter?" Jesse grinned in answer to Will's laughter. "The ginger goes by Masen. He's a bartender."

"Where did you meet him?"

"He tends bar at a bistro near my apartment that I stop into now and again when I need food and can't be bothered to cook. Kyle and I want to bring someone on a few nights a week, and I think Masen would fit in here, so he came in to talk to Kyle and check the place out. That's his partner, Cullen, with him, and they've got a few more friends coming. One of them is a DJ who may be interested in spinning some music a few nights a week."

Will nodded. "Cool. I had no idea you guys were expanding the staff."

"Under is a lot busier than either of us ever expected." Jesse poured bourbon, amaro and a variety of ingredients into a shaker he'd filled with ice. "Obviously, we wanted the place to turn a profit and neither of us is complaining about it. But Kyle's working a lot, even with two other bartenders on staff. I think we need to bring on some more help before he gets burnt out."

David furrowed his brows at Jesse's choice of words. "Doesn't Kyle agree?"

Jesse shrugged. "He didn't at first. Thought I was being too Mama Bear for my own good. Then he fell asleep on my couch after dinner last week and I practically had to carry him to bed. That's not as easy as it sounds, by the way, because Kyle works out a lot and he weighs a fucking ton."

Jesse shook the container of drinks as the others laughed, then popped the top off to pour the contents into the glasses. "He slept for ten hours straight that night and I think that finally convinced him I wasn't running my mouth. Kyle can be a stubborn ass, but he realizes even Captain Bartender needs a helping hand now and again."

"Uh-oh." Isabel glanced between Jesse and David, then back to Will. "Something tells me my brother's shown his comic book collection to your friends."

Will cocked a brow. "Honey, those boxes come out every time these boys show their faces in Freeport. Anyone who spends time with David discovers their inner nerd."

Jesse set glasses in front of Isabel and Allen. "My nerd is totally out, just like the rest of me. But what about you two?" he asked, glancing between them. "Do you also share David's affection for comic books?"

Allen made a so-so motion with one hand. "Affection yes, obsession no."

"I'm not obsessed," David scoffed. He hid a smile as Will mussed his hair. "Quit it."

Isabel sipped her drink and pursed her lips at his declaration. "Davey, you go to Comic-Con every year in New York and Boston and you *used* to go to San Diego with Dad, too. And wow, this is delicious." She stared at the glass in her hand. "What the heck am I even drinking?"

"It's called a Gold Rush," Jesse replied with a smile. "Kyle makes this killer ginger syrup and it makes the drink. I'm still trying to decide if I should make another round for your brother and Will or switch up to something else Kyle has been playing with."

Will turned to David. "You didn't mention going to Comic-Con last year."

"I couldn't get away to Boston," David replied. "I had a lot going on, gearing up for the election. It got even crazier when September and October rolled around so I skipped New York, too."

He cleared his throat against the unpleasant feeling curling in his gut. True, he'd been too busy for travel in August, but September was a different story. Only Isabel knew he simply hadn't been up to going to NYC Comic-Con. Dejected over the breakup with Will, he'd let his tickets go unused. The flash of understanding in Will's gaze told David he'd guessed the reason, but David quickly leaned over to kiss him. What was past was past, and he and Will were together here and now.

"We should go this year," Will said. "I've never been to Comic-Con before and it sounds equal parts amazing and terrifying."

"That sounds about right," Kyle cut in as he stepped up to join them. "Hello, all." He aimed a smile at the crowd. "More than half the city dresses cosplay the whole time the Con is happening, and somehow I always end up mixing drinks for both Hobbits and

Orcs. I'm kind of curious, though, so I'm in. And make sure you tell Carter."

"Tell Carter what?" a new voice asked, drawing everyone's attention as Carter and Riley joined the crowd.

"There's a plot afoot to crash David's trip to Comic-Con this year," Kyle explained after another round of hugs, kisses and hellos were out of the way.

"David will be cosplaying as Senator Sexy, by the way," Jesse threw in, and his face crinkled up in a grin when Will burst out laughing. David poked Will until he squawked.

"Anyway, I had a feeling you and Dyl Pickle would be down to go, too, Car," Kyle explained.

"So down," Carter replied. "Dyl Pickle is my son's code name, by the way," he said to Isabel and Allen. "Dylan will be eight this year and his Uncle Max got him into comics. The rest of us are all kind of along for the ride."

Riley smiled at his partner. "I've never heard you complain."

"And you never will." Carter returned the smile, though he appeared careworn to David's eyes. There were dark circles under Carter's eyes and David had made up his mind to ask if he was feeling well when the rattle of Kyle's shaker distracted them all.

"What are you mixing up there, McKee?" Will asked.

"Bourbon, bitters, orange juice and maple syrup." Intense satisfaction crossed Kyle's face as he popped the top off the shaker. He poured the contents of the shaker into four glasses. "I ran across the recipe a couple of weeks ago and tinkered with it because it seemed like a drink this crew would appreciate."

He topped the drinks with lemon slices and presented the first to David. "Maple Bourbon Cocktail."

David sipped from his glass, humming as the sweet and sour flavors of maple and lemon exploded over his tongue, carried by the smoky, deep cherry notes of the bourbon. "Son, this is dangerously delicious."

Kyle rubbed his hands together with a grin. "Now that's what I like to hear."

Under was never crowded — as Jesse maintained, they didn't have to let anyone in they didn't want. Patrons claimed spots on the guest list to receive a passphrase each evening, and the number of guests on a typical evening never passed forty. After the hand-mixed cocktails, the small crowd was part of Under's appeal and made it easy to feel at home in the bar's relaxed environment.

Kyle and Jesse's monthly parties were even more intimate, as their guest list didn't often extend beyond good friends and family members. That night, David met Jesse's brother and sister-in-law, Eric and Sara, who soon fell into conversation with Isabel and Allen. He also met Masen, the bartender Kyle and Jesse were considering hiring, and his friends. The striking and stylish group were all so young, David couldn't hold back a grimace as he and Will joined Carter and Riley in a seating area near the bar.

Riley chuckled. "Why the face?"

"Oh, it's nothing. Just feeling my age around that cluster of bright young things Jesse and Kyle are talking to." David waved vaguely at the bar. "I'm not sure any of them is over twenty-five."

"Now you know how I feel being surrounded by students most of the time." Will gently tapped his glass against David's. "It's even weirder when you consider I'm their teacher. They stare at me like I'm about to spout wisdom at any moment."

"Does that make you a wisdom whale?" Riley wondered, and smiled when Will stuck out his tongue. He glanced over his shoulder at Masen and his friends, then back to David. "I don't know. I suppose they're a bit young, but nothing out of the ordinary, right?" He blinked, clearly struck by something. "You know, there are children under ten in my life, so maybe my perspective is off."

"You and Sadie had a fifteen-minute conversation about Minions last weekend, Ri—your perspective is completely shot." Carter grinned when the others laughed. "But, David, you must work with lots of young people when you're campaigning, right?"

David nodded. "That is true, actually. A part of me still identifies with their passion too, and their conviction we can get out there and change the world."

Carter furrowed his brow. "So, you believe it's possible?"

"I used to, definitely," David replied. "That why I got into my line of work. I wanted to improve people's lives, make our towns and cities better and stronger." He glanced at Will and smiled. "I've mellowed over time, of course, and learned some lessons."

"Gained perspective?" Will guessed.

"Yes. I'm not sure we can change the world anymore, but we can change ourselves and *that* is the key to progress."

Will bit his lip against a fond smile. "Now who sounds like a wisdom whale?"

"That would be me." David raised his hand and laughed. "But I still remember why those kids who show up to campaign offices are fired up and I think it's great. That kind of energy is invaluable to any cause."

"I agree," Carter chimed in and raised his glass of limeade to David. "When I took the job at Corp Equality, they gave me carte blanche to hire some new staff and I absolutely wanted people with fire in their bellies. In the interest of full disclosure, by the way, we could afford to do that because I donate my salary back to the organization."

David blinked but kept a straight face. Before meeting Will's friends, he'd never known anyone who could afford to waive a salary. Of course, Will could do the same now, too, and David was still getting used to the idea he lived with someone who could choose a life of leisure.

"How many people did you hire?" Will asked. "And are any of them over twenty-one?"

"Only two, and yes, they are. Or at least, I know one of them is. Hah." Carter shook his head. "I hired my former assistant away from my old man's company. Malcolm was totally underutilized there."

"Absolutely," Riley agreed. "I can't tell you how many times Carter told me Malcolm kept him sane — he was Carter's right arm around that place. I wasn't sure the guy wanted to be an assistant, either. He seemed...I don't know, like he was ready for more? I'd have tried to steal him for myself, but I knew Carter would retaliate by smothering me in my sleep."

Carter laughed. "You're right about that. Anyway, Malcolm contacted me about coming to work at CEC at exactly the right time, because I could offer him something different. We needed a social organizer and that job had his name written all over it. I'm not sure what got him so fired up, but he's got enough energy for two people."

"I'm sure putting up with Bradley Hamilton's bullshit after you resigned had a lot to do with getting Malcolm fired up." Riley ran a hand over his partner's close-cropped hair. "We heard through friends there that Carter's father went on a bit of a tear after Car left," he explained. "He rearranged departments, moved staff all over the place, all without a clue, because his son ran the place for years. The old fool made such a mess he's gotten himself sued."

David raised both brows. "No shit?"

"Seems he set his sights on the wrong people at Hamilton Ad," Riley replied. "And, to no one's surprise, several of the plaintiffs are gay." He shook his head, lips pressed tight as Will cursed under his breath.

Carter cleared his throat, his discomfort clear. "Well, at least the lawsuits will keep Brad busy and out of our hair for a while."

"Praise all the holy things for that." Riley sounded fervent. "Your old man stresses you out way too much for someone you don't even see anymore and I hate that. *Especially* when the stress messes with your sleep."

"Yeah, insomnia sucks." Carter wrinkled his nose. "But I'd rather talk about how Will and David are settling in. Did you ever find a place for all those books of yours, Will?"

David smiled as the banter turned to the house in Freeport and Will's continued efforts to stuff his things into every nook and cranny of his office. Riley's words about Carter's father stayed with him, though.

Unlike Will, Carter and Riley, he'd never known the pain of being shunned by family simply because of whom he loved. His parents and sister had always supported him, even when he'd said and done things they didn't fully understand. His heart hurt to know that a man who should have loved Carter had spurned him instead, and even now made Carter unbearably anxious.

Thankfully, Bill and Agnes had reached out to their son before it was too late. The Martin family would never get back the ten years they'd lost to anger and intolerance, but they'd been given a gift last year, one that had grown to encompass and enrich David's life, too. Neither he nor Will would ever take that gift for granted.

"Hey, Senator Sexy."

David rolled his eyes at Will's toothy smile. "That's not going away anytime soon, is it?"

"Nope. But if it truly makes you uncomfortable, I promise to call you that only within the confines of these walls. Or when we're getting naked." Will waggled his eyebrows and made David laugh.

"Kinky. Is that what you've been thinking this whole time? Getting me into bed?"

"Not the *whole* time, no—don't be conceited." Will ran a hand along his forearm, the gentle touch countering his teasing words. "You've had a thinking kind of face on since we sat down over here, though, and I wonder what's on *your* mind."

"I was thinking about families, actually." David turned his hand palm up to take hold of Will's. "Yours and mine, your friends'…the families to which we're born and the families we build. That kind of thing." He paused to sip his drink.

"Hearing about Carter's father, I can't help thinking how differently last year could have turned for you. I'm glad you don't have to live with the anger anymore,

Will. Obviously, I didn't know you before you came back to Long Island, but I'm sure that anger wasn't good for you. *Or* for the rest of your family."

Will nodded. "You're right. I never forgot how much it hurt when my father turned me away. I think it held me back emotionally, too. I met men and dated, but they were always distant when I needed them not to be. I never felt truly connected to anyone — in my heart and head — until you.

"I think that's what made me so bitter when things didn't work out with Riley," he said more quietly. "I wanted that connection and he did too. I thought if we kept working on it, we'd eventually get there. I didn't realize Riley was already connected to someone else." Will shook his head.

"You're not alone. Lots of people have been in the same position, searching for someone they feel most in sync with." David shrugged at Will's questioning glance. "I'd include myself in that group, but, honestly, I'm not sure it ever occurred to me that I wanted more."

"Really?"

"I didn't mind being unattached. Work kept me busy and I had good friends who made my life full. I dated and had a healthy sex life but after Nik, I never got attached enough to anyone I dated to be hurt when it didn't work out."

David smiled wryly. "That's how I knew what you and I had was different. Nothing about us was supposed to be serious but the idea of you disappearing bothered me. Probably because there was a real possibility one day you wouldn't come back."

"I'm not sure I ever truly left after coming back." Will exhaled. "I told myself I didn't belong on Long Island and only stayed for Mom and Liv, but there was more to it than helping take care of Dad. Sure, I traveled back into the city and complained about missing home, but you said it once yourself—there was nothing tying me to Garden City. I could have commuted back and forth without much fuss, and my family would have accepted that decision."

David considered Will's words for a moment. "You're right. So, what made you pull up stakes and move back in with Bill and Agnes?"

"I wanted to reform connections with my family. And I forged a new one with you," Will replied with a smile. "I didn't recognize what was happening until we'd split and I realized what I'd *lost*."

Heat bolted through David's body. He leaned over and pressed a fervent kiss to Will's lips. "I have a theory," he said when they broke apart again. "Your father asked me to his house for brunch in an effort to try to throw us together. Maybe because I was the only other gay man he knew well, but maybe because he hoped we'd end up more than friends. Wouldn't that be a twist?"

Will laughed, his eyes sparkling. "You know, I wouldn't put it past him. William Martin Sr. was a crafty fucker and he *always* had an agenda. But it doesn't matter why he did it, because we figured it out on our own.

"I'm still not sure what changed for him to make this okay," Will added, pointing first at himself then at David before he pressed his palm over David's heart.

David took that hand in his own and twined their fingers together, sure Will could feel his heart pounding. "Maybe it doesn't matter, as you said. Or maybe your dad finally decided to change himself instead of the world."

"Maybe." Will gave him a sweet smile. "That's certainly a nice idea."

David drew Will close, and wrapped him up in a hug that felt like coming home. "Your dad definitely changed my life—I'd say he was capable of changing the world after all."

Want to see more from these authors? Here's a taster for you to enjoy!

The Speakeasy: Extra Dirty
K. Evan Coles & Brigham Vaughn

Excerpt

April 2015

Jesse Murtagh set down the packet of financial statements he'd been reviewing and smiled. He was seated in the back office of Under, a speakeasy in Morningside Heights, and life was good.

With Under approaching its one-year anniversary, the bar's earnings surpassed expectations each quarter. They boasted a full guest list every night, and Under appeared as a "must visit" on New York's fashionable lifestyle blogs and guides. Business was booming. And its success meant everything to Jesse and his business partner, Kyle McKee.

In addition to being Under's co-owner, Kyle also happened to be one of Jesse's favorite people in the world and one of his favorite partners in bed. Jesse would bet he'd find Kyle out in the speakeasy right now, too, readying the place for opening.

Jesse got to his feet. He locked the papers in the desk, then exited the office and moved toward the long bar that ran the length of the room. Under had a masculine, sophisticated vibe. Sleek leather seating areas dotted the room and open shelves lined the walls, backlit with amber lamps that cast a warm glow over bottles of rare and high-end liquors. On a typical evening, house music throbbed through the air by now, but Jesse and Kyle were holding a private party tonight, and silence reigned, save the sounds of Kyle at work.

"Hey, gorgeous," Jesse drawled. "When did you get here?"

Kyle glanced up at Jesse's approach. He smiled and the quirk of his full lips sent a ripple of heat through Jesse's body.

"About an hour ago." He shrugged easily. Kyle had dressed in black, as he always did for work, and rolled his shirtsleeves up to the elbow. His muscled forearms flexed as he polished a rocks glass. "I saw Matt upstairs when I came in. He told me you were here, but I figured you'd be busy counting the money. Thought I'd leave you to it."

Jesse rounded the bar with a laugh. "You know me too well."

Opening the speakeasy had been a departure from his usual business of running a growing regional media conglomerate with his family. Jesse had never even worked in a bar or restaurant, let alone owned one. But Kyle had mentioned the idea of opening a bar one night over dinner and drinks, and the way his dark eyes had shone had captured Jesse's fancy.

Jesse had mulled the idea over for several days, then brought it to his brother, Eric. He'd hoped Eric would talk him out of it and had thrown up his hands when Eric merely smiled.

'I'm not sure who you think you're fooling, Jes,' Eric had said. *'I can already tell you've made up your mind to do it.'*

And so, Jesse had found himself working with his accountants and his lawyer to create a business proposal. Within two weeks of that fateful dinner, he'd presented it to Kyle. They'd celebrated by screwing each other senseless, then started scouting for a location the very next day.

Jesse stepped up behind Kyle now and molded himself against his body. He wound his arms around Kyle's waist, careful to avoid the glass in his hands.

In many ways, Kyle appeared to be Jesse's opposite. His elegant, clean-shaven features and dark hair contrasted with Jesse's short beard and dark-blond, blue-eyed coloring. Jesse broadcasted his emotions, whereas Kyle was more reserved. Both men stood at six feet and were built long and lean, like runners. But where Jesse could be coltish in his movements, Kyle's were deliberate and graceful. Kyle, Jesse liked to say, had found his Zen.

Jesse nuzzled the side of Kyle's neck. "I take it last month's numbers are good?" Kyle's voice went low and throaty.

"Indeed." Jesse pulled him closer. He angled his hips and pressed his groin against Kyle's muscular ass, and his body paid immediate attention to that firm heat. "The numbers are so good, in fact, I think we should celebrate." He pressed a lingering kiss to Kyle's throat.

Kyle leaned back into him with a rumbling noise. He set the glass he'd been polishing on the bar. "What did you have in mind?"

"Next weekend off—Masen can handle things in your absence."

"Well, he'll like that."

Kyle sounded amused. They'd hired Masen Jones earlier in the year to help out, and he'd quickly become Kyle's right-hand man.

"A whole weekend, though... I don't know, Jes."

Jesse dropped one hand and palmed Kyle through his trousers, and, oh, yes, he was hard. Kyle let out a soft gasp.

"Friday and Saturday, then," Jesse bargained. He closed his eyes, heat flashing under his skin as Kyle pushed back and ground against him. "We'll go to that club in Chelsea you told me about."

"Oh, fine." Kyle turned in the circle of his arms. "I'll bring Jarrod and Gale as backup," he added, then looped his arms around Jesse's neck. "They can walk me home after you find someone to disappear with."

Jesse grinned. "You really do know me too well," he murmured and covered Kyle's mouth with his own.

The kiss deepened and Kyle groaned. Jesse palmed him again, his touch rough, and pressed Kyle backward hard into the bar. Kyle's cock twitched under Jesse's hand, and he broke away with a sharp inhale.

"Jesus."

"Jesse will do."

Jesse let Kyle go and leaned back enough to get his hands on Kyle's belt. Desire pulsed through him. Quickly, he opened Kyle's trousers and pushed the dark fabric down his legs. Kyle's eyes were wild when Jesse looked up again and a flush stained his cheeks and neck. He uttered a soft moan as Jesse sank to his knees.

Jesse kissed Kyle's thighs. He kneaded the soft, fair skin with his hands and dragged Kyle's boxer briefs down. Kyle sighed as his cock slipped free of the underwear and jutted up onto his abdomen.

Jesse pressed his face into the juncture between Kyle's thigh and groin and inhaled the smell of almond-scented soap and sweat and man. "Damn," he said, his voice low. "You always smell so good."

Kyle ran his hands over Jesse's head, then twined his fingers into his short hair. That possessive touch sent a jolt of lust zigzagging down Jesse's spine. He loved it when Kyle got rough.

Shifting, he held tight to Kyle's hips and opened his mouth at the base of his cock. He slowly dragged his tongue along its length.

"Oh, God." Kyle's low whisper set a fire in Jesse's belly.

He licked and teased the shaft before he ducked down and caught Kyle's balls with his tongue. He lavished them with attention until Kyle moaned steadily, then looked up and locked eyes with him. The dazed bliss on his face made Jesse's dick throb.

"Suck me," Kyle rasped out.

Jesse pulled back. He braced one arm across Kyle's abdomen and wrapped his free hand around his base. Very, very slowly, he slid his lips over Kyle, reveling in the bittersweet taste and weight of the hard, velvety flesh on his tongue.

He took Kyle deep and waited until his nose brushed the curls of hair on his groin before he swallowed. Kyle's eyes went wide. Jesse pinned him against the bar, and he bucked his hips forward, a strangled noise tearing out of him.

Kyle tipped his head back as Jesse sucked. He closed his eyes and swore, and his ragged tone went straight to Jesse's groin. Jesse dropped his free hand and palmed himself, past caring if he shot in his pants.

He worked Kyle hard with his mouth until a shudder racked his frame. Jesse moved the arm pinning Kyle's hips, which left him free to fuck Jesse's mouth. Kyle opened his eyes again and stared at Jesse, his gaze filled with fire. He started to thrust and desire rattled down

Jesse's spine. He groaned with need and closed his eyes when Kyle gasped.

"Gonna come, Jes," Kyle said, his voice rough and desperate. He tensed at Jesse's moan. Then Jesse pressed the fingers of his free hand into the soft skin behind Kyle's balls, and Kyle fell apart with a cry.

He tightened his grip on Jesse's hair and his knees buckled. Jesse used his shoulder to hold Kyle up. His balls tightened as Kyle pulsed in his mouth, and he swallowed, tasting bitter and salt.

Kyle's panting breaths echoed through the silent bar. Jesse pulled off, his head swimming, and Kyle freed his shaking hands from Jesse's hair. He bent and hauled Jesse to his feet, and Jesse stumbled and clutched at Kyle.

"You okay?" Kyle asked with a smile.

"Dizzy. And I wanna fuck you right now," Jesse muttered. Jesus, he needed to come. He pulled Kyle in for a messy kiss and ground his erection against Kyle's thigh until Kyle broke away with a breathless laugh.

"I think we've violated enough health codes for now," Kyle said. "Besides, we don't have any lube or rubbers."

"There's some in the office."

"We used them up last weekend."

Jesse whined and rutted harder into Kyle. "Fuck."

"I said no," Kyle scolded, his tone playful and his brown eyes gleaming. He pulled his trousers up. No sooner were they buttoned than he sank to his knees and reached for Jesse's belt. "Lucky for you, there's time for me to suck you off and clean up."

Kyle worked Jesse's fly open and leaned in. He spread his palms over Jesse's thighs and mouthed him through his boxer briefs. Goosebumps rose along Jesse's arms at the press of damp heat and cotton against his erection. Leaning forward, he braced his hands against the gleaming bar, arrested by the sight of his friend. Kyle shut his eyes and nuzzled Jesse through his clothes. His long, dark lashes fanned over his fair skin, and his lips were parted and wet. He looked unbelievably erotic.

Jesse cupped his jaw. "Mmm, baby."

Kyle opened his eyes. He hooked his fingertips under the waistband of Jesse's boxer briefs, then pulled his trousers and briefs down. Jesse hissed. He bit his lip hard when his cock sprang free, and Kyle swallowed him down.

Jesse's world exploded in a roar of pleasure that wiped his mind clean.

Life was very good indeed.

PUBLISHING

Sign up for our newsletter and find out about all our romance book releases, eBook sales and promotions, sneak peeks and FREE romance books!

About the Authors

K. Evan Coles is a mother and tech pirate by day and a writer by night. She is a dreamer who, with a little hard work and a lot of good coffee, coaxes words out of her head and onto paper.

K. lives in the northeast United States, where she complains bitterly about the winters, but truly loves the region and its diverse, tenacious and deceptively compassionate people. You'll usually find K. nerding out over books, movies and television with friends and family. She's especially proud to be raising her son as part of a new generation of unabashed geeks.

Brigham Vaughn is starting the adventure of a lifetime as a full-time writer. She devours books at an alarming rate and hasn't let her short arms and long torso stop her from doing yoga. She makes a killer key lime pie, hates green peppers and loves wine tasting tours. A collector of vintage Nancy Drew books and green glassware, she enjoys poking around in antique shops and refinishing thrift store furniture. An avid photographer, she dreams of traveling the world and she can't wait to discover everything else life has to offer her.

K. and Brigham love to hear from readers. You can find their contact information, website details and author profile page at https://www.pride-publishing.com

CPSIA information can be obtained
at www.ICGtesting.com
Printed in the USA
BVHW031548070422
633577BV00002B/181